For Francesca

Chapter 1

'Nina! One of the fridges is making a weird noise.' Gloria's voice is a welcome distraction from my latest attempt at flower arranging. At least, until I realise what I've just heard.

Shit.

I abandon the cornflowers, delphiniums and rust-coloured foliage, dash through to the back room, and hurtle down the stairs that lead to the basement storage area. With every step I take, a measured 'beep, beeep, beeeep' – like the sound of hospital machinery hooked up to someone in a coma – grows louder.

'Something must have tripped the alarm! What did you do to the fridge?' I ask as Gloria comes into sight.

'Nothing.'

Gloria is unruffled by my accusatory tone. She's my house-mate.

'I was looking for the cleaning spray,' she says. 'To take the whitewash off the window.'

The fridge's mournful signal of distress continues.

'Maybe buying my equipment on eBay wasn't such a good idea,' I manage. 'But at least there's nothing in it yet.'

As if to prove it, I open the door to the beeping fridge.

The noise stops and is immediately replaced by the sound

1

of a wooden object being hit – repeatedly – by a hammer. 'That must be Edo!'

Gloria hears the relief in my voice. She manoeuvres herself around the fridge, squeezes my shoulder and says, 'C'mon. Let's go see.'

My hand is still on the fridge door. Tentatively, I close it.

Beep

Beeep.

Beeeep.

The damn thing isn't even cold enough to keep an ice lolly from melting.

Whereas I am shivering with anticipation.

This is going to be an amazing day and I'm not going to let a dodgy fridge spoil a single moment. I shrug, and reopen the door to silence the skull-piercing sound. I'll deal with it later. For now, I follow Gloria back the way I've just come.

Presuming we're not being burgled and it really is Edo, the rhythmic hammering means he's been as good as his word. He's made me a shop sign and it seems he's fixing it in place. He's been hugely secretive about the design – 'Nina, I'm an artist! It'll be awesome!' – and I'm finally going to get to see what he's done.

Except Gloria can't get out of the door.

She's inched it open, only to find herself nose to nose with a hulking white Transit van parked extremely illegally and mostly on the pavement.

It's Edo's van and I realise he's standing on the roof of it to put up the sign above the door. A good idea because it's a lot cheaper than scaffolding. And as it's before eight o'clock, when the Primrose Hill traffic wardens begin their daily rounds of terror, he'll get away with it.

Gloria steps back from the door. 'Best to let Edo get on with it,' she advises. 'Anyway, how are you feeling, sweets? Ready for the off?'

Everything's been such a rush, there's been no time to arrange those delphiniums let alone smell the roses. But there's no need to pause for thought.

'I'm ridiculously excited!' I declare. 'It's like being a five-year-old on Christmas Eve. I'm so impatient for everything to start happening.'

I don't know why I didn't do this years ago. I must have thought about it a thousand times, but never dared.

'What about the fridge?'

'Let's not talk about the fridge.'

Gloria begins to clean the display window she helped me whitewash when we started fitting out my shiny new shop. I watch the murky coating that's kept the outside world from seeing how I've transformed the space disappear and think about my own transformation.

I still can't believe it. Only a couple of months ago, I was snuggled deep inside my own little comfort hole. It wasn't until change started happening all around me that I even began to realise I'd been snared. Then fate gave me a push – although at the time, it felt more like a mighty kick up the arse – and after that everything fell into place.

Now here I am. Captain of my own ship. In charge of my own destiny. Queen of my own little slice of heaven.

I am a shopkeeper. Owner of a small business.

It's a tiny business in every sense and, although I have no idea where my first customer will be coming from, I'm determined to be properly prepared. Fortunately, I have more than one fridge.

I do a slow three-hundred-and-sixty-degree turn and survey my miniature kingdom. Everything looks right. Better than right. Perfect. Between us – that's me, Gloria and especially Edo – we've done a great job.

The shop had been empty for ages and we've definitely breathed new life into it. Floorboards sanded, filled, and painted white. Walls in a soft shade of blue. Gentle, subtle lighting. A small reception desk to the right of the door to make the shop look friendly and approachable to passers-by. A pair of comfy couches on either side of a fashionable low table. The whole effect is warm and inviting, and today, even before any of the lights are turned on, it seems the place is brighter than I'd imagined.

Ah, that would be because Gloria has finished with the window, and Edo has shifted the van. Which means—

Before I can complete that thought, Edo appears. Dressed in his usual uniform of ripped jeans and tight black T-shirt, his shaggy black hair frames a baby face that makes him look more like a sixth-former than a recent art school graduate. Swinging a hammer from his left hand he throws his surprisingly muscled right arm around my shoulder. Cheeky!

'Come and look,' he says. 'I know I'll be in trouble if the sign's not dead straight. And I'm worried you're not going to like it.'

Him and me both.

Most of the work in Edo's portfolio is what you might – politely – call 'out there'. Installations that make Tracy Emin's 'Bed' look more sedate than a watercolour by Degas.

And all I need is a shop sign.

But my doubts disappear the moment I take in Edo's work. Wow! He's done me proud.

4

'I don't like it,' I say in my best Simon Cowell impersonation, complete with theatrical pause. 'I absolutely love it!'

It feels … it feels *official*. There for all the world to see. Classic hand-painted lettering. A shop sign that manages to be cool, clean, chic and somehow rather sexy – at least I think so – and announces: 'HAPPY ENDINGS'.

I'm still admiring the sign when I realise my feet are no longer on the pavement. Edo has scooped me into his arms and we're crossing the high street, dodging a dustcart and – as I begin to struggle – almost bumping into a Boris bike.

'Put me down!' I insist. 'I'm about to become a pillar of the community.' Edo laughs and carries me, undaunted, over the threshold of Happy Endings.

Gloria watches with a smirk that says, *Didn't I tell you Edo's got a giant crush on you?* But I figure he's just grateful I let him continue to live in the shop between the time I signed the lease (he was squatting there, called it one of his own installations) and today, when I open my brand-new business.

'Put her down and go sort the fridge,' Gloria orders. 'The alarm comes on every time you close the door.'

Edo retreats – I think he's scared of Gloria – and a moment later, the beep-beeep-beeeeping resumes.

Gloria turns to me and says, 'So what's next?'

'I need to get changed before Mum and Dad arrive.'

'Before you do, I want to say how proud I am of you. The way you've pulled everything together so quickly. You're going to be a huge success, sweets!'

'I couldn't have done it without your help—'

I'm interrupted by Edo yelling, 'Great! I can see what's wrong. Don't worry. It's an easy fix.'

A moment later, Gloria and I flinch at the sharp thwack of

a hammer against metal. Then silence. As if Edo has murdered the fridge with a single blow.

For some reason – nerves, most likely, because the destruction of a key piece of equipment really isn't funny – I laugh. Then say to Gloria, 'You know what? This is the best day of my life!'

'Really?' Gloria looks surprised. She knows I'm not the sentimental type.

'Well, maybe apart from the day Mum and Dad finally weakened and let me have a kitten … or that time at uni with Lin, when we took an impulse trip to Dieppe and ended up in Brussels. And the day I passed my driving test. Sixth time lucky.'

'Didn't know that,' she says. 'But it explains a lot!'

Before she can tease me any further, Edo's back. 'Loose connection with the fan,' he says. 'Fixed. Shall I sort out these flowers?' He notices my doubtful expression and adds reassuringly, 'I used to arrange them at college when we did the still-life module.'

'That would be great.' We haven't known Edo very long, but he's a definite asset, and fast turning into a friend.

I go through to the back room and begin to change out of my paint-stained denims and into my working clothes. I've been dithering for days about what to wear. I finally settled on tapered black linen trousers, teamed with a turquoise top and my smartest black jacket. The one with turned-back cuffs lined with turquoise and pink patterned silk. And, of course, my lucky silver earrings. I'd feel naked without them. It's an outfit that makes me look professional but still me. I give myself a final once-over in the mirror, quickly apply a fresh coat of lip gloss, then rejoin my friends.

Edo has worked magic with the flowers. Gloria has finished with the windows. The fridge is behaving itself.

In less than an hour, Happy Endings will be open for business. And any moment now Mum and Dad will arrive to inspect what they've taken to calling 'The Investment'.

Dad stepped in after the bank took all of three minutes to turn down my application for a start-up loan. 'You're to take my pension pot and put it into your business.' After he left the navy, Dad went into the construction business. Without his help, Happy Endings would never have got off the drawing board. He's got so much faith in me it's scary. Then again, as he says, I've got a great location on a busy high street, slap bang in the middle of London, how can I fail?

And I know I can do this. It's what I want more than anything. From now on I'm devoting myself to business. Nothing else matters. Not that there is much else, to be honest. Other than Gloria and Edo, I don't exactly have a red-hot social life. My choice, I know. Over the past five years, I've become a bit of a recluse.

But today, I can't even begin to describe my sense of purpose. I'm nervous, yet exhilarated.

In short, I've never felt more alive.

Which is a bit odd perhaps. Because I see dead people. All the time.

It's an occupational hazard.

Chapter 2

Whenever I meet someone new and we get to the bit where they ask me, 'So what do you do?' and I say I'm an undertaker, I get one of three reactions:

1. 'You're kidding!'
2. 'Eeuw.' Usually accompanied by that two-fingers-down-the-throat gesture.
3. 'So, okay, when you were small did you pull the wings off flies?'

I wish I could make people understand. It's not torture. Quite the opposite. I love my job. And is it really so strange?

Think of it this way. I'm an organiser. An event planner. A good listener. A shoulder to cry on. A public speaker. A nego-tiator. A seamstress. An accomplished multi-tasker. A stylist. I can remove a stain from almost any fabric, I'm a dab hand with a make-up brush, and I'm full of good advice. For example: never wear lip gloss when you're scattering ashes.

When the unexpected happens, I am expected to rise to the occasion. And I do.

Do I touch dead people? Yes, of course.

What do they feel like? Mostly, they feel cold.

Am I weird? I don't think so ...

I'm just a typical millennial who enjoys shopping, movies,

holidays and – mysteriously – housework. I probably keep myself to myself a bit too much but I've always enjoyed my own company and I've never been great in a crowd.

More than anything else, I'm proud to be an undertaker. Not to mention enormously proud to be opening my own shop. It's the biggest leap of my life and it still seems unreal – particularly when you think that until recently, I was a semi-disgraced ex-employee.

My life started to go pear-shaped late last year when the business I worked for, a firm of undertakers run by the original owner's great-great-great-grandson, was taken over by a huge funeral group with headquarters in New York and branches on every continent.

As soon as the deal was done we were summoned to meet our new manager, Jason Chung. 'Nothing's going to change,' he promised us.

But everything did.

Being accountable to a manager who'd never even carried a coffin was a huge change in itself. And that was just the beginning.

My former boss, the great-great-great grandson, was gone in a matter of weeks. He quit the day our new owners announced that from now on we would only be offering headstones made from Chinese granite, a decision that was all about profit rather than the best interests of our clients.

Even while two sets of lawyers continued to argue about whether or not the name of the family firm could be removed – it's there to this day, because the new owners know the public prefer to deal with supposedly genuine local firms – our professional vocabulary began to change. At staff training sessions, words like 'care', 'service', 'respectful' and 'time of need' were cast aside in favour of sentences that were strong on 'sales', 'targets', 'commission' and 'underperforming'.

That sort of mindset makes me want to throw up. In fact, at a subsequent regional training day, I was overheard during the coffee break saying something to that effect – how was I supposed to know it was Jason Chung's mother standing behind me? – and my comments resulted in me being sent to Siberia.

Not the place. Even though the new owners have business interests all over Europe, so far as I know, the people of Russia are not yet obliged to be commemorated with slabs of Chinese stone. No, Siberia was our name for the back office. To call it an office was actually an insult to offices.

Thanks to Jason's mother's need to overshare my private conversation, I spent ten days there, closeted in a small windowless space that used to be a store room, with only the low throb of the mortuary fridges on the other side of a thin partition for company.

Jason himself cloaked my punishment with a mirthless smile. 'This is an excellent opportunity for Nina to focus on her administrative skills without any risk of distraction,' he told everyone.

In practical terms that translated as one mountain of paperwork swiftly followed by another. A cross between school detention and prison. Gloria insisted my incarceration breached several employment laws, and since she's almost a qualified lawyer she's probably correct.

Then again, my solitary confinement wasn't entirely bad. I enjoyed breaking the office-hours monotony by going through all the product catalogues and samples that got sent to us in the post. I didn't usually get to see these – although I have stacks of them now – so it was interesting to discover you could pick up a third-hand hearse for under four grand. Which I seriously considered once I got into the preparations for Happy Endings, although in the end I splashed out on a simple pale blue van with my business name and contact details discreetly on the side and a properly equipped interior from a company that was offering a cheap finance deal. I think it looks uplifting yet still properly respectful.

Happy Endings may be a shoe-string start-up, but if it weren't for what happened on my final day at work, it probably wouldn't exist at all. So I shall always be grateful Jason Chung's mother is a sneak.

Here's what happened on that last day.

I'd spent most of the morning on the phone, unenthusiastically informing recent clients that by completing a customer satisfaction survey they could win a weekend in Devon. Then, having finished with the post, I moved on to the next batch of papers, and discovered a pile of burial applications in need of processing. They were going to take me at least forty-five minutes – always supposing the Wi-Fi in Siberia wasn't playing up again – and I was so not in the mood.

It was a quarter to one, fifteen minutes before my lunch-break was supposed to start, and I was feeling peckish. I'd been trying to stick to the 5:2 diet and this was one of the days when I was not required to starve myself.

I straightened the applications, grabbed my coat and umbrella – the April showers were in full flood – and prepared to make a dash for the deli next to Queen's Park tube station.

I knew that if Jason saw me leave so early, he'd do that annoying looking-ostentatiously-at-his-Rolex-while-tapping-the-glass thing that was supposed to remind me he's the boss.

Happily, he was nowhere in sight and by the time I got safely beyond the reception desk I was weighing the relative merits of tuna and cucumber on sourdough versus a jumbo salt beef hot wrap. And a chocolate orange cupcake, of course. Or maybe the vegetarian choice: a trio of chocolate orange cupcakes.

There was only the door standing between me and seven hundred calories, and I flung it open, umbrella at the ready. This particular April shower had turned into a full-blown downpour and the raindrops were bouncing off the pavement so hard I could actually hear them.

It must have been the thought of my lunchtime cupcake that made me fail to look where I was going. I stepped onto the street and literally fell over a woman for whom the phrase 'drowned rat' could have been invented.

She was sitting – slumped was probably more accurate – in the doorway.

Before I could apologise and ask if she was okay, I realised she was anything but.

And before I could speak the woman grabbed my leg and looked up into my face. She was about my age, dressed in a jacket and skirt that looked as though they'd been left out to drip-dry. Her pretty face was framed by two bedraggled blonde tendrils and her mascara was in ruins.

The pressure on my leg increased. 'Please,' the woman sobbed. 'You have to help me.'

Chapter 3

'So two years we are here. My husband Grigor and me. We are sad to leave home but things are better in England ...'

Whenever I think about the drowned rat – her name is Anna – which is often, I am grateful I took an early lunchbreak that day. It's as if fate decided our two paths needed to collide.

Sitting in the deli with her, I had remembered her story right away. 'Grigor Kovaks,' I said. 'I read about it—' I stopped myself from reciting the details of the horrific accident that had left Anna's husband in hospital with life-threatening injuries.

'Yes, Grigor. My lovely Grigor.' Her smile was so full of love it pierced my heart. 'We find a flat in Camberwell and Grigor works nights for a bank in Canary Wharf. Security guard. And I am a cleaner. Then three weeks ago, on the Tuesday, Grigor is offered an extra shift, and of course we say yes.'

I listened carefully. It's so important not to interrupt. Being there for someone at the worst time in their life, letting them tell their own story in their own way, can make it just a tiny bit better.

'He is so proud of his bicycle,' Anna continued. 'Cleans and polishes it like it is a sports car. He needs his bike. The fares on your underground, they are so expensive. Not like in Budapest ... After the accident I am living more or less at the hospital. Grigor stays in the coma. He looks asleep and I keep waiting for him to wake up. But nothing. And ... last night I agree with the doctors that the machines are turned off. Then later the nurses were so kind but I could not speak to them. I need a little time on my own. So I go to the hospital chapel to pray for my man and when I come back to the ward, Grigor is not there.' Anna started to cry. Fortunately, the deli was filling up fast, and nobody took any notice of us.

She took a sip of her now cold espresso, composed herself, and continued. 'And that is when they tell me he has been taken already to the funeral place. Your funeral place.'

Oh God.

Please.

No.

I think I know what's coming next. It shouldn't happen, but it does.

A phone call to a 'friendly' undertaker during the night.

Money changing hands.

And someone like Anna Kovaks, a woman who's just lost someone she loves and who has not slept for thirty-six hours, delivered like a lamb to the slaughter into the grubby paws of a business that sees every new client as a cash machine.

If this were BC – Before Chung – it would have been unthinkable. Our standards were always so much higher.

Gently, I encouraged Anna to continue.

'When I arrive, the man seems very nice. Very full of sympathy.'

Full of something else if you ask me, but I keep my professional face in place.

'He takes me into his office, and asks me many questions about my Grigor.' For a moment, Anna's voice faltered, but then – as is so often the case – she summoned her inner strength. 'I tell this man, this Mr Chung of yours, how Grigor and I meet when we are both twelve years old. That we grow up together. That we have so many big dreams. And how our life begins when we come to London. And now Grigor has been accepted to do teacher training in September. He is so good at mathematics. They put him on the fast track and he will work at a big school in Beckenham.'

Anna drained her coffee cup, then fumbled in her bag and produced a soggy linen handkerchief. I recognised it at once. Jason orders them by the dozen. 'Quality handkerchiefs make a statement about our business,' he informed us at a staff meeting. I happened to agree, but in this case Jason's largesse meant we were putting up our prices. Again.

Anna continued, 'Then Mr Chung tells me it is an honour and a privilege that your firm has been chosen to make the arrangements. That is how it works in England. The hospital decides on the funeral place, right?'

A million times wrong.

'So first of all, he invites me to choose the ... the coffin. I pick the one that costs the least. But Mr Chung tells me that as Grigor is going to be a professional man, a teacher, it is a bad choice. He wants me to pick the one made of ma ... ma—'

'Mahogany,' I supplied.

Anna nodded. 'And then he tells me about embalming. It needs to be done, right?'

Absolutely not.

'Mr Chung says I will want Grigor to look his best when relatives come to visit him before the funeral. I tell him that everyone is in Hungary, and he seems very glad. Before I say anything, he picks up the phone and talks about re ... re—'

'Repatriating the body.'

'Yes. But I can tell from the conversation that this will be much too expensive. I explain we have started saving for the deposit on a flat, but only recently. And that I must do what Grigor wanted for us most. Stay here in London and raise our child to have the best chance in life.' Anna noticed my startled face and softly added, 'Fourteen weeks. The two weeks before ... before the accident ... they were the happiest time we ever spent. Now I truly believe that the peanut – that was our name for the baby – is a gift from God. I have to think that. Or ...' Anna was unable to continue.

'So what did Mr Chung suggest?' I prompted.

'He said he would find Grigor a nice home at a cemetery in a part of London called Kilburn. He says it is a very nice district, right?'

Anna has obviously never been there.

'And there will be many flowers. And car for me to ride in alone. And a stone to remember Grigor that will come all the way from China. I want to ask questions, but your Mr Chung, he talks very fast. He tells me we shall need a double plot so we can be together always. And that it will be a good idea for me to take out a funeral plan for myself at the same time. He makes me very nervous, Mr Chung, because I can tell all this will be very expensive.'

I'm surprised only that Jason didn't insist on a horse-drawn hearse accompanied by the skirl of bagpipes and a juvenile chimney sweep.

Anna resumed, 'In the end I tell Mr Chung that I shall spend all our savings for the flat deposit. Every penny. We have eleven hundred pounds in the Santander account. And you know what?'

16

Sadly, yes.

Having snatched Grigor's body from the hospital in order to hold it to ransom in the corporate fridge, Jason Chung had been deeply unimpressed with the size of Anna's life savings.

'I knew it was expensive to live in London. But I never imagined it will cost so much to die.' Anna's bottom lip wobbled. 'But Mr Chung says he wants to help me give Grigor the ceremony he deserves, and that he has a solution. I am not to worry because there is a nice organisation that will help me. They are called Doshdotcom. You know them?'

Kill me now.

Jason Chung actually suggested this poor woman, deep in shock on the worst day of her life – someone who was expecting a baby and had no regular income – should take out a payday loan?

I had no idea what to say.

'By now I am very worried.' Anna looked me in the eyes. 'Mr Chung says that in England a cheap funeral costs about eight thousand pounds. That is correct, yes?'

'No.' My single word came out as a whisper, because I could barely trust myself to talk at all.

A weak smile. 'So I do the right thing. When Mr Chung says he will fetch an application form for me to pay for the funeral I run away. I need time to think. But then I fall over outside your shop. And then you come. Like you are running away also. And you fall over me.'

I reached across the table and squeezed Anna's hand. 'I'm so glad that happened,' I said. 'Mr Chung .. Mr Chung hasn't worked for our firm for very long. Please accept my apology for your ... your experience with him. I hope you will allow me to put things right. Here's what we're going to do.'

I began by reassuring Anna that she didn't need to get herself into debt to give Grigor a respectful funeral. She might even be entitled to a government grant to help cover the costs. But then I realised she was no longer listening.

She was staring at Jason Chung. Marching towards us, a trail of plump raindrops scattering in his wake. His suit looked as though it was midway through an intensive wash cycle, and he was angrier than I'd ever seen him.

'Mrs Kovaks,' he said. 'Found you at last. So glad Nina's been looking after you.' A meaningful glare in my direction. 'Let me escort you back to the office, so we can sign those forms and ensure your husband has the dignified funeral he would have wanted. I've settled the bill,' he added. 'Coffees on me.'

So Jason Chung shepherded us out of the deli as if we were two felons under arrest. We were waiting for a gap in the traffic so we could cross the road when a cab pulled over a few yards in front of us and its passenger got out.

'Quick!' I grabbed Anna by the hand and dragged her into the taxi. 'Just drive straight ahead,' I ordered the driver. The cab had stopped on double red lines, so he didn't need to be told twice.

As our getaway vehicle sped away, I turned round in time to see my boss's furious face. His clenched fists were high in the air and he looked almost as though he was doing a rain dance.

In other circumstances I might even have laughed.

Chapter 4

That's what I said that night, when I told Gloria the story of Anna Kovaks. 'In other circumstances, I might even have laughed. Jason was bouncing up and down on the spot, waving his arms around as if he was putting a curse on me! Or a spell to make everyone believe that the more you love someone, the more you need to spend on their funeral.'

'So the whole thing was what you might call an R-I-P off?'

Gloria said it as though it were a pun I hadn't heard before. I scrubbed the cast-iron orange saucepan that went with my dad to the Falklands War (and came safely home again) even harder, removing the final traces of our bolognese supper.

Truth be told, I was a bit irritated. If Gloria hadn't wanted to know what happened to me at work that day, she probably shouldn't have asked. On the one hand, we both knew she was only making a rhetorical enquiry before launching into tonight's instalment of her Disastrous Relationship with Thrice-Wed Fred. But just this once, Fred's latest crimes could surely wait until we'd resolved something more serious.

My entire life.

I'm the first to admit I haven't exactly cracked the work–life balance thing. It's almost all work – not least because whenever there's the faintest whiff of romance in the air, I tend immediately to think about my husband's funeral. The only place my life is properly rounded is at the hips.

Gloria, to her credit, realised from my tense posture at the sink that despite my light-hearted remark about Jason, his behaviour towards Anna was no laughing matter. The two of us had shared a home long enough for her to know what I was going to say next.

'So you're going to resign,' she pre-empted me.

'What else can I do?'

'Let's back up a moment,' Gloria said. 'You did absolutely the right thing, taking Anna to the no-frills funeral services in Putney. Eight hundred and fifty quid as opposed to thousands of pounds she simply didn't have.' Gloria rose from the kitchen table and headed for our emergency supplies cupboard.

This was definitely going to be a two-bottles-of-wine Wednesday.

'I take it Jason will release the body?' she asked.

An invisible hand grabbed my stomach and twisted. Until then, I'd completely overlooked – repressed, more likely – the fact that the bloke who started up his budget cremations business because he was scandalised by the cost of his own mother's funeral would need to liaise with my employers if he was going to have Grigor's body to cremate. I folded a damp tea towel into quarters, gave the glass hob a quick polish, then sat down at our kitchen table and reached gratefully for my fresh glass of wine.

'Jason won't have any choice,' I said. 'Which means I need to hand in my notice first thing tomorrow. Otherwise, I'm as bad as he is.'

'What about the others? Surely when you tell them what happened, they'll help you take Jason to task? Force him to behave properly from now on.'

As if.

Our staff turnover had been horrendous since the business was sold. Apart from a couple of the senior drivers, I'd been there longer than anyone else. Five years.

The newcomers seemed to have bought into Jason's marketing-speak: monthly sales targets and promises of big bonuses. For all I knew—

No, surely it was impossible that everyone except me was up-selling in the worst possible way?

'I'm not certain I can count on anyone for support,' I said. 'So the only question is, how much do you get on the dole these days?' I managed to sound a lot less frightened than I felt, as I started to face up to the true cost of my good deed. Ah well, I'd experimented with just about every diet in the universe, so perhaps the Poverty Diet would succeed where the rest had failed.

'I won't be out of work for long.' It was a promise to myself as much as to Gloria, although I was already wondering where my next job was coming from. Independent funeral companies were becoming an endangered species, and my battle charge towards the moral high ground, in flagrant defiance of corporate policy, was unlikely to impress any of the big chains – none of which I had ever wanted to work for anyway.

Gloria broke into my alarming thoughts. 'Sweetie, I've been telling you for three years,' she said. 'You pay me too much rent.'

Gloria is – not to put too fine a point on it – rich. Which is to say, Gloria's dad is an ex-banker whose name was never far from the headlines a few years ago, usually alongside words like 'disgraced' and 'fat cat'. These days, he seems to spend most of his time playing golf and gently taking the piss out of his adored only child for choosing to work at a community law centre. 'Sins of the fathers are one thing,' he'd chided last time he visited, 'but surely you could do good in a more lucrative way? There's plenty of women eager to pay handsomely for good divorce lawyers.'

This house, the house we live in here in Kentish Town, was Gloria's eighteenth birthday present. (Imagine that. I thought I was really privileged when Mum and Dad celebrated my coming of age with driving lessons.) And since the community law centre no longer has any budget for staff, my rent money is what Gloria lives off. Topped up by her trust fund, admittedly. Then again, for someone who needn't work at all if she chose not to, Gloria is pretty damn dedicated to her various causes. It's one of the things I love about her. However, I wasn't about to become her latest charity case and I resolved that first thing in the morning I'd start putting out feelers for a new job.

I drained my wine glass. 'I'm going to go and compose my resignation letter. I'll send it by email.'

'First of all,' Gloria topped me up with a generous glug of Malbec before I could get my glass to the safety of the sink, 'listen to me a moment.' I knew what she was going to say, and sure enough … 'It's always easier to get a job when you're already employed.'

'Yes, but—'

'So why not go marching in there tomorrow and apologise for your momentary lapse in professionalism which interrupted his bereavement consultation, or whatever it is he's calling it this week …'

'Intake appointment,' I muttered.

'Whatevs. Anyway, my point is that you can stick to your

principles without becoming a martyr. Take your salary for a few more weeks, while you get yourself sorted somewhere else. And leave with a good reference.'

I could see the logic in what Gloria was saying. And thinking about it, none of my erstwhile colleagues had gone to work for rival funeral directors. One took a job as a cosmetics consultant at the Westfield Centre, another went travelling, and the third member of what used to be our team said there were no decent jobs out there, just junior positions with zero hours contracts, so he went off to retrain as a hotel manager.

None of that was for me. I couldn't imagine not doing what I do.

My job is part of who I am.

What was I going to do?

What *was* I going to do?

I closed my eyes for a few seconds and visualised. It's a really useful technique I use whenever I need to adjust to change. In my mind's eye, I saw myself going off to work as … as … all I could see was Siberia, the miserable little back office at work where, less than twelve hours ago, I had been – frankly – a lot happier than I was right then.

So maybe my brain was telling me change was unnecessary. But in my heart I already knew that if I kept drawing my salary, even for a little while, it would be a betrayal of my profession.

'Tell you what,' I said. 'Maybe I'll just go and type my resignation letter. See how it feels to put into words the fact that Jason is a blemish on our industry. Perhaps I'll suggest he's the person who should quit, rather than me.'

Before Gloria could say anything more, the doorbell rang.

So far as I knew, we weren't expecting visitors. Not unless …

By the way Gloria leapt to answer, I wondered if Thrice-Wed Fred had decided to pay an unscheduled nocturnal visit.

But no, Gloria came back alone. An envelope in her hand. 'Came by courier,' she said, sliding it across the kitchen table to me.

Inside the big brown envelope with my name on it, there was a small white envelope with my name on it. And inside that, a single sheet of paper. Also with my name on it.

Dear Ms Sherwood,

Please accept this letter as formal notice of your dismissal for a wholly unacceptable act of gross misconduct committed today.

Our HR Department will calculate any outstanding salary and holiday pay and remit to your bank account in due course, and your personal belongings will be forwarded to you by courier tomorrow. I should add that you are no longer welcome on our premises.

On a personal note, I am extremely disappointed by your behaviour and respectfully suggest you are probably better suited to employment in a not-for-profit enterprise.

Jason Chung

There went my chances of a glowing reference. Wordlessly, I handed the letter to Gloria.

By unspoken mutual consent, we opened a third bottle of wine. And since there was no longer any need to debate whether or not I needed to resign, we soon moved on to discuss Gloria's favourite topic of conversation. Fred Carpenter QC. Visiting Professor of Law at one of London's most prestigious universities. Older than Gloria and me by at least ten years.

George Clooney hair. The fathomless brown eyes of a Labrador puppy. A silver tongue that effortlessly charms juries, judges and almost every woman under the age of eighty. And an ego the size of Uranus.

Also answers to the name of Thrice-Wed Fred. Or rather he doesn't. That's what Gloria and I started to call him when he appeared on the scene late last year, before Gloria got embroiled with him. Foolishly embroiled, if you ask me, although whenever I've tried gently to remind Gloria that Fred's a married man, she turns somewhere between defensive and downright shirty.

Then again, who am I to judge?

Two months ago, I had a one-night stand with Jason Chung.

Chapter 5

Jason and I happened because of a train strike. That and a serious, alcohol-fuelled misjudgement.

I was supposed to travel to Nottingham to collect a hearse from another business in our group. (We'd acquired a National Logistics Director who continually shuffled vehicles from one branch to the next, 'To ensure maximum capacity at all times,' as he so charmlessly put it.) The strike meant I couldn't go, but rather than leave it an extra day, Jason announced the two of us would drive there together.

'A great opportunity for me to brief you about the new commission opportunities from engraving,' he threatened. 'We've partnered with a firm that's going to pay us by the letter.'

I'm afraid my immediate thought was that Jason's Holy Grail of a client would be a recently deceased nanny whose compliant relatives could be persuaded to put 'supercalifragilisticexpialidocious' on her tombstone.

'Okay,' I said.

Okay is one of the most useful words in my vocabulary. It can cover a multitude of sins. On that occasion, it meant that since I had no choice in the matter, I'd do my best to behave like a good employee.

As it happened, our journey up the M1 was a revelation.

Jason's A–Z lecture about payment-by-the-letter – all I remember now is that capitals were apparently more valuable to the firm than words in lower case, so make that 'SUPERCALIFRAGILISTICEXPIALIDOCIOUS' – drew thankfully to a close just before we reached Dunstable. Then, to my surprise, the further we got from London, the more he started to relax.

I'm a good listener – another part of the job – and Jason is a great talker. Most of what he says is total bollocks of course, but on this occasion, he chose a topic that aroused my curiosity. He started talking about himself.

'I know you think I've got it easy, Nina.' Jason shrugged his shoulders and gave me a sidelong glance that also incorporated the interior of his ridiculous, show-off Porsche. 'But at least you're doing this job because you choose to.'

'Okay.'

'I don't have any choice. It's either this or my parents threatened to banish me to bloody Beijing.' That was the first time I'd heard Jason swear. 'It's not as if I've ever set foot in China in the first place,' he continued. 'We're the American side of the family.'

My wet-behind-the-ears boss was a nephew of the ultimate owners of our business and beneficiary of unimaginable wealth, luxury and jobs for the boys. Or so the office grapevine had it. But once Jason started talking, a different picture emerged.

Boarding school in New Hampshire. Business school in Pennsylvania. 'And then they told me – *told me* – I'd have to do this job for the next three years. And that unless my sales figures were fifteen per cent higher than every other manager in the group, I wouldn't have any say in my next assignment.'

'Okay.'

'Not okay, at all. I wish you'd stop saying that. It really pisses me off.'

Blimey. Jason Chung was suddenly turning into a human being, right before my eyes.

'Okay.' But this time, I giggled as I said it, and Jason laughed, too. 'So what is it you'd rather be doing?'

'What I really want is to be a landscape gardener. When I told my parents, you'd have thought I wanted to run away and join the circus. Or the Democrats.'

By the time we arrived in Nottingham, Jason was babbling on about the joy he gets from growing flowers and vegetables in containers on his balcony. I'd learned about the correct time of year to set out poppies, plant onion sets, and seed sweet peas. Also about a bumper crop of strawberries, fit to grace Wimbledon. And then there was Jason's relentless fight against super-slugs the size of a prizefighter's fist. It was almost like having a conversation with Gloria, whose latest project involved making a wildflower meadow in a dustbin lid.

Once we'd arrived at our destination, the paperwork for transferring the hearse to our branch took about twenty minutes.

Back in the car park, Jason watched me get into the hearse and adjust the vehicle's seat and mirrors. I wound down the window and said, 'I'll race you back to London!'

Jason produced the keys to his Porsche. 'Okay.' A grin. Then, 'Tell you what. We're almost into the rush hour so the M1's going to be really busy. I know a nice little place just off the motorway. Follow me there and we'll grab a bite to eat.'

'Okay,' I said. Driving in the slow lane surrounded by packs of impatient lorries and white van fleets isn't my idea of fun, so I was super happy to agree to divert myself with food until the traffic thinned out.

Twenty-five minutes later, I was beginning to wonder if Jason had changed his mind. I had no idea where we were – maybe he'd decided to take the scenic route back to London – but just as I heard my stomach rumble, he pulled over into a little red brick development that boasted both a Little Chef and a Travelodge.

I got out of the hearse and said, 'You certainly know how to spoil a girl.'

'Sorry.' Jason was flustered. 'The place I was looking for seems to have disappeared.'

He obviously wasn't about to tell me he couldn't find it.

'Never mind,' I said. 'I'm starving. Let's see what the Little Chef has to offer.'

It turned out the Little Chef was able to come up with a decent glass of wine, which washed down quite well alongside our meal. I'd meant to have mushroom soup, but when the waitress arrived to take our order, the words that came out of my mouth were, 'I'll have the foot-long hot dog with a side of beef chilli and as many chips as you can fit on the plate.' Jason opted for a more sedate plate of ham, eggs and chips.

By the time we'd finished eating, it was dark outside. Jason excused himself from the table and I thought he was settling the bill, but then our waitress arrived with another glass of wine. Five minutes passed ... ten. Had Jason done a runner? No, there he was outside, talking intently on his phone. Ah well. I had nothing on that evening, so I might as well relax.

I sat there thinking about my plans for the weekend – a trip to the cinema and Sunday lunch with Mum and Dad in Southampton – until Jason returned, accompanied by a pancake stack fighting for space on the plate with a giant dollop of vanilla ice cream.

'Really sorry,' he said. 'Office stuff. I thought you'd be able to manage dessert, though. What's that you were singing to yourself?' he added. 'Ah, got it! *Mary Poppins*! My mum loves that movie!'

After we'd finished, we made our way back to the car park. 'I've had a good day,' Jason said. 'Much better than being stuck in the office. See you tomorrow.' He stood and watched me get into the hearse.

But when I turned the ignition, nothing happened.

'Must be the battery,' Jason said. 'Let's take a look.' A minute or so later he confessed, 'I haven't got a clue what I'm doing. We're going to need a garage.'

And that was how – once we'd discovered the hearse needed a new alternator that couldn't be located until the morning – we came to spend the night at the Travelodge.

One thing I liked about Jason was that he seemed unruffled by the fact our simple errand was not turning out as planned. He took charge of the situation, booked us a couple of rooms and invited me to join him in the bar.

Three drinks later, I was bold enough to say, 'I'm surprised you didn't tell me to sleep in the hearse while you drove back to London. Maybe I've misjudged you.'

'Oh, I'm probably as bad as you think. Although not entirely without manners.' Jason topped up our glasses. 'But Nottingham can pay for the repair bill and the cost of our accommodation. And our dinner. I'm damned if it's coming off my bottom line.' This sounded much more like the Jason Chung I knew and was obliged to tolerate for forty hours a week. 'But let's not talk about work. Tell me about you, Nina. I know nothing about you.'

As someone who's much more comfortable operating a spotlight than basking in its glow, I hate it when I'm invited to talk about myself. But more than that ... if I'm honest, my personal life has been a wilderness for longer than I care to confess.

I'm an only child. I gave up line-dancing when it became evident I have two left feet. Apart from Gloria, I have a few close friends I met at uni – people I can call at four in the morning and know they'll be there for me – but unfortunately none live in London. The pancakes I rustle up on a Sunday morning are infinitely superior to those of Little Chef. And the nearest thing I do have to a personal life, by which I mean a romantic life, is listening to Gloria's ill-advised adventures with Thrice-Wed Fred.

My continuing silence was becoming uncomfortable for us both.

'Okaaaay,' I finally began. 'I live in Kentish Town ...' And within five minutes, I was telling a story about Gloria's plan to infiltrate the Regent's Park Garden Festival with a pop-up edible hedge that involves bareroot blackberries, cherry plums, crab apples and wild pears, all the while hoping Jason had forgotten he asked about me.

Sure enough, it worked. Soon, he was jabbering about the ins and outs of sweetcorn, and I was beginning to think he might even shape up into a suitable replacement for Thrice-Wed Fred.

But Jason had other ideas.

And I had no inkling, until he walked me to the door of my room, took me in his arms and kissed me. Rather well.

'I've been wanting to do that for hours,' he murmured. 'Mysterious Nina. Beautiful Nina.' Then he kissed me again.

It wasn't the right time to tell my boss I hadn't had sex for five years.

Ever since ...

An image of my husband's funeral. Ryan. His coffin, draped in the regimental colours, danced in front of my eyes. Was I really going to spend the rest of my life as a born-again virgin?

Apparently not.

Work 101: Never sleep with the boss.

Never.

Ever.

(Not that we got much sleep.)

When I woke the next morning, I felt ...

More than anything else, I felt reassured to know my body hadn't seized up through lack of use. But I was under no illusion. The night before had been about opportunity and circumstance rather than any genuine emotional connection.

And that suited me just fine.

I know Gloria thinks it's time I moved on with my life, even though she's never put it quite that way. Mum and Dad, for their part, would be thrilled if I turned up with a new man, although they know better than to say so. We had that particular discussion the Christmas before last and it ended with me sobbing that unless I could be sure of a relationship as strong and long-lasting as theirs, I'd far rather spend the rest of my life alone.

After all the pain I've been through – not to mention the guilt, however misplaced, that I was in some way to blame – why take any more risks? I only have to think how often

Thrice-Wed Fred fails to deliver on his empty promises to Gloria. At least if I'm alone, the only person with the power to disappoint me is myself.

I was having this conversation with myself because, thankfully, I had woken up alone. Jason was long gone. His Porsche, too. An hour or so later, while I was still waiting for the alternator and the mechanic to show up, I discovered a note in my jacket pocket. That was wonderful. You look beautiful when you're asleep and I can't wait to see you again. J xxx

No!

There was only one thing to do.

I sent Jason a text. *Last night didn't happen*, it said. *Please delete*.

Chapter 6

Jason was never the same after that. He was worse. Never missing a chance to criticise my work, berating me for missing sales targets, and even giving me a verbal warning for being five minutes late.

And yet ...

It's Jason I have to thank for this huge makeover in my life. If he hadn't fired me, Happy Endings wouldn't exist and I wouldn't be standing here in my new shop today.

Actually, I'm sitting at my reception desk. It's been two hours since Gloria and Edo left to take Mum and Dad out to breakfast, and I flipped the sign on the door from 'Closed' to 'Open'. I've passed the time by making sure I understand the various software packages that came with my new computer, dusting the display shelves (twice) and making sure the fridge in the basement continues to behave itself.

I'm on my fourth cup of coffee, which means I need to run to the loo again, but before I can leave my desk, the door opens and a woman comes in.

She's five foot nothing, dressed head to toe in a bright orange ensemble of blouse, skirt, tights and clumpy boots. Her outfit clashes magnificently with her thick, shoulder-length hair, dyed in that unfortunate yet ubiquitous shade Gloria and I always refer to as menopause red, topped by a purple fedora that adds several inches to her height.

'Good morning,' she says. 'I'm Sybille Newman. Your neighbour.'

The shop next door to mine is The Primrose Poppadum – 'Modern Organic Indian Classics, Free from Dairy, MSG, Wheat & Egg' according to its sign – and Sybille Newman doesn't fit my image of a restaurateur. Then again, I'm probably not her idea of an undertaker.

'Very pleased to meet you,' I say cautiously.

'So you're the owner, are you?' Sybille Newman has a cut-glass accent and she sounds cross.

'Yes, I'm Nina Sherwood. Today's my first day and—'

'Never mind that. I've come about the roof.'

'Pardon?'

'The roof. My husband and I live above the dreadful Indian restaurant.' Sybille gestures towards The Primrose Poppadum with a flash of her Guantanamo orange fingernails. 'Make sure you never go there – I've seen them arriving with carrier bags full of stuff from Asda. Organic my foot! We're trying to get them shut down because of the dreadful smells. My husband has a respiratory disorder and they're making it so much worse. But that's not the point. The roof is leaking and we need a new one.' She looks expectantly at me.

'I'm sorry to hear that,' I say. 'But I don't understand why your roof is any of my business.'

'It's a single structure that covers both properties.' Sybille Newman frowns at me as if I'm being deliberately obtuse. 'Ned and I have lived here for twenty-three years, and even when the betting shop was downstairs, back in the nineties, there was trouble with the roof.' She leans on my reception desk and adds, 'We've had it replaced twice, but now there's water leaking into our living room again every time it rains. We've got a good jobbing builder who's been patching it up, but we shouldn't have to be doing that at our own expense. Not when it's supposed to be a shared cost. I wouldn't be at all surprised if the purlin's rotted. And there's a ticking noise coming from the rafters that keeps us awake every night. Woodworm probably. Or beetles.' Sybille smiles slyly. She seems almost pleased at the prospect. 'So I'll get some roofers round to supply estimates and let you have copies.'

'Okay.' I presume she wants me to pass them on to my managing agent.

'And you need to complain to the council about the restaurant smell. Not that they'll do anything about it.'

There's something about the way she says this that makes me think Sybille Newman enjoys being a victim, that she's the sort of woman who is happy only when she's got something to complain about. I've already got a feeling that no matter how hard I try to be a good neighbour, nothing I do will be ever good enough.

Our conversation seems to have run its course and I'm wondering if I should walk Sybille to the door when she says, 'I take it your stock will be arriving soon?'

I'm not planning to carry a supply of coffins. The shop's too small. But it's a weird question.

Sybille continues, 'Ned intends be your first customer.'

Ned? Didn't she say her husband's called Ned?

I'm still working on the implications of that sentence when she continues, 'Ned's always got his nose buried in a novel. I presume you'll give him a discount. The old bookshop always did. So sad when they closed. Business rates went through the roof. But don't let me put you off.' Sybille has noticed my startled expression. 'I'm sure you'll make a huge success of Happy Endings.' She says this with an almost-sneer that suggests precisely the opposite. 'There's plenty of children around here, and it's so important to get them reading at an early age, stop them frying their brains with electronic gadgets.'

'Yes, reading's important,' I agree. 'But actually ... Actually, Happy Endings isn't a bookshop.'

'Not a bookshop?' Now it's Sybille who is perplexed. 'Everyone's been saying that's what's opening. If it's not a bookshop, then what *is* it?'

'A funeral parlour.'

'A *WHAT?* Really? That's totally unsuitable. No-one asked Ned and me about this. I'm sure we were entitled to be consulted. My husband's health is very fragile, and having an undertaker's downstairs ... Well, it's hardly going to cheer him up, is it?'

With that, the woman turns abruptly on her orange heel. At the door, she shoots a baleful look in my direction.

'Poor Noggsie.' She says it as if she's spitting a pair of marbles from her mouth. 'He was always so helpful about the roof. He'd be spinning in his grave if he knew about this. About *you*.'

Funeral Number One

†††

In Memoriam
PETER JAMES NOGGS
1933–2019

†††

T he vicar looked nervous, Gloria thought. And under-standably so. Everyone present in the church had known Noggsie, whereas few of them, including Gloria herself, knew the vicar, who seemed to be an earnest young man, clearly overwhelmed by the many famous faces staring back at him.

A final rustle of his papers, and the vicar began. 'Peter ...' he said. 'How strange to call him Peter, when all of us here knew him as Noggsie. He was the beating heart of our community for as long as any of us can remember.'

Primrose Hill royalty had turned out in force to pay their respects, and were now sitting in clusters surrounded by many of their less recognisable neighbours. A tribute to the fact Noggsie always treated everyone exactly the same, celebrity or not. To him, the famous customers were just ordinary people who happened to be doing a bit of shopping on their local high street. And there was nothing celebrities liked more than being treated as ordinary people – at least when they were off-duty and on their home turf. As a result, a surprising number of high-profile diaries had been cleared, with filming schedules rearranged, recording sessions postponed and fashion shoots put on hold. Even Tottenham Hotspur had to manage at training that morning without their most famous striker.

Outside the church, private security, police and paparazzi hung around in their separate tribes. Passers-by stopped to see what was happening and any number of teenage truants – almost exclusively female – tried unsuccessfully to blag their way inside.

Jamie Oliver and James Corden were seated three pews in front of Gloria, suited and booted, heads close together, cook and comedian whispering for all the world like a pair of overgrown schoolboys. Probably, Gloria thought, discussing recipes for Cornish pasties. At the front of the church, Chris Evans and Nick Grimshaw were bookending a pair of elderly women both wearing black hats that wouldn't have looked out of place at a state funeral.

Gloria felt a ripple of movement behind her and turned in time to see Mary Portas – her recognisable-at-two-hundred-paces auburn bob a little longer than usual – arriving in time to swap 'Good mornings' with Harry Styles.

But no sign of rock-god Jake Jay. The man who'd won more Grammys than anyone on the planet was said to be back in rehab, this time at a facility somewhere north of New Mexico, accessible only by helicopter. Maybe Robert Plant would show up instead, and treat everyone to a verse of 'Stairway to Heaven'.

Double Oscar winner Kelli Shapiro was also conspicuous by her absence. She had sent her regrets – accompanied by an arrangement of peonies the size of Kew Gardens – and the word was that she was in Geneva, waiting for the scars of a neck lift to heal, rather than suffering from the sudden and unfortunate bout of food poisoning that was her official reason for failing to attend.

Gloria was surprised to see Eddie Banks had been prepared to sacrifice the sunshine of Monte Carlo – along with one of his ninety tax-free days in the United Kingdom – to attend Noggsie's funeral. Bit of a surprise that he dared show his face at all, given the havoc his double-decker, nine-thousand-square-feet basement dig-out was causing along Chalcot Square. Banks and his giant underground extension had been the talk of the Primrose Hill Easter Festival the weekend before. Everyone knew the man was richer than God, but could it possibly be true that he'd instructed the builders to line the walls of his new chill-out zone with solid gold sheeting? Rumour also had it he'd offered his neighbours a week on Richard Branson's Necker Island by way of an apology for the noise, the dirt, the disruption and the damage caused by his building project, but they weren't to be bought off so cheaply, and were holding out – politely but with vicious determination – for the title deeds to luxury lodges at a Banks development in the Lake District. Gloria knew that piece of gossip was well-founded. Her parents were among the neighbours.

The Primrose Hill of her childhood had been a different place. Back then it was just another anonymous London backwater, albeit one with a bohemian edge, and the family had moved there only because her father's fast-track junior banker's salary wouldn't stretch to a house in Hampstead.

Just look at it now. Home to so many of the best-known people in Britain. And, increasingly, overseas owners who boasted to their friends about their charming home-from-one-of-their-other-homes in a neighbourhood that had grown stealthily into Britain's answer to Beverly Hills. Gloria, however, retained her affection for the Primrose Hill she had once known, and especially for Noggsie, whose General Hardware Store had been a local landmark for longer than she could remember.

As the years passed, Noggsie's business had survived and thrived. Car showrooms, coal merchants, computer shops, curry houses, coffee shops ... butchers, bakers, bookshops, betting shops, builders' merchants ... dry cleaners and drapers ... fish-and-chip shops, furniture shops, florists ... laundromats and lending libraries ... glaziers, greengrocers, Apple Stores ... Their custodians came and went, but the General Hardware Store was a permanent fixture, a family business that continued undaunted by the changes happening around it, rather like Ian Beale in *EastEnders*, which was one of Gloria's many guilty pleasures.

This time last year, Noggsie's shop was still a much-loved anachronism, its green-tiled façade a shabby yet proud island in the present sea of Michelin-starred restaurants, cupcake shops, art galleries, pampering places, frock shops, interior designers, more cupcake shops (mostly gluten-free; some of them also vegan), wine bars and – briefly – a pop-up shop that specialised in miniature replicas of fairground attractions whose price tags might reasonably have been thought sufficient for the full-size originals.

Noggsie himself had remained in excellent health for eighty-five of his eighty-six years. 'It's the work and the customers that keep me going,' he insisted whenever Gloria or anyone else asked whether it wasn't time he relaxed and took it easy. 'Besides, if I weren't here, who else would sell you a couple of curtain hooks or half a dozen nails?' In Noggsie's opinion, blister packs were the work of the devil. No matter what you needed, from a kettle to a casserole dish, from a single tap washer to a wooden toilet seat, the chances were high that Noggsie had it in stock.

He had been a kind man, too. 'Hear you're involved in some urban gardening project,' he'd said to Gloria when she popped in on an errand to collect dishwasher salt for her mother. 'Take these.' And Noggsie had produced half-a-dozen planting troughs along with three bags of compost, refusing all offers of payment.

Now Noggsie was gone and the General Hardware Store along with him. It had been shut for several months, ever since the day its proprietor collapsed across the counter with the first in a series of strokes, and was one of several shops in the high street that continued to stand empty. It had come an unwelcome surprise to many of the locals – Gloria included – to discover that even Primrose Hill was not immune from the toxic effects of hard times, greedy freeholders, ridiculous business rates, and the residents' own growing tendency to go shopping without ever leaving home.

Whoops!

Gloria realised she had been lost in her trip down memory lane and stood up hastily, a second or two later than the rest of the congregation. She fumbled for the order of service and stood in respectful silence as the three members of a boy band whose strategic failure to win *Britain's Got Talent* a couple of years earlier had launched them on the path to international stardom (and adjoining mansions in Regent's Park) began their acapella arrangement of 'Praise My Soul, the King of Heaven'.

The hymn's final notes died away and everyone sat down again. All except for Eddie Banks. He inched out of the pew, negotiating around his two grown-up children, Zoe and Barclay, then walked purposefully towards the lectern.

'Noggsie was my neighbour, my friend, and my inspiration.' Eddie Banks paused as if he expected to be challenged about what he had just said. 'He watched me grow up, and I watched him grow old.' Unexpectedly eloquent for Banks, Gloria thought. He was a man who tended to call a spade a bloody shovel. Or worse. She wondered how many of his PR people had been working on the eulogy.

Everybody present knew the story of Eddie Banks. Local boy made billionaire. Born in a council house along Chalcot Road, and now reminding his captive audience about the car cleaning business he'd started aged nine, equipped only with a bucket-load of ambition, a green sponge and a jumbo bottle of Fairy Liquid, purchased with his Christmas money from Noggsie at the General Hardware Store.

'Noggsie taught me so many things,' Eddie Banks continued. 'But most important of all, he taught me to dream big. When I told him I had no time to clean more cars, he told me to recruit my friends to help out. And that wasn't just so he could sell more Fairy Liquid.'

A pause for gentle laughter. 'When I told him my first business was about to go bust and my best bet was to go work for someone else, he told me to get over myself. And fail better the next time round. Then later, once I'd stopped failing,' a modest shrug, 'and could afford to buy Noggsie a decent dinner or two, I asked him ... "Noggsie," I said, "you've told me I'm capable of conquering the world, and I believe you. But what about you? What is it that you dream of? What is that you want? And how can I help you have it?" You know what he replied? He told me, "I'm blessed to have found a way

43

to earn a living doing something that contributes to others, yet doesn't rob my soul. I'm lucky enough to have found my calling, which allows me to continue the tradition of helping my community and to know that in my own small way, I'm making a difference."'

Banks's excellent eulogy made Gloria think of Nina. She imagined her friend casting a professional eye over the proceedings. What was it Nina had said the day before? About the way funerals were changing, with more people drawing up plans for their own farewell appearance while they were still alive and well. A question of matching the occasion to the person, she had explained.

Gloria made a mental note to tell Nina the Traders Association had organised a wreath in the shape of a giant hammer.

Then she realised she could do so much better.

At the champagne reception that followed Noggsie's funeral, Gloria cornered Eddie Banks and told him about Nina and her ideas about dragging funerals into the modern era.

Banks immediately offered to do what he could to help, and Gloria had been impressed that someone so successful was prepared to go out of his way to help a woman he'd never even met achieve her dream.

Noggsie would definitely have approved.

And later, listening to the way Nina talked – enthusiastically yet respectfully – about the people she intended to help once she had refurbished Noggsie's shop, Gloria was convinced Happy Endings would have had his blessing.

Chapter 7

Here I am in Primrose Hill, one of the most fashionable parts of London, and it ought to be wonderful.

But it's not.

I've spent all morning watching the world stroll past my shop window oblivious to my presence.

All morning, feeling I don't fit in.

All morning, every morning.

Monday to Friday.

Afternoons, too.

It's been an entire week and I almost wish I was back in Siberia. When Jason banished me to the back office, at least I had a sense of belonging.

I keep reminding myself it's like being the new girl at school. Too soon to have made any friends, too shy to approach anyone, but knowing that before too long, someone will be kind.

Maybe Eddie Banks lulled me into a false sense of security. I've never actually met him because he's almost always in Monte Carlo. But I spoke to him on the phone after Gloria's brilliant idea about me taking over Noggsie's shop.

The moment their conversation ended, Eddie Banks had apparently marched right up to Noggsie's son and told him,

'I've got the perfect tenant for your father's shop. Young entrepreneur by the name of Nina Sherwood. I know you're back off home to Australia tomorrow, so shall I have my people sort out the lease and the terms on your behalf? Save you the hassle, and get that shop open again.'

The two men shook hands and Eddie Banks's team proceeded to process the paperwork in record time, which was just as well, because apparently another retailer was showing serious interest in opening a business. I felt especially fortunate that Noggsie's son had even been talked into letting me have an initial discount on the rent. All I'd had to do was sign the agreement.

It had felt like destiny. But now I'm not so certain. Still, it was foolish of me to imagine customers would fall into my lap. That only happens once a business has proved itself and the recommendations roll in. For now, it's important to get a proper feel for the neighbourhood. Which makes the people-watching important rather than just a time-filler or an activity to stop myself fretting about the future.

I've certainly seen one or two strange sights, including a family of four dressed all in matching tweeds riding along the road on a double tandem the length of a hearse. Then there's Sybille Newman, my neighbour with the roof issue. Always dressed in orange. She's just spent five minutes telling off a road sweeper for doing a sloppy job. (I've privately taken to calling her Mrs Happy, because she treats me to a scowl every time she marches past the shop, pretending not to look inside.) There's also a man on rollerblades who seems to be circling our block of shops ... I've seen him go past at least five times, and here he is again.

In between studying the locals, I try to knuckle down

and practise my daily exercises in creative visualisation. I imagine myself busy and productive, doing a good job for satisfied customers, opening bank statements that demonstrate increasing prosperity, then the look on my parents' faces when I present them with tickets for a luxury weekend in Sardinia to say thank you for their backing.

And the rest of the time? I'm scared I've made a dreadful mistake.

Marry in haste and repent at leisure, isn't that what people say? I begin to think I've achieved the retail equivalent, and that I should have looked a lot more carefully before I leapt into self-employment.

My watch tells me it's still far too early for lunch, although talking of food, word must have got out that Happy Endings has nothing to do with coffee or cupcakes. No-one's asked me if I'm selling either since Wednesday.

But I'm still being mistaken for a bookshop and every time I explain I'm an undertaker, the outcome is more or less the same. I get an, 'Oh, what a shame, dear!' as though I've missed out on tickets for Glastonbury or the Latitude Festival. And that's on a good day. There have been two or three others who, like Mrs Happy, have made no secret of the fact they believe my business has no business being here.

'How dare you give your shop such a misleading name?' The woman who berated me for that didn't hang around long enough to let me explain my conviction that the best funerals are those that honour someone's life and give a true sense of who that person really was – and are far from morbid or mysterious affairs – which is why I think 'Happy Endings' is such a great choice.

Not, of course, that anyone's showing any signs of choosing

me. I still have no idea when I'll be called to action. I firmly remind myself this is par for the course. In my line of work, there's mostly no lead time.

Obviously, I feel sorry in advance for the person who's going to be my first customer, because organising a funeral is a distress purchase. But at least when it happens, I'll know how to help them and the people they leave behind. It's what I'm best at.

In the meantime, there's no point drooping around an empty shop like one of my wilting delphiniums. I've got plenty to do. The cremation urns are still down in the basement. I'm incorporating them into my inaugural window display – the empty window has turned out to be a mistake rather than the minimalist statement I had been aiming for – to eliminate any further misunderstandings about the nature of my business.

Edo promised to help me haul everything out front this afternoon, but there's still no sign of him, so I might as well get on with the admin instead of wallowing in procrastination.

In particular, I need to compose an email to Zoe Banks.

Zoe is not only Eddie Banks's daughter but also a fellow retailer – her shop is called The Beauty Spot – and she's the driving force behind the Primrose Hill Traders Association. I really want to get to know my fellow shopkeepers, and I need to get cracking. I activate my computer with a flick of the mouse and begin.

Dear Zoe Banks,

My name is Nina Sherwood and I am the new kid on the block. As you may know, my shop is called Happy Endings, and in many ways, it is thanks to your father that it is here at all. My friend Gloria was present at Noggsie's funeral, and afterwards, when she was talking to Mr Banks, my name came into the conversation.

There goes that man on the rollerblades again, whizzing past the shop. On the pavement this time. Close enough to flash me a smile. And for me to grin at his T-shirt, which declares, *Always be yourself. Unless you can be Batman.* I'm probably imagining his smile, but he's certainly around a lot. Training for some sporting event, perhaps. Anyway, back to my message ...

Mr Banks generously used his powers of persuasion to ensure I could get the lease, and without this initial help, my business would never have got beyond the dreaming stage. In case you're wondering, I previously worked for an established funeral director in Queen's Park but this is my first solo venture and I am hugely excited about it all.

Gloria says The Beauty Spot is one of Primrose Hill's most successful shops, so Zoe must have inherited her father's business acumen along with an appetite for hard work and the ability to be both popular and profitable. I hope that as we get to know one another, she might teach me some of the secrets of maximising income without ripping anyone off.

I hope you will wish me well and I look forward to meeting you in the near future. I am also very keen to participate in the activities of the Primrose Hill Traders Association. Could you please advise me of the procedure for joining? Is there a meeting coming up some time soon that I could attend? Finally, I am sure you are very busy, but if you

fancy a break, then I would love to have a chat with you.
Shall we meet in the wine bar? Drinks on me!
  Best wishes,
  Nina Sherwood, Happy Endings

I send the email and try to convince myself I'm having a good day at work. Now for those cremation urns ...

Chapter 8

The next morning, I wake to discover two significant additions to our household.

First off, I hear footsteps crashing up and down a flight of stairs so I get out of bed, shrug into my dressing gown, nudge my bedroom door and realise Edo is here. On his way to the little room at the top of the house. He's juggling an assortment of bin bags and holdalls plus a red and white 'NO ENTRY' sign that is still attached to the mid-section of a lamp-post.

By the time I am decently dressed he's on another trek, this time laden with a bunch of canvases. I observe that Edo's favourite colour is purple. And that he has at some stage persuaded at least four different women to pose for him while naked. One of them – a curvy redhead with spectacular breasts – has her cellulite-free thighs teasingly splayed around the 'NO ENTRY' sign.

'Morning,' I say. 'Are you storing your stuff in the attic?'

Edo looks puzzled. 'Didn't Gloria tell you I was moving in? That's why I didn't get to the shop in time to help you yesterday. Sorry about that.'

Um, no. Gloria's said nothing. 'Want some coffee?'

'Awesome!'

I get my head around Edo's news as I make my way to the

kitchen. He did say the place he found after he moved out of Happy Endings was a bit too dirty and a touch too noisy for his liking. Typical Gloria to say he could stay – she's both generous and impulsive, and it's her house, of course – but I'm surprised she didn't at least discuss it with me first.

An even bigger surprise awaits me in the kitchen.

A dog.

Eating breakfast.

Actually, he appears to be on his third breakfast.

The creature is almost the size of a Shetland pony. It looks as if it's been dreamed up by Disney, but is acting out a script from Tarantino – working title *The Andrex Puppy on Drugs*.

The pristine kitchen I remember from last night is a wreck. Two chairs have been overturned. The floor is covered in a collage of broken breakfast bowls, with several million breadcrumbs and a gooey patch of what looks like blood but is hopefully nothing more sinister than strawberry jam added for texture. A steady trickle of milk is dripping onto the floor from an overturned carton on the table. And, unless I'm very much mistaken, the roll of paper towel we keep on the kitchen table in lieu of napkins has three Shetland-pony-sized chunks bitten out of it.

The dog gives me a cursory glance then shamelessly returns to the plate of ham, cheese and salami that's occupying his attention. In fairness, his table manners seem to be improving with every chomp. He's figured out he's the perfect height so that his head – and jaws – can get to the food without the need even to flex his paws, let alone knock food to the floor. Perhaps he's cleverer than he looks.

A split second later, just as the dog's inhaling the final scrap of meat, Edo arrives in the kitchen. 'Oh no,' he says. 'Maybe this was a mistake.'

I give him a look.

'There was this bloke in the pub last night.' Edo has got himself a part-time job pulling pints. 'Said he and his partner had come to the conclusion their place was too small for Chopper. That's his name, Chopper. They took him to Battersea, but the people there admitted that if they couldn't rehome him, he'd be put down. The guy was literally sobbing into his beer, so I called Gloria and she said it would be okay. Then today, I wanted to get off to a good start and be a good housemate, so I put breakfast together before I moved my stuff in. Which turned out to be a mistake. Do you know anything about dogs?'

'Only that they appear to enjoy granola and salami. But I guess I'll learn.' The truth is, I've always wanted a dog.

'He'll be my responsibility. I promise this will never happen again. I'll clear up all the mess. And he'll sleep in my room. I'm going to make him a bed out of wooden crates. And then I thought I might paint him.'

'Purple?' I enquire.

Edo's enthusiasm is somehow infectious. Even though Chopper has wrecked our kitchen, he is trying earnestly to make amends by hoovering the floor with his tongue, which is the size of a rump steak.

'How old is he, anyway?'

'The guy said he's a year old. And fully grown.' Even as he says it, Edo sounds doubtful. He looks at me, then back to the dog. 'I'm really grateful to you and Gloria for agreeing I can move in, you know. I've promised to help out around the house, with odd jobs and that. And I'm going to be paying rent, of course.'

Immediately, I feel guilty. Gloria insisted I should only pay

half-rent until Happy Endings is on its feet – an offer I gratefully accepted. She's probably delighted Edo needs a place to
live, and can help make up the shortfall.

'I'll clean up the mess,' I offer. 'Then maybe, once we've had
breakfast, we can take Chopper out for a walk.'

After breakfast, during which I observe Gloria sneaking
morsels of still-warm croissant under the table to our new
dog, the four of us – Edo, Gloria, Chopper and I – head for
Highgate Ponds.

It's beautiful late spring weather, and Gloria is excited to
see the lilacs in full bloom. Edo keeps Chopper on a stout
leash, offering him no further opportunities for misbehaviour.

'So what sort of dog is he?' Gloria asks. She's spent the
past ten minutes complaining she's fed up with having her
social life dictated by the schedule of Thrice-Wed Fred's wife,
whose latest crime is to surprise her cheating husband with
a weekend jaunt to Berlin.

'Half-Bernese half-poodle,' Edo says.

I can see the poodle in Chopper. Woolly coat in shades
of black, brown and white, with a head of hair that reminds
me of those long wigs worn by the old codgers who populate
the House of Lords. But Bernese? Isn't that a type of sauce?

'So that makes him a Bernedoodle!' Gloria is amused by
the thought.

'Or a poodlenese,' Edo suggests.

I take another look at Chopper. Edo let him off the lead
when we got to the woods at the back of the ponds, and the
dog is celebrating his freedom by enthusiastically turning a
fallen branch into a pile of matchsticks. Chopper is about four
times the size of any other dog out on a Saturday walk, so all
I can say is that the Bernese must be a very big dog indeed.

'That's interesting,' Edo says.

'What?' I enquire. 'A dog chewing a stick?'

'No. Taking one thing and transforming it into another.'

Before I can say something about dogs doing that every time they sink their teeth into something, Edo continues his thought. 'Shapeshifting.'

'Is that what they taught you at art school?' Gloria's tone is only faintly mocking.

'As it happens, I've got a postgraduate tutorial with Joshua Kent next week,' Edo retorts. 'If I'm lucky, he'll mentor me on my next project.'

Wow! Edo must be an even better artist than he is a sign writer. Joshua Kent is a real big shot. His art is on display in galleries and private collections all over the world. It's not my kind of thing – call me a philistine, but I like a painting to look like a painting, with a nice frame and everything – but winning the Turner Prize three times has made Joshua Kent properly famous.

Edo is looking suitably modest. 'I've got a couple of ideas,' he says, 'but I think they're too ordinary. Can we talk about something else, please? I'm terrified. Nina, what do you think Gloria should do about Fred? Dump him, or what? What would *you* do?'

I'm about to reply to Edo's penultimate question in the definite affirmative, but Gloria is faster. 'I've told you,' she says to Edo. 'Nina doesn't do relationships.'

The pair of them exchange a glance, and I realise Edo has been briefed about the reason for my lack of a love life. Gloria must have told him about Ryan – his funeral and all that – and my decision to prioritise my career over relationships.

An awkward pause, while we watch Chopper take a breather

from his labours, then spit out the final shreds of wood and begin to paw furiously at the ground, digging a hole in which to bury his matchsticks.

'If anyone needs advice,' I finally say, 'it's me.'

'The business?' asks Gloria, and I suspect this is something she has also discussed with Edo.

'It's only been a week,' Edo chimes in. 'And besides, the weather's too good for dying.'

Even though he is being facetious, Edo has a point. More people die during winter than summer. But that's not the issue. Every time I think about my parents, I feel sick. Sticking all their pension money next to the matchsticks in Chopper's freshly dug hole in the ground is beginning to seem like a far better idea than allowing them to keep their investment in Happy Endings.

I feel Gloria's hand on my arm. 'Remember your business plan, sweetie.' She's doing her best to reassure me. I've estimated thirty funerals in the first year, so with only one week gone, I'm not even behind schedule. But neither have I earned a single penny.

'My business plan wasn't much more than guesswork,' I confess. Guesswork, moreover, that didn't even include any budget for advertising and marketing. 'I should have thought things through more thoroughly. Maybe there's a good reason why the shop was empty for so long after Noggsie's first stroke left him unable to carry on – and it wasn't just because the council rejected change-of-use applications from a bunch of hipsters who wanted to turn it into yet another café.'

'Rubbish!' Edo jumps in. 'Remember what Noggsie's son said.' The son who lives in Australia and gave me a good deal on the rent. 'He wanted you to have the lease because he reckoned the high street needs some proper shops again. There's only so many cupcakes a person can eat.'

Edo's wrong about that. Especially when they incorporate marshmallow frosting. But his intentions are good.

Enough of this.

I'm behaving like a complete wimp.

All doom and gloom and Poor Little Me just because things aren't happening as fast as I'd hoped. Yes, when I was an employee, we could more or less guarantee how many funerals we'd handle every week, but the business had been there for decades. My empty shop window has evidently led to misunderstandings about the nature of my business but it's sorted now: my collection of ceramic urns are modern and tasteful, although from what I've seen of Primrose Hill so far, there's a danger the locals will think I'm running an art gallery.

'You know what?' I confess. 'I was hoping in my heart of hearts that business would just fall into my lap. But I need to make myself known.' There have to be cheaper ways of advertising than buying space in the local paper, which every undertaker seems to do as a matter of routine. 'I've made a start already.'

I'm telling my friends about the email I sent to Zoe Banks when my phone pings. I look at the screen.

'Ha!' I tell them. 'Talk of the devil, and the devil appears!'

It's a message from Zoe.

I'm going to meet her on Monday.

Can't wait!

Chapter 9

Truthfully, Zoe's email reads more like a summons than an invitation. *Yes, we need to discuss what you're doing. Monday 7.15am. Home not spa.*

My own email is repeated underneath. Taking another look, it does seem to ramble a bit. But never mind that Zoe hasn't replied at length. The important thing is that she has replied at all. Promptly, too, which is good business etiquette. Zoe must be one of those scarily efficient women who has successfully tamed her email mountain by keeping responses – even to warm and friendly messages like mine – to the bare minimum.

That fits in with Gloria's extended briefing about Zoe and her day spa. The Beauty Spot is part of a chain that also has a presence in other wealthy pockets of London, plus outposts in Zürich, Rome, Dubai and Los Angeles. Our local branch is hidden away inside a beautiful Regency townhouse, just off the high street. I've always been too scared to go inside, but I've given the website a good going-over in preparation for this meeting.

Turns out the rumours that Zoe sells nothing that costs less than £35 are true. *Really?* For a bottle of bubble bath *that* small? And do women honestly pay three figures to have their eyebrows tidied? Especially when the first figure's not even a one! Back in my student days, I spent less than that on a weekend in Berlin, and my eyebrows always look just fine.

I know I ought to be grateful Zoe has prioritised our meeting, but instead I'm faintly resentful I needed to be up at half past five this morning to make sure I had enough time to dither about what to wear. And redo my eyebrows four times.

I arrive at Zoe's home – a leafy turning on the far side of the park going towards Swiss Cottage – at ten past seven. Which is just as well, because I squander the next three minutes trying to make the intercom system work. In the end, I resort to punching random numbers on the keypad, and this finally does the trick. A disembodied male voice instructs me, '*Step AWAY from the gates and state your name.*'

'Nina Sherwood,' I announce, startled.

'*Correct.*'

What is this, an intelligence test?

'*When the gates open, please make your way to the main entrance.*' The voice sounds like Carson out of *Downton Abbey*, scolding one of the servants for being ungrateful.

At first glance, the gates – sandwiched between high brick walls – could be mistaken for a piece of sculpture, all curves and swirls, with a hint of Art Deco. Then they glide soundlessly open, and I get my first glimpse of Zoe's home.

So this is how the one per cent of the one per cent lives ... As I read online last night – doing my Zoe Banks homework before explaining to Chopper that my bed is not *his* bed – I am now eyeballing a piece of prime central London real estate worth £14 million. Which buys you (I continued my online research via Zoopla, Google Earth and Vogue) seven bedrooms, a private cinema, a wine cave, staff quarters and one of the largest gardens in North London, complete with its own tropical pagoda. All that, plus a ten-metre infinity pool that incorporates both wave machine and rainforest shower.

'*This way please, Ms Sherwood.*' Carson's disembodied voice again, sounding even less pleased than before. I'm obviously over-gawping, so I jog the final few metres to the front door, crunching a spray of gravel in my wake. The door opens immediately, even before I can work out where the bell might be located.

I'm almost surprised *not* to be greeted by Carson. Instead, a man about my own age, dressed in a perfect charcoal suit – I'm guessing it costs more than the average funeral – teamed with white shirt, blue silk tie and black-rimmed round glasses is looking me up and down. The expression on his face is exactly as I had anticipated: disdain underpinned by disapproval.

But maybe I'm just flustered, because his voice is considerably more warm when he tells me, 'This way, please.' I follow him across a vast expanse of highly polished wooden flooring. 'Ms Banks is running late this morning,' he says. Late? At seven fifteen? Is this code for 'Ms Banks has overslept?' Apparently not, because the man continues, 'A meeting with her architect is taking longer than anticipated. If you wait here' – I am ushered into a space that is bigger than every room of Happy Endings put together – 'I'll fetch you a coffee.'

Carson leaves the room before I have a chance to say, 'White, please, with three sugars,' and I'm about to make myself at home on a squishy black leather couch when I hear voices coming from the adjoining room. A man and a woman speaking softly yet distinctly. I find myself heading towards a not-quite-closed door and begin earnestly to study a huge canvas on the wall. Blue splodges placed at indeterminate intervals against a backdrop of what looks like green and yellow electricity pylons, encased in an ornate frame that could easily be proper gold, although I'd have to bite it to be sure.

'So we should hear back from the planning department in the next four to eight weeks.' The man's voice.

'Why does it take them so long?' The woman – presumably Zoe Banks – is verging on shrill. I can almost hear her stamping her foot. 'Can't we fast-track it? Pay them extra? Anyway, it's going to be a formality, so might as well get cracking straight away. Right?' Before the man can reply, Zoe continues, 'You realise I'm still unhappy with the north-east elevation. If we're building a neo-classical palace we might as well get it right and have the columns properly hand-carved. Agreed?' A pause. 'I'm paying two hundred thousand for this, after all. Plus your fees.'

'Of course. And you're happy with the design of the frieze?'

'Let's have another look at the plans.' A rustle of papers. 'Yes, I like that. Lovely idea to call the extension a small temple in the trees. And our garden's so big, no-one will ever spot it. You know, life's too short to wait for the bloody planners, so let's get the builders in next week and pay the fine for going ahead without permission if we get caught.'

Temple in the trees? I'd assumed the people on the other side of the door were discussing plans for a holiday home. Greece, perhaps. Or Croatia. Surely even someone like Zoe Banks wouldn't spend two hundred grand on a tree house. Especially someone who, according to my research, doesn't have children. I'm worried Carson's going to come back and catch me eavesdropping but I've never heard a conversation like this before and I can't tear myself away.

That's weird. In one breath, the man is saying something about a multi-level dwelling with geometrically perfect proportions. But now he's describing a wirelessly controlled fox-proof security system. Surely he means foolproof. And what's this about an automatic sliding roof above the nesting box suite? Is that what rich people call a bedroom?

I'm wondering if I'm going deaf, and if I dare to push the door open just a tiny crack further, when Zoe says, 'We've had our skirmishes with this project, Marcus, but I've always known you were the man to create the Taj Mahal of hen houses.'

'That's very kind, but by the time we're done, I hope it will look more like Le Petit Trianon.'

Two smug laughs, followed by packing-up sounds. I retreat to the sofa, bewildered. What is this I've stumbled into? It feels like the set of *The Good Life* mashed with *Grand Designs*. Don't get me wrong, I love chickens, especially when roasted to a golden crispness, accompanied by Mum's silky gravy and fluffy potatoes, and I have no doubt the hens that are destined to roost legally or illegally in Zoe's extension will truly appreciate the clean lines and the modern aesthetics. Come on, though. Admittedly two hundred thousand won't buy you a garage in London. But a hen house? *A hen house?*

When I think how hard my dad worked, and how proud he was to be able to lend me the fifty thousand pounds I needed – more than half his life savings – to open Happy Endings ... I wonder what it must be like to be able to buy whatever you want ... anything you want ... *everything* you want ... without stopping to think how much it costs.

Zoe Banks enters the room with a face that suggests all the cash in the world can't buy you happiness, and I feel a little bit better about my current credit card balance.

'Marcus, I'll expect your confirmation that the builders will be on site by Monday latest,' she says before disappearing into the hallway. With that, the architect is dismissed. He fails to acknowledge me, and sidesteps Carson, who has arrived carrying a tray with my promised coffee and a plate of fancy biscuits. Silver icing! I follow him past the blue-splodged painting and into Zoe's office, which turns out to be a surprisingly austere space, dominated by a metal and glass desk as big as a ping-pong table. Behind it, there's a chair that reminds me of the Iron Throne, softened only by the addition of a scarlet cushion – Zoe's presumably – and on the other side, a considerably less impressive ladder-back chair. Carson gestures towards it, then gathers a bunch of envelopes from the desk and leaves the room.

I'm still taking in my surroundings – half a dozen floor-to-ceiling free-standing metal shelves in a geometric pattern that would make them almost sculpture were it not for the dozens of aluminium box files they hold – when Zoe returns. Instinctively, I stand up and take a few steps towards her.

Zoe Banks towers over me. I'm five six and she's at least three inches taller, even before you take into account her skyscraper heels. We exchange a firm handshake – I notice Zoe gives my home-manicured nails a beady once-over – then retreat to our respective sides of the giant desk.

'So you're Nina.' She looks square at me, pronouncing my name as though she's just captured something nasty on the tip of her tongue. 'One moment.'

Zoe busies herself with some papers, which gives me a chance to get the measure of her. She's actually rather beautiful. Model slender and impeccably dressed in a grey linen dress that accentuates long legs, bronzed in a shade that didn't come out of a spray can. She's got one of those Julia Robert mouths

– you know, the length of a pillar-box slit – and impeccable white teeth. But she's overdone the Botox or the collagen or whatever it is she's had someone squirt into her glistening lips. Unfortunately, they look like a pair of scarlet bananas. No, I'm just being mean. Zoe Banks is as high-end and glossy as everything else in this perfect house. Everything except me.

Before I can berate myself any further, the scarlet bananas begin to speak. 'Thank you for popping by,' they say. 'So, tell me about your little shop.'

And I'm off! Explaining that although the undertaker I used to work for mostly organised traditional funerals – black clothes, white lilies, newspaper notices, Bible readings, etc. – the funeral industry is starting to change.

'Relatives want something more personal,' I say. 'Services as individual as the person who has died.' I recall a photo emailed to me last week by Anna Kovaks. Grigor's family cycling through woods on the outskirts of Budapest, following one of his favourite off-road treks on their way to a river where they scattered the ashes Anna had repatriated. Zoe continues to stare at her papers, which is a bit rude, but undaunted, I persevere.

'It definitely helps families to grieve when they're able to do something that properly reflects the person they loved. Say, putting a favourite book inside the coffin. Or a cigar. Or notes from the grandchildren. I mean, you only have to think about the way weddings have changed in the past few years, with services on the beach, or at the top of the London Eye ...'

Zoe has picked up a gold fountain pen and is writing something down, so I trail into silence. Once she's finished, I'll ask her to guess some of the most popular music tracks that are played at crematorium services. Start a dialogue instead of lecturing the poor woman.

I watch Zoe's elbows move in, out and back in as she signs her name, cutting a Z into the paper. Then she leans forward on her throne thing and moves her perfectly made-up face closer to mine.

'It all sounds very undignified,' she says. 'If you have to have a funeral, much better to get it over and done with as quickly as possible, then get back to normal life. But that's hardly the point. The thing is.' Zoe purses her banana lips and pauses for emphasis. 'The thing is, Nina, we don't do death in Primrose Hill. Michelin-starred restaurants, yes. Designer handbags, absolutely. Health and beauty ... well of course, that's my job. We have a huge local demand for ethical foie gras, even though those smelly protestors were out on the streets demonstrating against the butcher *and* the fur shop last weekend. Which reminds me, I need to speak to the police commissioner to make sure it doesn't happen again. Look,' Zoe tries – and fails – to smile, 'we even sell chocolate and perfume. Everyday essentials the local community can't manage without. We give people what they want. And there's just no demand for death, I assure you. I can't imagine what possessed my father to encourage you. A clear error of judgement if you ask me.'

Wow!

And without further ado, Zoe's on her feet, her arm under my elbow, walking me to the door. I want to retort with a bold statement, explaining Happy Endings is here to do a job, to cater for a need, just like the chocolate shop. Or, indeed, the spa. But my cheeks are burning as if I've been slapped in the face and I know I'll struggle to speak without crumpling. Which means Zoe has the last word.

'If you like, I'll do what I can to help you get out of the

lease,' she offers. 'Otherwise, you'll be gone by Christmas. I bet on it. In fact, I already have. We're running a sweepstake to guess the date you'll close. We all thought it was a great way to help fund the Christmas lights.'

Chapter 10

Thank goodness for Chopper! If it weren't for him, I'd find it hard to get out of bed in the morning. After my humiliating meeting with Zoe Banks, I just wanted to lock myself away and hide. But Chopper's having none of it. He expects to be in the park at eight o'clock, wreaking havoc, so I've got into the habit of walking him before I open the shop, although walking is hardly the right word. Chopper is a force of nature – as soon as I slip his lead, he's away! Eager and surprisingly elegant for such a huge creature. Paws pounding like hooves, at least until he comes across some delicious distraction, such as rearranging the flowerbeds with his paws, chasing a wheelchair, or joyfully demonstrating his superpowers by turning a flock of pigeons into fifty black specks in the sky merely by lumbering towards them.

I'm now on 'Good-morning-how-are-you?' terms with a whole bunch of other dog owners, which is something to cheer me up first thing. In fact, it's often as much conversation as I get during the entire working day ... because it's still 'No Business as Usual' at Happy Endings, and I don't know what to do, short of entering Zoe Bloody Banks's sweepstake in the hope of winning back the fifty grand I owe my dad for foolishly investing in me and my stillborn business.

It's been a month. Time enough to stop kidding myself that all I have to do is raise awareness.

I've put leaflets through every door in Primrose Hill announcing my arrival. Then, when I called the local paper to see if they'd run an article about Happy Endings, they put me through to someone who insisted I could transform the fortunes of my business simply by spending two hundred and fifty pounds a week on advertising until I foolishly surrendered my credit card details.

Response? Zero.

I've also introduced myself to most of the other shopkeepers – none of whom went out of their way to be friendly, not even the florist, who's usually an undertaker's closest business ally – and confirmed my worst fears by reading the latest edition of our trade paper, whose front page declared Britain now has an 'over-supply' of funeral directors. By which I strongly suspect they mean me.

Perhaps I should look for a part-time job. Evenings in a pub or restaurant. At least that would keep some cash trickling in. I was talking to Edo last night about the possibility of—

What the hell!

Someone on a scooter is racing down Primrose Hill. Far too fast. Directly towards Chopper.

'Mind my dog!' I yell, as I run towards the accident that's about to happen.

Chopper, unaware of the danger, is on the main path at the bottom of the hill, head deep inside a carrier bag that's been abandoned next to a rubbish bin. The idiot on the scooter, meanwhile, responds to my anguished cry by taking one hand off his handlebars and waving at me. What am I supposed to do? Move Chopper out of the way?

Much too late to do anything at all.

Chopper is lumbering up the hill, greeting the scooter as if it's another dog out to play. I can hardly bear to look ... a millisecond before impact, the idiot dodges Chopper with the insouciant panache of a slalom skier, only to career head-first into a tree trunk on the other side of the path.

I sprint towards his body. 'Are you okay?' I yell.

Serves him right if he's not.

The scooter has come to rest on the grass, wheels still spinning. Its owner is picking himself up off the ground, and brushing grass from his skinny jeans. He runs an index finger along one of his cheekbones to wipe away a trail of dirt, then rotates his shoulder blades, as if to check nothing's broken. He looks vaguely familiar, although I can't imagine why.

'I'm fine, thanks,' he says. 'Just a bit winded. Sorry if I scared you.'

The idiot's pleasantly deep voice and immediate contrition catches me off-guard. I'd been all set to tell him off for dangerous driving. But that was when I'd assumed he was a teenage boy, rather than the man of about my own age who is now stroking Chopper.

'She's right,' he tells the dog. 'I was going much too fast. But it's such a wonderful feeling. Like flying.' Then he looks up at me. 'Buy you a quick coffee, by way of apology?'

I mean to say no. But the idiot is in possession of a mischievous smile, sparkling grey eyes, and a T-shirt that says, *Honk if You're About to Run Me Over.*

It's not as if I need to get to work on time to begin another soul-destroying day of no clients, so thirty minutes later we're still sitting outside at one of the cafés on the high street, across the road from Happy Endings. Chopper is refuelling on ice-cold water from a bucket-sized bowl. I'm on my second latte, wishing I'd followed suit when the idiot ordered himself a breakfast butty that overflows with dripping butter, bacon and HP sauce. It smells delicious.

'Okay if I give some to Chopper?' The idiot breaks off a generous portion of his breakfast and lobs it in Chopper's direction. The dog rises with gravity-defying grace, captures the snack before it hits the ground, and proceeds to chew daintily.

I sit and salivate, trying – and failing – to look elsewhere as the final sliver of buttery bacon disappears. He's got nice hands, the idiot. It's one of the things I always notice about a man. Assessing their suitability to carry a coffin. These are strong, capable hands. Well-manicured, too.

The idiot evidently cares about his appearance and if I'm not mistaken he's even wearing a splash of cologne, fresh and spicy, with a hint of fir. Doesn't smell as good as the bacon, but not a bad second.

'So do you live around here?'

'No,' I say.

'Professional dog walker?'

'Still no.' I'm not meaning to be unfriendly so I say it with a smile. 'How about you?'

'Oh, my dad's got a house up the road, and I was just popping in. I work for the family business. Property management mostly, and boring stuff involving corporate law. We've been doing a lot of insolvencies lately.'

He says this as though it's a good thing and I can't help but think of Gloria. If she were with us now, she'd say, 'You're the type of lawyer who makes rich people richer. The type of lawyer I never want to be.'

Disloyally, I realise the idiot would most likely scrub up pretty well if he swapped his jeans and T-shirt for a business suit.

'Do you like it?' he's asking me.

'Pardon?'

'My T-shirt. You were staring at it.' Before I can apologise he continues, 'I got a brilliant one yesterday. Going paintballing next week, and I came across one in Camden Market that says, *Why Should You Date a Paintballer?*'

He leaves the question hanging.

'Go on, then,' I encourage him. 'Tell me why I should date a paintballer?'

'Because we've got a lot of balls. That's what's written on the back. Convincing, huh?'

There's something about the guileless way he says it that makes me laugh. His company is an unexpected treat on what's bound to turn out to be another lonely day.

'I'm in desperate need of another bacon butty and more coffee. Say yes this time?'

'Yes,' I say. 'Yes please.'

Just as our refills arrive, something slots into place. 'Haven't I seen you before?' I ask.

'Is that the best you've got?'

'Pardon?'

'You're flirting with me, right?'

'Me? No! Of course not. I *have* seen you before. On roll-erblades. Going past my shop.'

'Which shop would that be?'

'Over there.' I point towards Happy Endings, sit back and wait for the inevitable response.

But the idiot proves the exception to the rule. 'Noggsie's old shop, right?' he says pleasantly. 'So how's business?'

71

'Okay.' I'm not about to confess it's non-existent. I pause for a strategic mouthful of bacon butty, while I attempt to swallow the accusation of flirting. He's sort of right. I'm definitely enjoying his company. Since that night with Jason, I've started noticing men again. There've been one or two who I – admit it, Nina – actually fancied.

And the idiot makes three.

'I'd better go to work,' I say.

'Why? Are there some dead people I don't know about? Did I miss the news story about the avalanche in Tufnell Park last night?'

'You're a very bad man.' It's the sort of remark I'd expect from a colleague rather than a civilian, and the mock shock-horror way he says it is actually quite funny.

'I try not to be. Stay a while.' The idiot brushes my wrist with his fingers. 'More coffee?'

Last time I drank four lattes for breakfast I was still awake at two o'clock the following morning.

'Go on then,' I say. 'And why don't you tell me about the paintballing?'

He needs no second invitation. 'There's this huge woodland site between Edinburgh and Glasgow,' he begins. 'All sorts of scenarios. The village hostage rescue looks the most fun. That's where you get to use the paint thrower.' He sees my puzzled expression and clarifies, 'It's basically a huge water cannon filled with paint. The ordinary paintballs are a mixture of oil, gelatine and dye, and we fire them through nitrogen-powered compressed air.'

'Does it hurt?'

'I have no idea.' The idiot looks puzzled. 'No-one's ever marked me. I always win.'

'You do this a lot, then?'

'Once before. When I was seven. If it works out I'm going to sign up for this place in Oklahoma where you spend a week recreating the D-Day battles. With paint. If you pay a bit extra, you can lead the French Resistance.'

By the time the idiot has finished telling me about battle packs, paint pods, flag capturing, defensive bunker play, ravine negotiation and a legendary character called The Paint Punk, I'm thinking I'd love to go paintballing. With him.

And then I realise what's really going on.

All this military talk ... well, for a few minutes, it was just like old times.

Old times with Ryan.

My husband.

Captain Ryan Sherwood.

That day I watched him being presented with his Afghanistan Operational Service Medal was one of the proudest of my life.

And now?

I'm ashamed to realise that instead of thinking about Ryan's funeral, I've been imagining myself on a date with a man who knows absolutely nothing about the savage realities of military life.

The idiot has stopped talking and for the first time in more than an hour the silence between us feels awkward.

'You're not how I imagined a corporate lawyer,' I blurt out.

'Says the lady undertaker. Sorry ... there's nothing I'd rather do than sit and talk to you for the rest of the day. But it looks like you've got a customer.'

I turn to see a man peering through the window of Happy Endings, then rattling on the door.

Business at last!

And a timely reminder that my priority is work.

Not relationships.

'I'd better dash. Come on, Chopper. Thanks for breakfast. Good luck with the paintballing, and drive that thing,' I point at his scooter, 'more safely in future.'

'Bye for now.' He hesitates. Then, 'Look, let me give you my number. Perhaps we can have dinner.'

I punch his details into my phone. Rude not to. Not as if I'm ever going to call him. But as I walk briskly across the street, rubbing the finger that used to wear a wedding ring, I acknowledge the idiot is charismatic in a man-child kind of way. Far too old to be riding a child's toy, but at least he has good manners.

And Barclay is a pretty cool name.

Chapter 11

'Ah, there you are.' The man who's been looking into my shop hears me approaching and turns round at the sound of my footsteps.

I recognise him. Gareth Manning. Runs one of our neighbourhood's abundance of estate agencies. I've overheard him several times in the street, braying with his colleagues about soaring house prices, boasting that if he learns a few phrases of Japanese he'll be able to add a further thirty thousand to the price tag of a studio flat. He looks from me to his watch.

'Thought you weren't coming,' he says.

'So sorry I'm late.' I quickly unlock and usher Gareth in through the door. Chopper and I follow. 'Just give me a few moments,' I say. I walk Chopper down to the basement and settle him onto his day bed, next to the fridges – which have been behaving themselves perfectly, although gobbling vast amounts of electricity since they have yet to accommodate anyone – and then retrace my steps.

'Gareth, isn't it?' I say. We shake hands. 'So how can I help you?'

'I've come to measure up. And take pictures.'

'For what?' I'm bewildered because Gareth has the look of someone who's made an appointment to see me.

'The shop.' Gareth flicks open the catches on his briefcase

and produces a camera plus some gadget that shoots out a laser of light when he points it at the wall.

'For what? Why?' I'm baffled.

'You know.' Gareth sounds embarrassed, whereas before he was merely impatient to get on with his work. 'The lease, and that.'

'What about the lease?'

Now Gareth looks shifty. 'Well, aren't you surrendering it at the end of the month?' He keeps his eyes studiously to the floor, then mutters, 'Personally, I think you've made a good decision. No call for your kind of business around here, is there?'

If I weren't so shocked, I'd tell Gareth that more people will die in our neighbourhood this year than will buy homes. And that we have only one undertaker, as opposed to half a dozen estate agents, all of whom seem to make a handsome living.

At least, that's what I wish I'd said when I rerun this scene in my mind hours later. But for now, I'm dumbfounded. I can feel my face turning the colour of a pillar box. 'Who told you that? About the lease?'

Before I can discover the source of Gareth's misinformation, we are both startled by the sound of a ringing phone.

'Excuse me,' I mutter. Then, 'Hello, Happy Endings. This is Nina speaking.'

Probably yet another cold caller trying to convince me I'm owed a fortune for payment protection insurance I know I never had in the first place.

But there's nothing brash about the voice on the other end of the line. It's female, shaky, and a bit muffled. 'Is that ... the undertaker?'

'Yes, you're through to Happy Endings,' I repeat. 'May I help you?' My heart is racing. This is the call I have been waiting for. Gareth is fiddling with his laser pointy thing, and I'd like to order him to leave, but I don't want to break off from this important phone call to speak to someone else, so I turn my back on him and listen.

'I need to arrange a funeral.'

'Of course. Might I have the name of the deceased, please?'

'Kelli Shapiro.'

'Kelli Shapiro?' *The* Kelli Shapiro? The famous Kelli Shapiro? The woman who declared her two Oscars make splendid bookends, at least according to what I once read in *Grazia*. I'm relieved I've managed to keep the shock from my voice. 'Let me just check the spelling on that,' I say. 'Kelli with a double l? And S-h-a-p-i-r-o.'

'That's right.' A whisper.

'I'm so sorry for your loss.'

'Thank you. If I give you the address, would you be able to come round to make the arrangements?'

'Of course.' I scribble it down. The big blue house facing the park. 'What time would be convenient for you?'

'Could you come now?'

'Of course.' I put down the phone.

Gavin has been packing up his briefcase. 'Kelli Shapiro, eh?' he says, trying and failing to quell his excitement. 'Suicide? Drugs?'

Coldly, I escort him the few steps to the front door and seize the advantage. 'Who told you to come here today?'

'Can't tell you that. Client confidentiality. You know how it is.' Gareth hesitates, then adds, 'Tell you what. Get me an introduction to sell Kelli's house, and I'll cut you in on my commission.'

I shut the door in his face.

Chapter 12

Kelli Shapiro's home is only a few minutes away. I force myself to walk slowly, although my mind is racing and my heart is hammering. Kelli's next-of-kin must have seen my advert in the local paper, so it turns out I wasn't squandering my start-up funds, after all.

Kelli Shapiro! Growing up, Mum was always teasing my dad about Kelli Shapiro. He had an enormous crush on her. 'It's just that she's got magnificent comic timing,' he'd protest. 'Britain's answer to Meg Ryan.'

'And such a fine actress. Especially when she's fighting the Mafia, dressed only in a chain-mail bikini,' Mum would retort. 'Shall I book tickets for Friday?'

Which means ... I do some rapid mental arithmetic. Kelli Shapiro couldn't have been much more than sixty. Part of me is shocked, as it always is when you hear someone famous has died. I wonder if Dad's listening to the news this morning.

Okay, enough of being starstruck. Time – at last – for me to do my job.

Organising a funeral is very much like organising a wedding, except you've got far less time to make everything perfect ... and a body instead of a bride. Just like a wedding planner, my top priority is to make sure it's all as stress-free as possible. I wonder if Kelli left any instructions for her funeral? There's no way of knowing whether it will turn out to be a huge, celebrity-filled gathering, or a private ceremony for family and close friends. No matter, whatever the family wants, I'll make certain it happens.

At Kelli Shapiro's townhouse, I push open the metal gate and walk the few yards to the front door. I run my fingers through my hair and adjust my jacket to make sure I look neat and tidy before taking a deep breath and pressing the doorbell.

Footsteps on the other side of the door, then through a panel of opaque glass, I see a shadow walking towards me.

The door is opened by a casually dressed middle-aged woman. Dirty-blonde hair in a pixie cut that reminds me of Kelli herself – I've seen several of her films on TV – and I notice a definite family resemblance, although there's nothing movie-star glamorous about the woman who's standing in front of me.

'Come on in,' she says.

I follow her along the hallway into a comfortable, shabby-chic kitchen. The scrubbed pine table, chintz-covered chairs and abundance of wild flowers seem more seaside cottage than metropolitan London. There's even a wonderful smell of freshly baked bread coming from the Aga.

'Take a seat,' the woman says. A moment later, she places a jug of coffee in front of me, then sits down on the other side of the table. 'I suppose we ought to get started.' She looks at me expectantly.

'Yes,' I begin. 'As I said on the phone, I'm Nina Sherwood. And you are ...' I pull out a notepad from my bag, and take the top off my pen.

'Kelli's my name,' the woman says. 'Kelli Shapiro.' She looks at me then adds, 'You've gone terribly pale, my love. Everything all right? If you're not feeling well, we can leave my first Italian lesson for another day.'

'Italian lesson?'

'Well, you're an hour early. But *sì*.' The woman pauses. 'Darling, you're staring at me as if I've got two heads. What on earth's wrong? Did they not tell you that I'm ... well, I'm in the public eye.' Kelli pulls a self-deprecating face.

Even though I'm sitting down, my legs are shaking. 'Did someone from this house just make a phone call to the ... the shop down the road called Happy Endings?'

'Happy Endings? The new funeral parlour that half my neighbours are up in arms about?' Now it's the woman – Kelli – who looks nonplussed.

A full ten seconds of silence.

Then she asks, 'Why would someone from my house call your business? Especially as I'm the only person here.' A note of steel enters her voice. 'You had a phone call?'

I nod.

'And?'

I'm unable to speak.

'Did someone put you up to this?'

Kelli's tone has shifted from steel to fury, and I do something I have done only once before in all my years as an undertaker.

I start to cry while I'm at work.

Kelli sits across the table, watching. I feel her pale blue eyes scrutinise me as though I am some particularly hideous insect, floundering in its own liquid.

I'm reaching for a handkerchief to wipe my eyes, when I feel a hand on my shoulder.

'Nina, tell me what happened. Please,' Kelli says, all anger gone from her voice. 'I'm sorry you're so upset. Whatever's happened, I'm sure it's not your fault. Not unless you're a better actress than I am.' Kelli goes back to her seat on the other side of the table, then gently asks, 'Who called you?'

'A woman.'

'What did she say?'

'That she needed to organise a funeral.'

'For whom?'

My tear-stained face tells Kelli Shapiro everything she needs to know. 'For me,' she says softly. 'Wasn't it?'

I manage a nod. 'I'm so sorry.'

'First of all, whatever this is, it's not your fault. Second of all, I'm going to pour myself a vodka. Join me?'

Another nod.

Kelli mixes two giant vodka tonics quickly and efficiently. She places a crystal tumbler in my hand, sits down next to me and raises her glass. '*L'Chaim!*' she declares. 'To life!'

I'll definitely drink to that. I take a gulp and feel the alcohol burn a fiery trail down my body. Better.

Kelli has taken charge. 'So here's what I think has happened,' she says. 'Someone's played an extremely cruel practical joke. The question is, are they trying to get at me, or at you?'

'Oh me, definitely,' I say. 'You would have been my first client.' Oh Lord, the vodka's got my tongue. I *so* should not have said that.

To my surprise, Kelli lifts her head back and laughs. A genuine, throaty chuckle. I remember how much Dad loves that laugh.

An infectious laugh that sets me off, too.

'Reminds me of a funeral I went to,' Kelli splutters. 'Someone started with the inappropriate giggles. Well, next thing you know, two hundred people are trying not to join in. We were all stood there with our heads down, biting on our lips, faces contorted, Botox notwithstanding, pretending to hold back the tears. Contagious hysteria, or what?'

'You'd be surprised how often it happens.' The professional in me reasserts itself. 'It's a displacement for grief. Funerals force people to think about their own mortality.'

A shadow passes across Kelli's face. 'Can I trust you?' she says.

'Well ... yes. Of course. Despite evidence to the contrary.'

'I feel I can,' Kelli says. 'I'm very intuitive. Look, it's possible this joke wasn't aimed just at you. I've not been entirely well.'

Oh my God.

'They've been treating me in Switzerland and everything's fine again. For now. But it's all been kept terribly hush-hush. If it gets out, I'll never work again. Film insurance and all that. The thing is, I'm chasing a big part at the moment. Me and every actress of a certain age on both sides of the Atlantic. So there's a possibility that tricking you into coming here is actually sending a message to me. That someone's found out about my ... condition, and this is their way of threatening to tell the movie people.' Kelli looks thoughtful. Perhaps she's going through a mental list of her rivals.

I'm about to thank Kelli for trusting me with such a big secret when her phone rings. She looks at the screen. 'Contact of mine who does showbiz for TMZ,' she says. 'Maybe he knows something about the movie. Do you mind if I take it?'

'Of course not.'

'Robert, darling.' Kelli listens intently for a moment. 'Well yes, of course I'm answering my mobile. What were you expecting?' She flicks her phone into speaker mode, and puts it on the table.

'We had a release that—' The man on the other end of the phone is stammering. 'According to the Press Association, you've, er, passed away. All I've got is your mobile number and I was hoping someone would answer the phone.'

Kelli doesn't miss a beat. She does her wonderful laugh again then says, 'Sorry to disappoint you, Robert. Anyone would think it's April the first. I think someone's got their wires crossed. Sorry to kill the story, darling. But – and I've always wanted to say this – I think you'll find reports of my death have been greatly exaggerated.'

With that, Kelli ends the call. 'I need to talk to my management,' she says. 'But I'm glad to have met you. Weird though it is. Good luck with your business, and I'll tell my neighbours you're just a normal person trying to do a difficult job. I can tell you're very good at it, too.'

We walk together to the door. Kelli's phone is ringing again but she takes no notice and kisses me on the cheek. 'See you around,' she says.

I walk slowly back to work, deep in thought. Even though Kelli seems to think this horrible trick was aimed at her, I'm not convinced. What with Gareth Manning appearing out of the blue to measure up my shop ...

And then it hits me. I still have no business.

The hundreds of pounds I've spent on those bloody adverts have had no effect. I might just as well have poured Dad's pension money down the drain. Maybe I should give up now while I'm still in a position to return some of his savings.

I'm back on the high street, where there's some sort of commotion going on. A scrum of at least ten people in a huddle at the café where I had coffee this morning with Barclay.

I hear one of the guys shout, 'There she is.'

Then they all swarm towards me. In a pack. Pointing cameras.

'Why did you do it, Nina?' bellows someone I've never seen in my life. How come he knows my name?

'Was it just a sick PR stunt? Trying to get your business on the map?' shouts someone else.

'And what about Kelli Shapiro? Is she in on it too? Trying to get herself back in the spotlight because her career is on the skids?'

Jesus. Now I get it.

'Kelli had nothing to do with it!' I sprint the final few yards to the door of Happy Endings. I fumble with the lock – the key wobbles all over the place in my trembling hand – until I'm finally able to let myself in. Then I lock the door from the inside, and flee to the basement.

Only when I am cuddling Chopper, who is delighted to see me, do I realise I was so flustered that what I just said to the paparazzi could easily be interpreted as an admission of guilt.

Chapter 13

Ten minutes later, I feel brave enough to go back upstairs and into the shop.

Mistake.

If anything, there are more journalists and photographers than before. It's a sunny afternoon and the good weather has tempted twenty or thirty passers-by to join the crowd to see what's going on.

I spot several familiar faces, including my roof-obsessed neighbour Mrs Happy, who has cornered a couple of members of the media. She's standing with them in the road, lips moving as if she's chewing on a lump of gristle, one hand constantly pointing towards the sky, like a Hitler salute, only higher. I hope she's treating the hacks to a lecture on tanalised battens or the relative merits of Spanish and Welsh slates.

Oh, no. Someone's spotted me through the window.

'Nina! We're from the BBC! Can we come in and have a word?' A man whose face I recognise from the television is bending down outside Happy Endings' front door and yelling through the letterbox.

He's soon joined by a crop-haired woman rapping her knuckles on the window. The moment we make eye contact, she presses a sheet of paper against the glass. I take a few steps forward to read what it says. *The Sun: Tell us why you killed Kelli Shapiro. Give us the exclusive and we'll be sympathetic.*

What the— I shake my head in despair. In response, the woman gives me the least sincere smile I've ever seen.

I'm under siege and I don't know what to do. If I hide at the back of the shop, it's going to look like further evidence of whatever it is they all think I'm guilty of. Maybe I should Uber myself home. But what if they follow me and find out where I live? I could set Chopper free in the hope he'll lick them all to death. Or I could— My list of unsatisfactory options is interrupted by the piercing wail of a siren, growing louder and louder.

A white van pulls up outside the shop and one ... two ... three ... six officers emerge.

I'm about to be arrested in full sight of the BBC cameras. Will they put me in handcuffs? Will my parents be watching tonight's news?

It's all gone eerily quiet outside, with the exception of Mrs Happy, whose voice is so shrill I can hear it even from inside, saying something about the unsurpassable merits of copper nails.

A police officer rings the bell. I'm not going to argue or struggle. My reputation is in ruins, but I can try to preserve my dignity.

I open the door.

'Good afternoon. I'm Sergeant Hartley. And you're Ms Sherwood?' The woman is about my age. She's tall enough to be a catwalk model and her black hair is tied in a bun.

'Yes,' I whisper. 'Will someone be able to look after my dog?'

'I beg your pardon?'

We stare at one another in confusion.

The officer pivots on her flat heel, shoots a disdainful look at the rubberneckers, then turns back and says, 'I wanted to reassure you these people will be leaving immediately. All of them.' Her voice is firm, and several of the locals begin to melt away. But the media is more resilient.

A man with a camera round his neck taps the officer on her shoulder. 'You can't tell us what to do,' he says. 'Freedom of assembly.'

'Familiar with the law, are you?' Before the man can say any more, she continues pleasantly, 'If so, you'll know you've just assaulted a police officer. I'll overlook it this time, so long as you round up your mates and leave Ms Sherwood to get on with her day.'

The photographer doesn't like being humiliated by a woman young enough to be his second wife. He looks as if he's about to reply, then thinks better of it and says, 'Okay everyone, we've got our pictures of *Mizz Sherwood*' – he says my name sarcastically – 'and since she doesn't want to tell us what happened, we'll draw our own conclusions.' His words sound like the threat they're meant to be.

I wonder if I ought to explain I've done nothing wrong, but the policewoman says loudly, 'I'll be giving Ms Sherwood details of the Independent Press Standards Organisation. So I suggest you all get your facts straight.'

Within a couple of minutes everyone has been shepherded away by the policewoman's colleagues. 'Thank you so much, Sergeant Hartley,' I say. 'I was scared.'

'You were right to call us,' she tells me. Before I can deny I made any such call, she continues, 'I've worked with lots of undertakers over the years. You're a decent bunch and I know you'd never pretend someone's dead when they're not.

I loathe the way the media hound people. Talk about a sense of entitlement. Anyway, there's no real story to be had, so fingers crossed they'll all be gossiping about someone else by this time tomorrow.'

'You really think so?' I explain to her about the phone call that started this whole thing off. 'Kelli Shapiro was so kind about it,' I say. 'Really lovely.'

'I didn't realise she lived around here. Did you see that film where she played the girl who—'

The policewoman is interrupted by one of her colleagues. 'RTA in Tufnell Park,' he says. 'Sounds bad. Good to go?'

The officer is about to get on her way when she is accosted by Mrs Happy. 'I need to talk to you about a dangerous structure,' she says in that imperious, cut-glass accent of hers. 'My roof is—'

'Your roof is a matter for the council rather than the police,' the officer replies politely. 'Goodbye Ms Sherwood,' she adds. 'I'm sorry you've had such a bad experience.' She gets inside the white van which departs, sirens screeching, leaving me and Mrs Happy standing awkwardly together on the pavement.

My neighbour is drawing breath and I can tell she's planning another onslaught.

'Got to get on,' I tell her briskly. And with that, I go inside Happy Endings. I turn the key in the lock in case any journalists decide to return, then join Chopper in the basement and make myself a much-needed cup of tea.

Sitting in an armchair, I do what I always do when I'm stressed out. I guide myself through a series of visualisation exercises. In my mind's eye, all the photographers and journalists form an orderly queue and vanish through a set of airport departure doors. Next, I stroll through the streets of

Primrose Hill and people nod and smile at me. I picture Mrs Happy, dancing with her husband – I've seen him a couple of times, but we've never spoken – beneath a watertight roof. And Chopper, gazing at me as if I am a goddess. Licking my hand as if it's been dipped into a vat of melted cheese. No ... Chopper *is* licking my hand. For real. Twenty minutes have passed and I've definitely calmed down.

A bit later and I'm back at my desk out front, wondering if the policewoman is correct and I will escape being featured on TV or in the papers. The doorbell rings again. I look up from *Funeral Director Monthly* – an article describing how the Unknown Warrior's coffin was fashioned from the oak of a tree grown at Hampton Court – fearing Mrs Happy is about to treat me to another of her roofing lectures.

Instead, it's the welcome sight of Gloria. I get up from my desk and she rushes in.

'What's happened to your phone?' she greets me. 'I've been calling you over and over. Did the police come? Really unlike you not to pick up.'

Gloria's right. A ringing phone often means work, or at least a customer enquiry, so I always divert my business line to my mobile whenever I'm out of the office. But today has been – to say the least – distracting and I've forgotten to check for calls. I fish my phone out of my bag. I'd set it to silent mode on my way to Kelli's home.

Seven missed calls from Gloria.

Four missed calls from Edo.

Thirty-two missed calls from unknown numbers.

Eight voicemails from unknown numbers.

I've never been so popular. But I doubt any of these are business enquiries. It's more than I can deal with for now so I keep the phone in silent mode and put it on the desk. Immediately, it begins to vibrate. I feel as if I'm being menaced by a hand grenade that's lost its pin.

'Yes, the police came and got rid of everyone,' I finally answer Gloria's question. 'But how do you know they were here?'

'I called them.' Gloria flops down on the couch, where she is joined by Chopper. 'I popped in to see my mum this morning. We were just having coffee when her cleaning lady came in and told us Kelli Shapiro was, um, dead. Not dead, I mean,' she adds hastily. 'And that you were ... well, never mind ... Anyway, I raced over here and saw the vultures gathering like a bunch of spectators at the French Revolution. Bastards. Your phone kept going straight to voicemail, so I told the cops there was a disturbance that was likely to result in a breach of the peace and that I feared for my safety. I pretended to be you because I thought that would be more effective.'

'Well,' I mumble, 'you know what happened, then.' You and the whole damn world.

'I know exactly what happened.' Gloria spits out the words and her whole face flushes. Last time I saw her so angry was when Thrice-Wed Fred texted to say he wouldn't be able to keep their dinner date at the fancy restaurant she'd chosen as a birthday treat because he was scared he'd bump into people he knew and that word would get back to his wife. 'Gareth Manning. That's what happened.'

'The estate agent?'

'Him. He was with you when you got the call about Kelli, right?'

I nod.

'So he went back to the office and phoned a mate of his

90

on the *Standard*. He's got some deal going with one of their property hacks. Gets a name-check for his business every time he leaks information about celebrities who are buying, selling or renting in the neighbourhood. Manning tipped off his mate that Kelli's dead and it all snowballed from there.'

'How did you find out it was Manning?'

'After he called the *Standard*, he rushed round to Julie in the florist's. Told her to get ready for a bumper sales day.'

I wince.

'And after that ... well, you know how it goes. When it comes to gossip, Primrose Hill makes *EastEnders* look like a Trappist monastery.'

'So everyone thinks I'm to blame?' Even worse than I feared. 'That I made it all up? What are they saying?'

'I've just come from the estate agents. Spoke to Manning himself.' Gloria's expression darkens. 'He said you got a phone call. But once he realised none of it was true, he changed tack and said it was Kelli herself who called you. That the pair of you were in it together.'

'You didn't happen to find out who made the appointment for him to be there in the first place?'

'The measuring-up business, you mean?'

I nod.

'He was even more cagey about that.'

'Wouldn't tell me, either,' I say. 'Just gave me some crap about client confidentiality.'

'Oh? He eventually told me he thought it was you who'd called to instruct him. Another lie, obviously. I soon put him right about that. In fact, I took the liberty of telling him he's never allowed to set foot inside Happy Endings again. Unless he's no longer breathing. And that my mum's been expecting a four-figure donation to the Chalcot Square Summer Fair from his mucky business. Payable in advance. I made him write them a cheque on the spot. Look!' Gloria triumphantly produces it from her purse.

Despite myself, I smile. I'm about to thank Gloria for being such a wonderful friend – and sharp-witted opportunist – when Chopper barks, anticipating the doorbell by a clear five seconds.

Gloria gets up to greet our visitor. 'Hi, Julie,' she says. 'You've saved me a trip to your shop. Mum needs her flowers for the weekend.'

'That's not why I'm here.' The woman who's ignoring Gloria's amicable greeting is in her mid-forties. Poker-straight blonde hair, burnished with impeccable gold highlights that come from days spent on a Caribbean or Mediterranean beach rather than overnight in a carton from the chemist. Suntan that hasn't come out of an aerosol nozzle. Flawless complexion. A brightly patterned silk dress with an asymmetrical hemline that screams designer label. And a huge scowl on her pretty, heart-shaped face. She's waving a large piece of paper in her right hand. 'I've come to see *her*.'

By which she means me.

Before I can say anything, Julie continues, 'I hope you've got business insurance. See this?' she thrusts the paper towards me. 'It's the order I placed with my supplier in Italy.'

I take the paper. 'Yes, I can see. But what's it got to do with business insurance?' Or me.

'I hope you're not going to be difficult about this. It's your fault, after all. I don't know where you worked before but you're not going to last five minutes around here if you go round making up malicious stories to promote your so-called business.'

'Now hang on, Julie.' Gloria stands up. 'Tell me what's happened.'

'Gareth Manning comes into my shop and tells me Kelli Shapiro's dead. So I send over a huge order to the growers in Puglia. To stock up for the funeral. By the time I find out it was a false alarm, the order's freighted up. At least, that's what they insisted, although I find it hard to believe. Anyway, it was too late to cancel, and I don't see why I should have to pay for something *she's* responsible for.' Julie wags a finger in my direction.

'My very good friend Nina Sherwood, you mean.' Gloria waits until Julie meets her eyes, then treats her to a glacial stare. 'Who is herself the victim of someone with a very sick mind. As well as an estate agent who ought to know better.'

'Yes, but—'

'Yes, but nothing. Nina is absolutely not responsible for your business decisions.'

'I'm trying to be nice.' Julie's tone of voice is anything but. 'Zoe Banks said I could sue Nina for the cost of the order but I'd rather settle this pleasantly.' Chopper picks this moment to rub himself against Julie's dress and she pushes him roughly away. 'I presume you've got insurance?'

'Look,' Gloria says. 'Once you've calmed down, I think you'll realise you owe Nina an apology. You're both in business, and the traders around here need to work together for the good of us all. If anyone should reimburse you, it's Gareth Manning. And if you put the flowers out for a sensible price, I'm sure you'll more than cover your costs.'

But Julie's having none of it. 'No, I want my four thousand pounds,' she insists. 'You should count yourself lucky I'm willing to charge you wholesale rather than retail.'

Chapter 14

Gloria spends the next ten minutes telling me Julie's always been a bit of a firebrand and that once she's flogged the flowers she'll calm down and apologise. Even though I know the damn order isn't my fault, I feel sorry for Julie. As for Zoe Banks, though, encouraging a fellow trader to sue me ...

Chopper's body clock is telling him – and us – it's almost time for his second walk of the day, but I'm too timid to show my face outside.

Gloria fiddles with her phone. 'I've just cancelled Mum's order with Julie,' she says. 'That'll give her something to think about. My mum's in and out of the florist's all the time.'

'Isn't that a bit mean?'

'Nina, you're going to have to toughen up. Consider this a baptism of fire. At least now everyone in Primrose Hill knows you're running a funeral parlour rather than a knocking shop. You know what they say. No publicity's bad publicity and all that. Give it another day and word will be out that you were simply trying to do your job.'

I think immediately of another old saying. Mud sticks.

I'm also beginning to wonder who set me up. One name in particular keeps rising to the top of my mind ... Zoe Banks. Would she be capable of this?

Before I can voice the thought, Gloria looks up from her phone and says, 'FYI, I've just checked the BBC and the *Standard*. No mention of you. Or Kelli. See, this is just a two-minute wonder. Nothing more.' She turns to Chopper and adds, 'Come on, let's get you outside before you disgrace yourself.'

'I'll stay here and check my messages.'

'You so won't! Delete the voicemails without listening then let's get back to normal.'

It's a sensible suggestion and I do as Gloria says.

Out on the street, I'm convinced everyone's staring at me, but Gloria insists I'm delusional. 'No offence, but you're probably the least well-known person in Primrose Hill,' she laughs. 'No-one knows your face in the first place.'

By the time we reach the park, I feel more relaxed. Such a relief not to be splashed all over the news. But two minutes later, when my phone starts to ring, I feel a sinking feeling in the pit of my stomach.

'Just ignore it,' Gloria says. 'Enough for one day.'

I force myself to look at the screen. Ah!

'Where are you?' Edo's voice.

'In the park with Gloria. What about you?'

'Outside the shop.' Edo sounds out of breath. 'On my way. Meet you at the gate.'

We retrace our steps. Chopper spots Edo first and lollops ahead to greet him. But Edo sidesteps the dog and runs towards me.

'Nina! I'm so sorry.' Edo wraps his arms around me and pulls me close. 'It's going to be all right,' he says. 'I'll take care of everything, don't you worry.'

My body stiffens.

Then relaxes.

95

It's been so long since anyone has held me.

I feel Edo's hands through my jacket, stroking my back, then his fingers gliding through my hair. I snuggle deeper into his embrace.

'I was thinking I should take you away for the weekend,' he whispers. 'Get you out of London and stay somewhere nice and quiet till all this blows over. I promise you it'll be all right,' he says again.

'It's already all right,' Gloria says crossly. 'Put her down, Edo. Stop taking advantage.' Still with an edge to her voice she adds, 'You've heard what happened then.'

I pull myself reluctantly away from Edo. 'Thank you,' I say softly.

The three of us walk to a bench and sit down, accompanied by Chopper. The dog makes two attempts to clamber up alongside us before sighing deeply and settles for blocking the path in front of us.

'So how *did* you find out?' Gloria asks Edo.

Edo looks shifty. He fiddles with his trainers, then encourages Chopper to make another futile attempt to mount the bench. Finally he mumbles, 'It's on Twitter.'

I'm not much of a social media butterfly. It's a miracle if I check my Facebook more than once a week – I use it mostly to keep in touch with a few cousins and uni friends – and I vaguely remember setting up a Twitter account a year or so ago although I never got into the habit of actually tweeting. So Gloria is faster on the uptake.

'How bad?' she asks Edo.

'Trending across London.'

I can tell from Gloria's horrified expression this isn't a good thing.

'Show me,' she demands.

Edo whips out his phone and starts stabbing the screen. 'There.' He hands the phone to Gloria, who looks intently.

'Kelli Shapiro RIP. Primrose Hill. Kelli Shapiro false alarm. Fake funeral.' Gloria seems reluctant to continue but finally adds, 'And, um, Nina Sherwood. All hashtagged. Bloody hell!'

Even though the sun's still out, I shiver. 'Does hashtag mean what I think?'

'Probably,' Edo says. 'You tag a tweet so other people can search by topic. Then the most tweeted topics rise to the top of the popularity list.'

'Let's have a look.' I brace myself.

'No!' Gloria and Edo speak in unison.

'It's that bad?'

'Worse than you can imagine. And spreading like Ebola.' Edo takes his phone back from Gloria. Keys in a couple of commands, then invites her to take another look.

'Oh Lord. Nina, when did you set up a Twitter account?' She turns to me. 'Do you know your password?' Then softly to Edo, 'Have you seen this one? Should we report it to the police? And this. Vile.'

While they are engrossed in the tweets, I take out my own phone. I'm not a baby. I need to see what's being said. I launch the Twitter app and type in my password. Easy to remember. RYAN28 – his age when we married.

I have two hundred and seventeen notifications, which means a lot of people have been sending messages directly to my account as well as gossiping with one another.

I brace myself, then pull up a fresh screen.

It's even worse than Gloria made out.

97

Three people hope I die of cancer. No, four ... five ... seven. One of whom spells it canser.

I think I'm going to throw up.

Another message expresses the wish that I should be gang-raped by a group of baboons. Followed by another from someone in Norfolk who hopes terrorists will behead me, 'because you're not worth the waste of a bullet'.

I spot three more from fellow undertakers saying I have brought shame on our profession.

One from Jason Chung, asking me to call him.

I know I should stop reading ...

#itsyourfuneral seems to be pretty popular.

Someone tells me I'm a worthless piece of crap. Here's a whole bunch of people instructing me to go kill myself.

... But I can't lift my eyes from the screen.

Four in succession saying I'm a slag.

Oh.

This one's different.

It says: I am certain none of this is @NinaSherwood's fault. Get your facts right. #pitifultrollsbeveryashamed. From Edo.

My eyes well up and the screen begins to blur. This is the most horrendous day I've ever had. Apart from when Ryan—

'Nina! I *told* you not to look.' Edo tries to grab my mobile, but clumsily I jerk my hand away and it clatters onto the path.

Chopper is quicker than any of us. Surprisingly nimble, he gets to his feet, marches up to the phone, cocks his leg and releases a strong, steady stream of urine.

'Take that, Twitter!' Edo says. 'Exactly what they all deserve. Nina, the internet's not the real world and tomorrow they'll spew their vitriol on someone else. Tell you what, I've got a hacker friend who can find out who they are. Then we can tweet about their strong desire for kiddie porn. What do you say?'

Through the tears, my laugh, I realise, is the laugh of a hysterical woman.

Chapter 15

That night, I sleep with Edo. More precisely, I mean simply that we share a bed. I know Gloria thinks Edo fancies me, but she's barking up the wrong tree. It's all completely innocent and I'm grateful for the comfort.

The three of us had supper – Chinese takeaway accompanied by medicinal amounts of alcohol – then Gloria went to the cinema with Fred (presumably, there's less chance of him being spotted by anyone who knows him when he's sitting in the dark) while Edo watched four episodes of *Game of Thrones* and I sat with him pretending to understand what was going on, grateful not to be on my own.

So when, at my bedroom door, Edo suggests in a gentlemanly way that he keeps me company, it seems a far better idea than staring at the ceiling all night alone with my thoughts. Also, we have Chopper as a chaperone and he takes up most of the bed, stretched out peacefully between the pair of us.

Edo's telling me about his meeting with Joshua Kent. 'This mentoring business,' he says, 'it's not a foregone conclusion. I've got three rivals, so I hope I impressed him. He was friendly enough. Quite ordinary really, when you consider his reputation. Wearing a cardigan.'

'Maybe it was a post-modernist statement?'

Edo takes me seriously for a moment, then gets the joke and says, 'Joshua Kent described that installation where the guy nailed himself to a car in the middle of Leicester Square as timid. Said he should have had the courage of his convictions and hired a mate with a blow-torch.'

'And this is the man you want to mentor you?'

'You bet!'

'So what did you talk about?'

'It was pretty informal. He asked me where I was living. Who I was living with. Actually, he seemed pretty interested in *you*.'

'Me? Don't you think I've suffered enough?' Despite myself, I giggle. 'What did the man in the cardigan want to know about me?'

'Don't panic. It was more about death and dying, really. And that's the thing. He's set me a test. I have to come up with some new ideas. Designs for death, I'm calling it.'

'Okay.'

'So I was wondering if I could pick your brains?'

'What's left of them!' Actually, I'm interested in what Edo's saying. And a bit terrified, in case it's going to involve blow-torches. Or worse.

'Well, you've said before how funeral services are starting to change.'

It's been almost four months since I last attended a funeral. The longest gap in my career.

'You mean with the baby boomers – that's people over sixty to you – wanting ceremonies that are more about them and less about God? Humanist funerals where family and friends celebrate someone's life as much as mourn their death.' Edo nods, and I continue, 'The industry's starting to get a lot more family requests, such as burying someone in their favourite football strip. And making sure they take their mobile with them to wherever they're going. That sort of thing?'

'Kind of. Joshua Kent told me about some latte lover who was buried in a Costa-Coffee-style coffin. I think it was painted maroon, like their cups. Even had their logo written on the side.'

'Really?' I wonder if I'll ever arrange another funeral.

'Hope she got them to sponsor it!' he says.

No-one can fault Edo for his lack of enterprise. I doubt he'll be an artist slash barman in ten years' time. 'So have you made a start on your project?'

'Still at the ideas stage. Been thinking about a sculpture made up of individual urns in a public space. Or maybe mixing people's ashes with cement to make bricks for affordable homes. That would be transformative, sustainable, and a great alternative to the woodland burial grounds I've been researching. What do you think?'

I think Edo is talking in the matter-of-fact way of someone young who has encountered death only ever as an abstract concept. He has yet to learn what it's like to lose someone you love ...

But it would be unkind to say so, and it's not my place to dampen his enthusiasm.

'Okay,' I say. And you never know, the relatives of a deceased builder might think the brick idea is good. 'Keep me posted.'

'I will.' Edo yawns. 'Good night,' he says. 'Sleep well.'

I'm certain I spent the next five hours listening to the rhythmic snores of the two males in my bed. Although in the morning Edo had the temerity to tell me I snored, too.

Cheeky pup!

* * *

Over breakfast, Edo asks me, 'So what are your plans for the day?'

The same question I've been asking myself.

What should I do, now that I am known locally – and quite likely nationally – as The Woman Who Pretended Kelli Shapiro Was Dead in Order to Fool People into Thinking Her Business Is Successful?

I've got the beginnings of a plan. 'Edo,' I say. 'I need you to give me a crash course in social media.'

'Sure.' He looks pleased. 'But there's one condition. You have to go to the shop. We'll do it there.'

Edo knows me better than I thought. I'd intended to keep my head down and keep Happy Endings closed.

But he's right. I've done nothing wrong, and I've got nothing to be ashamed of. So it has to be business as usual, or at least, lack of business as usual. The important thing is to show my face.

'No problem,' I say.

'In case you're wondering,' Edo says, 'I've already looked at today's papers. Nothing. And the Twitter trolls have moved on to abuse that Arsenal player who scored an own goal last night.' Edo's a Chelsea fan so he doesn't look especially dismayed. 'You're yesterday's news, Sherwood. C'mon, let's grab Chopper and go see the world.'

Our first port of call is the phone shop in Swiss Cottage, where my mobile is declared dead on arrival. I discover I have no insurance, no chance of an early upgrade, and no choice other than to buy a new phone. I do so, wincing at the price.

'Bad dog,' I chide Chopper. I know it was an accident, but I'm horrified at the way I'm haemorrhaging money.

We walk to the shop the pretty way, via the top of Primrose

Hill. I'm getting to know a few of the dog-owning locals – inevitable when you're in charge of an unguided canine missile – and several people greet me as usual. And down there. Isn't that the idiot on the scooter? Barclay. Walking in the direction of the canal. Stopping to talk to a couple of girls who are probably asking him why he's got a canoe slung casually over his shoulder. He looks good in shorts. Remarkably long legs.

Edo realises my attention has drifted elsewhere and taps me on the shoulder. 'See, I told you everything would turn out fine,' he says. He casually winds his arm around my shoulder as we stand there looking at London spread out beneath us.

Equally casually, I move beyond his reach and bend down to pick up a stick. I hurl it into the air, and Chopper sets off in eager pursuit, catching it in his strong jaws before it hits the ground.

If only my life were as uncomplicated as Chopper's.

Chapter 16

I start to feel tense once we reach Regent's Park Road, but no-one takes the slightest notice of me. And by the time we've been sitting inside Happy Endings for an hour, I'm so wrapped up in completing the task Edo has set me that I jump at the sound of his voice.

'How are you getting on?' he asks.

Blocking the Twitter trolls so they can never contact me again is liberating. Today, their taunts and insults seem merely infantile. And while I've been tidying up my account, my brain's been at work. Old-fashioned newspaper advertising costs an arm and a leg – as I know to my cost – but social media is free.

'I'm going to make a fresh start with Twitter,' I tell Edo. 'Open a new account for Happy Endings. I'll use Facebook and Instagram, too. And I need to build a website.'

'Awesome! I can definitely help you with the website.'

'Then I'll need to start following local people, so I can get to know them and they can get to know me. I want everyone to get used to the idea that I'm just another local business and that I'm here to stay and become part of the community.'

'Sounds like a plan.'

'There's tons of Londoners on Twitter. Who knew!' Edo

looks at me in a way that suggests I'm an elderly relative who's extremely late to the party. 'But first,' I add, 'I'm going to fill in the paperwork and sign up for the Traders Association.' Zoe Banks might not be convinced about my business but the Traders Association can damn well fund their Christmas lights some other way. I've always hated bullying and I'm not going to let Zoe or Julie browbeat me into slinking away.

Edo's nodding his approval. 'Good move,' he says.

Before I can make a start, my landline starts to ring. Edo looks at my anxious face and picks up the phone. 'Hello, Happy Endings,' he says.

I watch his face while he listens to the person on the other end of the phone. 'I'll pass on your message. Yes, and your number,' he says curtly. Then he slams the handset back on its base and throws his pen on the desk without writing anything down.

'Another member of my fan club?' I pull a face.

'Not sure.' Edo looks puzzled. 'Some bloke with a stupid name. Barclay. Sounded more cocky than crazy. Says he wants to take you out to lunch. Who is he?'

The idiot on the scooter.

The good-looking idiot on the scooter.

The good-looking idiot on the scooter who is of no interest to me whatsoever.

'Oh, just someone I met the other day in the park,' I say. 'He probably feels sorry for me about yesterday.'

'Are you going to go?'

'What?'

'To lunch?'

'Doubt it.'

Edo seems mollified by my answer. Sweet of him to be so protective.

I spend the next twenty minutes locating the online application form for the Traders Association and supplying the details required.

'There!' I press the computer keyboard to send the form on its way. This is turning into a good day, after all.

Before I can do anything else, I hear my email ping. That was quick. An almost-instant reply from the Traders Association. Probably an automated acknowledgement. I open the message.

Dear Ms Sherwood,

Thank you for your application to join the Primrose Hill Traders Association. In anticipation of your request, members of the Executive Committee met last week and have made their decision.

As local businesses, we strive to maintain the character and feel of our lovely neighbourhood and to supply our residents with appropriate services and goods. Had you properly done your research before foolishly acquiring the lease on Noggsie's shop, you would have been aware of this requirement.

What the neighbourhood needs at present, along with an increase in casual and weekend footfall, is, at one end of the spectrum, outlets for discretionary spending in the luxury goods sector, and at the other, high quality artisan outputs. For example, we would very much welcome the arrival of a vintage fashion shop, a stained glass specialist, a craft cider store, or perhaps a lovely, old-fashioned, sugar-free sweet shop.

The Traders Association is the retail guardian of the

village and as such, we have entered into a pact of trust with our customers to maintain a quality standard that must not be compromised.

So far as we are aware, the undertaker of choice for any local residents who should be unfortunate enough to experience the end of life is Leverton and Sons. Not only do they date back to 1789, they were also good enough for Margaret Thatcher and the Princess of Wales. Moreover, their presence gives us a valuable opportunity to create employment by outsourcing to Camden Town any occasional requirement we might have for their services.

In conclusion, Ms Sherwood, your wish to peddle death on our charming high street is ill-judged and unwelcome. We therefore have no hesitation whatsoever in rejecting your application to join the Traders Association. Please note that this decision is final and that you have no right of appeal.

Sincerely,

Zoe Banks (Chairman)

'Wow,' I say. Zoe must have drafted the email after we met, so she had it ready and waiting to send.

'Wow what?'

'Let's just say I won't be joining the Primrose Hill Traders Association any time soon.'

I turn my screen so Edo can see. He scans Zoe's response, then shakes his head. 'So bad it's funny. Peddle death on the high street! They're such a snotty little clique, Zoe and her chums. Think they run the show. You're so right, Nina,' he adds. 'What you were saying last night. People round here need you to help them come to terms with death being part of life.'

'Thanatophobia. That's what it is.' Edo looks blank. 'Extreme fear of death,' I explain. 'It's not so uncommon, but I never dreamed anything like this would happen.'

Before I can say anything else, Edo groans. 'Uh-oh.' He points towards a figure in the street outside.

Julie, the florist. Obscured in part by an elegant bouquet of long-stemmed yellow roses almost as big as she is. I brace myself for the next onslaught in the battle of the misordered flowers for Kelli's non-funeral. The first thing to hit me, though, is a heavenly scent that wafts in with the summer breeze while Julie successfully negotiates the shop door.

'I've come to say sorry,' she says at once. 'I was too hasty. I've taken Gloria's advice and put out the flowers at slightly above cost. Selling like hot cakes, and I might even make a small profit. I just panicked yesterday. Got myself into a right state over cashflow. And Zoe really wound me up, kept saying it was all your fault. But it wasn't. Everyone knows that now.'

This is reassuring.

'Julie, do you belong to the Traders Association?' I ask.

She has the grace to blush. 'Yes, I heard they had a meeting about you last week. Sorry to hear they've turned down your application.' She twirls the yellow roses awkwardly in her hands. 'I don't know why Zoe's got such a bee in her bonnet about your shop but if it's any consolation she gave the betting shop a rough ride when they arrived and they're doing all right now.'

'Well that's good to know.'

'Mind you,' Julie continues, 'Zoe's not entirely wrong about Happy Endings. The thing is, Nina, people around here … they just don't die very often.' Julie clocks my baffled expression and explains, 'You'd be amazed how many of the old

109

brigade have two or three homes. They tend to pop off to the sunshine of the Caribbean or Florida before they pop off for good. Then they get buried abroad for tax purposes. And you realise how much the neighbourhood's changing? All those rock stars, teachers, accountants, journalists, doctors, writers and the like who came here in the seventies and eighties ... they're all coming up to retirement, selling their homes for a fortune, and moving out of London. It's a young people's place now.'

Julie's not making me feel any better, but she's in full flow. 'You only have to stick your head round the door of the wine bar at six thirty every night. More hedge fund managers than you can shake a stick at. Technology entrepreneurs who look like they're not old enough to drink. You know, the clever boys who've just sold their businesses to Google for more money than I'll earn in a lifetime. Accompanied by supermodels who make me want to slit my throat. Especially when I spot them running up the hill, chased by their hot personal trainers. And the expats, of course. Sometimes on the streets of Primrose Hill, you'd think the first language is Russian.'

'But your business is doing all right?' I ask.

'Touch wood.' Julie places a hand on my desk, almost dropping the roses as she does so. 'Thanks to the fact that so many people think of flowers as part of their interior design schemes. And the ladies who send flowers to one another on a regular basis, like they're playing pass the parcel, bless their little Amex gold cards. I do pretty well with weddings, too. Mostly second-timers and third-time-luckies. But not so often with the funerals. Not compared to other florists.' Julie stops to think. 'Noggsie's the only funeral we've done all year.'

'In that case, we must be due for another one soon,' Edo

says. He might have been tapping away on his phone, but he's evidently been listening carefully. 'Statistically speaking, of course.'

Julie gives a superstitious shudder. 'I'd better get back. Only popped in to give these to you.' She places the yellow roses into my hands.

'There's no need!' I protest.

'Oh, they're not from me. I'm just the messenger.'

Inside the small envelope there's a handwritten note.

Hope you're alive and well! Let's have supper the week after next. Can you do the Wednesday, 8pm at the Blueberry Café? Kelli xxx.

Dad would be so jealous.

Chapter 17

In the aftermath of what I've come to think of as #Kelligate, I've had plenty of time on my hands to meet the needs of anyone who requires a funeral. An entire week. And – as always – no takers. Yet I think I've spent my time wisely because you sometimes have to slow down before you can speed up.

My inspiration has come from Dad

Being ex-navy he's always impeccably organised and I've heard him talk on several occasions about the soldier who jumped on his horse and rode off in all directions.

With this in mind, I abandoned my usual routine – rushing round the neighbourhood with my thrown-together leaflets, posting a few random tweets, then polishing every inch of every skirting board in the shop and generally chasing my tail into a whirlwind of panic because the customers still aren't coming – and backtracked instead.

I forced myself to sit quietly and focus on the reasons why my business has failed to take off. And, in the end, I realised the answer was as simple as it was complicated. People don't understand what I'm offering.

With my old employers, this was never an issue. The shop in Queen's Park was part of the neighbourhood furniture with a reputation that had been built up decade by decade. People were familiar with its presence and there was never any hostility.

Whereas in Primrose Hill ... I mustn't get things out of proportion. It's probably only Zoe Banks who actively resents the sudden appearance of Happy Endings – and her extreme response is most likely the result of being too scared to confront what my shop's presence signifies. Everyone is going to die,

Anyway, I arrive at the shop this morning before eight o'clock, feeling enthusiastic. Optimistic, even. I need to stop feeling apologetic about the nature of my business. It's my immediate job to make sure the neighbourhood understands what I'm offering – or would like to offer – and why it's a little bit different. Sure, I can organise a traditional religious funeral, and if that's what someone wants, I'll gladly do it – won't I just! – but times are changing. Funerals, too. And from now on, I'm going to make sure Happy Endings gets the message across about the end-of-life choices that are available to us all.

Put it this way. I didn't know I wanted a red silk skater dress until I noticed one on Oxford Street when I was passing H&M. That was my lightning-bolt moment, when I decided to junk my own display of tasteful yet innovative cremation urns and replace them with a more arresting window display.

Or to put it another way, today is the day death comes out of the closet. Yes, it's Sunday but I can't wait to get started so I make myself a quick coffee, park it on my desk, then return to the basement to fetch my recent purchases. For two days, I ran around London like one of those manic candidates on *The Apprentice* doing the scavenger hunt challenge, collecting everything I needed and haggling for the best prices.

113

Now I begin by carefully unpacking a large flatscreen TV and bolting it onto its stand. After a couple of false starts, followed by a sausage roll from a family pack I've been keeping in the fridge (I've graduated to the Comfort Eater's Diet, with exactly the results you would imagine) and a YouTube tutorial that guides me through the set-up, I've got the new TV sitting in the shop window, facing outwards, with an onscreen message announcing it's connected to an equally new DVD player.

I insert one of the discs that arrived yesterday into the DVD player, then press a couple of buttons on the handset that comes with it.

Success!

For less than five hundred quid I've built myself what Edo would call a moving installation. Or, in my language, I've now got the beginnings of an attention-grabbing window display. At least, I hope so.

Let's take a look. I go outside into the street and pretend to be a passer-by. Yep, that picture on the TV is definitely going to get noticed and hopefully stop people in their tracks. I stand and watch a mini-movie unfold.

It begins with a beaming infant, dressed in white. The image morphs into a schoolboy, all big grin and missing front teeth. Now he's a teenager with a helmet of blond hair accompanied by a sulky expression. But adolescence is fleeting. Two seconds pass and the boy becomes a man. He looks confident and happy and I wonder if he's posing for his student ID card. The picture's so sharp I can see he's wearing eyeliner. I bet his mother loved that! Now the image of a startlingly handsome thirtysomething fills the screen but before you know it the hairline is receding. Next, dressed in an expensive jacket, shirt

114

and tie, the man is suddenly my senior. A few seconds more, and the bags that appear under his eyes fill me with unexpected regret. And look! Three deep sets of frown lines beat a path across his forehead. Whatever's happened to make his life such a disappointment as he enters middle-age? I don't have time to dwell on it because now there's a caption. '*Simon.*' I read. '*The first 49 years. Tune in for the next instalment in 2045.*' Then the screen goes blank. Until the beaming infant dressed in white reappears and the time-lapse sequence starts again.

Amazing what you can buy these days. I have no idea how something so brilliant has been created, but I say a silent thank you to Simon – whoever he is – and his photography project and go back inside the shop. That's phase one complete. Now for the fun stuff.

It takes me the whole afternoon, punctuated by another trip to the park with Chopper – this time, uneventful – before I'm satisfied. When I'm finally finished, my shop window is beyond transformed and Simon's changing face is a perfect backdrop to my collection of props.

I hadn't realised what a tight squeeze it would be to get everything in, but the vintage bike that came from a cycle shop on the Old Kent Road looks even better than I'd hoped with its fresh coat of black paint and newly white-walled tyres. It sits securely on a kick-back stand and is ridden by a life-sized skeleton I saw advertised on Gumtree. (One previous owner, who decided to study physics rather than medicine, persuaded to take fifty quid in cash when I met him at Colliers Wood for the handover. And yes, I did get a lot of strange looks when I brought it back here via the Northern Line.) The skeleton is dressed in a flowing black gown with a red lining that I discovered hanging from a rail in Camden Market and his costume is completed by a dented top hat and a jaunty bowtie.

How do you get a skeleton to ride a bike? With difficulty. It took two tubes of superglue to secure the skeleton's feet to the bicycle pedals, make sure his hands gripped the handlebars and get his bony backside stuck firmly in the saddle. Then his skull had to be fixed to the top hat, by way of three transparent strings attached to a window pillar, and tugged tight to make sure he has perfect posture. I pull back the gown to reveal the skeleton's naked right forearm, then turn my attention to the next element of my window display.

Getting the long brown cardboard tube to sit securely in the bike's front basket proves tricky but eventually I manage it. Another trip into the street – it's turning into a glorious evening – and I'm well pleased. This is even better than I'd hoped. The words on the tube are nice and clear. 'Imagine you could come back to life through nature'. And underneath, in a smaller but still easily visible font, 'This cremation urn will transform you into a maple tree'.

My final task is to fix a narrow black and white banner along the bottom of the shop window.

TWENTY-FIRST-CENTURY FUNERALS
Meaningful ceremonies that reflect the
life the passions and the personality
of someone you loved

I go back outside to admire my day's work. Have I overdone it? Simon's ever-changing face is intriguing and almost hypnotic. The skeleton on the bike should raise a smile. The biodegradable cremation urn echoes the trend for greener funerals. And the banner, while understated, leaves no room for doubt about the nature – or approach – of my business.

'Justin, look! That's so cool!'

I jump at the sound of a strange voice.

Standing behind me, a woman has paused to take a closer look at my window display. She's pointing at the cremation urn.

The man gives her a hug. 'I think you're more weeping willow than maple tree,' he teases.

'No! Have me turned into a cherry blossom.'

'That's easily done.' I've interrupted their conversation but neither seems to mind.

'Really?' The woman is intrigued. 'So how does it work?'

'The ashes go in first,' I say. 'Then you add soil, fertiliser, and the sapling of your choice, before planting the whole thing.'

'So long-term, we could replace cemeteries with forests,' the man muses. 'Plant generations of a family together somewhere beautiful.'

'And prove there's life after death.' The woman's tone is more playful. She turns to face me. 'It's your shop?'

'Yes.' Across the road I notice Barclay sitting at the café sipping a cold drink and chatting animatedly with a beautiful woman who looks to be in her early twenties.

Oh.

So he's got a girlfriend. Maybe even a wife. He's also got a huge red kite – almost the size of a hang-glider – which is attracting plenty of attention from passers-by, not least because the words 'I've never flown a kite' are written on it and it's blocking half the pavement.

With difficulty, I focus on the woman next to me. The potential cherry blossom.

'I keep telling Justin we need to make our wills,' she's saying.

'But it's one of those things we never get round to. Anyway, brilliant shop window. And it's good to know funerals don't have to be all about religion. You know, with vicars who don't even know how to say your name properly. That's what happened to my aunt. Her name was spelled R-O-I-S-I-N, and you're supposed to say *Rosheen*. But the stupid vicar turned her into a raisin.' The woman glances at her watch. 'We're going to be late for hot yoga,' she says. 'But good to meet you. And you should enter your window in a competition or something. I bet you'd win.'

'Glad you like it.'

That's the most positive conversation I've ever had about my business with anyone who is neither friend nor family. Please let it be a turning point.

I watch the happy couple stroll towards the hill. They pass the café where Barclay was sitting just a few moments ago. He's no longer there. Wife ... girlfriend ... whatever. I'm not going to let it spoil my day.

He was obviously just being polite when he offered to take me to lunch. And since I've forced myself onto a new diet that consists mostly of butternut squash and eggs I'd be a difficult date anyway.

I banish Barclay from my mind and drift back inside Happy Endings on a little cloud of happiness. I've achieved so much today. Just one funeral, that's all I need. Well, obviously not *all* I need but it would be a start. From now on I'm going to maintain the faith, spend more time building my brand and do plenty of positive thinking. In fact, I'll get started right away and map out the content I need for my website. I'm going to build it myself, which means I'll learn a whole new set of skills – and save a whole lot of money. In which case ...

maybe I *will* buy that red skater dress. It's been weeks since I allowed myself the luxury of new clothes.

Instead of building my business, I find myself checking whether the dress is available online, when I hear a text arriving on my phone. I fish it out of my bag.

Barclay.

Good to see you working on a Sunday. You looked too busy to interrupt. Let's have our business lunch next Friday, OK? Bx

Three minutes later and I've bought the red skater dress, feeling only moderately guilty about this misuse of Dad's money.

I spend the next twenty minutes overanalysing Barclay's text. Business, he says. Well that's okay. I can do that. Even if he is married. I'm pondering the significance of the '*x*' when the sound of the shop doorbell startles me.

I look up from my computer half-expecting to see Barclay. But no. It's a man who looks vaguely familiar. It takes me a moment to place him. That's right. Ned Newman. Mrs Happy's husband. I saw them together the other day in the pharmacy, where she was complaining about the quality of her eyedrop medication.

Ned Newman is peering impatiently through the shop door, and from the sour expression on his face, I don't think he's come to congratulate me on my window display.

The moment I open up, he thrusts a white envelope into my hands.

'For you.'

'Um, thank you. What is it?'

Ned looks shifty. 'Business correspondence.'

'About?'

'About the roof. We had another big leak through our

upstairs ceiling last night. The roofer's done his best, but we've had to put down buckets all over the bedroom floor. The whole thing needs to be replaced as soon as possible. It's all in there.' Ned gestures at the envelope in my hands.

'I still don't see why it's anything to do with me. As I told Mrs H ... your wife, I'm sure it's my landlord you should be talking to. Noggsie's son.'

'Read the letter and get back to us.' Without wasting any further words on me, Ned turns away.

I stand and watch as he goes outside and gets into the passenger seat of a white van. The words 'Sheet Hot Roofing' are written on its side.

Chapter 18

'Look, here's my bomb! What do you think?'
My response is to anxiously scan the café in case some-one's overheard what Gloria said. We're having breakfast across the street from Happy Endings because there's something she wants to celebrate with me. Thankfully no-one's looking nervously at our table even though Gloria has now produced what is unmistakably a bomb-shaped item – round with a fuse, like something you'd see in a cartoon –from her bag.

She places it proudly on the table and taps the rust-coloured outer covering with her index finger. 'It's made from recycled paper shell,' she says. 'We fill them with organic peat-free compost, and a gram of wildflower seeds.'

'Who's we?'

'My guerrilla gardening group. With a bit of help from Edo. He designed the bomb mould.'

'So how does it work?'

'You have to soak it first. Then throw it high in the air. Like a grenade.' Gloria grins. 'After a few weeks, you get billowing flowers wherever the seeds land. That's the theory, anyway. I'm going to experiment by lobbing a couple over the fence to brighten up that hideous piece of waste ground next to the school.'

'Is this what we're celebrating?'

Gloria's looking exceptionally pleased with herself. 'No,' she says. 'I'll come to that.'

My friend's fork is poised over a mountain of banana pancakes laced with maple syrup. I've gone for a plate of smoked salmon and scrambled egg, sacrificing the toast in an almost certainly vain hope that high protein will succeed where general willpower – let alone a diet of butternut squash and eggs – consistently fails to help keep me trim.

'So,' Gloria asks. 'What are you up to this week?'

Before I can answer her question, my phone rings. Every time I get a call I'm ready to spring into business mode. But as always, it's a name already on my contacts list that pops up on the screen – Dad. I'm not about to launch into a fresh series of reassuring lies about the success of my business while Gloria's listening so I switch the phone to vibrate and slip it into my pocket.

'Supper with Kelli Shapiro,' I tell Gloria. And lunch with Barclay on Friday, although I keep this to myself.

'Sounds like fun. Make sure you come home with tons of celebrity gossip. Now then.' Gloria pauses. 'Let me get the bad news out of the way first. About the roof.'

When I got home last night, I showed Gloria the nasty letter from Mrs Happy and her husband, Ned. Basically, they took seven single-spaced pages to tell me that under the terms of my lease, I am responsible for fifty per cent of the cost of maintenance and repairs to the 'common parts' of our two adjacent buildings – in other words, the roof – that complete replacement is urgently required, and could I kindly let them have a cheque for twenty-two thousand pounds at my earliest convenience. Surely, my neighbours are just plain crazy. In which case, why is Gloria looking so suddenly serious?

'I read the lease,' she tells me. 'I'm afraid they've got a point.'

'What? The guy who works for Eddie Banks told me it was a standard document. And don't you remember, I only had twenty-four hours to sign it because someone else was after the shop? You were in Milan for the weekend, where Fred was speaking at that conference, so I didn't think there was any need to bother you. I'm sure I told you that.'

Gloria puts my lease down on the table and leafs through the pages until she gets to a paragraph she's highlighted in yellow.

'Here,' she points. 'It says you've got a repairing lease, which means it's your job rather than the landlord's to keep the whole building in good order. It's a bit complicated because it involves the freehold, as well. Nothing unusual, although I really don't understand why your solicitor didn't take a pen to the clause and tell them where to stick it.' A pause. 'But it's worse than that.' Gloria seems reluctant to go on, and when I glance down at my plate, I realise I've completely lost my appetite.

'Tell me the worst.'

'It's pretty bloody bad, sweets. The flat above the shop is unoccupied, right?'

'Yes. It's kept empty in case Noggsie's son ever wants to come back to visit.'

'Hmm. In that case we might be able to argue the son still has some responsibility and get your liability reduced to twenty-five per cent. But as things stand according to this,' Gloria scowls at the lease, 'you're going to have to pay up.'

'But ... Twenty-two thousand pounds ...' The words

coming from my mouth are somewhere between a whisper and a groan. 'That's just not fair. If the roof needs replacing, it must have been falling to bits for years.'

'Your solicitor didn't point this out to you?' Gloria asks. 'We could always go after him.'

'He's a friend of Dad's. Retired. Did us a favour. Basically, we trusted Eddie Banks's team to sort out a legal agreement that was in everyone's interests.'

Gloria tries unsuccessfully to hide her disapproval. 'Well look, you've only got their word that a new roof's required. And that estimate from Sheet Hot Roofing,' Gloria manages a wry smile, which I am unable to reciprocate, 'seems pretty steep. But the fact that The Primrose Poppadum people have agreed to pay their share suggests Mr and Mrs Happy aren't making a fuss about nothing. I think your best bet is to tell her for now that you're going to get a second opinion. String things out a bit. See what happens.'

Am I imagining it, or is Gloria implying that she thinks my business is going to fail? I've been so full of hope these past few days. The window display is a huge success. Half a dozen people have taken the trouble to come inside the shop to tell me how much they like it – 'irreverent yet relevant,' as one of the locals put it – and I've been convinced my first funeral will happen soon.

Now this.

'Let's talk about something else.' I say. 'What's your good news?'

Gloria tactfully removes my lease from the table and tucks it into her bag. 'Double good news, actually. Remember the Regent's Park Garden Festival?'

'Isn't that soon?'

124

'Three weeks' time. They've priced the tickets at thirty quid each, which is a bloody disgrace. Not to mention the thousands of pounds they're charging exhibitors. All in a public park, too! So we've decided to do more than just plant an illicit hedge made of edible fruits.'

Oh Lord. Is Gloria planning to lead a bunch of demonstrators and picket the festival-goers? I wouldn't put it past her. 'So tell me. Is that where the seed bombs come in handy?'

'We're going to do something far more high profile. Our very own display. One of the park workers is going to sneak a few of us in the night before, to build a full-scale pop-up. Something that really stands out and makes people think about the migrant crisis. We're going to ring a plot with razor wire and dying plants that have been deliberately starved of water. On the inside, there's a flourishing wildflower garden with lots of non-native plants, representing hope and dignity. On the other side of the wire – beyond the checkpoint – we'll dig a moat, strewn with little wooden rafts. *England's Green and Pleasant Land*, we're calling it.'

Gloria's exuberance is impossible to fault, but I'm worried she'll make more enemies than friends with this new venture. The Regent's Park Garden Festival is a big deal, and I can't see the organisers taking kindly to an unauthorised contribution, no matter how well intentioned. Equally, I know from experience that Gloria will take no notice if I query the wisdom of her idea, so I nod and smile, then promptly change the subject.

'Is it true what I heard about Chalcot Square? That security guards armed with Tasers delivered forty square metres of gold sheeting to Eddie Banks's basement last week?'

'That's the least of it.' Gloria's happy to switch topics, too. 'My parents say people are staking out his house day and night, hoping for builders' offcuts. And Banks has gone back to the council to extend his planning permission. Everyone's furious. I mean, you can understand the need for a music room. An underground bike store, even. But a meditation room ...'

'Eddie Banks doesn't sound like the type to sit in quiet contemplation.'

'And that's before you get to the cigar room. But what really takes the biscuit is the salt grotto.'

We stare at one another in a moment's silent contemplation, then descend into howls of laughter.

'So the real good news,' Gloria manages to get a grip, 'is that I think there's going to be an addition to our house, as well.'

'Are you ... You're not—?'

Gloria looks affronted. 'Call me old fashioned, but when and if that happens, I'd prefer to be married. To which end, Fred's going to leave his wife.'

'You're kidding!'

'I think you mean, "That's wonderful news, Gloria." Well, maybe not so much for his wife, although Fred's sure she'll be delighted to be shot of him. But the two of us couldn't be happier.'

Gloria's sentence ends on a note of challenge. I sense the hurt in her fighting talk and realise, not for the first time, my friend is an interesting mixture of convention and rebellion.

'Sorry,' I say. 'You took me by surprise. Tell me everything.'

Gloria relaxes and begins to tell me about the misery of Fred's marriage, while I do my best to swallow the remainder of the bouncy scrambled egg on my plate.

'... Everyone's going to tell me I'm crazy even to contemplate setting up home with someone who's been married three times already. But I really do love him, sweets. I knew from the very beginning there was something special about him, that he was the person I'd been waiting for. And relationships are never straightforward, are they?'

Setting up home. What does that mean for me? Will I end up in a squat with Edo? Because there's no way I can afford to pay anyone a proper rent. But Gloria mistakes the stricken look on my face for something else.

'I'm so sorry, Nina,' she says. 'I understand how hard it is for you to talk about marriage. After what happened and that ...'

Ryan, she means. The man I knew from the very beginning was so so special. The man I knew I'd marry. Even before our first proper kiss. Even before our fourth date, when he went down on one knee slap bang in the middle of Trafalgar Square and proposed. But for the first time in a long time, thinking about my husband fails to produce the usual engrained image of his funeral pushing through the surface of my imagination. It must be because my brain is still in shock while I selfishly continue to calculate the implications of Gloria's happy news. How soon will I have to move out? Could I sleep in the shop? Or is this the final nail in the coffin, so to speak? Time to give up and let Dad have back what's left of his failed investment.

'Gloria, I'm truly thrilled for you and Fred. Of course I am.' A lie. Fred's handsome enough, but his moral compass is – at best – dyslexic. I don't trust him to leave his wife. And if he does ... well, Gloria deserves so much better. As does Fred's wife.

'That means a lot to me, sweets. You're the first person I've told.'

'So what's, er, the timescale for Fred moving in?'

'First things first,' Gloria says. 'He has to leave his wife. Before the end of the year, we think. That'll give me time to introduce him to Mum and Dad. Soften them up before they discover he's got a bit of a past.'

I suppose that's one way to describe Thrice-Wed Fred's emotional CV. It also means I'm unlikely to be homeless in the immediate future.

'Time for work,' Gloria announces. She settles the bill and we make our way out into the street, my friend with a bomb in her bag, and me with a legal booby trap still ricocheting around my brain.

Chapter 19

Gloria heads towards Chalk Farm, leaving me at the door of Happy Endings.

Once I've opened up, I'll check the trade press and see if there's any funeral-related news worth tweeting. I'm trying to do at least one tweet every day. Yesterday's was about a recent service in Yorkshire where the service was taken by an Elvis impersonator. Five of my growing band of followers favourited my link, so I don't think I'm wasting my time, while I wait for 'The Call' that will mean my business is actually in business.

I know. Only a few minutes ago I was thinking of conceding defeat, but the reality is that I'm still only six or seven funerals behind the schedule I set in my business plan and I just have to keep the faith.

Bugger. I've broken a nail taking my key out of the door lock. I wince at the pain and suck on my finger.

When the stinging has subsided, I examine my hands. They could definitely do with a spot of TLC. It's been far too long since I had a professional manicure and talking about Eddie Banks and his basement has made me wonder what's happened to his daughter, Zoe, and her posh hen house. You know, why not? There's no point sulking about being banned from the Traders Association. Perhaps if I go to The Beauty

Spot as a customer – I suppress the scary thought of how much it's going to cost – Zoe will realise she's misjudged me. And it won't hurt to have well-groomed hands when I'm sitting across the table from a customer. Or Kelli. Or Barclay ...

No time like the present. But I start to feel nervous five minutes later, when I approach Zoe Banks's shop.

From the outside it looks like just another Primrose Hill townhouse, freshly painted and impeccably maintained. A blue plaque above the door announces this was once the home of Karl Marx. And to the side, in lettering so discreet as to be almost invisible, a logo to reassure me I'm in the right place.

It takes me a few seconds to locate the door buzzer. I also spot a security camera tucked into the corner of a windowsill. What if Zoe takes a look and refuses to let me in? But no. A friendly voice with a Scottish accent comes out of the entry system's loudspeaker and beckons me inside.

Having seen Zoe's home, perhaps I should have been prepared for the opulence of her shop. The space is much larger than I'd anticipated. Lavishly modern, all marble flooring, artful lighting, rich colours, and a couple of sculptures that wouldn't look out of place in the Tate Modern. In the centre of the room sits a state-of-the-art nail bar. At first glance, you'd think it was made of ice, but I think it's solid glass. A couple of white-uniformed beauty therapists are giving treatments and I watch a woman of about my own age slide her hand inside a square machine that radiates a deep violet glow. I feel as if I've entered a foreign country, one with a heavenly scent of pine in the air, and I'm intrigued.

To my right there's a set of steps. A sign tells me there's a steam cabin and an infinity duo pool tucked away downstairs. I'm eyeing up something that could be mistaken for

130

an octagonal coffee table were it not for the line of flickering flames running through the centre when I realise there's a woman standing next to me.

'Hello,' she says. 'Do we have you booked in?'

'No.' Oh well, it was a nice idea, and at least I've seen inside The Beauty Spot. 'I only wanted a manicure.'

'You're in luck!' The woman's Scottish accent has a pleasant lilt to it. 'We've had a cancellation. If you don't mind waiting a few minutes?'

Before I can say, 'No thank you, I'd better be getting back to my empty shop,' I'm installed in an armchair next to the Coffee-Table-on-Fire-Thing. The woman – she must be the receptionist – hands me what looks like a restaurant menu. 'Have a look,' she says. 'We've got some excellent special offers at the moment. And several new treatments. I'll be back in a moment.'

It feels good to let someone else take charge, and I can see how professional the woman is. Friendly yet authoritative. I feel myself start to relax. This is going to be hugely expensive, so I might as well enjoy every moment.

My fears about cost are reinforced the moment I begin to read the list of treatments. The price of a crystal-clear micro-dermabrasion massage and manicure is roughly the same as I spend on groceries in a month. As for the eco-friendly heated massage using recycled shells from tiger clams 'hand-picked from a minor Indonesian island'... let's just say I've sold coffins that were less expensive.

'For you.' The Scottish receptionist is back by my side, bearing a tumbler of green liquid balanced on a slab of slate. 'Your complimentary welcome juice shot,' she says. 'Freshly blended fruits, spices, and seven organic herbs known for their

131

power to strengthen nails.' She sees me hesitate and adds, 'You'll love it.' I take the glass from her and she walks to a staircase at the back of the salon. I wonder what's upstairs.

The juice is a strange combination of sweet and sour. I think I've identified nutmeg, fennel and possibly sorrel, when my attention is diverted by a voice that declares, 'Darling, you absolutely should treat yourself to the vampire facial!' I do my best to look-without-looking at the two women sitting on the other side of the fiery coffee table. The woman who just spoke is American and I'd guess she's in her early sixties. 'I have a friend in Texas who swears by them,' she confides. 'And these days, having your own blood extracted is so routine. They separate the platelets and inject them back into your skin. Simple!'

'Maybe.' The potential vampire victim, a few years younger, and someone I think I've spotted in the street, says it in a tone that really means, 'Not on your life!' This is confirmed when she scans the treatment list and decides, 'For now, I'm going to stick with this one. The Cluckingham Palace Regal Facial. So important to support our local businesses, isn't it?'

The American looks bewildered, but I think I understand. My suspicions are confirmed when the other woman continues, 'If it's good enough for the Duchess of Cornwall, it's good enough for me. Zoe's built this amazing hen house in her own back yard. Can't get more sustainable than that ... although I have to admit the blood thing is pretty sustainable, too. Anyway, every morning at dawn, Zoe selects seven eggs, separates the yolks and blends them into a special moisturiser that's "overflowing with Vitamin A". That's what it says here,' the woman taps the treatment list with her already-immaculate

132

fingernail. 'She makes enough for two facials every day and there's a waiting list. It's taken me three weeks to get to the top, and I don't want to waste the opportunity.'

So Zoe's had her way with the hen house. She must have found a way round the planning regulations to be up and running so fast. Despite myself, I wish I could see how the architect's plans turned out. Cluckingham Palace is a fun name, I have to admit, and as for Zoe's sheer cheek at monetising her hens' output, I don't know whether to be impressed or appalled.

Another voice breaks into my thoughts. One I recognise immediately.

'... Well you know what my big brother's like.' Zoe Banks is walking down the staircase, arm in arm with someone who looks awfully similar to Kate Moss's sister. I strain to hear her continue. 'Different girl every week. I don't think he'll ever settle down, he's having too much fun. He's been on the *Tatler* list of most eligible bachelors for the past four years, and doesn't he know it!'

Zoe's voice gets louder as she walks towards the salon's main door. 'I'll certainly ask him. But I don't think polo's his thing. Other than the leg over.' Both women giggle. 'You're far too good for him! I'll be in touch.'

The woman who wants to date Zoe's brother leaves The Beauty Spot without any money appearing to change hands. Zoe has a quick word with the Scottish receptionist, then scans the salon.

Our eyes meet.

Zoe frowns – at least as much as the Botox will permit. I swiftly and solemnly bury my head in the treatment list, but it's no good.

Zoe marches up to my seat. 'What are *you* doing here?' she demands.

'I popped in for a manicure.'

'*Here?*' The way Zoe says it, you'd think she was sucking one of those sugar-free sweets she's so fond of. Her banana lips are bubblegum pink today – although they look as though they're sucking on a rogue sherbet lemon. 'You're not welcome here. You know that. You're not welcome anywhere around here.' Zoe's voice is rising and the woman who's waiting to have egg on her face makes no secret of the fact she's listening to every word.

This is ridiculous. I resist the impulse to get up and slink out. Instead, I say, 'Zoe, I'm well aware that having an undertaker in Primrose Hill makes you uncomfortable and I'm sorry about that. But be reasonable.'

Heads are turning. Everyone is eavesdropping. Undaunted, I carry on.

'There's no reason for us to be enemies. In fact, I was wondering if we might go out for a drink some time.' Where did *that* come from? But no worries, Zoe looks as if she'd rather sup her own blood – with or without platelets – than socialise with me. 'For now though, would you recommend the Haute Couture Manicure,' according to the treatment list it includes a mineral bath, 'or am I better off having the one with a salt and lavender scrub?' I stretch out my hand towards Zoe and I'm quietly proud – and relieved – to see it's not shaking.

Zoe takes three swift steps sideways, and for a hideous moment I think she's about to tumble into the Coffee-Table-on-Fire-Thing.

Without looking at my nails, she spits, 'You'd need the

antioxidant serum. Gets rid of age spots. But it's not going to happen.'

'Why not?'

A long pause. Then Zoe finally tells me – and everyone else in her shop – 'Those hands have touched death.'

'Not lately, they haven't.'

Someone at the nail bar laughs at my heartfelt retort, but our conversation isn't going anywhere good.

'You know what, Zoe?' This time, I do stand up. 'I came here with the best of intentions. I admire you as a business-woman, and I'm disappointed you'd prefer not to have my custom. But I wish you all the best, I really do.'

The Scottish receptionist intervenes. Gently, she touches my arm, and says, 'I'll see you out.' I walk with her to the door. She checks we're out of earshot. 'I'm so sorry about this, Zoe can be very ... how can I put it ... she can be very ... stubborn, at times.'

'Never mind. She's entitled to decide who she wants to do business with.'

'Talking of which,' the receptionist says, 'the hairdresser at the other end of Primrose Hill does manicures. Good ones. We recommend them whenever we're too busy. No welcome drink I'm afraid, but they're about a quarter of our price. Tell them I sent you.'

Chapter 20

'By the way,' Kelli Shapiro says, 'I adore your dress. Where'd you get it?'

Before I know it, I'm telling my new friend how I treated myself to the red silk skater dress as a reward for inspiring my new window display.

Friend? That's more wishful thinking than reality, but Kelli's got a gift for putting people at their ease. To think an hour ago I was nervous about having supper with someone who's delivered acceptance speeches at two Oscar ceremonies, but look at us now, chatting away like really close friends. Kelli's been keeping me entertained with a string of Hollywood indiscretions. My favourite is the story of the Ultra A-List couple – no names mentioned but I'm certain I know who she means – who spend their spare time swapping genders with one another. As Kelli put it, 'She gets to wear the leather trousers with the cowboy hat and shoots pool in the games room while he does a Nigella in the kitchen, dressed in ten thousand pounds' worth of Alexander McQueen and a set of sapphire earrings that belonged to Princess Diana. Only in the music business!'

The best I can manage by way of shoptalk, over the Blueberry Café's signature dish of wild garlic soup, is an anecdote from China, where apparently three hundred under-takers recently entered a national cremation competition.

Kelli's intrigued. 'Why would anyone want to do that?' she asks.

I explain how China is running out of space for cemeteries just like we are in Britain. 'The big problem is that cremation goes against the whole tradition of ancestor worship,' I explain. 'People are horrified by the idea of burning a body, they think it's the ultimate in disrespect. So the Chinese government is pulling out all the stops to make cremation less unpopular.'

'Competitive cremating.' Kelli rolls the words around in her mouth along with a tiny sip of Prosecco. 'But how do you win?'

'According to what I read, the bones needed to be burnt completely. So the ashes turn out white as ivory, without any impurities.' I realise what I just said and continue hastily, 'I'm so sorry! I don't mean to put you off your dinner.'

'Not at all.' Kelli daintily spears a final pillow of spinach pasta as if to prove her appetite is unaffected. 'Delicious,' she declares. Then continues, 'I'm fascinated. But what I really want to know, Nina, is why you became an undertaker.'

Ah. The million-dollar question. Sooner or later, it always crops up. I leave it hanging in the air for a few moments, giving Kelli the opportunity to ask if I spent my childhood dismembering insects or burying my Barbies at the bottom of the garden.

When she does speak, the words are a surprise. 'I do apolo-gise. None of my business. Let me tell you about—'

'No,' I interrupt. 'It's a perfectly reasonable question. It's just ... well, it's a bit of a long story.'

'The sort of story that requires more alcohol?'

I nod.

Once our glasses have been refilled, I begin. 'When I went to uni, I thought I was going to be a social worker. On my very first day at Sussex, I met this girl called Lin.'

A wave of nostalgia ripples right through me as I remember how I'd been queuing to join the photography society and Lin was standing behind me. We started talking. I'm a South Coast girl and she'd grown up in Glasgow, so the first joke we ever shared was about the need for either an interpreter or subtitles. After ten minutes of standing in a line that was going nowhere, we got fed up and joined the film club instead.

'We soon realised we didn't have much in common but it didn't matter because we were on the same wavelength. We had such fun, every single day. By the end of the first term, Lin had become the sister I never had.'

'I'm an only child, too.' Kelli senses I need to take a moment. 'I always think that's why I ended up in acting; I had so many imaginary friends, and I became whoever they wanted me to be. So, Lin?'

'It happened ...' I gulp, then concentrate on controlling my breathing. 'It happened three weeks into the start of our second year. A Friday. We were supposed to go on a double date with a couple of boys from my course. I really fancied the one we used to call Handsome Richard, and Lin was so fed up with me mentioning his name she got together with his mate and organised a curry night. Except at the last moment Lin thought she was getting a migraine. She insisted I went anyway ...'

My voice trails away, as I remember the last words my friend ever spoke to me.

'An early night won't do me any harm. Have a great time, and I'll expect a full report the moment you get back.'

'I stayed with Handsome Richard that night.' Even after all these years, I am still ashamed. 'Came back to our little flat on the Saturday lunchtime. Greeted by three police officers. Lin's body ... it had already been removed.' I shake my head in response to Kelli's unasked question. 'No, there was nothing suspicious. At the inquest, the coroner made a big thing about how the under-twenty-fives are particularly vulnerable to bacterial meningitis. And often, no matter how quickly treatment is given, it's impossible to save a life. I've always thought he said that for my benefit.'

'Well it certainly wasn't your fault.'

I acknowledge Kelli's emphatic tone with a wan smile. Lin's parents had said the same. Over and over. The more they repeated it the more it was clear that not one of us believed it.

'Her mother tried to make me feel better by taking full responsibility. After I went out Lin called her to say she'd been sick and her mother told her to keep warm and drink lots of water. Said she'd call her in the morning. She rang a dozen times or more. Then called the police. But yes, I did still blame myself. I always will. If only I'd gone home then at least she might have had a chance.'

Both of us have stopped eating and our waiter interprets the lack of activity as a signal we have finished our appetisers. Quickly and professionally he clears away the crockery and once he's backtracked towards the serving hatch I continue.

'I went to Glasgow for the funeral and even though I'd never seen a dead body before – unless you count a budgie and a couple of guinea pigs – I needed to see Lin beforehand. To say sorry ... and to say goodbye.'

'You poor girl,' Kelli says softly. 'And that's why you became an undertaker?'

'No. Sorry. Haven't got to the point, yet.' Despite myself, I smile. 'I was so terrified at the thought of having to go into that room and look at Lin. Didn't know if I was going to faint. Or throw up. My heart was thumping so hard they must have heard it in the Highlands. The coffin was set up beneath a window in the corner of the room. Eventually I managed to look. And there she was. Except she wasn't.'

I see it again, now. Yes, Lin did look as if she was asleep. People had been right about that.

But ...

'For a start, Lin hated pink lipstick,' I say. 'Cherry Lush was her colour. That was the first thing I noticed. Then the nails. She always wore navy blue nail varnish, but that was gone, too. And the silver earrings she wore every single day. As for her hair, someone had inserted a parting into her curls *and* flicked the ends. It looked so weird. And her clothes. All brand new. Lin looked as if she was off to a job interview.'

'*Git that skirt! I'd never be seen dead wearing anything like that!*' Through the years, I hear my friend's voice again. Clearly, as though she were sitting with us now around the table. Still indignant that someone had got it so wrong.

'I stood there desperate for her to wake up and tell me she was having a laugh. Lin was cheeky. Witty. Wild-haired. But there she was, dressed like a junior business executive. I felt I'd let her down all over again. How can I put it ... In death, she was everything she had not been in life.'

Kelli nods her understanding.

'As for the funeral itself, it was dreadful. Just plain wrong. They chose "All Things Bright and Beautiful", "I Vow to Thee My Country", and "Love Divine, All Loves Excelling". I stood there mouthing the words along with everyone else but all

I could think was how Lin would have hated her parents' playlist. She was so much more of a "Dancing Queen" kind of a girl.'

Kelli touches my hand, shakes me back to the present. 'When it's my turn,' she says, 'I fancy "Ring of Fire". Make sure everyone leaves with a smile on their face.'

'Yeah, well. Lin would never have wanted a church service. And her favourite flowers were pink peonies. Not white fucking lilies. So you might want to write down what you want and put it somewhere safe.'

Kelli ignores my angry words. 'So you became an undertaker after you graduated?'

'I dropped out. Couldn't handle seeing Handsome Richard every day. Did a backpacking thing to India. It felt good to be in a place where nobody knew me.'

And even better to be far away from well-meaning people who had tried to comfort me with crap like, 'You're strong enough to handle this.' (I wasn't.) 'I know what you're going through.' (They had no idea.) And worst of all, 'Can I do anything to help?' (Can you bring back Lin?)

'But eventually, I knew it was time to go home and work out what I was going to do next. I saw an advert that asked if I had ever considered a career as an undertaker. Which, until then, I hadn't. But it was my chance to apologise properly to Lin. I wanted to do whatever I could to make sure a funeral reflected at least *something* about the person whose life had ended.'

We sit in reflective silence, until Kelli says, 'Sometimes, you don't choose a job. It chooses you. And in a manner of speaking,' she continues, 'you became a social worker, with or without a degree. You do everything you can to protect the

141

integrity of someone who's died. You work with people who are going through a crisis. Help them come to terms with grief and loss. And I bet you're always there if they want to talk to you any time after the funeral.'

Social work for dead people. I've never thought of it quite like that. But Kelli's made a good point. Although I inherited Lin's collection of CDs and treasured silver earrings, her true legacy is that she changed my life forever.

Chapter 21

I've just finished telling Kelli the story of how Lin and I won a whole month's rent betting on a white horse called Hawaii-Five-Oh one afternoon at Brighton races when our main course arrives. Two large plates of veal shin slow-cooked in Chianti, sage and lemon peel with cavolo nero bruschetta on the side are brought to our table by Marcantonio, proprietor of the Blueberry Café.

'*Come stai stasera?*' Kelli greets him.

'I'm very well indeed. You?'

The two of them begin a conversation in fluent, quick-fire Italian, punctuated by vigorous hand gestures and magnificent shoulder shrugs. It ends with Kelli saying, '*Sembra buonissimo! Ah, ci porta un'altra bottiglia di vino.*'

I understand the final few words well enough and once Marcantonio has left in search of more wine I say, 'So those Italian lessons you were starting. The day we first, er, met. They seem to be going well.'

'Darling, you have no idea!' Kelli does that lovely throaty chuckle she does – it reminds me of Dad, I really must phone him – 'I never did get round to telling you why I need to speak Italian. You remember that film part I was up for?'

I nod.

'Well, the director. It's Roberto Ferrari.' He's serious box office. 'Even my agent didn't think I stood a chance. They'd already screen-tested half of Hollywood *and* London, but the word was it was all just a formality before they gave the role to Meryl. So I was tipped off that Roberto was going to be in Sicily with his family. Rediscovering his roots or something. I spent three weeks learning dozens of Italian sentences and phrases by rote, as I would for a film script. Then I pitch up in this tiny mountain village near Erice and, accidentally-on-purpose, bump into him. I launch myself at him in my best, fluent Italian. About how much I admire his work, my Neapolitan grandmother – may God forgive me, along with my two lovely, lovely grannies, both of whom came from Kent – my lust for pasta, and my devout wish to crown my career by inhabiting the role of a glamorous yet serious woman who, in late middle-age, abandons her comfortable life in Seattle because her Filipino housekeeper's father and his army general boss have been murdered.'

'You said all that in Italian?' I'm enthralled by Kelli's story. She certainly knows how to keep an audience – even an audience of one – on the edge of its seat.

Kelli nods gleefully. 'With the odd Filipino phrase chucked in. I wanted Roberto to know how much I loved the script. And you know what?'

I shake my head.

'Roberto didn't understand a word I'd said. Not a single bloody word! Once he'd stopped laughing, he told me I had the passion, determination, and enterprise the role demanded. Meryl hasn't spoken to either of us since, which isn't so surprising. It really is the role of a lifetime.'

'So tell me about the story. You go to the Philippines, right?'

'Yep. The two women travel to Manila, where they uncover a web of corruption that reaches to the heart of government. Our heroine – yours truly – is framed on drug charges and sentenced to life imprisonment. She spends the next two years teaching her fellow prisoners to speak English and transforms the prison work programme into a goldmine, to make sure those who are released leave with a decent amount of cash. Eventually, one of the ex-prisoners exposes the wicked government people, there's four days of fighting in the streets before the army seizes power, and then my character is given a royal pardon. Plus several medals.'

We are halfway through the bottle of wine – I realise I've been drinking a lot faster than Kelli – and even though I'm pretty full, I allow myself to be talked into a pear and grappa sorbet for dessert. I could easily get used to the Italian Diet.

'I know the film's going to be a huge success. Can't wait to see it!'

'And I can't wait for the first day of filming! But I didn't ask you here so I could boast, Nina.' Kelli sounds suddenly serious. 'I want you to know I'm rooting for your business to succeed. It won't happen overnight. Success doesn't work that way. But I see something of myself in you when it comes to the jobs we do.'

'Really? Actress and undertaker?'

'Think about it. So much of my career has been spent waiting for other people to make decisions. That's where you are right now, waiting for someone to choose your business. You'll do a great job, and the word will be out. But when you run a small business, which is what we both do, there are always going to be these lulls when you convince yourself you'll never work again. You need to get used to it. Accept it.

Learn to value the downtime. It's always a fine balance between making sure you're ready to do your job at short notice and lapsing into can't-get-out-of-bed lethargy.'

Kelli's making a lot of sense. And she's not finished yet.

'You have to keep going. Even when it seems hopeless. I believe in you and I'm sure there are plenty of other people in your life who'd agree. And I've been meaning to say, I think that window display of yours is genius.'

Before I know it, I'm telling Kelli how my dad's invested his money in Happy Endings. How hugely supportive Edo and Gloria are. How – and why – I came to be sacked from my old job. And how damn difficult it is to keep myself going day after day, waiting for the chance to show what I can do.

'That really does sound like my life!' Kelli says.

'I'll feel so relieved once my first job actually happens. Looking forward to that moment is what's keeping me going.'

'What about outside of work? Is there someone special?'

Kelli's caught me off balance.

'My husband ... I can't get his funeral out of my mind,' I say before pausing. I'm not going to spoil our evening by talking about Ryan.

Quickly, before Kelli can say anything sympathetic, I lob the question back across the table. 'How about you?'

My enquiry is met with a broad smile. 'You know what they say ... variety is the spice of life. There's a young man I see when I'm in London. Keir. An engineer. Early forties. Nothing too inappropriate. Proper action man. Hardly ever watches a film, because it means you have to sit still.'

Kelli's words make me think of Barclay.

'So last weekend, Keir persuaded me to get kitted out in a full climbing suit – boots, harness, the lot – so we could yomp across the roof of the O2 arena,' Kelli grins at the memory. 'I was terrified, but it made me feel properly alive. You get an amazing view of the London skyline if you're brave enough to look up from your feet. Ah, Keir. I love him because he makes me laugh. Then, when I'm in America, there's someone called Murray. He's in the business. Producer. Married. Always has been. Always will be. He and his wife, they have an arrangement. The two of us have known each other for thirty years. And I love *him* because he makes me think. Makes me reconsider my own beliefs and prejudices. Every once in a while we have very perfunctory sex together. I'm not entirely sure why. Habit, I suspect. I try not to get involved when I'm working, because it's too likely to get messy. But Keir and Murray, they're not the only ones.' Kelli looks directly at me, without hint of apology or embarrassment. 'I don't think we can get everything we need from just one person. Maybe I'm making excuses, or perhaps it's because my work means I've led such a nomadic life.'

'And have you ever been married?' I'm relieved the focus is back on Kelli, and loving her gung-ho attitude.

'Once. For about half-an-hour. Two actors. Fatal combination. Probably what put me off long-term relationships for good. And in case you're wondering, yes, I do occasionally regret not having children.'

Exactly what I *had* been wondering.

'I think we can all have anything we want. But not everything. The little choices we make almost without thinking can have huge consequences. That's something I didn't properly realise until it was too late.' Kelli seems to be talking as much to herself as to me.

'So here's a piece of unasked-for advice from an older

woman, Nina. Life is short. You of all people know that. I'm truly sorry for your terrible loss, my darling.' Kelli reaches across the table and brushes my hand with her own. 'But I want you to promise you'll never hide from what's most important. I don't mean your work. That's part of who you are. I'm talking about love. Big love. That's what completes us all and makes life worth living. Remember I told you I'm intuitive?'

Kelli's blue eyes stare directly into mine until she forces me to answer with the merest bob of my head.

'Well I sense you won't need to be alone too much longer. And I want you to know that almost always, there comes a moment when you can write yourself a complete new script. Redefine yourself and shift the course of the rest of your life. All you have to do is take the leap and let love in.'

'Yes, but—' I'm about to say something about protecting yourself from another dose of pain, but Kelli's having none of it.

'Yes, but—' she mimics my voice, not unkindly, but with unnerving accuracy. 'Yes, but ... And then there's "if only". Aren't they just the saddest words in any language? We meet someone. We feel the connection. And instead of thanking our lucky stars, we worry. We make excuses. We overanalyse. We step away. Or we run. When really, all we ever need to do is say yes. And talking of saying yes,' Kelli concludes, 'you said something earlier that's been playing on my mind. Nina, I need your help. Here's the thing ... Just hear me out.'

'Okay.'

'That first time we met,' Kelli begins, 'I told you it was possible the funeral hoax thing was aimed at me. Someone warning me off trying out for the new movie. Remember?'

148

'Of course.'

'As I said,' Kelli looks around the Blueberry to make sure no-one can overhear, 'there's an issue with my kidneys. Nothing immediately fatal. It's under control with medication. The doctors say I've got probably two, maybe three years of wriggle room before we have to even consider a transplant. So I'm fine to work. I've told Roberto, of course, and we agreed to keep shtum because of the insurance hassle. Bit naughty, I know.'

I'm shocked. Kelli looks a picture of health. 'But—'

I was about to say I'd never have guessed in a million years, but having cut me short, Kelli continues. 'Darling, this is the first time in months I've drunk alcohol,' she says. 'And it's mostly because I've been plucking up the courage to ask you something.'

'*Me?*'

'As I say, I'm hardly at death's door. But I've come to think there's a reason why we've met. Nina, since you came into my life I've given a lot of thought to my funeral. I know what I want when the time comes. And I can't think of a better person than you to be responsible for the arrangements. Would you do that for me, please?'

I gulp. 'It would be an honour. But you have to promise you're going to live for years.'

This time, Kelli's laugh is so loud a couple of people do take notice. 'I promise,' she says. 'How are you fixed tomorrow? Let's sit down and write the script for my final appearance. Three o'clock?'

Despite myself, I'm laughing too. I've never met anyone so enthusiastic about their own funeral.

'You're on!'

Chapter 22

M y life has taken a turn for the surreal.

Yesterday, I spent a hugely uplifting afternoon helping Kelli plan her funeral. To say she has something unusual in mind would be to do her an injustice.

Today, I was meant to be having lunch with Barclay.

And I am.

I think I am.

At any rate, he's promised I won't go hungry.

When he texted yesterday and said he'd organised a long lunch out of town, I was in the middle of a conversation with Edo, who was telling me about his plan to visit our local hospice and talk to a colleague of Joshua Kent – an artist friend who's suffering from lung cancer and has more than just a passing interest in Edo's Design for Death project. We got so engrossed I forgot to text Barclay back to explain I couldn't be away from Happy Endings for more than a couple of hours. In case a client turned up. So I've told Edo a white lie about needing to go to the dentist and he's agreed to mind the shop, which I strongly suspect he wouldn't if he knew I was out with Barclay.

And not only out with Barclay. I'm out of the country with Barclay.

As our cab threaded its way across town, I thought he was

taking me to lunch in Chelsea. But our destination turned out to be Battersea heliport. Barclay ushered me inside a helicopter, then plonked himself in the pilot's seat.

'No way!' I protested. 'Remember I've seen what you can do just with two wheels.' *And frankly, I'm intrigued about what you did with that canoe. And the kite. And that woman I saw you with last Sunday*, I added silently.

Fortunately, Barclay couldn't read my mind. In response, he simply fastened my seatbelt. As he did so, his hand brushed against my thigh but he seemed not to notice.

'Would you like to see my driving licence?' he offered. 'You *are* allowed to pilot helicopters when you've passed, right? Isn't that what Prince William did? Just sit back, my princess, and enjoy the ride.' A sidelong glance accompanied by a grimace that reassured me Barclay was sending himself up. 'We'll be there before you know it.'

I'd never been in a helicopter before, and I have to admit I loved it. Even when Barclay removed his sweater to reveal a T-shirt that announced, *Helicopter Pilot in Training*.

Or at least I was fine until I realised the land beneath us was about to change to water.

'Turn this thing round!' I squealed. 'You didn't say I needed to bring my passport.'

'Don't worry.' Barclay was relaxed, so I guessed we were going either to the Isle of Wight or the Channel Islands. For the remainder of our flight, I sneaked sidelong glances at his handsome profile – I think the broken nose adds character – while admiring his easy familiarity with the helicopter's controls.

'So tell me about your family, Nina,' Barclay says now. 'Live in London, do they?'

'Southampton. My dad works in construction and Mum's a teacher.'

'Long way to commute. Whereabouts do you live? Is there a Mr Nina I should know about?'

I do one of the things I always do when I'm with a man who's showing interest in me. I tell him in a single sentence that I live in a house share with friends in Kentish Town, and then encourage him to chat about himself.

'So how was the paintballing?' I enquire.

'Epic!' Barclay spends the next ten minutes telling me about the riotous time he had in Scotland. 'There was a split second when I thought I was either going to get hit or lose the flag, but I dived just in time.'

He puts his hand over mine, encouraging me to control the helicopter. 'Have a go,' he says. 'You know you want to.'

And for the next few seconds, I'm flying!

When Barclay resumes command he starts telling me about a recent case that obliged him to visit the Cayman Islands. I'm fascinated by the lengths some clearly rich people will go to make themselves even richer, which is probably why I'm focused more on Barclay than on the earth spread out below us. But when I do take a look at the scenery I realise I'm wrong about our destination. That's definitely not Ryde Pier I can see below us. And the scale of the city coming into view is much bigger than any of the Channel Islands ... until, after about ninety minutes in the air, Barclay lands us smoothly back on the ground.

'*Et voila*,' he announces.

I get out of the helicopter and gaze up at the Eiffel Tower, tantalisingly close to where we've landed.

Wow! This is much more like being on holiday than going out to lunch.

Once inside the terminal, a uniformed official walks towards us. Barclay says quietly, 'Leave everything to me.' Then, '*Bonjour François. Ça va?*' The two men exchange handshakes and a bit of banter and Barclay produces a red document wallet. The Frenchman gives it barely a glance before handing it back and waving us towards the exit where a taxi is waiting. No passport, no problem.

Barclay ushers me into a waiting car and to be honest I'm a bit disappointed we're not having lunch up the Eiffel Tower, as I'd been expecting.

'Want to guess where we're going?'

I shake my head. It feels good not to wrestle with any decisions. I don't mind admitting, at least to my 'holiday self', that Barclay's take-charge attitude is attractive. I also like the fact he doesn't have perfect teeth: one's got a slight chip on the side, perhaps the result of another of his misadventures on a scooter.

The Parisian traffic is light. Only a few more days to August, and it looks as though the residents have already begun to abandon the city for their traditional month out of town. It's not long before I see a sign that says we are on Avenue de la République, followed, a few minutes later, by another, when our car turns into Avenue Gambetta.

Bloody hell. Now I know where Barclay is taking me.

Chapter 23

'Have I done the wrong thing?' Barclay's face falls. It's the first time I've seen him look anything other than self-assured.

'Absolutely not. It's just that I'm ... well, it's not exactly where I imagined us having lunch.'

The car glides to a halt at what looks like steps that lead to a park.

But I know better.

This is Cimetière du Père-Lachaise.

While Barclay murmurs something to our driver in a mixture of English, French and laughter, I take in my surroundings. Okay, so this isn't how I imagined my day was going to turn out, but Père-Lachaise and New Orleans are meant to have the coolest, most interesting cemeteries in the world. And until now, I've seen neither.

This is also my first visit to Paris, and if I'd come for a weekend break, Père-Lachaise would have been high on my list of sightseeing priorities. So now's my chance to explore – although I'm not sure, exactly, where lunch is coming from. Maybe there's a restaurant.

'You might want this.' Barclay gives me a map. 'I've brought us in the back way,' he gestures. 'It means we get to walk downhill. The other way's pretty steep. Ready?'

154

Without waiting for an answer, he takes my hand. Together, we walk up a short flight of concrete steps and enter the cemetery.

'Most people make a beeline for Jim Morrison's grave.' I feel Barclay's pepperminty breath on my face as he speaks. 'But if you'll let me, I'd prefer to take you on a tour of some of the hidden gems. Unless, of course you've been here before?'

I know I'm supposed to fill the silence now Barclay's finished talking, but something's happened to my brain. I suspect it's been fried by the pulses of electricity that have been flooding through me ever since we started holding hands.

Surreal and surrealer. Here I am, on a gorgeous summer day, on the fringes of a famous French cemetery, with a man I know almost nothing about – not even his surname – when I ought, by rights, to be at work.

And it feels so good.

'Look over here.' Barclay finally releases my hand and points towards a tombstone embossed with elegant gold letters and adorned with a pair of deep red roses. Maria Callas. The opera singer.

'Fifty-three,' I say.

'Pardon?'

'Her age when she died.' I gesture towards the two dates on the stone.

Barclay gives me a quizzical look.

'I can't help it. I always calculate people's ages. Date of birth to date of death.'

'How about 1938 to 2012?'

'Seventy-four.' My answer is instant.

'1546 to 1603?'

'Fifty-seven.'

'1879 to 1999?'

'One hundred and twenty! You're teasing me.'

'Yes,' Barclay says solemnly, 'I am. Did you know that someone stole Maria Callas's ashes from the cemetery?'

'Are you still taking the piss?'

'No. I swear. She died of a heart attack here in France. The police eventually recovered the ashes, but rather than risk another theft, her friends had them scattered in the Aegean Sea.'

It looks like Barclay's going to be an excellent tour guide. I follow in his wake – careful to keep a small distance between us – and we work our way deeper inside the cemetery.

'A million people are buried at Père-Lachaise,' Barclay says. Everywhere I look, tombstones are laid out in orderly rows. Like the streets of a silent city. Even though we're still less than a hundred metres from Avenue Gambetta, the pathway has become as eerily quiet as it is beautiful.

Eighty-six. Fifty-three. Twenty-nine. Seven. I'm back calculating ages as we walk among the dead. Some of the graves are ornate, protected by metal railings, although I don't recognise any famous names; others are less distinguished but well-tended, often with fresh flowers. And every time I turn my head, I see angels. Angels clasping crosses. Angels with doves perched on their shoulders. Angels with their wings soaring into the sky.

Père-Lachaise surely contains more angels than there are in all of heaven and the older and more weathered they are, the more lifelike they seem.

'Keep up!' Barclay breaks into my thoughts. He's stopped beside a name I recognise immediately.

Oscar Wilde was forty-six when he died and his tomb is

as peculiar as it is impressive. It's huge, with a flying, naked angel at one corner, and looks almost brutal, like something that would be more at home in a Russian theme park. But the vision is softened by hundreds of lipstick hearts and kisses, along with graffiti tributes from visitors. *Thank you. I love you. Keep looking at the stars. Wilde child we remember you.*

'They put up the plate glass wall a few years ago,' Barclay says, 'when the cost of cleaning was getting out of hand. So now people decorate that, instead.'

We're joined at the grave by a group of excited, lipstick-at-the-ready German teenagers. Barclay attracts their attention by blowing Oscar an extravagant farewell kiss, then says, 'I'll take you to one of my favourites now. Ever hear of a guy called Victor Noir?'

'Nope.'

'Follow me!'

Barclay is such easy company, it feels as if we've known one another for years. We walk companionably along one of the many cobblestone lanes that crisscross the numbered sections of the cemetery in an intricate maze. Barclay takes a path that leads us gently towards the centre of Père-Lachaise. A distant honking duel between two irritable motorists is the only indication that it's business as usual for the living.

'Here.' Barclay has stopped at a grave unlike anything I've ever seen before. It's a life-sized sculpture of a man lying flat on his back. The bronze has a green-grey weathered patina. The prone man's top hat is upended just below his right knee, and someone has recently used it as a makeshift vase, placing a bunch of mauve freesia inside.

Twenty-one. Younger even than Edo.

'Let me introduce you to Monsieur Noir.' Barclay has the

innate charisma of a showman. And expressive, groomed eyebrows that remind me a little of Brad Pitt. His clothes are casual – white shirt and chinos – but clearly expensive. Brown, well-shined brogues. Dad says you can judge a man by his shoes, but should I be judging?

Is this a date?

Or lunch?

Or what?

'Victor Noir was an unfortunate young man, shot dead by Napoleon's great-nephew.' Barclay seems unaware of my scrutiny. 'But extremely popular with the ladies, to this very day. Can you see why?'

I take a closer look at the sculpture.

How did I miss *that*? Not only are Victor Noir's nose and lips unaccountably shiny – no wonder he seems to be smiling beneath his green toothbrush moustache – his, how can I put this … Victor Noir is still pleased to welcome visitors. To be blunt, there's something that's only too plain to see in the trouser department. Something that has obviously been very well-rubbed.

I drag my eyes back to meet Barclay's.

'Women come from all over France to visit Victor Noir. All over the world, in fact.' Barclay is amused. 'He's quite the fertility symbol. They say that if you kiss him on the lips, you'll be pregnant before you know it. Or if you give him a bit of a French polish, you'll be married within the year. Shall we give it a try?'

'Certainly not,' I say firmly.

'Don't say I didn't offer.'

Barclay is hard to read. Half the time he seems either to be teasing me, or taking the mickey out of himself.

Is he interested in me?

I'm so out of practice, it's hard to tell.

Do I want him to be interested in me?

Is this the sort of connection Kelli was talking about? Or exactly the opposite, and a case of crossed wires ...

'You hungry yet?'

I surreptitiously consulted the map while we were en route to Victor Noir and found no symbol for a restaurant or café, but I'm learning to expect the unexpected.

'I did skip breakfast this morning.' A decision made in expectation of a lavish lunch.

'No worries. This way.'

We stroll for five minutes, chatting inconsequentially about Chopper's insatiable lust for sticks, a new hip-hop musical that opened last week in the West End – Barclay's seen it already, and I can't help but wonder who was sitting next to him – and Camden Council's latest recycling initiative, which is so complicated, neither of us have a clue what's supposed to go where.

We arrive at a series of steps that lead into a small park, complete with brightly coloured flowerbeds, a well-kept lawn, and a perimeter lined with wooden benches.

Barclay zones in on one of the benches. 'Look,' he points. 'Over there.'

I swivel and take in the perfect view stretching across Paris all the way back to the Eiffel Tower. Barclay, meanwhile, continues until he reaches a thick, waist-high hedge. He bends down and fishes around inside the greenery until he finds what he's looking for, then returns to the bench – triumphantly – carrying a wicker hamper. How on earth did he manage that?

Before I can enquire, Barclay's saying, 'I thought it would be fun to have a picnic. Nothing fancy, just a few bits and pieces. Ready to dig in?'

Barclay opens the hamper, reaches for a linen tablecloth packed inside, shakes it out, and lays it on the grass beside the bench. He begins to arrange a magnificent selection of French delicacies. I'm particularly impressed when a white polystyrene box opens to reveal a platter of seafood, king prawns, oysters and smoked salmon, so fresh I can almost smell the Mediterranean, accompanied by juicy wedges of lemon, thick mayonnaise and crusty brown bread. I arm myself with a napkin, sit down on the grass, and get stuck in. Everyone knows French women don't get fat – people have written books about their lack of obesity – and I'm working on the basis that calories consumed in France don't count.

Barclay builds a stacked plate of ham, cheese, salami, salad and baguette, puts it down beside me, then reaches back inside the hamper to fetch liquid refreshments and glasses. He does the honours – chilled rosé for me, iced mineral water for him – and says, 'Cheers!'

We lock eyes and raise our glasses.

I'm starting to feel overwhelmed. No-one has ever been to so much trouble on my behalf. 'Thank you for organising this.'

'My pleasure. So good to be away from home, even for a few hours. Especially on a day like this. Helps get everything into perspective, wouldn't you say?'

I realise I haven't given Happy Endings a single thought for several hours and feel immediately guilty.

'So what would you usually be doing on a Friday afternoon?'

Barclay flicks away baguette crumbs while considering his

answer. 'Thinking about my plans for the weekend. Either that or dealing with last-minute work emergencies. Although, sadly, corporate insolvencies seem to be going through a dip.'

'Isn't that a good thing?'

'Not for me!'

I don't like what Barclay's saying, but there's something very engaging about the way he doesn't take himself seriously.

'Talking of which, Nina, how's *your* business going?'

'Much better, thank you.' I'm not going to sit here and whinge.

'Lots of people dying, are they?' Barclay sounds genuinely interested.

'Well no. Not exactly. But I've been busy getting everything into place. Website. Branding. Social media. Getting my name out there. That sort of stuff.'

'I heard there was a spot of bother with one of your neighbours. Something about the roof?'

'Oh, Mrs Happy!'

Barclay chokes on his water. 'Yes, that's her! Brilliant name. She's the most miserable woman in Primrose Hill. Always yelling at me when I was a kid.'

'What were you doing?'

'Breathing, mostly. What's her problem this time?'

'She seems to think I should pay thousands of pounds to get her roof fixed.' I explain about the shared roof and the lease, and Barclay listens intently.

'There's nothing so unusual about a repairing lease. But it does sound like bad news for you,' he says when I've finished. 'Expensive bad news. And it's an old building, so there could be other stuff happening. Dry rot. Wet rot. Woodworm. Subsidence, even.'

We both fall silent. Barclay begins to pack up the remains of our picnic. I pluck blades of grass from the earth while performing scary mental arithmetic. It all seems hideously unfair. I've been in the building for a matter of weeks. I don't own it yet I'm legally obliged to foot the bill for what's obviously years of neglect. And this is the professional opinion of the only two lawyers I know – Gloria, and now Barclay. Oh, and Dad's legal friend, who should have spotted the clause in the first place. Maybe he did, and thought nothing of it, if it's as common as Barclay says it is. That still doesn't make it right, though.

On the pretext of helping Barclay clear away, I pop a stray morsel of saucisson sec into my mouth, and wonder how I can spend even less on food than I already do.

The beep of a text alert. Mine. I check my phone. Edo.

Quiet day at Happy Endings So went up on roof. Big fuss about nothing. Slates & flashings all fine. Just a bit of cracked render on parapet. Few hundred quid max 4 proper repair. Done temp fix with special tape from Homebase, should last ages. Taken photos. Will send 2 Mr & Mrs Happy! Hope dentist not 2 painful xxx

Weird telepathy, as if Edo overheard our conversation. I text him a reply.

Fantastic! Thx xx

I feel bad about the dentist thing, even though Edo has nothing to be annoyed – or jealous – about. Gloria's told him, there's a reason why I don't do relationships.

'No need to be miserable, Nina.' I start at the sound of Barclay's voice. 'There's a solution to every problem, and I know how to fix yours.' Before I tell him I think Edo has already – literally – fixed it, Barclay continues. 'You have to cut your losses. Move into Kentish Town. It's on the up and up, thanks to all those French families who've taken it over. I'll find you a shop. Negotiate a cheap rent. Get you out of that lease, too. Just because you've failed once, it doesn't mean *you're* a failure.'

Bloody hell. Does Barclay have any idea how patronising he sounds? Talk about mansplaining. He might as well pat me on the head and say, 'There, there.' Or is it that he's used to people doing what he says, in that way that rich people are?

'Let me think about it. And I'd have to consult my father. He's an investor.' No point in spoiling the afternoon, especially as my financial circumstances have just taken such a reassuring turn for the better. 'How long before we need to head back to London?'

'No huge rush.' Barclay saunters across to the hedge and puts the picnic basket back where he found it. Then he adds, 'You do need to think about it, Nina. Burying your head in the sand when you're running a business with no clients isn't smart. It's how bankruptcy starts. Let's face it, Primrose Hill isn't the right spot for you.'

This time, Barclay sounds very concerned. As if I'm one step from debtor's jail. Whereas I'm still several steps away. And I don't think people get imprisoned any more.

'Thanks for offering to help. Where are we off to next?'

'You can't go home without visiting Édith Piaf. A woman after your own heart ... no regrets and all that jazz.' There's not even a trace of sarcasm in Barclay's voice. 'Did you know *piaf* is French slang for sparrow?' My lunch date has reverted to full-on tour guide mode. 'And that her great-grandmother was a Moroccan acrobat?'

We giggle our way towards the perimeter of Père-Lachaise, back towards Oscar Wilde. All I really know about Édith Piaf is that she had a gorgeous voice, and big problems with drink and drugs.

Forty-seven.

Piaf's tomb is a solemn slab of granite, decorated with a vase of slightly wilted flowers, and twenty or more individual red roses, each one hand-tied and cellophane-wrapped.

I notice Barclay is frowning at his phone.

'Something wrong?'

'Oh, just my dad. One of his projects giving me a headache. Neighbours complaining the burglar alarm's going off. Why do these things always happen on a Friday?' I'm about to make sympathetic noises when Barclay continues, 'I need to call our security people. There's gold on site, so we need to be careful.'

Barclay retreats to make a phone call, leaving me staring at Édith Piaf, and wondering what sort of building project uses gold.

It takes a few seconds for the penny to drop.

With a big fat clang.

Chapter 24

Barclay returns, looking relieved. 'False alarm,' he says.

'This building project.' I pick my words carefully. 'Whereabouts is it?'

'Just around the corner from your shop. It's why I'm in Primrose Hill so often.'

'In Chalcot Square, you mean?'

'That's the one.'

'Eddie Banks's basement?'

'We're way behind schedule. And the bloody neighbours say they'll invoke penalty clauses if we go over. Going to cost us a fortune.'

'But that would make you ...'

'Barclay Banks. Pleased to meet you.' He holds out his hand, in mock formality, then pulls a face. 'My mum's idea of a joke. But in her defence, my parents didn't have two pennies to rub together when I was born. As for the bloody gold in the chillout zone, that certainly wasn't my idea. More trouble than it's worth. Not literally, but you know what architects are like.'

I have no idea what architects are like.

'You're Zoe Banks's brother.'

It comes out as the accusation it's intended to be.

'Ah Zoe,' Barclay says her name fondly, reminding me of the

way I sometimes say Chopper's. 'She's not exactly a member of your fan club, is she?'

You know what my brother's like. Different girl every week. You're far too good for him!

'You're the playboy brother.'

Barclay considers this second allegation. 'Well, I do like the fine things in life. Who doesn't?' He looks me up and down, then treats me to a warm, innocent smile.

It should make me want to slap him.

But it's really hot.

'There's a lot to be said for money,' Barclay continues. 'Essentially, it buys you time. Like today. With the helicopter. I expect you think I'm bone idle, but I was in the office at five o'clock, and I'll put in another shift when we get back. Dad's drummed it into Zoe and me that there's no free rides. Work hard, play hard, die young, make a good-looking corpse. Right?'

I ignore Barclay's attempt to lighten the mood. 'Why did you bring me here?' I snap. 'What do you want?'

'To get to know you better. Anything wrong with that? I've heard from Zoe and Dad that you're a very hard worker, and I hate to think you're going to work yourself into the ground with nothing to show for it when your shop goes under. I meant what I said, Nina. You've picked the wrong location. I want to help you.'

'Why?'

Barclay considers the question. 'I've never believed it's wrong to combine business with pleasure.' And with that, he turns his back on Édith Piaf and me and heads towards a curving lane that wouldn't look out of place in the New Forest, calling over his shoulder, 'Jim Morrison or Marcel Proust?'

166

'Jim Morrison.' I'm still processing the fact that Barclay is Zoe's brother – Zoe's playboy brother – and figure there's safety in numbers. By all accounts, Jim Morrison's grave is usually the busiest place in the cemetery.

Today is no exception. I realise we're getting close when the distinctive smell of cannabis mixed with the excited chatter of American accents begins to fill the air.

'People always tell you his grave's hard to find. But in my experience, you just follow your nose.' Barclay waits for me to draw level with him and we begin to walk up a hill, then along one of the narrow paths. 'They say Jim Morrison visited Père-Lachaise a few days before he died and said he wanted to be buried here. His dad was an admiral.'

Twenty-seven.

Barclay sees me looking at the dates on Jim Morrison's tomb. 'Yeah, same as Amy Winehouse, Kurt Cobain, Jimi Hendrix and Janis Joplin. It's a dangerous age. But you know what they say – better to burn out than fade away.' There's something sombre, pensive almost, about the way Barclay says this.

'Are you a big fan of Jim Morrison?'

'Hardly. Always thought "Riders on the Storm" was a bit of a dirge. Seems to last forever. And I bet you most of this lot,' Barclay nods towards Jim Morrison's latest fans, 'would be hard-pushed to name another two of his songs. Give me Pharrell Williams any day!'

The grave itself is modest and nondescript, nothing much to look at, but the sightseers are undeterred, taking it in turns to do selfies and sing choruses of 'Riders on the Storm'.

'Seen enough?'

I nod. 'So what's your favourite grave in the cemetery?' I ask. 'Can we go see it?'

167

'I wouldn't call it my favourite exactly. But yes, there is one place I always visit. It's round the corner. Follow me.'

'Come here often, do you?'

I'm teasing, but Barclay's voice when he replies is serious. 'As a matter of fact, yes. I do.'

We turn right and make our way along a path shaded by a canopy of trees. I wonder who Barclay's taking me to see. After Victor Noir and his shiny bits, anything is possible.

'Here.'

A well-maintained grave. Black headstone, the lettering in gold.

'Twenty-two.' Barclay's voice, faster even than I can calculate the gap between the date of birth and the date of death. 'The only thing I remember is the way her hair used to smell. Like apples.'

I read what's written on the headstone, trying to work out what to say.

'She was born in Paris and her parents thoroughly disapproved of the marriage.' There's nothing of the tour guide or the showman about Barclay now. 'But back then, if you were pregnant, you got married. Even if you *were* only nineteen, and you'd met your husband three months earlier. But you know what ... sometimes, these things work out ... At least, until ...'

'What happened? Was it an accident?'

'Sort of.' Barclay stifles a bitter laugh. 'My mother died in childbirth. Ten days before my second birthday. Dad couldn't afford a decent burial, so the in-laws, my grandparents, stepped in and brought her home.'

Barclay's voice is getting thicker with every sentence. His every ounce of confidence has drained away. He looks twelve years old.

I wrap my arms around him and pull him towards me. A second in which the only sound is the beating of my own heart. Then Barclay wraps one hand in my hair, and the other around my waist.

He pulls me close and I look up at his face.

This is momentous. I'm stone-cold sober and it feels like the start of the rest of my life. It feels ... just ... right.

Barclay runs his fingers through my hair, and I close my eyes in anticipation.

'So tell me Nina.' His voice is soft, husky, urgent. 'Have you ever done it in the back of a hearse?'

Chapter 25

I don't know if my daily social media efforts are doing any good but at least when I'm doing them they keep my mind off Barclay Banks. It's been a week since Paris, but he's still flitting in and out of my thoughts.

One moment I picture him as a vulnerable boy – how dreadful to lose your mother when you're still an infant – and the next, I think of him as a presumptuous know-it-all, insisting I've opened my business in the wrong part of London.

Might he be right?

As if to ensure he's wrong, I return to my social media accounts. Two pieces this afternoon. One about Japan's equivalent of *Britain's Got Talent* for Buddhist monks. Yes, really. They were competing to see whose funeral sermon had real star quality and, according to the report I found online, they all gave it one-hundred-and-ten per cent. I follow this with a link to a news update about an unfortunate man arrested at an airport in Australia and accused of possessing ketamine – which turned out on closer inspection to be his younger brother's ashes, ready to be scattered on the Great Barrier Reef.

In my imagination, I'm telling Barclay Banks that if you want to impress a woman, asking a crass question at the precise moment she thinks the two of you are about to share a first kiss is *not* the way to do it. But my lecture is cut short by the phone.

I pick up on the second ring.

And finally, it happens.

'Hello? Happy Endings?' A man's voice. He sounds appropriately uncertain and upset, and I know in that instant that someone needs my professional services.

'Yes. I'm Nina Sherwood. How can I help?'

'It's just ... there's been a death ... my mother, she was ... she was ... there was blood ... everywhere ...'

'Sir, I'm so sorry.' I can hear a woman's voice, sobbing in the background, and I realise that in order to help, I need to take charge.

'Sir, whereabouts are you calling from?' St John's Wood. 'Would it be easier if I were to visit you there? So we can discuss the arrangements face to face?'

The man – his name is Roger Sanderson – sounds relieved at the prospect and next thing you know I'm on my way in my official Happy Endings van.

No hoax call this time.

Roger Sanderson turns out to be in his forties. I'm relieved to discover his mother – Lydia – is actually alive. And as well as can be expected in the circumstances.

I do my best to mask my horror as the events that took place late last night are described to me – this was a sudden, violent, death – and together with Roger, his wife, and his mother, spend the next hour sketching out a funeral plan, then adding in the detail.

Burial is out of the question, everyone agrees.

There's to be a viewing of the body, which will be available for release as soon as the papers are signed. Making the

171

corpse presentable will be tricky, but I think it's do-able. It's all a little outside my comfort zone, and it's crossed my mind that maybe the family would be better served by a specialist undertaker. But then I imagine myself telling Kelli – who's been sending me regular emails with upbeat messages such as *Smile! You're one day closer to your first funeral* – and I know I can pull everything together, exactly as the family wishes.

I'd forgotten what it feels like. The necessity to cancel your plans for the evening – not that I have any – and guide the Sanderson family towards good decisions that will give them no regrets in the days to come.

I sneak a glance at my watch.

'So if we collect Alice's body now?' I say gently. 'I can arrange cremation and we could scatter the ashes on Saturday. Does that look like the best plan?'

Three faces nod trustingly back at me.

'I'll do my utmost for Alice,' I promise. 'And for you all. Shall we get started on the paperwork?'

Funeral Number Two

††††

In Memoriam
ALICE SANDERSON
2008–2019

††††

'It was love at first sight. From the moment our eyes met, little Alice totally stole my heart. I remember it as if it were yesterday. Bringing her home then watching over her for hour upon hour, far too excited to sleep. Bewitched by her adorable face, and those intelligent, all-knowing black eyes. They were her finest feature. Alice loved life. And life loved Alice. Hers was a short life well lived, and I shall always be grateful for the wonderful adventures we shared.'

Barclay Banks had attended three previous funerals, but none had been like this.

The opportunity had presented itself when his friend Roger called to cancel their sailing date. The family spaniel had met an untimely end in the jaws of a Rottweiler, Roger explained. His mother was refusing to let the vet send its body for cremation, and he couldn't really bugger off and leave her to it.

Before Barclay knew quite what he was doing, he had recommended Happy Endings. Partly because he'd been curious as to whether Nina would be willing to take on a pet funeral, but mostly because he needed to see for himself if she was any good at her job. That, at any rate, had been his excuse.

'Just don't tell her I sent you,' he warned Roger.

'How so?'

'It's a business thing. If you let me have a full report, I'll pick up the bill.'

Roger had needed no further persuasion.

Now Barclay sat deep in thought, only half-listening while Roger's mother continued her eulogy. 'You might remember that time we travelled to Sweden to see the Northern Lights, and how Alice was invited to join the huskies as they raced across the frozen tundra,' she was saying. 'Truly a once-in-a-lifetime experience. And only three years ago, we climbed Ben Nevis side by side, raising over seven thousand pounds for Great Ormond Street Hospital. By the time we got to the top, I was utterly exhausted. But Alice ... she was barely out of breath and eager to do it all over again. I shall always be grateful we had eleven fantastic years together until the day she was—'

For the first time, the woman's voice faltered. She looked down at the grass, grinding her three-inch heels into the yielding earth and fighting for composure until she was calm enough to continue.

'All I will say is this. Alice had a sense of adventure few of us are fortunate enough to possess. She lived life in the moment. She made friends easily. Too easily ... Sweet Alice trusted everyone who crossed her path. And that's what got her ...' The woman removed her dark glasses, produced a dainty white handkerchief from her pocket and continued resolutely. 'I know people are saying this was an accident.

Just a tragic accident. But so far as I'm concerned, my darling baby girl was *murdered.*'

Barclay watched Roger race to the side of his youngest daughter, who had begun to wail the moment her grandmother said the 'm' word. The sadness and the sincerity of those who were gathered to mourn Alice made him feel like the voyeur he was.

Barclay swung round in his chair, took another swig from the bottle of Peroni that was keeping him company during the ceremony, then forced his eyes back to the computer screen on the makeshift desk – twelve bricks and a sturdy wooden plank – in front of him.

Ah! There was Nina, walking discreetly behind Roger and his family. The moment he saw her, Barclay knew the outrageous amount of money he'd paid a 'security expert' to rig up the sophisticated webcam and sound system that was live-streaming the funeral here to his hideaway was money well spent.

Nina! He'd been such a jerk. Whatever had possessed him? Especially when it had all been going so well. What had started out as just another piece of family business was turning into something entirely different. He'd known from the moment he heard Zoe bitching about how Nina had turned up at The Beauty Spot requesting a manicure that she would be no pushover. But Barclay hadn't expected his – frankly – wise advice about moving Happy Endings to a more suitable location to be dismissed out of hand. Especially when he'd gone to the trouble of taking her all the way to Paris to butter her up.

Nina! He'd presumed she knew who he was. Most people in Primrose Hill did. What had taken him by surprise was the way that when she found out, she clearly didn't give a damn. Unlike every other woman he knew.

'*You're the playboy brother!*' Nina hadn't meant it as a compliment, and it only made him like her all the more. He couldn't get her out of his head. Hence today's exercise in ... well, he'd justified it to himself as further research. But even though he could fool his father, there was no point in deceiving himself.

Back on the computer screen, the eldest of Roger's three daughters was speaking. 'Alice was born six months before me, so she's been in all of our lives forever.' The girl's sisters nodded solemnly. 'I can't believe we'll never see her again. Sunday walks will never be the same. But at least Alice died quickly, doing something she loved.'

'I'll drink to that,' Barclay mumbled to himself. He thought about the report Roger had delivered to him a couple of hours before the funeral began.

'Nina's been absolutely bloody brilliant,' Roger had declared. 'Nothing's too much trouble. Hadn't realised this is her first funeral, but if this is anything to go by, she's going to be a huge asset to the neighbourhood.'

Not exactly what Barclay had wanted to hear. But at least poor little Alice and her brutal demise had given him the chance to spy on Nina.

Or rather, to observe her at work. There was no way he could have attended the funeral in person, so watching from the privacy of his father's Chalcot Square basement was the perfect alternative. It also gave him a chance to do a sneaky Saturday check-up on the works in progress – the gold bloody cladding had been cocked up beyond belief.

Nina!

'Your turn now,' Roger was saying to his youngest daughter, who pulled out a piece of paper from her bag, and began.

'Alice stole more than Grandma's heart,' she said. 'There were sausages ... toilet rolls ... and remember last year, when she got into the kitchen and ate her weight in Christmas goose?' The mood at the ceremony was lifting, Barclay noticed, with smiles being exchanged. 'We're all very sad that Alice has gone to heaven, but we know she'll be feasting on geese every day now. And steak. And as many biscuits as she wants. Always.' The girl walked the short distance across the grass to her grandmother and gave her a big hug.

Barclay watched Nina place a narrow cylindrical tube into the old woman's hands. The ashes, presumably. Nina was like a stage manager, he thought, making sure everyone was on their mark and all the props were in place. 'So let's all take Alice on her final walk,' she said softly.

Barclay moved closer to the computer screen, as if to listen better. Pity the webcam didn't have a zoom function. Nina looked gorgeous. Not in that designer-clad-obviously-very-expensive-Darling-You-Look-Fabulous way he associated with Zoe and her friends. Nina had ... there was just something about the way she radiated – for want of a better word – goodness.

Imagine dedicating your life to helping other people come to terms with their grief. Barclay knew he wouldn't last five minutes. Not that Nina had said too much about her work, despite his best attempts to get her talking.

'Nina!' He wanted to say her name aloud, and he realised he just had.

That stupid crack about sex in the back of a hearse. There'd been no point trying to explain, telling Nina that whenever he felt himself on the verge of an important emotional moment – in the sort of situation where other people manage to let

177

their feelings show – he always sabotaged himself by saying something utterly inappropriate. Maybe it was just as well. He had a job to do. No point letting feelings get in the way of what needed to be done, and he wasn't exactly short of female company.

Barclay drained the remainder of his Peroni in two deep swigs while drinking in the sight of Nina bending down to collect a bunch of balloons that were about to be released on the summit of Primrose Hill, each one bearing a handwritten message that honoured the eventful life of Alice Sanderson.

Chapter 26

'Here's to Happy Endings!'

I pronounce the toast and clink champagne flutes across the table with Edo and Gloria. Chopper nods his approval. Actually, his head's bobbing up and down while he destroys a pig's ear, his favourite low-carb snack.

Gloria goes to the oven to see how our celebration meal of roast beef with all the trimmings is coming along. She opens the door and prods the sirloin with a meat thermometer.

'Another twenty minutes, and we're there,' she says. 'Who's going to whisk the batter for the Yorkshire puds?'

Edo shoots up to do her bidding, pausing only to top up our glasses. I stay sitting at the table, reflecting for a moment about the funeral.

No, there was nothing I could have done better. I'd accompanied Roger and his mother to the vet to do the paperwork and when I saw little Alice, I'd been shocked by the state of her. Small wonder the vet was so keen to send her straight for cremation.

As things turned out, Alice became the first corpse to ride in my blue van. I'd spent the next three hours cleaning her up, stitching multiple wounds – concealing the worst of them with cosmetics – washing and shampooing her stiff little body, then drying, brushing and combing her hair before snuggling her into a cashmere blanket supplied by Roger, who also brought along her basket. By the time Lydia saw her beloved pet, Alice looked as though she was asleep.

I'd kept Lydia company through the night while she said goodbye to Alice. A night filled as much with laughter and stories about Alice's deeds and misdeeds – she'd once chewed right through the rear seatbelt of the family Volvo, in protest at being left in the car while the rest of the family went shopping – as with sadness and the numbing shock of the dog's horrible end.

I knew from experience that grief would come soon enough. Lydia had seemed pleased when I invited her to join Chopper and me on a walk next week. It would be a chance to see how she was coping without Alice, and Roger had asked me to gently explore whether Lydia would welcome the idea of a new puppy.

Bugger. Up until now, I've had precious little time to think about Barclay Bloody Banks. Yet here I am on a Sunday night, celebrating the fact that Happy Endings is – at long, long last – a real, functioning business. And all of a sudden, he's turned up right here in my head.

Barclay.

The worst thing was how much I'd liked him. He intrigued me, recklessly riding his scooter in the park like a scruffy Herbert one day, then turning out to be some high-powered corporate type complete with his own helicopter. The insolvency lawyer thing wasn't the most compassionate of occupations but he said he worked hard. He'd been great company and there'd been real chemistry between us. I hadn't imagined that. I might even have been prepared to overlook the fact he was Zoe's brother. But—

'Nina! Didn't you hear me?' Edo is waving a fistful of napkins in my direction. 'Are you going to lay the table?'

'Sorry. I was miles away.'

'Planning a blog piece about your first funeral? Have you thought about cornering the market in animal funerals? There's a huge demand for it. You could be, like, a Doctor Doolittle for dead pets. Awesome!'

I give Edo an enigmatic smile, decide not to point out Doctor Doolittle's job was to keep animals alive, and instead start organising placemats, plates and cutlery.

Barclay.

Our helicopter ride back to London had been notable for its long periods of silence punctuated by frosty, stilted conversation. Our earlier, easy camaraderie had evaporated. So he'd turned out to be one of those guys for whom death was an aphrodisiac. Life-affirming, or so they always say. Like any undertaker, I've had my share of post-funeral propositions, but sex in the back of a hearse? Bloody uncomfortable. And no, I'm not talking from personal experience.

I line up three sets of knives and forks with geometric precision and contemplate folding the napkins into swans. Or roses. I go with the swans, although ten minutes later, my handiwork is instantly undone, and the three of us – four, if you count Chopper, which we definitely do – begin our slap-up meal.

Gloria and Edo begin to talk about a project in Liverpool where a bunch of artists, gardeners and architects combined to win the Turner Prize, redeveloping part of Toxteth in the process.

'I'd love to do something like that in London,' Gloria declares.

'Yes. But is it really art?'

'If it's useful, who cares?'

'Joshua Kent, for one. He's still furious. Convinced the Turner should have gone to the woman whose installation consisted of ten chairs draped with fur coats. Genius!'

Gloria and I choke on our wine. I think Edo's being deliberately provocative, but I'm only three-quarters listening.

Barclay.

He's sent me two texts since we returned from Paris. One with some rubbish about how I'm always welcome to come and talk to him if I need help with my business. The other asking if I'd care to accompany him to either the Royal Opera House or the Kilburn Bingo Hall – my choice – next week. I have silently rejected all three invitations.

'So the dude I'm visiting at the hospice – he's called Dele Dier – we've been having fantastic conversations about art. He was telling me about this new installation in Seoul. Involves a live goat lying up to its neck in a jasmine-scented bubble bath.'

'Sounds more entertaining than the man who spent a million euros on a print of an organic potato,' Gloria says.

'Really?' Edo is impressed.

'It was Irish. The potato. The photographer is someone famous.'

'He'd have to be. Is it the guy who shoots everything on a black background? Kevin someone?'

Gloria shrugs.

Chopper contentedly slurps shallot-and-rosemary-infused gravy from a bowl the size of a tractor tyre.

I refresh our glasses.

Barclay!

How come he's the person I most want to tell about Alice's funeral? This is ridiculous.

'Edo,' I say. 'How are you finding the hospice?'

'It's a great place ... considering. I was a bit scared about going there,' Edo confesses. 'But the staff and the volunteers are fantastic. As for Dele Dier – he's very angry about being there. Says his illness is interfering with his legacy to art. Although he certainly doesn't look like he's about to die.'

I hear the question behind Edo's statement. 'Some people spend weeks, months even, in a hospice,' I say. 'Depends on circumstance.'

Edo nods. 'Dele hasn't got any relatives to take care of him. He's going to look through my sketches for the Design for Death project, but we spent most of my visit talking about that Riverdance guy. Michael Flatley.'

'How so?' I ask.

'He's making a fortune, dipping the soles of his dancing shoes in acrylic paint, then strutting his stuff on giant canvases and selling the results. We both think he should use his feet as paint brushes. Or maybe his dick.'

Gloria decides to change the subject. 'So what are we going to do about Mr and Mrs Happy?' she enquires. The three of us exchange looks, and start laughing.

Edo's good deed has been punished by a fresh flurry of correspondence. This time, eight pages.

Handwritten.

Accusing 'you and your associates' – that would be Edo – of deliberately causing further damage to an already fragile roof ... using plastic materials totally unsuited to a conservation area ... undermining future insurance claims ... tampering with works carried out previously by the honest, skilled tradesman from Sheet Hot Roofing, who was now, apparently, in talks with a firm that had recently restored part of the main roof at Westminster Abbey. Then there was an entire page about incorrectly circumferenced corbels that I didn't even begin to understand ... along with a warning that Mr and Mrs Happy held me personally responsible for their rapidly deteriorating health ... followed by various threats involving leasehold tribunals, lawyers and injunctions. And a final sentence requesting I cough up twenty-two thousand pounds without further delay, using the envelope thoughtfully provided.

We've taken to reading Mrs Happy's letters aloud, which reduces us all to childlike laughter after only a few sentences. Edo's threatening to turn her tortured sentences into a rap and shoot a video of himself performing it to use as the centrepiece of a crowd-funded Roof Appeal.

'I've already replied,' I say. 'A few lines pointing out she failed to mention all the photos Edo took, and asking for evidence the repair hasn't worked. That seems to have shut her up. At least for now. Anyway, I've got better things to do.'

Gloria and Edo look expectantly at me, and while we start to clear away the remains of our feast, I fill them in on my new idea.

'I'm going to set up a funeral planning consultation service,' I announce.

'Cool.' Edo is immediately enthusiastic and Gloria returns from the sink to the table to hear more.

'How's it going to work?' she asks.

'Basically, people will be able to write down information about the kind of funeral they want and leave behind clear instructions for their families,' I explain. 'I'll talk them through

184

all the different burial and cremation choices that are open to then, like leaving your body to medical research or opting in or out of organ donation programmes. Clients can say if they want anyone to visit their body, and if so, what they want to be wearing, whether they want make-up and so on.'

Gloria nods her approval, and I warm to my theme. 'We'll talk about the kind of service they want. And the budget. That's really important. I'll give them an estimate that reflects their choices.'

'Asking if they want a traditional coffin? Or something more personal. Like one their friends and relatives can decorate? That's going to be hugely popular.' Edo speaks with surprising authority. I can tell he's been researching.

'Yes, that sort of thing,' I agree. 'They can decide who they want to speak. The music they want played. If they'd like to display photographs that tell the story of their lives. And so on. I'm going to call it "Know Before You Go", and charge ... I'm thinking somewhere in the region of a hundred and fifty pounds. What do you reckon?'

'Great name,' Gloria says.

'Definitely not enough.' Edo weighs in. 'Surely a service like that is worth more than you'd pay the plumber to fix a toilet?'

'It's only going to take me a couple of hours to help people make their decisions,' I counter.

'I suppose.' Edo considers. 'And if you can get two clients a week, that's fifteen grand a year straight onto your bottom line. Then you could commoditise the service with an online package for do-it-yourself downloads. And add on funeral pre-payment plans. I know you don't think they're a great idea, but you have to admit the income would be handy.'

Edo's loading the dishwasher while he speaks, assisted by

Chopper, who's busy rinsing the plates with his shallot-and-rosemary-imbued tongue as they go into the machine. As always, I'm impressed by Edo's entrepreneurial flair. Maybe I should make him my sales manager, although he's much better off working at the pub. They've already promoted him to shift manager.

'I know.' Gloria's eyes light up with that spark she gets when she's figured something out. 'We offer a free will-making service at the law centre. If you do me a leaflet that explains the things people need to think about, I could include it with the documentation. It might get you some business long-term, and from our point of view, it would be very useful.'

'I can do better than that,' I say. 'How about I come to the centre and give a group talk, as well? No charge, obviously. It'll help me fine-tune the service.'

'Cool.'

'So when does "Know Before You Go" get going?' Edo asks.

'I've already done my first client.'

'*Who?*' Gloria and Edo ask the question together.

'I can't tell you that. Client confidentiality. But by the time we'd finished planning, she seemed very pleased. Said it was a weight off her mind. And she paid on the spot.' With cash I've already spent on this lavish Sunday lunch. It feels so good to start paying my way again, and the Farmers' Market Diet with Prosecco is simply delicious.

'It'll be Lydia. Alice's owner,' Edo tells Gloria.

'Mmm.'

I can tell Gloria's not listening properly. She's zoned out, and I bet I know what she's thinking about.

Fred.

He's been reading her the riot act about her plans for the

Regent's Park Garden Festival. Says that if they're going to be properly together, then she needs to stop acting like – what were his words? – '*a spoiled little rich girl who always wants to be the centre of attention*'.

That went down well.

'Sometimes, he just doesn't get me at all,' Gloria told me when she recounted their conversation.

The only thing wrong with that sentence – if you ask me, which Gloria had not – is the first word. I'm no fan of Fred, and not only because when he moves in with Gloria I'm likely to be homeless. I just don't get what she sees in him.

Then again, I'm no judge of men ...

Barclay.

Oblivious to the fact that both our minds are now partly elsewhere, Edo is back on one of his favourite topics. The value of art.

'... It's something Joshua Kent and now Dele Dier keep drumming into me,' he's saying. 'Art – our sort of art – is all about pushing boundaries. When Andy Warhol hand-painted a single-dollar bill, what was he really trying to do?'

'Forge money in an interesting way?' I suggest.

'He was making a statement about our money-dominated society. And unearned wealth. And the transactionality of art.' Edo senses he's losing his already distracted audience and cuts to the chase. 'Fifty years later, Warhol's dollar bill painting sold at Sotheby's for twenty-one million pounds. What does that tell us about art and boundary breaking?'

Before either of us can make a sensible contribution to Edo's impromptu lecture, the doorbell rings.

Chapter 27

Edo gets up to see who's at the door. From the way Gloria's running her fingers through her hair and quickly checking her lipstick I can tell she thinks it's Fred, come to apologise for the error of his ways.

Which gives me a few moments more to berate myself for being preoccupied with Barclay Bloody Banks. How could he have possibly known playing bingo is secretly one of my favourite activities, dating back to childhood holidays at Center Parcs where I won all manner of gruesome ornaments and assorted tat.

I hear raised voices from the hallway.

Barclay!

This time I'm not imagining it. That's definitely his voice drifting down the stairs. And Edo's.

'I'm telling you. She's busy.' Edo sounds cross. 'You're interrupting.'

'Her phone's broken.'

'No. It's not. What do you want?'

'What's it to you?'

'Who are you?'

'Barclay Banks. Who are you?'

'None of your business.'

Chopper senses bad vibrations and begins to bark. I'd better intervene and find out what Barclay's doing here before the pair of them come to blows. Especially as I never gave him my address. How presumptuous of him to think my phone's not working, just because I ignored his texts.

By the time I get to our front door, the conversation has moved on. Barclay and Edo are across the street, next to a black sports car. They seem still to be squabbling. I watch Barclay take a large white envelope from his messenger bag. He shoves it at Edo, says something I can't hear, then mounts a purple skateboard and shoots off along the pavement.

Edo comes back to me. 'You went to Paris? With *him*?' He looks disgusted. 'On a date? I didn't realise you were that superficial.'

'It wasn't a date. Just lunch. A business lunch.' My explanation sounds lame, even to me.

'He said he'd come round on business.' Edo seems a little less certain. 'And that I was to give you this.'

The envelope.

'Let's go back inside and see what's in it,' I suggest. 'And Edo, it wasn't a date. I promise. I'm sorry I said I had to go to the dentist. I said that because I didn't want you getting the wrong idea.'

'It's nothing to do with me. It's just that ...' Edo looks uncomfortable. 'Look,' he says, 'I know you've, um, suffered in the past. With relationships. Gloria told me what happened. So I want to look out for you. You're like a sister to me, Nina. And that guy's bad news, I know he is.'

'You've got nothing to worry about. And as it happens, the business advice he gave me was rubbish.'

Edo looks cheered by this and we go back indoors.

Gloria's made us all coffee. 'What was that all about?' she asks. 'Did it come to blows? I didn't realise you knew Barclay Banks. That *was* him I heard yelling at Edo, right?'

'I don't. Not really.'

'He took her to Paris.'

'*Really?* You're a dark horse, Nina Sherwood!' Gloria's delight is enough to paint the scowl back on Edo's face.

'Enough,' I say firmly. 'Let's see what it is he's brought me.'

'Remember last time someone came round here with an envelope?' Gloria says.

Indeed I do. 'The one from Jason Chung, telling me I was fired ... that seems such a long time ago.'

'Maybe this one's an injunction, ordering you to stay away from Zoe,' Gloria jokes.

I open the envelope and pull out a bunch of papers. Before I have a chance to see what's written on them Gloria says, 'That's definitely legal stuff. Give it here.' I hand over Barclay's paperwork. Edo and I sit in respectful silence, while she scans the pages. A good five minutes pass before she is ready to deliver her verdict.

'Bloody hell,' she says. 'Where's that envelope again?'

Edo picks it up from the table and gives it to Gloria, who reaches inside and produces a second envelope. She tears it open and produces an oblong-shaped piece of pink and white paper, glances at it – poker-faced – then pauses for what seems like forever, collecting her thoughts.

Until at last she says, 'So here's the thing. The Banks Group – that's the holding company for the family's entire business interests – would like to invest in Happy Endings. They say their representatives have been monitoring your progress since they helped you acquire the premises, and now wish to acquire five per cent of your company. Their conditions are that you immediately surrender the lease in Primrose Hill and move to premises they have identified in Kentish Town. They will pay all costs and any penalty charges associated with the move, and also assume liability, if any, for the roof repairs.' Gloria is all business now, and I'm reminded what a good lawyer she is. Clear, incisive and effortlessly able to command the attention of any room. 'The Banks Group appears already to have valued the business, although goodness knows how. And they enclose a cheque.'

Gloria hands me the pink and white piece of paper.

I scrutinise it.

'This is a joke, right?'

'Apparently not. It's properly signed and dated and everything.'

'Enough to buy another bottle of Prosecco?' Edo is indignant. 'They've got a bloody cheek.'

'Yes,' I say quietly. 'We could definitely buy a bottle of Prosecco.'

I pass the cheque to Edo.

Gloria and I sit looking at one another.

'*RIDICULOUS!*' Edo looks as if he's denouncing Andy Warhol's dollar bill. 'Fifty thousand pounds? That would value Happy Endings at a million.' Edo's favourite show is *Dragons' Den*. He's also quicker than I am at percentages. 'Sorry Nina, this is awesome. But *wrong.*'

I stare at Barclay Banks's signature. His elongated, pointed initials look like a pair of daggers. Edo and Gloria, meanwhile, stare at me.

Before they have a chance to say anything, I tear the cheque in half.

Then in half again.

Chapter 28

This is the hottest summer we've had for years, and I'm starting to enjoy it. Business isn't exactly overheating – still just the one funeral to date – but things are definitely warming up.

It's been two weeks since I ripped up that cheque from Barclay Banks and, ever since, I've felt empowered. Yes, it would have been good not to have to worry that my income is still dwarfing my outgoings, but the freedom to run my business exactly as I want is priceless. And who's to say the whole thing wasn't some sort of a joke? Entirely possible – likely – that if I'd paid that cheque into my bank account, it would have bounced further and faster than Barclay Banks sitting on a space hopper.

Damn! Now there's a picture of Barclay in my head again. Good Barclay, tour guide extraordinaire, the entertainer who went to such an effort, taking me to Paris. Quick, flick the mental switch ... here comes Bossy Barclay, the know-it-all who wants to have a big say in my business and take it somewhere I don't want to go. In real life, I've heard nothing further from the man himself and, as I limit myself to thinking about him for no more than five minutes a day, that's today's ration all used up.

Still, it makes a change from thinking about my husband's funeral, as I've done in the past, whenever I wanted to switch off from any hint of romance in my life.

I pull up a spreadsheet on my computer. Let's see, the blog piece I wrote about 'Know Before You Go', accompanied by promotional tweets, led to a piece in the *Standard*, which in turn has generated thirty enquiries. I've done four paid consultations this week alone, with a further three to come.

So far, my favourite is the one where a husband and wife in their seventies turned up saying they'd heard about a company in France that's found a way to take someone's unique scent and turn it into perfume. I contacted the company in question and discovered it's doing a roaring trade with both the living and the recently deceased. All they need is an item of clothing, plus the know-how to extract the dozens of different molecules that make up an individual's scent, which they turn to liquid through some miracle of chemistry. My clients went away cheered by the thought that whoever survives longer will at least be comforted by the other's familiar fragrance.

They also wrote down their instructions for a humanist ceremony. Basically, they'd like family and friends to stand up and tell stories about them, followed by simple cremation. The gentleman asked for his ashes to be scattered at Lord's cricket ground – legally or otherwise – and wanted 'Ruby Tuesday' to be played at his funeral, because that had been blaring through loudspeakers the first time he kissed his wife. She, in turn, chose 'All You Need Is Love' because they'd walked down the aisle to The Beatles anthem, and said she didn't care what happened to her ashes. 'Just don't leave them in the boot of the car, darling,' she'd told her husband. 'You know I've never liked the way you drive.'

So that's another few hundred pounds in the bank. Which has helped take the sting out of Jason Chung's latest move. His company's taken over a funeral parlour up the road, in Belsize Park. As usual, there's been no change of name, just a big advertising campaign announcing £500 discounts on all funerals for the next three months. I wouldn't be surprised if this isn't a deliberate move, purely to stifle my business.

A ding on my computer announces the arrival of an email.

Darling, Greetings from Manila!

Even hotter than London, but there's driving rain to cool me down! I'm not needed on the set for a few days, so I'm off to Davao to check out the Kadayawan festival and the Pearl Farm resort while I get to grips with the rest of my lines. Should I send Meryl a postcard, d'you think?!? What's happening in P Hill? Take it Zoe Banks hasn't managed to run you out of town yet? And that poor little dog! You did a great job from the sound of it, and I loved the pictures on your blog. Been in any more helicopters, lately? Very Christian Grey!!!!!! Don't let Barclay tie you in knots, my love, but even if he was a bit of an arse, it was thoughtful of him to take you to Père-Lachaise. Maybe give him another chance? From what you said, you two really did connect. What's to lose? K xxx

Did I mention Kelli's become my confidante? We're exchanging emails several times a week.

I'm about to reply with the news that work on Eddie Banks's basement has been halted due to an invasion of moths when I notice the increasingly familiar sight of Sheet Hot Roofing's white van pulling up outside.

Is it my imagination, or does the man who's pulling a bag of tools from the back of his van (I've learned his name is Rob) give me a wry smile? He must be a saint, putting up with so many call-outs from Mr and Mrs Happy. Either that, or he's being well paid. But no matter which way you look at it – and right now, I'm enjoying the sight of him stretching his arms towards the sunshine – those are fab abs! Clambering across the roofs of London every day evidently gives the torso a better workout than merely toiling in the gym. I get up from my little desk and stroll to the window to check I'm not mistaken about Rob's six-pack.

Impressive. Although Barclay is a good three inches taller.

There you go again, Nina Sherwood!

Five years of celibacy. Then Jason Chung. And now ...

Now I wake up in the mornings, thinking about Barclay Banks. He torments me last thing at night. Maybe this is good. Perhaps I'm finally emerging from the deep-frozen emotional cocoon in which I'd wrapped myself in the wake of Ryan ... but relationships *hurt*. Men like Barclay, golden boys who can have whatever they want (including purple skateboards), don't choose women like me. They just don't. It's one of the laws of nature. A few dates, maybe. A romp. But as his own sister says, Barclay has a different girl every week. He's out of my league so why even think about it? Why put myself through all that again? Why ...

... Why is that man in a green uniform taking pictures of my shop window?

Not that it's so unusual for passers-by to take photos of my lovely skeleton on the bike and the clever cremation urn that transforms human remains into trees. Visitors to Primrose Hill frequently pose for selfies. But this man is different. There's something officious about him. Maybe it's his walrus moustache that's off-putting.

No. It's the fact he's using a proper camera, rather than his phone. And not taking photos on impulse, because he likes what he sees. There's something careful – methodical – about the way he's working. I back away from the window and watch him take a further six or seven pictures before he packs up his equipment.

Ah well, no harm done, and high time I tackled today's to-do list. I'm about to accomplish item one – make coffee – when I realise the man has opened my shop door and is halfway inside.

'I'm looking for Nina Sherwood,' he barks.

'You've found her. How can I help you, Sir?' This man is not here to organise a funeral.

'Joe Carter. I'm a senior inspector with Camden Environmental Health Department.'

'Okay.'

'We've had a report. A complaint.'

'Really? Would you like to sit down and tell me about it?'

'I'd prefer to stand. I'm going to need you to remove your window display. Immediately.'

'Pardon?'

'Did I not make myself clear? Your window display. You have to dismantle it.'

'But why?'

'As I say, there's been a complaint.'

'From whom?'

The man looks at me scornfully. 'I'm not at liberty to tell you that, Madam. Client confidentiality.'

'Then you can hardly expect me to take any action. Not

based on one anonymous complaint.' I struggle to keep my voice polite. This is outrageous.

'Madam, I agree.'

Result!

Then the man continues, 'I expect you to take action because I am an official acting on behalf of your local council. And because I agree with the complainant.'

'About what?'

'Your window display.' He's looking at me as if I am a tiresome child. 'It breaches anti-social behaviour legislation. On the grounds of taste and decency.'

'But ... but people like it.'

The man gives me a hard stare. 'I'm not concerned with people. I'm concerned that what's in your window will give children nightmares. And upset anyone with a sick relative.'

'And if I refuse? What happens then?'

Before the man can tell me, my landline starts to ring.

'You'll have to excuse me,' I say. 'Business.' I give him a hard stare of my own.

'I'll wait outside,' he says at last. 'But we need to resolve this at once.' The man bangs the door behind him, and I pick up the phone. 'Good morning,' I say. 'Happy Endings. How may I help you?'

'Nina! At last!'

'Dad!' The pair of us have been playing telephone tag for weeks and I feel guilty for not having made more of an effort. At least now I can arrange a weekend visit.

'So, I was wondering,' Dad says, 'how's your business getting along?'

And at least this time, I don't have to lie. 'The last couple of weeks have been fantastic,' I say. I begin to tell him about

Alice's funeral, all the while keeping an eye on the man from Camden Council. Who is now stomping up and down outside my shopfront, shaking his head and tutting his disapproval.

'... And pet funerals, are they especially lucrative?' Dad asks.

Less so than funerals for people. Customer Number One had been pretty generous and insisted on paying me more than I'd asked, but I'm still a long way from being able to treat my parents to a holiday in the sun.

'Worried about your investment, Dad?' I tease.

'Actually ... Yes. I am.'

There's nothing teasing about his words and I'm instantly on guard. 'How come?'

'I was going to warn you. But then I thought better wait and see. Just in case.'

'What's happened?'

'It's work. They've decided I'm past my sell-by date. Redundancy.'

'Dad, I'm so sorry.'

'Well, you know. Construction. It's a young man's business, these days.'

'But you're not even sixty!' I'm not sure if I'm arguing for Dad's sake, or my own.

'So anyway ...'

Dad's voice trails off and I say it for him.

'You're going to need your investment back.'

'They've put me on three months' notice. But because I've only been with this firm for a couple of years, the redundancy package is next to nothing. Still, you never know, Nina, maybe I'll find another job.' His voice lacks conviction. 'And even if I don't, I'm not asking you to pay me back what you've borrowed. That wouldn't be fair.'

Thank God.

'But Dad ...' I can't let myself off that lightly. 'How will you manage?'

'I think I've come up with a fair solution. That as of December, you pay me a regular income. Easier for you than paying everything back at once.'

'Okay.'

'Fifteen hundred a month. Does that sound reasonable? Now you're doing so well? Not too much?'

'Dad, don't you worry. But look. Right now, I have to go.'

'More customers, pet? I'm so proud of you. I always knew you'd succeed.'

'Dad, I *have* to go.' I can't bear the relief pulsing up the phone line all the way from Southampton. 'Everything will be all right. I promise. Love to Mum.'

Funeral Number Three

††††

In Memoriam
SYBILLE FRANCES NEWMAN
1965–2019

††††

Golders Green Crematorium. The final stop for Sigmund Freud, Victoria Wood and Ronnie Biggs, among hundreds of thousands of others. Now it was Mrs Happy's turn. And it appeared to Edo that it was going to be even worse than he'd feared.

'Where *is* everyone? Surely they should have turned up by now.' Edo looked anxiously at Dele Dier, who had insisted on waiting in the sunshine outside the red brick chapel, where he could continue to smoke.

'I've got a feeling this is going to be like Eleanor Rigby,' Dele Dier said.

'Pardon?' Edo was baffled. As if he didn't have enough on his mind, and now Dele was speaking in riddles.

'You know,' the older man said. 'The Beatles song. The funeral for the lonely old lady where no-one came.' Dele Dier reached into the pocket of his suit, produced a packet of Marlboro Lights, took out a cigarette and proceeded to light it from the embers of its predecessor.

'You really shouldn't be doing that,' Edo said. 'Or that.' Dele had extinguished the butt of his previous cigarette between two yellowing fingers, and was in the process of burying its remains in a conveniently located plant pot. 'I promised I'd take good care of you.'

'It's a hospice I'm staying in, not a prison,' Dele replied mildly. 'One of the very few benefits of lung cancer is being able to smoke without worrying you're damaging your health. More to the point, how are *you* feeling?'

Edo still felt like a murderer. If only he hadn't repaired that bloody roof, Mrs Happy would still be alive – and doubtless continuing to write threatening letters to Nina. Everyone kept telling him it wasn't his fault, but the fact everyone was so keen to reassure him he was blameless implied precisely the opposite.

'Ah, company.' Dele was first to notice three people strolling towards the red brick chapel. 'Anyone you know?'

Edo nodded glumly. 'That's Arjun and Navja, who own the restaurant next door to Happy Endings. And the one in the suit's a wanker.'

Even as he said it, Edo knew he wasn't being entirely fair to Barclay Banks. Nina insisted he'd been pretty damn heroic, taking charge at the scene of the accident. Still, offering to buy a share in Nina's business for a ridiculous amount of money ... something definitely wasn't right.

'Edo, isn't it?'

Edo forced himself to nod a second time.

'You really mustn't blame yourself,' Barclay said. 'She slipped and fell. That's all there is to it.'

'I know.'

Before Edo could change the subject, Dele helped him out.

'Was she really as ghastly as Edo says?' he enquired politely.

The four mourners tried – and failed – to keep their faces suitably solemn. 'Let me put it this way.' Arjun from The Primrose Poppadum rose to the challenge. 'Sybille spent more than ten years complaining about my restaurant. She did everything she could to help me lose my livelihood. She had a good word to say for nobody. But today is her funeral and we must all try hard to show our respect for her soul. At least now she is at peace.'

'Here they come.' Barclay shepherded everyone off the short stretch of tarmac that led to the chapel. Nina's blue van drove slowly through a pair of iron gates, followed by two cars. The van stopped in front of the chapel and the cars continued to the parking places nearby.

As if summoned by an invisible signal, four men appeared. Dressed in matching black suits with white shirts and black ties, they looked like members of a once-famous boy band, all set for their comeback concert, forty years on.

Mr Happy, meanwhile, had emerged from the passenger seat of a VW Golf and was waiting in the car park with half a dozen others. Edo recognised only one of them. Rob, the guy who owned Sheet Hot Roofing.

'Not quite Eleanor Rigby, then,' Dele murmured to Edo. 'Shall we go inside? Make sure we don't get trampled in the rush.' Dele led the way into the chapel and scanned the arrangement of seats. 'Back row, I think. Like the cinema. Always the best view. That, and the opportunity to behave badly without anybody noticing.'

Edo obediently took a seat next to Dele in the row of seats nearest the door. Then he asked, 'Doesn't this make you feel ... well ... nervous? Or scared?'

In the weeks since Edo and Dele had been introduced at the hospice by Joshua Kent, the two men had spent hours discussing topics as diverse as art, football, women, drugs, politics – Dele believed all members of the Green Party should be automatically placed on a no-fly list – and the interesting potential of the Latin American stock market. But never death.

Dele had never mentioned the subject.

And Edo had never been brave enough.

Until today.

The circumstances in which they now found themselves demonstrated starkly the gap between end-of-life theory and practice. Edo still couldn't believe he would never see Mrs Happy again. But what was far more disturbing was the thought that the next funeral he was likely to attend would be that of the man sitting next to him, the man who was wistfully fingering a cigarette between two of the fingers on his right hand, not – quite – daring to smoke it.

Dele took his time, weighing Edo's question. 'You know what?' he said finally. 'I'm with Peter Pan. I really hope death turns out to be an awfully big adventure. But scared? Not at all. Pissed off that I'll never know if Homer becomes president in the final episode of *The Simpsons*. Which reminds me, I've finally conceptualised my final work of art. My legacy.'

Dele Dier's career landmarks included a video loop of Hitler addressing a Nazi rally, subtitled to explain the Fuhrer was overseeing preparations for a football match that involved Bayern Munich travelling to Chelsea – a game destined, he declared, to culminate in a German victory, followed by a permanent occupation of Stamford Bridge. That one had spawned thousands of YouTube imitations.

Another installation featured what looked disconcertingly

like two freshly severed heads, each one bearing an uncanny resemblance to Tony Blair, gazing into one another's eyes and smiling. It had been promptly banned in four Middle Eastern countries although a gallery in Islington had given it a permanent home, insisting only that visitors had to be over eighteen.

But it was an earlier work that was Edo's favourite. *The Museum of Invisible Art*. Dele had rented an empty space in Venice and announced the exhibits on display existed only in his imagination. Collectors were invited to purchase a title card that described a piece of art and mount it on a blank wall. The exhibition had sold out in forty-eight hours, with Dele trousering the thick end of one hundred thousand euros. Global headlines followed, but Dele had failed in his ambition to win the Turner Prize. That year, it had gone to Damien Hirst and his pickled tiger shark. Dele had never forgiven him. Or the shark.

Edo was delighted to hear about something brand new. Something that would take his mind off death, and the fact that Dele was visibly shrinking, steadily losing weight, week by week.

'Awesome!' Edo declared. 'What's it going to be?'

'My final work will be a statement about the culture of intolerance.' When you knew Dele, it was easy to tell when he was sending himself up. 'Or rather, I should say *our* work,' he continued. 'We're going to do it together, and you're going to take all the credit.'

Before Dele could explain further, five men, ranging in age between twenty-five and fifty, entered the chapel. They walked, heads bowed, towards the front row of seats. Edo recognised none of them. They were followed a second or two later by

Barclay, Arjun and Navja, who, after slight hesitation, opted to sit together in one of the middle rows.

Dele nudged Edo. 'And we're off,' he said.

A man in a dog collar had appeared at the chapel door. He nodded towards the sparse congregation, a signal that everybody should stand. A sense of expectation filled the silence, broken only by a nervous cough from Edo.

The minister began to walk slowly towards to the front of the chapel, ahead of the coffin, which rested on the shoulders of the four freelance bearers Nina had hired for the occasion. Ned Newman – Mr Happy – head bowed, eyes hidden behind dark glasses, walked behind it, accompanied by Rob the roofer. With a casual ease that demonstrated their many years of experience, the bearers placed the pine box on the catafalque and disappeared through a side door, their work complete.

'I am the resurrection and the life,' the minister began. 'The one who believes in me will live, even though they die.'

Edo had never believed in God, not even as a child. He wondered if Mrs Happy had. He pictured her now, inside that box, dressed all in orange, hands crossed neatly against her cold chest. Astonishing to think that in a single moment, she had ceased to exist. If only—

Edo's thoughts were interrupted by an instruction to stand and sing 'Guide Me, O Thy Great Redeemer'. He did his best, aware the small congregation was no match for the taped organ music that drowned their voices, although Dele became unexpectedly enthusiastic when they got to the bit about heaven and bread.

A very simple no-frills funeral. That had been Mr Happy's brief to Nina. She had been gobsmacked when he asked her to make the arrangements, having assumed her name would be bottom of any list. Until it turned out Mr Happy had already contacted the Belsize Park branch of Jason Chung's company. Even with their £500 discount they were much more expensive than Happy Endings.

No, Nina had explained, hiring a hearse was actually not a legal requirement. The specially equipped Happy Endings van would be fine. And to trim costs even further, Edo knew Nina had quietly paid Julie out of her own profit for the beautiful orange and peach single-ended spray of roses, chrysanthemums and carnations that adorned the top of the coffin.

The minister had finished reciting Psalm 23 and was saying something about shadows lengthening, evening coming, and a busy world being hushed.

'Please all stand for the committal prayer,' he continued. 'We now commit Sybille's body to be burned, earth to earth, ashes to ashes, dust to dust, in the sure and certain hope of the resurrection to eternal life through our Lord Jesus Christ.'

There had been no eulogy. Not a single word to distinguish the life of Mrs Happy from everyone else who had been carried down the well-worn aisle of the chapel before her. The minister had murmured something about 'beloved wife' but that was about it. Mr Happy had insisted he wanted a short, traditional service, and Nina had delivered.

Sybille Newman was leaving the crematorium, her coffin on a conveyor belt that reminded Edo alarmingly of a supermarket checkout. He was first to leave the chapel, seconds after the ritual had ended, trying hard not to think about what would come next. He could hear Dele a couple of steps behind him, lighting up on his way out of the door.

'If my shindig's anything like that,' Dele said, 'I'll fucking kill you, Edo. I'm relying on you to put the fun into my

206

funeral. We need to pick some decent music, for a start. And since there's no chance of anyone describing me as a beloved husband – bloody husband yes, beloved ... definitely not – I need to write some nice things about myself before I go. And remind me to Google "professional mourners" once I'm back at the hospice. All those empty seats. Testimony to a bad life poorly lived, if you ask me. Still, where's the afterparty?'

'Shh!' Edo had noticed Mr Happy and Rob the roofer walking towards him, their arms around one another's shoulders for support. The moment Edo was dreading more than any other. He took a deep breath followed by a few paces forward. 'I'm so sorry for your loss.' He spoke directly to Mr Happy. 'I made a full statement to the police, and obviously, if I could only turn back the clock ...'

Edo faltered. It was the first time he'd come face to face with Mr Happy since the accident. He'd rehearsed this moment in his head over and over, but was damned if he could remember what he had planned to say next.

Mr Happy stepped into the silence. 'It wasn't your fault,' he said. 'Rob and I will never forgive ourselves. We were in the kitchen having a sandwich. Chicken and Marmite. Rob had promised to go out onto the roof and check your repair after lunch but Sybille must have decided to see for herself. I think she may have slipped on some fresh bird droppings and toppled over.'

Edo had the feeling that Mr Happy, too, had been rehearsing what to say – and had been better at learning his lines.

A few feet away, Dele and Rob the roofer were sizing one another up. Rob spoke first, 'So is he your partner?'

'Him?' Edo heard Dele demand with a dismissive snort. 'My partner in crime, that's for sure. But determinedly heterosexual, so far as I'm aware. Always banging on about the same girl. Gloria, isn't it, Edo? Still not getting any?'

But Edo was no longer listening. He was looking at Nina. And Nina looked as if she'd seen a ghost.

Chapter 29

Outside Happy Endings, everything is far from all right. The man from Camden Council appears to be denouncing my window display to a police officer. I recognise her. She's the one who rescued me from the media vultures in the wake of Kelli's funeral-that-never-was. I rush outside into the sunshine.

'Good morning,' I say to the woman. 'Sergeant Hartley, isn't it?'

'Yes, indeed. You've got a good memory, Ms Sherwood.'

'Nina, please. Good to see you again. I never got the chance to thank you.'

'No thanks necessary.'

'Were you just passing?'

Sergeant Hartley pauses. 'Actually no, Nina. I'm afraid there's been a complaint about your activities. But I'm sure we can sort it out.'

'The window display, is it?' The Camden Council inspector looks as if he's just won the EuroMillions.

Sergeant Hartley examines the window display more closely. 'Fabulous,' she says. 'Fascinating time-lapse photography, the way that man on the video goes from a baby to middle-age right before your eyes. And can you really have your ashes turned into a tree? You know, I think I'd really like that.'

Is it against the law to kiss a police officer when you're not actually at Notting Hill Carnival?

'But it's disgraceful.' The inspector splutters a glob of spittle on his own moustache. 'I'm here to ensure it's removed. Pronto.'

'Really? Are you empowered to do that, under local government legislation?' Sergeant Hartley seems genuinely interested. 'I can't imagine you are. I know Camden has a great deal of authority,' she makes it clear she thinks this is a bad thing, 'but so far as I am aware, you're not permitted to have an opinion on what traders keep or display on their own private property any more than you're allowed to disapprove of the colour of my curtains.'

'That's just not correct.'

'Then maybe you'd care to show me the legislation?'

'Legislation?' A shadow appears on the pavement in front of me, and a new voice joins our discussion. 'My middle name. Well, close, anyway. The truth is, I prefer litigation. Fighting in court's always such fun.'

Barclay Banks steps off one of those hoverboard things – the ones that look quite fun but can overheat and explode your kitchen if you leave them to charge on a power socket – and greets me warmly.

'Morning Nina,' he says cheerfully. 'Thought I'd pay you a social call. You remember how much I like to combine business with pleasure.' Barclay turns to the other two, shrugs his denim-clad shoulders and adds, 'She never writes. She never phones. Not even a text. And now the police. Has she been a *naughty* girl?' That sexy emphasis ... it turns me on and infuriates me in equal measure, even though I know anyone who's ever typed #metoo would disapprove.

Along the street, Julie is pretending to organise her flower display. I know she's hanging on every word. I appear to have two choices. Slap Barclay's chiselled cheekbones – hard – and add assault to whatever charges Sergeant Hartley may be about to bring, or invite everyone inside.

I plump reluctantly for option two.

I usher everyone inside Happy Endings and disappear to the basement to fetch a jug of water. As I come back up the stairs, I hear Barclay discussing the window display with the inspector.

'I agree with you entirely about the skeleton,' he's saying.

That's it.

I *am* going to hit him.

Kick him out of the shop.

Kick him out of my life.

But before I can move, Barclay continues. 'The bicycle just doesn't look right. You have to agree he'd look way cooler on a motorbike. Maybe something like a Flying Eagle. Vintage, but still good to go. Or if you're looking for something sleeker, how about an Ecosse FE Ti XX? That's a seriously shiny piece of kit. Want to see a picture?'

Sergeant Hartley giggles.

'Mind you,' Barclay continues. 'What if we put the skeleton behind the wheel of a car? Classic Aston Martin. British Racing Green. Open top. Nice and aspirational, even for Primrose Hill. And making a statement ... how you can't take it with you when you go, so you might as well splash out on a nice, expensive funeral.'

'You'd need to get the window reinforced,' says Sergeant Hartley. 'Too much of an insurance risk, otherwise.'

'That's easily done,' Barclay tells her. 'You know, I think the idea of the car is stronger. Metaphorical. Art, almost ... especially if we gave it a name. How about Rust in Peace? Perhaps we could put in for a grant. Is Camden still supporting the arts, do you know?'

I can hardly believe it. This is like my video in the shop window. Except Barclay is morphing into Edo right in front of my ears.

The inspector's heard enough. 'I'll excuse myself for now,' he says. 'I need to check the rules. It's possible that if eighty-five per cent of the skeleton is covered from public view by concealing it in a car, you might get away with it.' He makes it plain that I would still be committing a crime in all but name.

'You do that,' Barclay says. 'And if you could get back to me on the arts grant front, I'd be very grateful.'

By way of a response, the inspector slams the door on his way out.

'So, Nina,' Barclay acknowledges my return to the front of the shop. 'One down, one to go.' He takes the tray I'm carrying, sets it down on the table, pours three tall glasses of iced water and hands one each to me and Sergeant Hartley. Then he turns to the officer and says, 'Seriously, is there some sort of an issue, or are you here on a courtesy call?'

'Barclay,' I say firmly. 'I'll deal with this. If you don't mind.'

'No worries. Is it okay if I go downstairs and plug in my hoverboard for a few minutes? It's running out of charge.'

'Sure.' If that's the quickest way to get him out of the room. Barclay picks up his hoverboard and leaves us to it.

'So what's this about?' My conscience is clear and I'm genuinely curious to discover what I'm supposed to have done.

'I hope it's nothing, Nina, but as I said, there's been a complaint.'

'And you're not allowed to tell me who made it, I suppose?'

'Actually, it was a tip-off. Anonymous. But we're obliged to investigate, as I'm sure you understand.'

'Okay.'

Sergeant Hartley pulls out a notebook and takes a quick look. 'You're not under caution or anything like that. But we do need to get to the bottom of this. The allegation is that you were seen disposing of human remains in one of the Royal Parks. Namely, Primrose Hill.'

'That's priceless!' Barclay comes rushing from the back room, where he'd obviously been eavesdropping. 'Nina was conducting a pet funeral. The ashes belonged to a sweet little spaniel called Alice. She was savaged by an out-of-control dog on Primrose Hill. That's the crime you ought to be investigating.'

Sergeant Hartley puts away her notebook. 'That's fine. I have no further questions, and thank you for your time. Just be sure that silly man from the council doesn't find out, or he'll have you up on a charge of littering.'

We say our farewells and Sergeant Hartley departs, leaving me alone with Barclay. Who seems in no hurry to get out of the way.

'I hope that was helpful,' he says.

'How did you know about the pet funeral?'

For a moment, Barclay looks nonplussed. Then he says, 'I read about it. On your blog.'

'Good to know you're taking such an interest in my business.'

My sarcasm is wasted.

'"The Know Before You Go" service,' he says. 'That's clever, too.'

'Let me know if you'd like a consultation.'

'You're on! How soon can you fit me in?'

Whoops. That backfired.

'Anyway, the reason I'm here ...'

Hallelujah! Barclay is finally getting down to business.

'... Other than to charge my hoverboard. Which is truly amazing, by the way. Want to try it?'

'Look, I'm busy. Cut to the chase, won't you?'

'I'd love to.' A mischievous smile that I know I'll be thinking about for the rest of the day. 'First and foremost, pleasure. I know I screwed up last time. At the cemetery. Don't know what came over me.' Barclay is fiercely studying his shoes. 'Sorry about that,' he murmurs. 'I really enjoyed our day, and I know you did too. Right?'

Despite myself, I nod my head.

'I'm competing in a Go-Kart Derby,' he says. 'Will you come?' Before I can turn him down, he adds, 'Extreme sport and all that. You never know, I might be able to help you bag a few customers.'

So unfair.

Barclay Banks is making me laugh.

'I'll take that as a yes,' he says. 'As for the business. Nina, I'm impressed. You play hardball. I was sure you'd be smart enough to jump at the chance of securing investment. Think how much more quickly you could expand the business. Happy Endings all over London?'

I am thinking.

Hard.

It's one thing to tear up a cheque for fifty thousand pounds fuelled by righteous indignation, Prosecco and the fear that someone I really like is having a joke at my expense. But now Dad's about to lose his job.

'Tell you what.' Barclay mistakes my silence for a negotiating ploy. 'I'm authorised to increase the offer to sixty thousand. But that really is the limit.'

'Would you still insist I move to Kentish Town? I don't understand how leaving Primrose Hill fits in with the idea of expansion.'

'The thing is ... What was that? Did you hear it?' Barclay looks startled and he's already heading for the door. 'Sounded like one hell of a thud. Quick, let's—'

The rest of Barclay's sentence is drowned.

In the street, a man screams.

We hear several people shouting over one another.

I follow Barclay through my shop door to see what's going on.

On the pavement outside The Primrose Poppadum, a knot of people are standing in a semi-circle.

I see Julie from the flower shop. 'Don't move her,' she's saying. 'Has someone phoned for an ambulance?'

'On its way.' A man I don't recognise. 'Did someone go to the surgery to fetch the doctor?'

'Here.' A woman takes off her cardigan and begins rolling it up. 'Use this to elevate her head.'

The small crowd rearranges itself. Through the gaps, Barclay and I see a body slumped awkwardly on the ground. Face down. Orange trousers and a matching top, like an angry sun that has tumbled from the sky.

'Is she still conscious?' someone asks. 'Keep her talking. Ask questions. Get her to count to three, or something. Look, she's moving. Thank God! Shall we try to turn her over?'

'Absolutely not!' Barclay races from my side and immediately takes charge. 'I think she's impaled herself onto one of the spikes.' The pointed metal posts that line the high street so people can leave their dogs securely outside the shops, he means. 'If I'm right, it's a job for the fire brigade. They'll need to use cutting gear.'

Barclay kneels down on the pavement and puts his arm gently on Mrs Happy's shoulder. 'Sybille,' he says loudly. 'Sybille. It's me. Barclay Banks. You know who I am, don't you?'

No response.

So far as I can see, Barclay is taking Mrs Happy's pulse, talking gently to her all the while. Everyone else is silent, exchanging anxious looks. Then an ambulance siren, louder and louder. The vehicle comes to a halt outside Happy Endings and two paramedics get out.

'She must have fallen from the roof,' Barclay tells them. One of the paramedics begins to assess Mrs Happy, while the other takes Barclay out of earshot and is apparently asking a string of questions. I watch Barclay gesture towards the spikes.

When the conversation is complete, Barclay returns to my side, and pulls me into his arms. 'I'm pretty sure the only person who can help her now is you.' He says it in the quietest of whispers, so no-one else can hear.

Chapter 30

I can see Edo is looking at me, and I can tell my expression is shocking him. I probably look as if I've seen a ghost.

After all these years, that's what it feels like.

It does happen at funerals. Occasionally. A definite presence, as if the person who has died is still with us. I have seen rainbows appear from out of nowhere during burials. Lights flickering on and off at wakes. Even a hailstorm in the middle of August. All as if someone unseen is doing their very best to say, 'I'm here!'

This is not the same thing.

This is Ryan Sherwood.

My husband.

Large as life and twice as natural.

Leaning against my van in the car park.

Sweet Jesus, now he's waving at me. What if Edo sees?

I'm supposed to stay here until everyone has left the crematorium. It's my job to offer words of comfort to Mr Happy. I need to thank the vicar. Tell the bearers they've done a great job and that I'm sure I'll be able to offer them a lot more work in the future.

But none of that matters now.

I can't let Edo meet Ryan.

Edo believes my husband is dead. Just about everyone I've met in the past five years believes my husband is dead. Sometimes, I have even caught myself believing it. If the truth comes out now, I'll be mortified. And, worse, exposed as the liar I am.

My stomach is churning hard enough to produce a pack of Kerrygold, but it's essential to behave as if nothing's wrong. I manage to catch Edo's eye and half-wave to him. 'See you later,' I mouth. Before he can respond, I turn and walk towards my vehicle.

This is how Marie Antoinette must have felt on her way to the guillotine. There's a part of my brain telling me to run the other way, fast as I can. But I also know there's no chance of escaping my fate.

Almost there.

Yes, it's absolutely definitely Ryan.

I thought I would never see him again.

Not for real. Not like this.

My husband – the ghost – is a few pounds heavier than I remember. With a suntan and longer hair that suggests he is no longer in the army. And smiling, for all the world as if he's just come home and is pleased to see me after a difficult day at work.

'Hello Nina,' he says. 'How've you been?'

His voice flows over me like a bowl of tepid washing-up water. Not exactly unpleasant, but somehow it makes me feel sullied. I want to rinse my hands. That doesn't make sense. Nothing makes sense.

Ryan ...

'Ryan.' This time, I manage to cough out his name, although my own voice seems to be strangled somewhere deep inside

218

my throat. 'What are you doing here?' I'm fumbling in my bag for my car keys when something that does make sense occurs to me. 'Did somebody die? Your parents?' I've been too busy to check the crematorium's daily funeral list.

'No, they're both fine.'

I open the door of the van. 'What are you doing here?' I recognise I'm stuck on repeat, but anything more complex is beyond me.

'Let me in and I'll explain. Shall we drive to Hyde Park?' Our old stomping ground. 'Take a pedal boat out on the Serpentine? God, Nina, you're looking great. Black was always your colour!' One of our standing jokes. The way he says it – warmly and with what sounds suspiciously like affection – you'd think we'd been apart for a couple of hours.

It's been five years.

Five years since my husband left me.

And now he wants to take me *boating*?

All I can manage by way of response is, 'You'd better get in.'

I slump into the driver's seat and flick the lock for the passenger door. Ryan slides into my van, as if that was always what he had expected would happen. I start the engine and head slowly towards the Finchley Road, aware I'm in no fit state to drive. We travel in silence for a couple of miles. Ryan keeps sneaking glances at me, and I feel I'm being X-rayed.

Are you looking at my heart? It's not broken, not any more. But look closer and you'll see the scars. The permanent damage.

When Ryan finally does speak, I jerk in my seat, lurching dangerously close to a lorry on the inside lane. 'So whose funeral was it?' he's asking me.

'Her name was Sybille Newman.'

'And?'

219

'And what?'

'So tell me about her. I always enjoyed your stories, Robin. What was it you used to say ...'

Robin.

My nickname. As in Robin of Sherwood. That and the fact that on our honeymoon there was a naturist island twenty minutes by boat from St Tropez, where I got sunburned so badly my new husband couldn't touch me for the rest of our holiday. I had never been more in love ...

My brain freeze is starting to thaw, and I am finally able to answer Ryan's question. 'Sybille Newman was my neighbour.' I feel like a child who has correctly passed a test. The early afternoon traffic is light, and I finally manage to get the van into top gear.

'What happened?'

'She died in an accident.' There's a shortcut ahead that will take me up through West Hampstead. Mirror ... indicate ... I indicate right and concentrate on my driving.

Mirror, indicate, manoeuvre.

Mirror.

Indicate.

Manoeuvre.

I'm getting into a rhythm, saying the three words over and over in my head. Calming myself with every repetition. I need to branch left once I've passed Swiss Cottage Odeon, then—

Then I become aware that Ryan is talking again.

'Your sense of direction never was great,' he's telling me, 'And that's not how to get to Hyde Park. You need to go straight ahead. Otherwise we'll end up in Regent's Park.'

I slip into the nearside lane and turn left, feeling the tiniest thrill of defiance. 'We're not going to Hyde Park,' I say.

'Oh?'

Mirror, signal, manoeuvre. I turn right, past the Marriott Hotel.

'I hope you're taking us somewhere interesting.' The way he says this, with just the slightest hint of a fake laugh, stabs my memory. Ryan is irritated but doing his best not to show it.

At the final junction I go straight across. And – it's a miracle – find a parking space right outside Happy Endings.

Chapter 31

I get out of the van and push the door shut, giving Ryan no choice other than to follow suit. 'If there's something you want to tell me, we'll do it here,' I tell him. I'll feel safer once I'm inside my shop.

As I unlock, I look upwards, as I always do, half expecting to see Mrs Happy spying on my comings and goings. That will never happen again.

Ryan is checking out my shopfront and window display. He grimaces at the skeleton. 'Happy Endings, huh? Well there's a name that's open to all sorts of interpretations, hun.' A smirk as he follows me inside the shop. 'But seriously, it's great you've opened your own business. Doing well, are we?'

Has Ryan come here looking for a cash handout? If so, he's well out of luck. But that was never his style. My husband was always generous with money.

'Let's talk downstairs.' I lead the way. 'I'll put the kettle on. Then you can tell me why you're here.' I busy myself with cups, saucers, teabags, and milk.

Another routine that makes me feel calmer. Until I realise Ryan has settled himself into the couch and the only place for me to sit is next to him.

I procrastinate with teaspoons, while my brief – and

spectacularly unsuccessful – career as a military wife comes flooding back to me. There was a time when I wasn't so bad with army sayings, and the one I remember now is: *Never show fear, even when you're in a tightly contained space.*

'Do you take sugar?' I enquire. Ryan has – had – a sweet tooth and always went for three heaped spoonfuls.

'You can't have forgotten!' For the first time since he reappeared, Ryan sounds rattled. 'Still three,' he mutters.

I put two teaspoons of sugar into his cup, pass it to him, finish making my own brew, put it down on the table in front of the couch, and then sit down next to him.

Into the lion's den.

Close enough to touch.

Okay.

Here I go.

'So, Ryan. Lovely to see you and all that.' I think I sound suitably casual and composed even though I'm anything but. 'I'm still waiting to hear what exactly you're doing here? What is it you want with me?'

'What is it I want?' Ryan sets his cup and saucer down on the table. 'Well, if you put it like that ...' I'm still waiting for an answer when I feel his index finger painting a trail down my cheek. 'Your skin is just as soft as I remember,' he whispers.

I push his hand away.

Never show fear, even when—

'Look.' Ryan's voice is back to normal volume. 'I've been abroad a lot, lately. But I'm in London for the next little while, and I wanted to see you. Catch up. I've always felt bad about what ... what happened. I was such a fool, Nina. You were the best thing that ever happened to me. And I blew it.'

I don't know what I had been expecting Ryan to say. But not this.

'I did, didn't I?' Ryan takes my hand in his own.

This time, I don't pull away.

Connection.

It's still there.

Like a broken electric circuit that's been repaired.

Inside, I'm glowing like the Blackpool Illuminations.

If only you'd said all this five years ago …

I shift position and turn towards Ryan.

A face I once knew as well as my own.

A body that used to be my personal adventure playground.

An uncertain smile playing on those über-kissable lips.

'Yes, Ryan,' I say finally. 'You blew it.' Actually, he threw me away like a half-smoked cigarette.

'So you've moved on?'

'As you can see.' I gesture at the room.

'With, um, relationships, I mean.'

'After five years? You'd think so! What about you? Have you moved on?'

'I suppose.' Ryan shrugs.

'Okay.' We're still holding hands, and I need to be the one who severs the connection. But not quite yet.

'Anyway,' Ryan continues. 'Small world that it is, we have a mutual friend.'

'Oh?'

'Yeah. Kelli Shapiro.'

'You know Kelli?' I'd be less surprised if Ryan announced he'd become a brain surgeon. 'How do you know Kelli?'

'I'm the military adviser on her film. In the Philippines. We were all in a bar one night, cast and crew, and I overheard her talking about her friend, Nina. London's coolest undertaker, she called you.'

'Military adviser?' So I'd been right about his longer hair meaning he was no longer in the service. 'When did you leave the army?'

'Couple of years ago. Resigned my commission and got headhunted by an old mucker who was setting up a specialist firm to work with the big studios. I'm a partner. Out in Manila, I've been teaching the guy who's supposed to be an army general how to act like one. Tough gig, because the actor in question is accustomed to having everything done for him. Definitely lacking in leadership qualities.'

And just like that, it really is as if we've never spent a day apart.

Ryan starts telling me about the movies he's worked on. One with Brad Pitt. Another with Samuel L. Jackson. Locations as diverse – and glamorous – as Australia and Brazil. And now the Philippines. With Kelli Shapiro.

Somewhere between the Gold Coast and Rio, I finally manage to tear my hand away. Ryan interprets that as a signal to move a little closer, and drapes his hand around my shoulders. Where it remains.

'So how *is* Kelli?' I ask.

'Here's the thing,' Ryan says. 'There was a bit of a misunderstanding on the set. Won't bore you with the details. But the upshot is that I got fired. They're refusing to pay up the contract, and I can't afford for that to happen. They've even threatened to have me blacklisted across the entire industry. So I want you to help me, Nina. For old times' sake. Will you do that for me? Have a word with Kelli. Tell her I'm basically a good guy. She's got enough clout to get me reinstated.'

Ryan might as well have poured a bucket of ice over me.

I'm such a rubbish judge of character. Until this moment I really did believe he'd sought me out to apologise. Maybe even to suggest we make a fresh start. What's that saying ... *Fool me once, shame on you; fool me twice, shame on me.*

I unwind myself from Ryan's embrace and start clearing away our cold cups of tea. 'So did you tell Kelli we used to be married?' I ask.

'Thought I'd leave that to you. You've got her email and phone numbers, right? If not, I can give them to you.'

'I've got everything I need, Ryan. And now if you'll excuse me, I've got tons to do.'

'Yes, well look. It's been great seeing you. Dinner next week? You'll probably have heard back from Kelli by then, right?'

'I'll be in touch,' I say. 'You've still got the same personal email?' Mine is different.

'Yes. Nothing's changed, Nina. Nothing. I realise that now. Thank God I met Kelli and found out where you'd gone.' Instead of turning towards the front of the shop Ryan walks towards me and folds me into his arms and kisses me. 'There's never been anyone else who mattered.' His voice is soft, hypnotic. 'Only you. I still love you. I've never stopped caring. You have to believe me.'

Chapter 32

I want to believe him. I really do.
 But I don't.

If Ryan had ever tried to find me it would have been so easy. Just pop my name into Google and up I come on LinkedIn. And if he wanted to ask for another chance – something I once fantasised about – how come it's taken him five years?

No, Ryan has come back into my life only because he needs my help. Remembering that when I was his wife, I'd do whatever he wanted, immediately and without question. He trained me well, as if I were one of the soldiers in his command. Making Ryan happy was so much more important than making myself happy.

Except I am no longer that person.

When we parted, I was convinced my life was over. I coped only because the counsellor I saw at the height of my misery taught me to visualise myself moving forward in a Ryan-free life. Soon, he would just be a speck in the distance, she promised. Just so long as I took the time to build a detailed picture in my head.

At that first session, the counsellor also quoted an old saying that stayed with me. *Those parted by death can wipe away tears. Those parted by life must cry and cry forever.*

I'd already done enough crying for several lifetimes and the words gave me an idea. For many weeks and months afterwards I survived by pretending to myself – and then to anyone who tried to get close – that my husband had died. It became a bad habit.

I never hated Ryan enough to wish him truly dead, but now, sitting here in my shop, I realise I'm pretty much indifferent to the fact that he is alive. So yes, I did feel something when he kissed me. But I expect I'd also feel a frisson if James Norton kissed me. Or Barclay Banks ...

Sleeping Beauty.

That's who I feel like.

Not because I am beautiful, but because I have woken up to the fact that my husband – my ex-husband – is an irrelevance to the person I have become. Doing what he wants and carrying out his orders isn't important any more. A simple yet shocking truth.

It has taken five years – and about fifteen minutes – to understand I am finally free from Ryan Sherwood.

I go back to the front of the shop and fire up my computer. I need to tell Kelli the truth about Ryan and me. And not only because he might well take my name in vain once he realises I'm no longer marching to his beat.

Hi Kelli

There's something I need to tell you. Plus I owe you an apology. It's a bit of a long story, but here we go. It's about Ryan Sherwood. The Ryan Sherwood who's been working as the military adviser on your film. You know who I mean? Well six years ago, Ryan and I got married. He was in the Household Cavalry Mounted Regiment – the

bit of the army you see on TV strutting their stuff at
the Queen's Birthday Parade and the State Opening of
Parliament – and we were living our dream in married
quarters at Knightsbridge Barracks, slap bang in the middle
of London. It was eight months into our marriage and I
thought we were blissfully happy, right until the moment
Ryan told me we weren't.

It began one ordinary Thursday afternoon with an out-of-
the-blue text that said simply, *We need to talk tonight.* Ryan
did most of the talking. Our marriage wasn't working, he
explained. His fault as much as mine. He'd thought he'd be
able to cope with the demands of my job. But working long,
irregular hours had apparently caused me to fail in my role
as a military wife, and my last-minute absence from a recent
Mess Ball (death pays no respect to an undertaker's social life)
had reflected badly on him. He'd been agonising for weeks, he
said, and I'd surely agree it was better to cut our losses now,
painful though it was, rather than continue in some sort of
a loveless sham. This from a man who two nights previously
had spent the better part of three hours shagging me joyfully
senseless.

It still hurts, but at least now it feels more like a paper cut
than being stabbed with a pair of scissors.

Ryan was about to deploy to Afghanistan and we agreed
that by the time he came back I'd be living elsewhere and
he would take care of the divorce paperwork.

More accurately, Ryan had already made the decisions. He
was calm. Clinical. His words gentle but cold as a bayonet.

By the time he got to the bit about hoping that, in time, I'd be grateful to him, and that we would always remain friends, it felt as though I was being crushed by a tank.

And then I did something I'd never done before.

I begged.

Slid off the couch – it was yellow and had been on sale in IKEA – got down literally on my knees and pleaded with Ryan to give us ... me ... another chance. I'd volunteer for army committees. Make jam. Sack the cleaner and do all the housework myself. Have children sooner rather than later. Even my final roll of the dice, that I'd give up the job I was born to do, made no difference.

'Hun, don't,' Ryan said. 'Don't humiliate yourself. I don't want to have to remember you like this. You're being pathetic. If I wasn't sure before, I am now.'

Eighteen hours later, I'd moved out. Gone to a Gumtree flatshare in Cricklewood with nothing more than a single suitcase. In the weeks that followed, I realised I'd lost more than my husband ... the army closed ranks behind Ryan, and the wives and girlfriends I'd regarded as friends didn't really want to know me. I couldn't eat. Lost a stone, which was the only good thing to happen that entire year. I couldn't sleep more than three hours at a time. You should have seen me at work, Kelli. I was like a zombie. And all the while, I was in physical pain. My heart actually ached. Then I discovered why our marriage 'hadn't been working'. Bonnie, the wife of Ryan's best friend, took pity and finally replied to my string of messages. You'll think I was stupid not even to have suspected anyone else was involved. Suzi Brenanden she was called. Worked for the Royal Household, and I imagine they met in the line of duty. Bonnie thought I deserved to know.

The next day, my boss caught me crying all over a corpse. He was great. Organised a counsellor. And that was where it all went wrong. As well as right. The counsellor taught me how to visualise. 'It's like playing a film in your head,' she explained. 'The more detailed the better.' So I planned out a little horror movie, frame by frame. Ryan's funeral. A military funeral. All I have to do is show up. His light oak coffin is shouldered by strong, stoical men, immaculate in their No. 2 service dress. Pale sunlight bounces off the highly-polished toe caps of their echoing black boots. Weeping parents. Traditional words of kindness from a vicar and the Commanding Officer. A lone trumpeter's final mournful note, then silence. Precision-folding of the maroon and blue regimental flag, which is then handed to me. I'm dressed in black and dry-eyed. Always dry-eyed. That visualisation became my comfort blanket. Whenever I thought of Ryan, I pictured him dead, in the coffin. And you know what? I DID find it easier to get on with my life.

I told the counsellor the visualisation exercise was hugely helpful, although I never quite get round to saying what it was I saw. Did it really matter? After only four or five sessions, I was down to a packet of Kleenex every other week

People at work knew what had happened so I never needed to lie there. But the following year, February I think it was, I met Gloria at a supermarket checkout. We were both surreptitiously checking out one another's trolleys, exchanging smiles that acknowledged a shared liking for red wine, pink prawns, and orange peppers. Gloria was ahead of me in the queue, shopping all bagged up, when she realised she'd come out with her Oyster card instead of her debit card.

'Let me help,' I offered. I paid for her shopping, then my own, and our friendship began.

Gloria was the first good thing to emerge from the wreckage of my marriage. The second time we met, the conversation turned inevitably to our love lives – just as it did when you and I had supper in the Blueberry Café. I told Gloria the same as I told you. That my husband had died. I might not have used exactly those words, but it was what I wanted you to think.

Kelli, I'm so sorry I lied to you. In the beginning, when I'd explain to new people that my husband left me for another woman, I felt diminished by pity and sympathy. Then one day, someone was being particularly nosey, so I just blurted out that he was dead, and embarrassed them into talking about something else. Worked a treat! By the time I realised Gloria was going to be a close friend, it was too late to own up, so I gave her the whole funeral visualisation thing – without mentioning I'd imagined it all. And she's told other people, people I've met, like her mum and dad, and they all treat me with kid gloves, tiptoeing around my past. And because I don't think I'll ever trust another man ever again, not properly, I go with the widow thing – in my head usually – whenever someone shows interest in me.

Except Barclay, I realise. I haven't done that where Barclay's concerned.

I think of myself as an honest person, but over the years, it's become a habit. Sometimes, when I visualise Ryan's funeral, it's as if he really did die. So when I'm caught unawares, as I was when you asked about my personal life, I just say the words husband and funeral in the same sentence, then change the subject. I've already promised myself I'll never do it again.

And here's the thing ... assuming you're not so cross you've already deleted this email. Ryan's back here in London. He turned up today at Mrs Happy's funeral. Which went okay, although it was a very small turnout. He told me he's been fired from your movie, and basically asked me to ask you to get him reinstated. But I absolutely don't want you to do that. I realise that with Ryan, you never know the whole truth, just the parts he wants you to see. He's basically dishonest. Which is rich, coming from me! I'll understand completely if you decide to ignore this email, and again, I'm sorry. Love, Nina xx

I hit send and wonder what Kelli will make of it all.

I try to remember if Gloria said she'd be home tonight, so I can own up to her, too. Will she and Edo ever trust me again? Now I come to think of it, what on earth was I thinking when I left the pair of them alone with my parents the day I opened my business? Imagine the confusion if either of them had said anything about me being a widow!

I'm just about to lock up and leave Happy Endings when my iPhone pings Kelli Well that didn't take long! Is that good or bad? My heart thumps as I open the message.

Darling!

I was just about to give you the heads-up on a BIG announcement about yours truly. But you poor thing! Yes, I know Ryan. Complete dick. Don't know how much he told you, but Roberto fired him for trying to shag half the woman on the set. He caused absolute havoc, and all while his wife's stuck at home, seven months pregnant, with their third child. I'm sorry he hurt you so badly. But you know what they say about living well being the best revenge and all that. So far as you and I are concerned, there's nothing to forgive. As for my news ... Nina, you'll never guess what I did last night! In the circumstances, it's a teeny bit ironic. I GOT MARRIED!!!! More soon. XXX

Chapter 33

So here I am in Hyde Park. Ryan has always been compulsively punctual – that's army discipline for you – and I intend to arrive at our rendezvous comfortably ahead of schedule.

It's been an eventful two days since Mrs Happy's funeral and Ryan's reappearance. For a start, Kelli's email made me realise it was time to think hard about my own life. I wasn't ready to confess to Gloria and Edo, so I texted to say my parents needed to see me.

Then I drove to Brighton, a pre-Ryan place where I'd done so much of my growing and been happy until Lin died ...

I found a small B&B not far from the station, checked in, and slept for eleven hours. When I woke up, I knew what I needed to do.

I needed to go shopping.

I wandered around the Lanes, startled at how posh the little retail paradise had become. In my student days, the area was edgy and creative. Now it's a maze of upmarket traders and, if I were on speaking terms with Zoe Banks, I'd ask if she reckons an 'erotic boutique' that specialises in 'high-end fetish couture' would do better in Primrose Hill than the sugar-free sweet shop of her dreams.

Eventually, I found the type of shop I was looking for and made my purchases, complete with gift wrapping and stashed inside a jaunty red and white striped carrier bag.

Next, I drove to Lewes Road and parked outside the house where Lin and I used to live. The property boasted new window frames, a fresh coat of paint, and a well-established scarlet fuchsia hedge in the small front garden. The single doorbell indicated it was now a family home rather than student accommodation.

I sat outside for a while, thinking about my friend. And how random life is. You can put two plants in the soil side by side. One will flower and flourish while for no apparent reason the other shrivels and dies. Lin had been unlucky. And I'd grown rooted in my past ... Would Lin and I still be friends today, or would our lives have taken us along separate paths? It was the first time I'd ever asked myself the question and, while there's no way of knowing, I'm pretty sure we'd still be in touch. I'm certain she'd have seen through Ryan's bullshit much faster than I did. Part of me hopes Lin knows how I'm doing.

Fighting back.

The next thing I had to do was go talk to my parents. The journey from Brighton to Southampton didn't take long and Dad waited a whole ten minutes before he asked – while Mum was out of the room – 'So how's business?'

I took a deep breath.

'Much slower than I'd been hoping.' I looked Dad in the eye. 'I've spent roughly thirty-five thousand of your pension pot, and I've done two funerals. A dog. And my neighbour. Net profit just over sixteen hundred quid. I'm going to give you back the rest now. Is a cheque okay?'

236

'Steady on,' Dad said. 'I've still got my salary coming in until Christmas. If you give me back my money, what's going to happen to Happy Endings?'

'I think I can get another investor.' Barclay Banks. Even if the cost of his money means I'll have to move out of Primrose Hill and start all over again.

'An investor?' Dad suddenly looked ten years younger. 'That must mean you can't be doing everything wrong. I'll take my chances. What I was going to say is that I probably panicked about my own job.'

'They're not going to make you redundant?'

'If only! No, I've been asking around and even if I can't get another job in site management there's a good chance one of my ex-navy mates will take me on as a labourer. Part-time to start with.'

Before Dad could elaborate on his career prospects, Mum came into the room carrying a tea tray. 'I hope you're not filling Nina's head with nonsense about working on sites in January,' she admonished. 'Minimum wage for a man of your experience? I don't think so!'

An imperceptible shake of Dad's head signalled we should change the subject. Over home-made cherry pie and whipped double cream with a generous hint of vanilla (the Family Diet), I entertained my parents by telling them about my friendship with Kelli. A heavily edited account of how we came to meet – 'She lives just a few minutes from the shop and we were introduced by a local estate agent' – but even though I was tempted, nothing about her marriage. I'd checked online, and the news had yet to break.

Mum and Dad wanted me to stay, but I told them I needed to get back. 'Work,' I said. 'You know how it is.'

Dad walked me to the car.

'So about your investment,' I began.

My father placed a gentle finger over my lips, the way he used to shush me when I was little and he needed to get a word in edgeways. 'Will you have spent the whole fifteen thousand by Christmas?' he asked.

'Shouldn't think so. And if I get any more funerals between now and then, definitely not.'

'Well look. Don't go killing any more neighbours. Or pets. Not on my account. Spend what you need to and let's see where we are in a couple of months. Like I said, if you're already attracting backers, someone else believes in you and your business. And I'd much rather we keep the profits in the family. What do you say?'

I said thank you, and drove back up the M3, feeling relieved I'd seen my parents, instead of just pretending to.

When I arrived back in London in the early hours of this morning, the house was in darkness. I felt my way upstairs without turning on the lights. Chopper must have been asleep too – a mega-fail in his duties as a guard dog – so I got to my room without disturbing my housemates. I slept badly, too wired thinking about what I intended to say to Ryan.

In my head, our meeting was going to be short and – at least, for me – sweet. Over and over, I've visualised what's going to happen.

Ryan remains at the table absorbing the shock. I watch, without regret. Better than that, I walk away and go forward knowing the long period of mourning for my failed marriage is complete. A huge burden lifted. I am smiling.

It's taken a long time, but finally my counsellor can be proud.

'Hang onto that thought,' I tell myself now, at the top of the steps that lead to the terrace restaurant in Hyde Park.

A moment's hesitation. Then I choose a table that gives me a clear sight line. I sit down, and stare at my watch.

I'm ten minutes ahead of schedule.

Chapter 34

Ryan arrives four minutes early and the face he pulls when he sees I'm already seated gives me an extra little shot of confidence. He's wearing fashionably ripped-at-the-knees jeans, a yellow polo shirt and a leather jacket and his hair is still damp from the shower. I wonder for a moment where he lives now, then realise I don't care. He hesitates, waiting to see if I'm going to stand up so he can kiss me. When it becomes clear I'm staying where I am, he slides into the seat opposite me.

'Well, this place brings back happy memories,' he says. 'Great choice!'

When we lived at Knightsbridge Barracks we often came here for Sunday brunch, followed more often than not by a boat trip on the Serpentine.

I push a menu across the table. 'What are you going to have?'

Ryan doesn't even glance at it. Instead, he takes my hand in his. 'Full English and a double espresso, of course. And you'll be having the French toast with streaky bacon and maple syrup. And a latte.'

A statement, rather than a question.

Call me slow on the uptake, but having thought about it for the past two days, now I see so clearly how controlling

Ryan has always been. The annoying thing is that I really do fancy the French toast. But it's a small sacrifice to make.

I remove my hand. 'Fruit salad and a flat white for me,' I declare.

Ryan leans back in his chair and looks at me properly for the first time. 'Good call,' he nods. 'You can probably get back to your fighting weight in about ten weeks if you try hard enough.'

A remark that would once have had me rushing for the nearest salad bar. Now I'm gagging to tell him I'm not the only person sitting at this table who needs to watch their waistline. But what the hell. Let him get fat.

After we've ordered, and after we've made small talk about the weather, Ryan leans forward in his seat. I take both hands off the table, carefully out of range.

'Thank you so much for speaking to Kelli,' Ryan says. 'To be honest, I'm surprised you've managed to sort out everything so quickly.'

I say nothing.

'And grateful,' Ryan adds. 'That goes without saying. When do they want me back?'

'That depends,' I tell him. 'What about you and me?'

'Us? Well I thought after breakfast, we'd take a pedalo out on the lake. Then, maybe ... well, you could show me where you're living. Or we could book into a hotel.' Ryan shoots me the sexy smile that used to make my heart flip. Now it only makes me feel queasy.

'That's not quite what I meant,' I say. 'I was thinking longer term.'

Fortunately for Ryan, our food arrives, which gives him time to come up with a plausible reply.

'About us. We need to take it slowly,' he says. 'What with the job, I'm away a lot. I'll be back in the Philippines for the final month of filming. And I'm probably in Turkey in November, now I'm not blacklisted. Which is all thanks to you, my lovely little Robin. Are you sure you don't want some of my toast? Shall I butter it for you? Maybe a few days in Istanbul if you're not too busy with your business?'

I detect more than a hint of disapproval in Ryan's final word. 'November's a long time away,' I muse. 'Anything could happen.'

'I'd forgotten how good the food is here.' Ryan bayonets a plump wedge of sausage, dips it in egg yolk, and pops it into his mouth. His way of changing the subject.

'Do you realise you haven't actually asked me how I see our future?'

'I know you want to try again. But hun, it's not that straightforward.' Ryan destroys a slow-roast cannonball tomato with a flick of his fork and tiny fragments of basil float into what's left of the egg.

'No-one's life goes in a straight line,' I say. 'And has it crossed your mind you might be wrong?'

'About what?' Ryan looks startled, and it's satisfying to know I have his full attention.

'About what I want to happen between the two of us.'

'So spell it out, why don't you? And drink your coffee before it gets cold.'

I ignore both ex-husband and coffee in favour of my fruit salad.

'Just so we're on the same page,' I say between dainty mouthfuls, 'it *was* you who suggested we get back together.'

I resist all temptation to fill the silence and wait until Ryan responds by way of a curt nod before I continue. 'That's what you told me on Wednesday, right?'

Ryan's looking wary, as if he suspects an ambush. Another long pause, then he nods again, intently focused now on me rather than what's left of his full English.

'Although now you're saying it's my idea to try again.'

'What is it with you and these word games, Nina?' Ryan picks up the pepper grinder and detonates a vigorous spray of black dust over his bacon. 'Does it matter who said what? The most important thing is that this is a new beginning for us. After I get back from filming. When do they want me, by the way?'

A new beginning. Ryan's right about that.

A final piece of our relationship puzzle has snapped into place. What I once took for military authority – charisma, even – is borderline bullying. My ex-husband is like a spoiled child. Delightful when he's having his own way, nasty when he's not.

It's not that I was a bad wife.

Ryan was a rubbish husband.

And he still is.

'A new beginning sounds great.' I drain my coffee cup. 'A new beginning for us both. Tell you what, I'll just nip outside and give Kelli a call. See what she knows about your return.'

'Great.'

'Oh, and I've got a little surprise for you.' I reach beneath the table and produce the red and white striped carrier bag that contains the items I bought in Brighton.

'For me? Fantastic! You've always been great at presents. Let's see!' Ryan's charming child mask is back in place.

I stand up, move the remainder of my breakfast to one side, and place the bag on the table.

'All yours,' I say. And with that, I turn my back on Ryan and walk towards the door. 'Let's see what Kelli has to say.'

'You're the best!' Ryan calls after me. 'Tell them they need to book me into business class, won't you.'

I wonder if those are the final words I'll ever hear him speak.

I leave the restaurant, go down the steps and walk quickly across the grass until I've got a view of Ryan at the table, engrossed in his surprise packages.

I take out my phone and put it to my ear, in case he spots me. Then I wait.

And watch.

I'd spent ages in that toy shop before making my selections. First, I chose something called a 'Despicable Me Fart Blaster', a gun that not only makes disgusting noises but also gives out a rotten banana scent every time you press the trigger. Ryan is about to remove a layer of green wrapping paper from its box.

After he's finished puzzling about my choice, he'll progress to the oblong box covered in blue paper with a galaxy of stars printed on it.

Inside, is an electronic drum kit. The lovely man in the toy shop warned me it's louder than a burst of gunfire, and virtually guaranteed to cross the adult pain threshold when the base drum, snare and cymbals are played at the same time. It's hard to suppress a smile at the prospect. I try, and fail.

Ryan looks up from his fart gun. Our eyes meet and I move my lips, so he'll think I'm talking to Kelli. As I do so, I turn my back on the café and amble across the grass. By the time I'm out of the park, Ryan will also have unwrapped the final – smallest – package.

I admit it. My final choice was heavily influenced by

244

Barclay and the variety of slogans he wears across his chest. Nevertheless, it's Ryan's face I'd quite like to see when he claps eyes on the baby-sized T-shirt that tells the world, *I Don't Want to Grow Up. Neither Does My Dad*, but I could always visualise it. Although I doubt I'll bother.

Will the penny have dropped by this stage, or will Ryan need to read the note at the bottom of the carrier bag? In which I explain how Kelli filled me in about his wife. And children. And his lecherous behaviour on set. I explained the film company was glad to be rid of him because his mind was never properly on the job. That the gifts are actually for his kids. And a final paragraph saying he needs to tread very carefully from now on. Unless he fancies another divorce.

If he chooses to interpret my advice as a threat, so much the better.

At the tube station, before I disappear underground, I send Ryan a text: *I wish you well. Have a happy life.*

245

Chapter 35

I get off the tube at Chalk Farm.

Procrastinating, when what I need to do is face the music, fess up to Gloria and Edo that I'm not a widow after all – just an idiot who invented a sad story because she couldn't face the reality that her cheating husband had dumped her.

I know they'll both be at home, because Gloria and her band of guerrilla gardeners are meeting tonight to rehearse their forthcoming assault on the Regent's Park Festival. Edo and I have promised to help her get everything ready. But I still need a little time to myself so I'm going to drop by the shop.

When I've let myself in, I collect the post from the doormat. Two envelopes. One white, one brown. The white one has a stamp on it and looks official. The other's handwritten, and I open it first.

A card from Mr Happy, thanking me for ensuring the funeral went off smoothly. And adding that 'in view of the circumstances', he has decided not to pursue putting a new roof on the building. My friend Robert, who you met at the funeral, will make it properly watertight at no cost to yourself and we will embark on the works immediately.

Huge relief! By way of celebration, I go to the kettle, brew myself a coffee and then immerse myself in my various social media accounts. Last night when I drove back from Mum and Dad's I had the germ of an idea to promote Happy Endings. What if I could organise some sort of exhibition about funerals and the way they're changing? Practical information mixed with cutting-edge ideas that concentrate on celebrating a life as well as mourning a death.

I could pull in some favours from the contacts I made at my old job. There's Carol, a celebrant I used to work with on a regular basis. I'm sure she'd be keen to come and explain how she works with bereaved families to organise funeral services that, yes, are full of sadness, but also bursting with inspiration and happy memories.

I check out her Facebook page and see she recently officiated at a jazz guitarist's farewell. The service featured live music from his friends, who shouldered him in and out of a garden marquee in a white customised coffin, featuring lyrics including 'You may say I'm a dreamer but I'm not the only one', 'Go your own way', and 'Thank you for being a friend'. Perhaps I could ask Carol to do a slide show about coffin art.

On the subject of coffins, I've been reading about a firm that wants to turn them into storage space. The idea is that you buy your coffin now and it doubles up as a piece of furniture for – hopefully – many years. Before you know it, I've found a retired carpenter who runs 'Build Your Own Coffin' workshops. Might be fun!

We could even have a Death Café, a casual get-together where people of all ages chat about dying over tea and cake. There was a pop-up at the Royal Festival Hall and hundreds of people showed up. I imagine Zoe Banks will self-combust if I bring the concept to Primrose Hill.

I scribble down a few more ideas, then close my eyes and

start to visualise what an exhibition might look like. I see a market place of workshops, displays, discussions and cakes.

Cake …

All I've had so far today is that small fruit salad. And I've been playing with this new idea for an hour now, which means it's high time I went to see my housemates to eat humble pie.

I click 'Shut Down' on the menu bar. While the computer is going through its farewell routine, I remember my other piece of post, still sitting unopened on the desk. I slit the white envelope, pull out two pages of closely typed white paper, and start to read.

What the hell.

A firm of West End solicitors writes to inform me they are acting on behalf of a group of concerned Primrose Hill residents. Who are accusing me of devaluing their properties.

… Estate agents confirm that homes and commercial free-holds within a five-hundred-metre radius of your address have lost approximately one per cent of their value since your business opened in April. This equates to £10,000 per million, and for your information, the average value of the properties concerned is £2.75 million.

We would prefer to avoid legal action and imagine you share this objective. My clients are not unreasonable, and provided you give an undertaking to relocate 'Happy Endings' elsewhere no later than 31st December, we can resolve this matter amicably.

We look forward to receiving your compliance, in writing, at your earliest convenience. However, should this not be forthcoming, we will not hesitate to initiate litigation.

Talk about swings and roundabouts! No sooner have I been spared the expense of a new roof than another bunch of neighbours are gunning for me. Can they really pin the blame on Happy Endings in particular, rather than the economy in general? I'd love to throw the letter in the bin, but I've got a feeling this latest hassle isn't going to disappear so easily, so I stuff it into my bag and head for home.

I'm barely through the front door when Gloria yells, 'Nina! Is that you? At last! You'll never guess what's happened.'

Gloria greets me – Chopper at her heels – brandishing her iPad. 'It's Kelli Shapiro! She got married!'

I hug Gloria in greeting and say, 'Let's see.'

So Kelli married the engineer. Keir. My money was always on him, given that the other man in her life was already married.

Kelli looks glorious in a simple white dress with sequin beading, and her husband looks dashing – not to mention extraordinarily handsome – in a traditional Filipino embroidered tunic and black trousers. Kelli's quoted in the text. *'We've known each other a good few years,'* she says. *'It was a spur-of-the-moment thing. What you might call an arranged marriage. Keir said we were going to a black and white party at White Beach, not far from where we're filming in Manila. I thought we were kicking off with a walk on the sand at sunset. Then I realised I'd pitched up for my own wedding. The entire cast and crew were there to wish us well. It's the best surprise I've ever had!'*

I scroll through more photos. The beach looks like paradise. Here's Kelli being given away by her director, Roberto Ferrari. A close-up of a white gold amethyst and diamond ring. Non-traditional and very Kelli. Someone's even rustled up an elaborate four-tier wedding cake that wouldn't be out of place at a society wedding in Chelsea.

I can feel Gloria looking over my shoulder. 'Definite eye-candy!' she says gleefully. 'More than a hint of Christian Bale. Let's hope he comes to live in Primrose Hill.' Then, 'You don't seem terribly surprised.'

On our way to the kitchen, I admit Kelli had already been in touch. 'You're so good at keeping secrets!' Gloria says, mostly, I think, in admiration.

I seize my opportunity. 'Talking of which, there's something else I need to tell you. You and Edo.'

'Someone mentioned my name?' Edo is kneeling on the floor, presiding over what looks like the wreckage of a plane that nose-dived into a war zone. Mangled lumps of rusting metal, a waist-high pile of rubble, two coils of barbed wire, and lethal shards of glass are spread out on a tarpaulin along with an array of three-quarter-dead plants and a few toys that look as if they've been snatched from a skip.

Edo – wearing heavy gauntlets to protect his hands – is decanting the haul into numbered boxes and rubble sacks, in preparation for its unscheduled appearance at the Regent's Park Garden Festival. Gloria quickly shuts the door behind us, to keep Chopper safe from harm.

'Nina's got something to tell us,' Gloria says. 'C'mon, spill the beans! What's up?'

'It's not your parents?' Edo stops what he's doing and looks anxious. 'Is that why you dashed to Southampton?'

'No. It's about my husband,' I begin. 'There's something I need to tell you. And you're not going to like it.'

Gloria and Edo listen intently, letting me speak without

interruption, until I get to the bit about how I accomplished my counsellor's well-intentioned suggestion that I visualise life without Ryan.

'You mean ... you mean you put him six feet under in your *imagination*? Awesome!' Edo's face lights up with laughter.

'It's not funny.' Gloria leaps in. 'She must have been in real pain to do something that drastic.'

'I had a really hard time accepting what had happened,' I acknowledge. 'I was so used to doing whatever Ryan wanted. It was as if keeping him happy was how I measured my own value.' A feeling I've never managed to put into words until now. 'I think I became addicted to his approval and that's why I crashed and burned so hard when he dumped me.'

My friends hear me out, all the way to this morning's final meeting in Hyde Park.

'Good on you,' Gloria says. Almost as an afterthought, she adds, 'He's properly dead to you now.'

Edo chimes in. 'I don't know why you thought we'd be cross with you. He cheated on you. Now he's cheating on his wife. Dirtbag! He never deserved you in the first place.'

I think Edo's slightly missing the point — I've been apologising for my behaviour, not Ryan's — and on the other side of the room, I notice Gloria flinch. She'd been stuffing empty tinfoil containers into a sack, but stops what she's doing and looks up.

Our eyes meet and I know we're thinking the same thing. Fred.

Finally, Gloria understands why I've got reservations about him. It's not that I've been trying to protect my friend. Well, up to a point that's what I've been doing, of course. But mostly, I've always felt sorry for his wife.

251

Edo carries on, oblivious to the tension in the room. 'So now you're a born-again divorcee, rather than a tragic widow,' he says lightly, 'does that mean men are back on the agenda? Are you going to start dating?'

'You're punching above your weight,' Gloria snarls.

'I know.' Edo looks at Gloria with an expression that reminds me of Chopper when he's being told off. A mixture of hurt and unquenchable optimism.

Wow! I always knew it wasn't me Edo fancies. He's got a crush on Gloria. Poor lad!

'I'd better start loading the van,' he says.

Once Edo's left the room, burdened with a heavy box of shrapnel, Gloria says, 'Fred always says his wife's going to throw a party when he moves out.'

'Maybe she will,' I say carefully. 'But are you sure *you* want to be someone's fourth wife?'

'I've not been thinking that far ahead,' Gloria admits. 'Fred's got a brilliant legal mind. But he thinks that makes him special. That the normal rules of life don't apply to him. When you were talking about Ryan, I realised that so long as I do what Fred wants, he's all sweetness and light. But whenever there's something I want that he doesn't, he accuses me of putting pressure on him.'

'Like the living together?' I ask gently. Gloria's been pretty quiet on that front, lately.

'He's come over all pompous,' Gloria confides. 'Says I should be concentrating on my law exams rather than the Garden Festival. Sometimes he sounds more like my father than my actual father. And he always manages to make everything about him. Last night, he was banging on about how my "guerrilla gardening activities"' – Gloria drops into an accomplished Fred-like tone – '"are hardly going to advance my progression up the legal ladder". As if I care about that!'

I pick my way across the kitchen floor, through the mine-field of unorthodox garden display materials that separates us, and give Gloria a big hug. 'I love who you are,' I say. 'And I never want you to become the wife I worry about. You're far too good for that.'

After we've disentangled, Gloria says quietly, 'Fred's told me he doesn't mind getting married again. But he says he couldn't bear another divorce.'

Not the most romantic proposal I've ever heard. But Gloria needs to find her own way.

'What about you? Are you going to start dating again?' she's asking me.

'Well ...'

'What?'

'Don't go getting ideas.' I know I'm saying this to myself as much as to Gloria. 'It's nothing serious. But just for practice, just to make sure I've learned to take heartbreak in my stride, I'm going out on Sunday night. With Barclay Banks.'

Chapter 36

'Put this on first.' Barclay hands me a matte black helmet. 'Then get your leg over.'

Perhaps I've led a sheltered life, but I've never been on a motorbike before. This one is all chrome, leather, and big wheels. Barclay's already in the saddle, and the engine is running. I adjust the chin strap on the helmet, and after a moment's hesitation, jump on behind him.

'Keep your arms wrapped around me. And remember, don't fight the bike. Always move with it.'

At least that's what I think he's saying. Impossible to be sure with the helmet muffling my ears, and before I can ask for further instructions, we're off.

I cling to Barclay's waist, trying not to think about the dozen or so motorbike fatalities whose funerals I've helped to organise during my career, clutching him even tighter as he accelerates, and only just resisting the temptation to lean backwards at the first corner.

There's not much traffic and by the time we get to the bottom of Highgate Hill I'm starting to relax. Barclay's no boy racer, although the first time he moves onto the wrong side of the road, to overtake a bus, I dig my nails into his midriff. Not even a single ounce of belly fat lurking beneath tonight's T-shirt, a skimpy white number that modestly declares, *Go-Kart Champion*.

We pull up at traffic lights in Crouch End. 'Nearly there,' Barclay yells, and I try to figure out where this Go-Kart Derby is taking place. It's only when we're driving through a sudden stretch of parkland that I get my bearings.

Alexandra Palace looks stunning at this time of year. High on a hill, dressed in its summer best, with beautiful mature trees and fabulous views all the way to east London. I wonder if they've built a track especially for the derby. Barclay steers the bike into a parking space, kills the engine, dismounts, and removes his helmet. I follow suit.

'That was fun,' I say.

'I've got the scars to prove it!' Barclay turns and lifts his T-shirt and I'm alarmed to see two sets of red marks tattooed on his smooth torso. My tense response to that bus he overtook. 'I've heard of love bites,' he continues, 'but this looks like I've been attacked by fleas.'

'Sorry.' How come I've never noticed the laughter lines that crinkle around his eyes before?

'At least you can't keep your hands off me. I'd say that's a promising start to our evening.'

'It's just that I've never been on a motorbike before.'

'I get the feeling you're more comfortable as a driver than a passenger,' Barclay says. 'Anyway, we're about to find out. This way.'

He slings his arm around my shoulder and steers me towards the ice rink.

I'm confused on several levels.

Did he just say I'm bossy?

Or is he suggesting I'm literally about to drive something?

A go-kart?

As if!

And what are we doing inside an ice rink?

We stroll past a sign that says 'Closed for Private Function' and down a corridor that – yes – leads out onto a vast expanse of ice.

In the middle of the rink, yellow and white safety cones mark out a figure-of-eight race track. A dozen or so go-karts are neatly lined up. I'd been expecting something that looked like a fairground bumper car, but with their open cockpits, single seats and sleek body shapes, these are more menacing, like scaled-down Formula One beasts.

At the edge of the ice, about twenty people – mostly male – stand chatting. One of them notices Barclay and waves.

'Do you want to meet the gang first? Or get suited up?' Barclay enquires.

The look on my face tells its own story.

'You didn't think I invited you here just to sit and watch me?' He looks perplexed. 'That would be plain rude. Not to mention sexist. I thought you'd enjoy driving something with a bit more oomph than a hearse. But not if you don't want to. We can go out to dinner instead. Your call.'

I look at Barclay, his *Go-Kart Champion* T-shirt, and his concerned expression. 'It's not dangerous,' he adds. 'Not really. Just a chance for you to give it a whirl before the racing starts.'

The fact he's making no attempt to cajole me onto the ice encourages me to reconsider. I look towards the rink and notice a couple of karts are out on the ice. I watch them negotiate their way safely round the circuit, encouraged by a few cheers from the crowd. 'They've got brakes, and things?'

'Of course. But sometimes they freeze, so better to accelerate your way out of trouble.'

Barclay's advice isn't entirely reassuring. I watch one of the karts slither to a standstill. The driver gets out. A girl. About fourteen years old.

'That was brilliant!' she shouts. 'Thanks, Dad! Best birthday present ever!'

'Okay.' I've made up my mind. 'Where do I go to get changed?'

'Really? You're sure?'

'Absolutely.'

Barclay leads the way towards the crowd. 'Everyone,' he says, 'this is Nina.'

A couple of his friends nod hello.

Then one says, '*The* Nina?'

Barclay looks embarrassed.

I try to help him out. 'No, I'm the other Nina,' I say.

Everyone looks confused, Barclay included.

'Joke.'

Barclay squeezes my hand, and introduces me to one of the rink's staff members. 'This is Simon. He'll get you kitted out and walk you through the safety stuff. Then off you go! Wait,' he adds. 'Who did you say's your next-of-kin?'

'Quit while you're ahead,' I retort, and follow Simon towards the changing rooms.

Twenty or so minutes later, I retrace my steps. Dressed in head-to-toe thermal overalls, boots, gloves, goggles and a full-face helmet over a balaclava, I feel like The Stig. Barclay whips out his phone and takes a picture.

'You on Instagram?' he enquires. I try to grab the phone from him, but the heavy gloves make it impossible. He presses a few buttons. 'Hashtag brave. Hashtag beautiful. Do you think we need hashtag blessed as well?'

I pull a face at him – not that he can see me through my helmet visor – turn and walk towards my go-kart and cautiously lower myself into the hot seat.

Chapter 37

I settle myself into the go-kart – dismayed to discover my bum is so close to the ice – and run through Simon's briefing again. My right boot grazes the two pedals. Brake and accelerator. Seatbelt on. Studded tyres ... roll bars ... head rests ... all designed for maximum safety.

Steer into the skids (am I really going to skid?), keep to under thirty (seems way too fast), and slip sideways into the bends. (*SIDEWAYS?* How is that even possible?)

I take a deep breath, exhale slowly, gun the engine and creep out onto the track. At least I meant to creep, but I've overdone it on the gas, so here we go! The first bend is rushing towards me and it's hard to resist the impulse to close my eyes, count to three and see if I'm still alive. For a moment, I don't know if I'm sideways, upside down, or back to front. Then the bend's behind me and I hear a voice.

My own. Laughing!

That's the first circuit safely negotiated. Four more to go. By the time I whiz round again, I feel brave enough to lift my eyes from the track. There's Barclay, giving me a thumbs-up.

Ah. So that's what Simon meant about not even trying to drive in a straight line. You just go with the ice. Let it lead the way. It's leading me past Barclay again, and this time I lift a gloved hand from the wheel and wave at him.

Mistake! I've steered too far to the right. The kart lurches to the left and does a figure-of-eight spin. By some miracle I'm still pointing the right way. Onwards and sideways, snaking into the next turn, I've never been so terrified yet so thrilled at the same time.

For some reason, I'm thinking about Gloria when I enter the next straight. Last week, she attended a workshop for something called laughing yoga. Where you do yoga and, um, laugh while you're at it. Well, this is laughing go-karting. On ice. Everyone should try it.

One final lap. My hands and muscles are starting to ache. My overalls are soaked through from the spray of the ice. And my thighs are numb. But I savour every metre, until I slither to a reluctant standstill.

Barclay's on the ice to greet me. He extends a hand to pull me out of the kart, then wraps me in a bearhug.

'Nina Sherwood, you're a real speed demon!' I bask in his admiration. 'Didn't you hear me tell you to slow down? You took that last bend like a real pro. Will you take part in the proper racing? On my team.'

I've gone weak at the knees. Not because of Barclay's proposition but at the aftershock of having egged myself on to do something seriously scary and living to tell the tale.

The racing is about to begin. Four teams. One of them captained – naturally – by Barclay. I walk carefully on the ice, back behind the barrier and into the changing room where Simon is waiting with a hot drink.

'That was fantastic.' I taste blackberries. 'Thank you so much for telling me what to do.'

'You ignored most of my instructions.' Simon smiles wryly. 'Particularly the one about speed. Here.' He thrusts a piece of paper into my hands. 'Look at the lap printout times. Fastest I've ever seen for a first-timer. Even our Barclay's going to be hard pushed trying to beat that!'

By the time I return to the rink, the racing is in full swing. By now, there are more than fifty people watching, and I soon feel self-conscious. They all seem to know each another and are chatting merrily away but I haven't got a clue who's who.

For one horrible moment, I think I've spotted Zoe Banks. But the woman who turns round as I'm contemplating hiding behind a pillar turns out to be someone else entirely.

'Hello. You're Nina, right?' I'm startled to hear a voice behind me. 'I'm Rosie.'

The girl who was karting before I had my turn. The one whose exuberance gave me the courage to risk it. Close up, she looks even younger than fourteen. Before I can reply, she continues, 'Barclay asked me to watch out for you. Told me to introduce you to people, and stuff. I'll do that if you want, but they're mostly boring old farts come to watch, when they could be racing.'

I take another look at the crowd. The boring old farts seem to be my age. And younger. A quick change of subject seems in order.

'So how do you know Barclay?'

'He's my godfather. How about you?'

'We kind of ran into each other.' I start telling Rosie how Barclay almost mowed down Chopper on Primrose Hill.

She frowns. 'That doesn't sound at all like Barclay,' she says. 'He's brilliant on a scooter. Showed me how to do a three-hundred-and-sixty-degree jump on mine. He made it look so easy but I still can't do it.'

Ten minutes later I'm showing Rosie pictures of Chopper on my phone – trying a bit too hard not to be an old fart – when we're interrupted by loud cheering, and shouts of, 'Go *onnnnn!*'

We look up to see two karts side by side on the track as they go into the straight no more than an inch between them. For five gut-clenching seconds it seems they're going to collide. Then one jousts past the other and accelerates towards the finish line.

Barclay leaps from the victorious kart.

'Same old, same old.' Rosie sounds much older than her years. For my benefit she adds simply, 'Barclay always wins. Except when it comes to his father. At least that's what *my* dad says.'

'How'd you mean?' I'm intrigued. After all, if Eddie Banks hadn't put in the good word that helped me start Happy Endings, I'd never have been in Primrose Hill, and I'd never have met Barclay.

'Well, according to Dad, Barclay doesn't really want to work for the family business. But his father blackmailed him.'

'Oh?'

'Says it'd kill him if Barclay walked away. So now the pair of them are always having terrible rows about how things should be done.'

Before I can find out any more, Barclay's at our side. Holding a silver trophy. 'Not a bad night's work,' he says.

'How much did you raise?' Rosie asks him.

'Close on fifteen grand. It's for the care home down the road,' he adds for my benefit. 'We do it every year. Pays for a few day trips to Whitstable and the Isle of Wight.'

We say our goodbyes to Rosie. Then Barclay says, 'So I can either introduce you to my mates – I think they're going for curry in Muswell Hill – but I'd much rather keep you to myself for the rest of the evening. What d'you think?'

'Rosie says your mates are old farts,' I tease.

'So long as she didn't include *me* in that description.'

Barclay and I make a quiet escape.

Even though it's well into the evening, the air outside is still warm and humid. We're back at Barclay's motorbike. He unlocks a pannier and places his trophy inside.

'Quick walk up to the Palace?' he suggests. 'While we decide what to do next?'

Since curry is off the menu there can be only so many possibilities. We walk uphill to the Great Hall. On the summit, Barclay says, 'I love the way the view is always changing. So many new buildings springing up across the capital.'

He's brought me up here to talk about architecture? Maybe I've misread the situation and Barclay simply wants to be friends. Just because I've finally stepped out of the shadow Ryan cast over my life, it doesn't mean Barclay's going to—

'I really enjoy your company, Nina,' he's saying. He sounds almost cross about it, which confuses me all the more.

'We have fun together,' I say cautiously.

'I had a private bet with myself tonight,' Barclay continues. 'Two private bets, in fact. And I've lost both.'

'Oh?'

'I didn't think you'd get on the back of the bike.' Barclay stares at the horizon rather than me. 'And I didn't think you'd go go-karting.'

'You're saying I'm dull?'

'Absolutely not!' Barclay looks at me in amazement. 'The

opposite. You're not like any of the girls I hang out with. That's the point.'

'Maybe you're mixing with the wrong kind of girls.' Barclay's a player, I remind myself. *The playboy brother with a different girl every week.* Am I this week's girl? Even if that's all I am, is that the worst thing in the world?

'Double or quits?' Barclay asks.

'Is that like truth or dare?'

'More or less.' He shoots me a smile that hits my heart like a dart on a bullseye. 'You up for it?'

'Okay.'

'Is that a yes?'

'Probably.'

'Let's find out.'

What's Barclay up to?

'I want you to turn your back on me,' he continues. 'Then I'll count down from three. When I get to one, you take off your shirt.'

'You what?'

'Trust me. Now turn around.'

I do as he asks. Which isn't the same as agreeing to take off my clothes in a public space.

'Three ...'

Barclay's correct. The view up here is amazing. Look, there's the Shard. And St Paul's Cathedral.

'Two ...'

When Barclay shouts '*ONE*', the whole of London seems to come to a halt. What the hell. My fingers are steady as I undo the two buttons on my white shirt and pull it quickly over my head. At least I'm wearing one of my most presentable bras.

'Now turn around again,' Barclay says.

I do so, without overthinking it, and find myself confronted with a topless Barclay. He holds out his T-shirt to me. The one with *Go-Kart Champion* printed across the chest.

'For you,' he says. 'You deserve it more than I do.'

I take a tentative step towards him. Our eyes are locked upon one another, as we both enjoy the view.

'Did you lose again?' I ask.

'Oh no.' Barclay's look of admiration makes me feel ridiculously happy. 'This time, I've definitely won.'

I maintain eye contact, stretch out my hand, and take the T-shirt. 'Will you be needing mine?'

Barclay considers. 'Probably on the small side.'

I watch him lace the fingers of both his hands together. Then, in a single fluid movement, he steps forward, raises his arms as if he's about to do a pirouette, drops them over my head and quickly pulls me in.

'I've been dreaming of this since I messed up in Paris,' he says. 'Of you.' Then – slowly and confidently – he eases his way into a kiss that tells me everything I need to know.

For the second time in a single night, I realise I've never been so terrified yet so thrilled at the same time.

Chapter 38

Barclay insists on driving his motorbike bare-chested. 'It's perfectly legal, so long as I'm wearing my helmet. Besides, I need to cool down.' He shoots me a playful look.

We leave Alexandra Palace in a roar of exhaust fumes. Barclay drives with a greater sense of urgency than before, although when we slow down to make a right turn he shifts backwards in the saddle, moulding his body into a single shape with mine.

I have no idea where we're going. Yes, this is the same way we came, but is Barclay planning to drop me off at home – I hope not! – or has he decided where we're going for supper?

In Kentish Town, we ignore the turning that leads to my place and keep going through Camden. A mile further down the road we encounter a batch of speed bumps. Barclay negotiates them like a stone skimming the surface of a pond.

A moment later, we're in Primrose Hill.

Chalcot Square, to be precise.

Barclay parks the bike between two cars and we remove our helmets. 'Did I mention I'm living here for the time being?' he says.

'Nope.'

'Means I can crack the whip with the builders. Seems like the quickest way to get this bloody basement finished. We're a bit sparse on the furniture, but I thought we could do takeaway and a grand tour?'

'Great!'

We debate the merits of curry from The Primrose Poppadum versus kebabs from the Greek.

'You decide. I'd better nip inside and grab a shirt,' Barclay says.

By the time I've chosen kebabs with feta salad, Barclay has reappeared in a new T-shirt. This one says, *Lucky Man!* I try not to look too pleased.

In the end, we take our supper to the park, then walk hand in hand back to Eddie Banks's palatial home.

'Let's start with the basement,' Barclay says.

So he wasn't kidding about the grand tour.

'Is there really a salt grotto?'

'It'd be quicker to go to Siberia and cut the rocks myself,' Barclay groans. 'I don't know what my old man's playing at. I mean, we've done some great developments. Very profitable. But this one ...' he pauses to press something on his phone. In response, golden light appears from translucent walls that glow a soft amber orange. The colour reminds me disconcertingly of Mrs Happy.

'This one's beginning to make the Taj Mahal look understated,' Barclay sighs.

'What's going to happen when it's finished?'

'I'm going to get very drunk indeed. Seriously? My father insists he's coming back to London full-time. He's been negotiating for months with HMRC about doing a tax deal that means he can afford to leave Monaco. Every time I tell him he should just pay what's due and enjoy the rest, he looks at me like I'm a huge disappointment.'

Barclay sounds fond yet exasperated. I remember what Rosie said about him and his father not seeing eye to eye.

'Do you enjoy working for the family business?'

'It's not exactly my life's ambition,' Barclay sighs. 'The legal work's a lot more fun than the property stuff. Anyway,' he presses his phone again, and this time a door slides open. 'Welcome to the chill-out zone in all its solid gold glory. Ta da!'

'It's hideous!' The words tumble from my mouth before I can stop them. 'I mean—'

'You mean it's hideous.' Barclay's face is stern for five very long seconds. Then he roars with laughter. 'Yeah. Ghastly. I tried to talk him out of it. I try to talk him out of lots of things, but ...'

By the time we've finished in the basement – the banana-scented wallpaper in the meditation room is a particular highlight – Barclay is telling me about his plan to take a sabbatical when the building works are finished.

'My life's on hold till then,' he says. 'But once we're done, I need to stop coasting. Time to reassess my priorities. I'll be thirty-five next year, and that's too old to keep being the playboy brother, wouldn't you say?'

Barclay's smile scores another bullseye. It's followed this time by an arm looped around my waist as we walk into the upstairs part of Eddie Banks's home.

Five flights of stairs. By the time we get to the roof terrace – the view is almost a match for Alexandra Palace – I'm out of breath.

Barclay and I sit alongside one another in comfy, wicker armchairs, cold beers in hand. He finishes a story about the time he challenged a Serbian builder to a wrestling match – 'It wasn't until I was in hospital on morphine having my collar-bone mended that I discovered the old bugger had an Olympic bronze medal!' – and suggests we go inside.

All at once, I feel nervous. It's that time of night when you either go home ...

... Or stay.

I hesitate, waiting for Barclay to make his next move.

'Another beer?' he asks.

Three hours later, we're still chatting. I'm stretched out on a couch the size of a small yacht, my head in Barclay's lap, while he gives me a light head massage.

'You're very good at this,' he says.

'Isn't that what I should be saying to you?' I tilt my neck to one side and look up at him.

'I mean, here I am, spilling all my secrets' – it's true, Barclay has just finished a story about the girl he wanted to marry when he was twenty-five, who turned him down in favour of a career as a zoologist in Borneo – 'and you're such an easy person to talk to. You've told me all about Gloria and her good works at the law centre. Not to mention Edo and his art. And Kelli's extended honeymoon, now that film of hers has wrapped. But the person I really want to know about is *you*!'

'Like what?'

'What's the most embarrassing thing you've ever done?'

'That one's easy.' Barclay resumes his head massage and I'm glad I don't have to look at him. 'When my ex-husband dumped me, I pretended he was dead.'

'Pretended?' Barclay seems amused. 'Well, I suppose that's marginally better than killing him. I didn't know you'd been married.'

'Why would you?'

'So what happened?'

I start telling Barclay about my marriage and its demise. He peppers my story with remarks like, 'What a bastard,' 'That must've been hideous,' and 'Remind me never to cross you!'

By the time I get to the bit about watching Ryan unwrap his farewell gifts, we're both snorting with laughter.

'A little baby T-shirt you say. Nice! Glad to know I'm having a good influence on you.'

I hope Barclay can't see me blush.

'You're blushing!' he says.

I pull myself upright.

'Too much beer.'

'Me too.' Barclay fixes me with an intense stare. Is this the bit where he says he's over the driving limit? And offers to Uber me home. Or—

'I'll make us some coffee,' he says.

I follow him down two flights of stairs and into the kitchen of my dreams. Oversized light fixtures crisscross the high ceiling, shining pools of light onto pristine granite surfaces and a wealth of cupboards. While Barclay busies himself with coffee, kettle and cups, I prowl the edges.

A brace of steam ovens, each one large enough to roast a haunch of venison. Induction hobs with no visible controls. Glass-fronted wine fridge. Warming drawers galore. One of those big spray taps – the sexy ones that look like a shower attachment – stands sentry over a sink that's easily big enough to bath a baby. Everything in mint condition, and probably never been used. The whole look is stunning, yet peculiarly soulless.

Barclay puts two mugs of coffee on a glass dining table. 'I know,' he says. 'Big enough for a good game of table tennis. Maybe we'll try that next time you're over.'

Next time.

Two words full of promise.

'So how's business? Sorry, I should have asked you before.' Barclay sips his coffee. 'I meant to say, you did a good job with poor old Mrs Happy. Do you think she's made her first complaint to God yet?'

I laugh at the thought and I'm soon telling Barclay about my ideas for a Funeral Expo.

'Cool,' he responds. 'I was just reading about a Liverpudlian, one of the first Beatles tour guides, whose mates came to his send-off dressed in Sergeant Pepper jackets. Hired the original Magical Mystery tour bus, too.'

'Glad to know I'm having a good influence on you,' I deadpan.

'I'm guessing you haven't changed your mind about accepting investment in Happy Endings?' Barclay counters.

'Not going to happen.' Behind my back, I cross my fingers. 'But you know how you like to mix business with pleasure?'

The moment I start telling Barclay about the solicitors who wrote to say Happy Endings is devaluing property prices, I have his full attention.

He looks furious.

'Do you have the letter?'

I fish it out from my bag and Barclay speedreads.

'Ridiculous,' he says. 'Leave this with me.' He puts the letter to one side. 'I promise you don't need to worry about it.'

'You mean they haven't got a case?'

'Let's just say they'd be foolish to try it on in court. Don't waste another second worrying.'

'If anything, it makes me even more determined to make a go of things,' I say. 'I don't understand why people are so hostile.'

271

Barclay considers. 'The sort of people who live round here. They just don't do death. Happy Endings makes them uncomfortable. Dead bodies on the high street – even when they're out of sight – they remind them there's some things money just can't buy.'

'All the more reason for me to get on with the Funeral Expo,' I say. 'Clear up some misconceptions. Not the one about death itself, obviously. But if I can help even one person to accept death is part of life, make it a tiny bit easier for them to deal with future losses by planning ahead and knowing what their loved ones want, then I'm in the right business.'

I see Barclay's smile reflected in the glass top. 'You're really quite something,' he says.

Ryan was never so interested in my work, not even in the early days.

Barclay stands up. 'End of consultation?' he asks.

I nod.

'So about payment ...' He's standing behind my chair. 'I'm thinking a few more kisses. Followed by—'

I tilt the chair and look up at him. 'Didn't realise you were that cheap!' I tease.

'I'm thinking I might persuade you to put me on a retainer.' Now Barclay's hand is stroking the back of my neck in a way that sends shivers down my spine. 'But seriously ... I don't want you to get the wrong idea. You're far too—'

This isn't sounding good. But before Barclay can let me down gently, I am saved by the bell.

Inside my bag, which is lying on the floor, my phone is ringing.

I check my watch.

Almost two o'clock in the morning.

An unknown phone number.

Which can mean only one thing.

'Guess someone's died,' I say. 'Sorry, but I'm going to have to go to work.'

'No need to sound quite so pleased about it,' Barclay says ruefully.

I press the reply button on the phone screen and say, 'Hello, Happy Endings. This is Nina Sherwood. How may I help you?'

The woman on the other end of the phone is sobbing.

Eventually, she calms down enough to blurt out, 'Nina, it's me. Gloria. I'm at Kentish Town police station. I've been arrested.'

Chapter 39

Luck had been on our side, that night. When we'd arrived at Kentish Town police station, a familiar face had happened to be in the reception area.

'You two again.' A weary greeting. 'To what do I owe the pleasure?'

'Sergeant Hartley.' Impressively, Barclay remembered her name, and was rewarded with a cautious smile. 'One of our friends called. I believe she's been banged up in one of your cells.' He made it sound as if a dinner party host had just learned the guest of honour was allergic to food – regrettable, but not insurmountable.

'Name?'

'Gloria O'Sullivan,' I supplied.

A police officer loomed up from his computer. 'Arrested in Regent's Park. Broke into the Garden Festival area. Criminal damage.'

'Oh.' Sergeant Hartley considered. 'Has she been charged?'

'Not yet,' the other officer said. 'Busy night. And the girl keeps insisting her lawyer's on the way.'

Barclay took a step forward. 'And indeed, here I am,' he announced. 'So sorry for the delay. Please may I see my client?'

'I'll deal with this,' Sergeant Hartley decided. 'This way. Not you,' she added to me, 'just the lawyer.'

I sat there in reception for forty-five minutes before Barclay emerged with Gloria.

'We're out of here,' was all he said.

So it wasn't until we were back home – Barclay dropped us off in a cab – that I got the full story. Just after midnight, Gloria and her guerrilla gardening chums had snuck into the park, hauling the components of their protest installation through a strategically placed gap in the festival fencing. Everything was fine until a security guard turned up and raised the alarm. At which point, Gloria started a diversion – she told the guard that being Albanian he, better than most, should sympathise with the plight of migrants – to give her friends time to escape.

In the back of a police car, she'd managed to exchange a string of texts with Fred. Who, to put it mildly, couldn't have been less interested.

In bed with his wife, he said. Gloria knew the rules, and served her right for getting into trouble.

'Then he turned off his phone.' I'd never seen Gloria so furious. Or so hurt.

By the time she'd been formally arrested and offered a phone call, Gloria realised she was in deep trouble. 'Even if I managed to get away with a caution, my law career would be over before it began,' she said. 'That was why I was so upset when I called you. I'd forgotten you were going out with Barclay. Thank God the date went well!' Gloria had sounded a little more cheerful.

Barclay had been nothing short of magnificent, she insisted. 'When the cop reappeared, he said that yes, I was unquestionably guilty of criminal damage, along with unlawful entry, conspiracy, and most likely theft of materials, too. I wanted to kill him! But then he went into this long spiel about my good works at the law centre – although how he knew about that I have no idea – and how I was saving the police a lot of time, effort and money by giving out sensible advice on a voluntary basis. And that the world needed more lawyers like me, and less lawyers like him. Nina, I thought he was never going to shut up! In the end the policewoman told me I was fortunate to have such an eloquent friend and that she hoped I would treat this serious matter as a learning experience. Then she wished me all the best with my career, and we legged it.'

In the three weeks since that night, Gloria had broken up with Fred.

Meanwhile, my relationship with Barclay had begun. We're officially an item, and there are moments when I think I'm going to burst with happiness.

Barclay Banks might like to pretend to himself that he's a ruthless business type, but he's actually very sweet.

After the night of Gloria's arrest, he told me that since I was only just free of Ryan, I was vulnerable. Said we should take things slowly. Get to know one another properly. I asked if that meant he didn't fancy me and just wanted to be friends.

'Absolutely not.' He was shocked. 'I mean, of course I want to be friends. But since I come with a bit of a ... how can I put it ... a bit of a *playboy* reputation' – that teasing smile I am already growing to love – 'I want you to know you can trust me. There's no-one else in my life, Nina. Only you. Well, you and forty-five builders, all of them giving me the bloody runaround.'

Barclay has set up headquarters in the kitchen in Chalcot

Square, which means most days he pops into Happy Endings for a coffee. Sometimes, if I've got Chopper with me, we go for a stroll at lunch. And tonight – in fact, any moment now – he's coming round for supper.

Can't wait to see him.

Mostly because I can't wait to see him, but also because I have good news to share. Oh, and because this evening, Barclay is cooking for us all, to make up for cancelling on me at the eleventh hour last week, after promising dinner at the Shard.

'Hurry up, Nina,' Edo shouts from downstairs. 'I'm opening the wine. I need a drink before lover boy arrives.'

Despite the fighting talk, Edo is no longer hostile to Barclay. They bonded over Sky Sports. Chelsea versus Manchester United. Both of them letting the barriers down enough to confess they missed the old manager – the one who's always so well dressed – and thought he'd had a raw deal.

The doorbell rings and I go bounding down the stairs to answer, pipped at the post by Chopper.

Barclay is not alone. 'This is Kenji,' he says. The smiling man next to Barclay is carrying an assortment of carriers and cool boxes. 'He's going to teach us how to make sushi. You'll like that, won't you?' he adds to Chopper. 'Seaweed's good for your coat. Salmon, too. And,' he whispers conspiratorially, 'I've bought you a pig's ear. Shall we stuff it with rice?'

I'm not sure about Chopper, but sushi is Gloria's favourite food. An inspired choice, particularly as I mentioned to Barclay the other day that she's been too upset even to eat a Chocolate Orange from our emergency supply.

Thirty minutes later, Kenji has us set up with aprons, boards and knives, and is teaching us the correct way to cut cucumber for the shikai maki.

'Imagine it's Fred you're slicing and dicing,' Barclay encourages Gloria. It's the first time in three weeks I've seen her smile like she means it, and I want to kiss him.

'See the marbling on that salmon?' Kenji points to the peachy orange flesh with a chopstick. He has a strong – and incongruous – Scottish accent that reminds me of Lin. 'That's what makes it melt in your mouth like butter.' He cuts it with such precision, he could double as a surgeon.

While we are put to work washing the rice – it needs to be rinsed five times – Kenji produces two bottles of saké. And several more as the evening progresses.

Little by little, we learn not to overstuff our sushi rolls. Or press too hard when we roll using the bamboo mats. There's a method to make paper-thin omelettes that involves sieving the eggs and adding potato starch. Who knew! And the secret ingredient of perfect sushi vinegar? Kelp.

By the time we're finished, colourful platters of delicious fresh food abound. And Chopper's breath smells strongly of fish.

Kenji inspects our handiwork. 'Not bad for one night,' he says. 'Especially considering you need at least seven years of training to become an expert sushi chef. Well done everybody. I'm going to leave you to enjoy, then come back later to clear away.'

We demolish our feast in a lot less time than it took to create.

'Delicious!' Gloria says. 'I could get used to this.' She and Barclay start talking law to one another – Gloria is trying to radicalise Barclay into joining a protest march against cuts in legal aid – and Edo chimes in with a story about Dele Dier spending two full days closeted with an intellectual property lawyer, discussing his artistic legacy. I can tell Edo's miffed because Joshua Kent was invited to the marathon meeting, and he wasn't.

'How's Dele doing?' I ask.

Edo considers. 'Mrs Happy's death seems to have given him a whole new lease of life.'

'That happens more than you'd imagine,' I say gently. 'People with a limited lifespan finding the energy they need to sort out their affairs.' Edo's already told me Dele's got very firm ideas about his funeral and I've agreed to act as undertaker when the time comes. I ask, 'What about your Design for Death project?' Edo hasn't mentioned it lately. 'Has Dele been a source of inspiration?'

'We've come up with an idea that meets Joshua Kent's approval,' Edo says cautiously. 'But I'm not sure we'll be able to pull it off. *I'll* be able to pull it off,' he corrects himself. 'Anyway, for the moment, Dele's talking about a weekend in Amsterdam with Joshua. Wants to get some decent weed to help himself through the pain barrier. More wine anybody?'

After Edo's topped up our glasses, I say, 'I've got good news to share.' Three faces turn towards me. 'My Funeral Expo. I've finally found a place to hold it. The community centre's given me permission.' My friends know I've already been turned down by the local church, the library and three schools. 'So it's all systems go!'

'When's it happening?' Barclay looks impressed.

'Sooner than I expected. They've given me a slot in six weeks' time.'

'Can you pull it together that fast?' Gloria says.

'I'm going to have to. Otherwise I have to wait till next April and that's too far away. I need a big PR blast this side of Christmas.'

I sound more confident than I am. I didn't want to approach any exhibitors until I was sure I had a venue so there's a ton of work ahead to pull off a decent event in such a short space of time.

'If you need any of my builders to knock up some stands or whatever, just say the word,' Barclay offers.

The sound of clattering from the kitchen announces Kenji's return.

Barclay stands up and stretches. 'I'll help him clear away, then I'll be off,' he says.

I wonder if Barclay and I will ever spend the night together. He seems content to take things very slowly indeed. It's a puzzle I'm still thinking about when I eventually fall asleep.

And it's Barclay I'm dreaming about – he's trying to persuade me to ski *up* a mountain – in the middle of the night, when my phone begins to ring.

Funeral Number Four

††††

In Memoriam
KELLI JULIETTE SHAPIRO
1961–2019

††††

'So first, the *tragic* death of Kelli Shapiro ... ten days ago ... on *honeymoon* in the Philippines. And now today ... these *extraordinary* arrangements for her funeral.' Nina noticed the Sky News reporter kept interrupting his own words with frequent – scripted – pauses and inflections, as if to increase the gravity of his words. Kelli, she suspected, would have accused him of overacting.

'We'll be bringing the entire funeral service to you and an audience of millions across the *globe* ... live ... here from Osea Island,' the reporter continued. 'But next, we go to *Chelmsford* ... where a crowd of at least *twenty thousand people* ... fans of Kelli Shapiro who have travelled from all over *Europe* ... awaits a glimpse of the funeral cortege as it arrives from North London en route to the *causeway* that links this beautiful little island to the mainland of *Essex* '

The reporter turned his back on the camera and started discussing cricket with a colleague.

This must be what it was like to be on a film set, Nina

thought. Bursts of tightly focused energy and activity punctuated by lengthy interludes of waiting while everything that needed to happen behind the scenes was taken care of. And none of it seemed real, even though she herself was the person who had organised every tiny detail.

Darling! I can't wait to see you. My husband and I (oh, how I love sounding like Her Majesty The Queen!) will be home in ten days. We're about to fly north to an amazing place called Luzon for our honeymoon. Keir's arranged everything. You're going to love him! Kxxx

Nina knew Kelli's final email to her off by heart. She had read it for the first time twelve nights ago, only a few hours before she was woken from her sleep by the shell-shocked voice of Keir Mahoney who had related – almost trancelike – the facts of his wife's death.

A freak accident in the ocean, Keir had said. The two of them frolicking in warm, waveless waters. Kelli had cried out in pain when she bumped against the monstrous creature for just a single second. A sea wasp, the locals called it. Officially, the box jellyfish, which looked no more menacing than a white plastic bag, discarded in the sea.

Even before Keir could help her back to shore, a vicious red rash was spreading along Kelli's arm and by the time the ambulance arrived she was unconscious although the red rash continued to feast on her skin. At the hospital, Kelli was declared dead. A doctor confessed that twenty to forty people died every year in the Philippines from jellyfish stings, although it was very unusual for the time of year. As though that might be some consolation. The British Embassy in

Manila had explained Keir would need an undertaker back in England and Kelli had spoken about Nina a lot. Please, he'd asked on the phone, would she be able to help?

After the call, in the darkness – equally trancelike – Nina had dressed, left the house and driven to Happy Endings. There, she opened and printed off the computer documents with Kelli's name on them.

To whom it may concern. I, Kelli Shapiro, place on record that in the event of my death, the arrangements for my funeral shall be as specified below.

That was as far as Nina was able to read before the words blurred. Through her Niagara of tears, she saw herself, only a few weeks ago, sitting in Kelli's comfortable kitchen. The pair of them giggling their way through Kelli's instructions. Toasting the success of 'Know Before You Go' with vodka tonics. And after they'd had three each, working out how to use Nina's iPhone to shoot video while Kelli gave an improvised performance.

'Much better than doing it in a studio,' Kelli insisted. 'Someone would be bound to leak it online and that would ruin everything.'

Afterwards, the pair of them, heads close together, squinting at the screen, reviewing Kelli's mini movie.

'It's not me you'd need for this!' Nina protested when Kelli was finally done. 'It's more of a job for David Copperfield!'

'How about David Blaine? I've got his number right here,' Kelli had offered. Then, 'But seriously, Nina. This is hugely important to me. Can I rely on you to make it happen?'

Now it was about to happen.

Nina had set her own grief to one side. Like anyone else who'd been freshly bereaved, a frenzy of displacement activity cushioned the hammer blow. The first job had been to arrange Kelli's repatriation, which took a mountain of paperwork and long-distance phone calls to achieve. While she waited for the necessary permits to arrive, Nina faxed Kelli's wishes to Keir. He agreed immediately. Cost was absolutely not an issue, he added. 'Do whatever it takes. Hire whatever you need. Tell me what I can do help.'

Nina summoned the UK's premier entertainment event management company. A team of fifteen people was assembled and – under Nina's meticulous stewardship – took control of everything, including the all-important media agenda.

It didn't matter that so many of the headlines and talking heads were critical; in fact, the more the better.

Kelli had been branded a diva. A spendthrift. The worst sort of movie star. A very poor example. And – Nina's favourite – 'the Queen of Excess'. The object of the PR exercise was to ensure that Kelli Shapiro, *tragic* Kelli Shapiro, was the only show in town for ten consecutive days.

Now the show was about to reach its final curtain.

'*Darling! Go out there and enjoy every moment.*' Kelli's voice and her wonderful throaty chuckle rattled inside Nina's head.

'Are you ready?' The production assistant's question brought Nina back to the job in hand.

'Absolutely.' She allowed herself to be placed in the line of camera fire and the Sky News reporter began.

'I'm joined now by the *funeral* director, Nina Sherwood,' he said. 'Is it fair to say this is the biggest funeral we've seen in the United Kingdom since that of *Princess Diana*?'

'There have been comparisons, yes.'

'But equally ... how do you respond to those who say this is a *vulgar* demonstration of ostentatious *wealth*? People who are saying ... no matter how *tragically* Kelli Shapiro died, this funeral demonstrates ... she had ... more money than *sense*. Or *taste*.'

'First of all, I'd say Kelli is to be congratulated for having planned ahead, and making sure her funeral is a true reflection of who she was. I'd also suggest people shouldn't be quite so quick to judge.'

'One *moment* ...' The reporter paused theatrically. 'Here are the first pictures of the funeral cortege approaching the causeway.'

Nina could see what was happening on a small monitor to the left of the camera. She assumed the images were now being shown on live TV.

'Are you able to confirm ... that the *mourners* in these cars following the hearse include Brad Pitt, Helen Mirren, *Madonna* ... David Beckham, Sir Elton John, Meryl Streep, Benedict Cumberbatch and Dame Emma Thompson? Yes ... look,' the reporter began to answer his own question, 'that is *indeed* Sir Elton John we can see in the limousine. Join us after this very quick break ... when we will see a *galaxy* of celebrity mourners walk the *red carpet* that leads to the *incredible* graveside of Kelli Shapiro.'

Nina's interview was over. A member of the event team was waiting at the wheel of a Jeep to drive her the short distance to the graveside.

'Everything's in place,' the young man reassured her.

'And still no-one knows what's really going to happen?'

'You can count on it.'

Twenty minutes later, Nina was staring out at the sea of celebrities from her vantage point high in the control booth.

A hush of expectation.

Until the silence was broken by 'Spirit in the Sky', performed by a one-time-only supergroup consisting of Elton John, members of Coldplay, Justin Timberlake, and fifty per cent of Simon & Garfunkel. Followed by debatably inappropriate whistles and cheers.

An impromptu burst of 'Bridge Over Troubled Water' by way of an encore while the starriest of the star-studded cast of mourners arrived finally to claim their front-row cinema-style seats, then the funeral of Kelli Shapiro began.

A large outdoor screen – the type used at football matches to replay goals and other highlights – flickered into life.

Followed by a collective gasp, when everyone realised what they were seeing and hearing.

'Hi. Yes. It's me!' Kelli had been staring directly into the camera lens of Nina's phone that day in the kitchen. What was lacking in Hollywood production standards was made up for in shock value. 'And I'm dead.' She sounded remarkably – disturbingly – cheerful about it. 'As you've probably heard, I'm going to be buried in my car. My very expensive car.'

Eyes dropped from the screen to the deep hole that had been dug underneath it at centre stage in front of the assembled congregation and at the huge pile of dirt alongside it. All against the backdrop of a huge golden curtain.

A gasp as the curtain lifted to reveal the car that Kelli had specified as her final resting place. An electric blue Rolls-Royce Ghost.

'And there you *have* it,' the Sky News reporter was telling his global audience. 'List price just under a quarter of a *million* pounds. And this at a time when funeral poverty in the United Kingdom – people who can't *afford* to give their

loved ones a *decent* funeral – is approaching record heights.'
He might just as well have been saying Kelli Shapiro was a
spoiled, wicked woman.

An elaborate stainless-steel coffin expertly shouldered by
six of Nina's most trusted pallbearers was slowly making its
way along the red carpet that divided the sea of mourners.
Even at a glance, you could see it was the funereal equivalent
of Kelli's Rolls-Royce.

At the graveside, the pallbearers gently placed their precious
cargo onto a makeshift altar made of natural rock.

Then silence.

Those present began to exchange glances, their unanswered
questions hanging uneasily in the air.

Would Kelli's coffin actually fit inside the car?

Did they plan to rest it in the back seat?

In the boot?

Were there going to be prayers?

More live music?

Traditional hymns?

What about a eulogy?

And presumably it was going to take a crane to manoeuvre
the Rolls-Royce into the grave?

Just when the mood was shifting from uncomfortable to
unbearable, Kelli's home movie resumed.

'Don't worry, I'm not actually inside the coffin.' Nina sobbed
into her handkerchief as Kelli's glorious throaty chuckle filled
the outdoor auditorium. 'And I'm not so daft as to bury a
car. Especially one we've borrowed from the lovely people at
Rolls-Royce. No. Here's the thing. A while ago, I was diagnosed
with kidney disease. When they told me, I did exactly what
you'd have done. I got straight onto the internet!'

Ever the accomplished professional, Kelli paused to allow a ripple of nervous laughter.

'And that was when I realised that what's far more absurd than burying yourself in a car is burying – or burning – your organs just when you have the opportunity to save someone else's life, instead. Sorry to mislead you. But I bet the media's have been having field day talking about how rich and spoiled I am, and hopefully, that's given my funeral more publicity than it would otherwise have got. Which has given me a platform to beg for your help.'

Kelli's beautiful face dissolved on the screen, replaced with a montage of hospital shots, children on dialysis machines and ordinary men and women, who appeared with a subtitle that declared: 'Kidney Donor'. Meanwhile, her voice continued on the soundtrack.

'Over six thousand men, women and children are waiting for a kidney transplant,' Kelli said. 'One-third will be on the waiting list for two years, which means their whole life goes on hold while their families pray for a match. They are the lucky ones. Because one person in every ten will die before a suitable match comes up. So here's what I want you to do. I beg you to recycle yourself. Become an organ donor. You can do that right now.' A website address filled the screen. 'Get yourself on the national register. Sixty per cent of kidney transplants go ahead because someone volunteered to become an organ donor before they died. I'm here to tell you ... there is life after death. Please help.'

The screen faded to black and the golden curtain silently closed.

Kelli's widower stood in front of the audience. 'My name is Keir Mahoney,' he said, 'and I had the great privilege to be married to Kelli for nine days.' His voice was strong and his trembling hands were buried deep inside his jacket pockets. 'My wife was an incredible woman who believed passionately that more of us would volunteer to donate their organs if we knew it was as easy as going online and filling in a form. I hope you'll do that today, no matter where you are in the world, in memory of my wife, Kelli Shapiro.' Keir's voice faltered. 'We also have a stack of donation cards right here and I'm hoping some of you will be generous enough to fill them in. And please, if you can, lobby your government, so that organ donation becomes the norm. We can save thousands of additional lives if we switch to a global opt-out system, and that's exactly what we should do. For now, though, it's essential to opt *in*.'

David and Victoria Beckham were first to reach Kier Mahoney. Followed by Meryl Steep and Sir Elton John. Sky News continued its live broadcast for ninety minutes longer than scheduled, its reporter and studio pundits naming and chit-chatting about the celebrities who stood patiently in line, most of them experiencing the novelty of queuing for the first time in years, while they waited to complete and autograph an organ donation card.

'And *finally* it is *my turn* to honour the life of the *brilliant* Oscar-winning actress, Kelli Shapiro.' The Sky News reporter signed his name with a flourish. 'Now back to the studio.'

Chapter 40

'Nina, where's the coffin-making workshop going to happen? Main hall or side room?' Gloria's voice drags me back to the land of the living. Which is to say real life, rather than the imaginary world where I spend so much time holding long – usually angry – conversations with myself about Kelli.

Yes, being an undertaker means you learn how to compartmentalise. But no amount of professionalism can protect you from the agony of losing a friend. Death sucks.

The grief comes in waves and, at first, I felt I was drowning. I couldn't bear to walk past the Blueberry Café. Vodka burned like acid in my mouth. Even the news that eighty thousand people had joined the organ donor register in the thirty-six hours following Kelli's funeral left me feeling ... empty.

One month on, it's more as if I've survived a shipwreck. The waves aren't so high and there are interludes of calm. But the ocean is a lonely place and treading water is the best I can manage for now. Every day, I do my best to join in with life's basic requirements and, occasionally, I succeed.

Like now, when I drag myself into the moment and answer Gloria's question with one of my own. 'How many sign-ups have we had for the workshop?'

'Eleven.'

'Then let's put the workshop at the end of the main hall. To entice people past the photos. And that man with his collection of miniature tombstones for aquarium owners who want to commemorate their dead fish.'

'My favourite exhibitor,' Gloria says. 'Did I ever mention that when I was seven, I was a goldfish serial killer? I'd have been that guy's best customer, for sure. Do you think that's why the smell of cod always makes me feel like I'm going to throw up?'

I don't know what I'd do without Gloria. Or Edo.

After we got back from Kelli's funeral, my only ambition was to cancel the Funeral Expo and stay in bed for the rest of my life. Gloria and Edo had to work hard to convince me that wasn't an option.

'But I've been prancing about like Pollyanna,' I mumbled. 'Making out funerals can be joyful. They're not. Kelli didn't deserve to die.'

I paused to blow my nose again, and Edo leapt in. 'Only one part of that's true,' he insisted. 'Yes, Kelli was so unlucky. But you honoured her wishes to the letter. I'm so proud of you, Nina. And I know Kelli would be, too. As for cancelling the exhibition, that's just bollocks.'

Gloria chimed in. 'He's right,' she said. Then to Edo, 'When did you get to be so wise?'

'And eloquent.' I felt the glimmer of a smile twitching on my lips. 'But you know what? I just can't. I'm going to postpone until next year.'

'You're not!' My friends spoke in unison. 'We're going to help you.'

I could tell Edo and Gloria had already discussed this

and sensed it would take less energy to agree than it would to fight them.

Instead, I steadied the life raft by immersing myself in hard work. Sixteen-hour days interspersed with interludes of patchy, restless sleep have become the new normal.

And the expo – now branded 'The Final Celebration' – is about to happen, which means there's still far too much to do before the first of the exhibitors arrive tonight to set up their stands. Thirty separate displays, which is double the number I had hoped for, and largely thanks to Edo.

In the first few days after Kelli's funeral while I either sat in a shell-shocked haze, refused to get out of bed, or took Chopper on aimless walks through the streets of Camden, Edo worked office hours at Happy Endings. It was just as well, because after six months of silence my business line was finally starting to ring.

Journalists, mostly, wanting to talk to me about Kelli. Instead of telling them to bugger off, as I almost certainly would have done, Edo said I was too busy to be interviewed because I was organising a – what did he call it? – a unique event to help everyone be the star of their own funeral. Not exactly how I'd have put it, but the journalists lapped it up, and everything snowballed from there.

When I learned Edo had charged two exhibitors four-figure sums to participate – accountants keen to drum up business with a seminar about inheritance tax, and solicitors offering will writing and power of attorney services – I didn't know whether to be horrified or delighted, although the arrival of the shop's electricity bill helped me climb off the fence.

'I'm going to make a start on The Wall of Death,' I tell Gloria now. 'It's going next to Funeral Foods, right?'

Gloria nods. 'Have you spoken to Edo?' she asks.

'No, why?'

'He had a call from the hospice yesterday. Dele's taken another turn for the worse. I think Edo stayed there overnight.'

Sad news that comes as no surprise. Two weeks ago, Dele paid me a professional call, and I could tell he didn't have much time left. I'd helped him choose a coffin – large, traditional, mahogany – and when I broke the news that a plot in Highgate Cemetery was going to set him back more than twenty thousand pounds, he wrote a cheque on the spot.

'You might want to tell them that in a year from now, this cheque will be worth at least five times more than the amount it's made out for. Death isn't going to be the end of me, I promise.'

It was comforting to know the flame of Dele's artistic self-worth was still burning brightly, although I was concerned by the sheen of perspiration across his face and neck, and the nasal cannula attached to his portable oxygen supply.

'I've left my funeral instructions with Edo,' Dele had added. 'Things might get a little rough for him when I'm gone. You'll take care of him, you and Gloria, right?'

'Of course,' I promised.

'I'm looking forward to your exhibition,' Dele continued. 'Edo's been telling me all about it. I love the banner that's going by the entrance.'

The one that declares: 'It's not that I'm afraid to die. I just don't want to be there when it happens.' A quote from Woody Allen.

I look at it now, hammered into position to greet people as they come through the door.

'Bloody hell!' Gloria looks up from her laptop. 'We've

293

had another two hundred and thirty registrations since nine o'clock alone. That makes seventeen hundred. It's a good job you decided to go for a three-day event.'

Originally, I'd have been thrilled if three or four hundred people had signed up for 'The Final Celebration'.

'It's all thanks to you,' I say quietly to Kelli. 'You're the reason for all the publicity. And I still can't believe you won't be here to see it.'

A throaty laugh of appreciation, heard only by me. '*I'll be watching all right,*' says Kelli in my head. '*Wouldn't miss it for the world. But Nina, I'm worried. What about Barclay? Is he actually going to be there?*'

Barclay.

I'm pretty sure it's my fault, but Barclay has become somewhat elusive. Immediately after Kelli's funeral, when I told him I needed time alone, he took me at my word and disappeared for a week. On business to see his father in Monaco, he said. When he returned, we managed a trip to the cinema, then he was off again, doing something called horseboarding, which apparently involves standing on a fancy skateboard while being towed by a thoroughbred that gallops across the sand at thirty miles an hour. Although we talk or text most days, it's as though there's frosted glass between us and I'm not the only one who needs their space.

But surely Barclay wouldn't miss the opening night of my show?

Chapter 41

In any event, it turns out that Edo rather than Barclay is missing the first night of The Final Celebration. He got a phone call two hours ago. The hospice ...

'I'm scared,' he said. 'I've never seen ... well, I've never seen anyone die before. Not in real life.'

I assured Edo it was normal to be apprehensive. 'One of the most helpful things will be talk to Dele,' I advised. 'Even if you think he's unconscious, it's quite likely he'll still recognise voices.'

'And just for once, he won't be able to contradict me.' Edo did his best to summon a smile but his chin continued to tremble. I gave him a big hug, while silently chiding myself for feeling envious that – unlike Kelli's – Dele's death wasn't going to come as a colossal shock to anyone who knew him.

I'm still thinking about Dele while I stand here in a corner of the hall, trying to work out how many people have already arrived. At least two hundred. Some I recognise as locals but most have been attracted by social media and all the press coverage. I startle to the touch of fingertips brushing against my shoulder.

'Here you go, gorgeous.' Barclay slides a glass of Prosecco into my hand. 'You've achieved so much in such a short time, it's absolutely amazing and I'm very proud of you. And your mother and father are lovely.'

What?

I hadn't realised Mum and Dad were already here. I'd been planning to introduce Barclay to my parents at some stage of the evening. Preferably as they were on their way out of the door and saying goodbye. And definitely without mentioning the B-as-in-boyfriend word ... no need to get them excited about the prospect of romance re-entering my life until I'm sure Barclay and I have a future together.

Oh Lord. Across the room, Mum and Dad are watching our every move. That's not good.

'I really must congratulate Julie,' I tell Barclay. 'Her flowers are spectacular. See you later.'

'Okay, I promised your father we'd try out the cremation simulator as soon as the queue gets smaller. Oh, and Zoe says she's going to drop by, so keep an eye out for her.'

Whaaaat?

I try to decide which of those two sentences is more horrifying while I nudge my way to the front of Julie's stand. Our local florist has created dozens of remembrance tributes – not a traditional wreath among them – chosen with local residents in mind, and tongue firmly in cheek. And she's done an amazing job.

The centrepiece of her stand is a sleek Aston Martin, crafted from hundreds of black dahlias.

Then there are the items no-one in Primrose Hill can live without: Bollinger Champagne (white wisteria blossoms), Chanel No. 5 (winter marigolds) and Châteauneuf du Pape (wine red geraniums) plus a vintage Rolex with numbers made from tiny bits of hydrangeas, an iPhone whose replica apps are made from mosaics of individual flower petals, and a large recycling bin crafted from rhododendron leaves and featuring three plump floral rats peeping out from the half-open lid – a protest at the council's recent decision to switch to fortnightly rubbish collections.

Julie herself is deep in conversation with a couple who are commissioning her to do their wedding flowers, so I save my own congratulations for later and head for the small side room where Carol, the professional celebrant, is talking about some recent funerals at which she has officiated.

'There was a man called Tom who loved greyhounds,' she's saying. 'He rescued and rehomed them once their racing days were over, so he'd made a lot of friends along the way. Tom's relatives encouraged people to bring their dogs to the ceremony, out in the country, on a natural burial site. We had forty-two greyhounds in all, and the family said it really brought it home to them how many people Tom had helped to make happy by sharing his passion for the dogs. Next ...' Carol presses a button and the screen behind her changes from greyhounds to butterflies. 'We had a woman who adored butterflies, so we released three thousand of them at the gravesite. As you can see, it was stunning. And here's one of my personal favourites, for a Harley-Davidson lover.'

Carol's audience nods its approval at pictures of family, friends, flowers, and biking memorabilia all in Harley orange and black and I slip away, past a bicycle hearse that used to travel between cemeteries in Copenhagen and has been given a new lease of life by an eco-funeral firm in Buckinghamshire.

I'm curious to discover how the exhibition zone that specialises in what the American trade unattractively calls 'cremains' is going down. If anything is likely to cause controversy or consternation – other than the cremation simulator and/or Barclay having further unsupervised conversations with my parents – it's probably going to happen here.

I arrive just in time to eavesdrop on an earnest man in a suit talking to an elderly woman I recognise from the local cafés.

'There's so much more you can do with ashes than just scatter them or keep them in an urn,' he's telling her. 'Martin here,' the man nods to his colleague, 'all you have to do is send him a few ounces of ashes and he'll incorporate them into a special pressing of that person's favourite music. In vinyl and fully playable.'

'So I could be recreated and have copies sent to my friends? Something like "I Remember You" by Frank Ifield?'

'Great choice!' The pair of them break into a song I've never heard, all smiles and laughter.

A few metres beyond the stand, a video catches my eye. At first sight, it could be one of David Attenborough's marine documentaries, but then the picture cuts to a workshop where someone is carefully stirring ashes into concrete. 'This creates what we call a pearl,' the voiceover explains. 'The pearls are taken by boat out into the ocean where they form part of an eternal reef, creating a new habitat for fish and other forms of sea life.'

'Whatever will they think of next!' the woman standing to my right asks a lanky teenager who might well be her grandson. 'I bet it would appeal to some of the people I met when I went on that Baltic cruise last year.'

'How about this?' The youngster is eyeing up the next stand. 'Isn't that way cool?' He's zoned in on a series of pictures showing how tattoo artists can sterilise ashes and mix them into their ink, so you can live on with someone who loved you, beneath their skin.

'Over my dead body!' comes the frosty riposte. 'Although you do have my permission for the one over here.' A nod towards a neighbouring service that promises to take your ashes and turn them into a box of two hundred pencils. 'I've always wanted to write a book.'

I'm still smiling to myself as I walk to the next set of stands when I feel a sharp tap on my shoulder. I turn round and find myself face to face with Zoe Banks.

'There you are,' she says. 'I've been looking all over for you.'

Chapter 42

It's the first time Zoe and I have crossed paths since she chucked me out of The Beauty Spot back in the summer.

'Hello,' I say warily. 'Thanks for coming.'

'Barclay said I ought to.'

Zoe's tone is not unfriendly. I've realised she and Barclay are close, talking most days, and I wonder what else he's been telling her.

'Have you had a look around?' I ask.

'A bit,' she mumbles. 'I'm not very good around death. As you know. But I have to admit, some of this stuff is quite interesting.'

It crosses my mind – not for the first time – that Zoe's line of work and my own have more in common than she might imagine. Botox and embalming, for example, both involve injecting poison into the body. But this doesn't seem like the ideal moment to exchange professional confidences, so instead I ask Zoe, 'You're comfortable with the idea of taking someone's ashes and turning them into something else?'

'Surprisingly so.' Zoe has dressed down for the occasion. Designer jeans, midnight blue velvet top and three-inch heels. Her trademark scarlet banana lips seem more in proportion with the rest of her face than before. In fact, here, on my territory, Zoe looks less poised, more vulnerable.

'With my mother ...' she continues. 'All I've ever known of her is a gravestone in Paris. That and a few photographs my father hides in a cupboard. No videos. I don't even know what her voice sounded like. I spent the whole of the year I turned twenty-two thinking I was going to die like she did. That's how Barclay and I differ from one another. We both know how short life can be. He's grown into a thrill-seeker who wants to pack in as much as he can, always tempting fate and laughing whenever I beg him to be careful. As for me, you wouldn't believe how much time I spend thinking about death. Barclay says I let it get in the way of my life, and he's probably right.'

Zoe shifts her gaze from the floor and looks directly into my eyes. 'What I'm trying to say is that I'm sorry. I know I haven't behaved very well towards you. Your shop really freaks me out, but Barclay's made me realise that's down to my own issues. He really wanted me to come tonight. Aversion therapy, he called it. Now I'm here, I'm understanding a bit better that people grieve in different ways. And that there's nothing wrong with that. Nina, you deserve to succeed.'

'Thanks, Zoe. What you say means the world to me.'

'Well, you seem to mean the world to Barclay. I've never known him so keen on anyone. He's even cancelled his plans to go travelling, and that's definitely a first. Can't say I'm sorry. Barclay's hugely important to me and that's why I needed to come here and talk to you.'

Barclay's said nothing about travelling and I'm about to ask Zoe for details when I realise she's looking right past me, towards one of the stands.

'Come and have a look,' I suggest, and we walk towards what looks like a display of expensive jewellery.

'*Really?*' Zoe looks more fascinated than afraid.

'It's becoming more and more popular,' I say. 'Remember, the human body contains lots of carbon. Just like diamonds.'

'And they do say diamonds are forever.' The woman in charge of the stand joins our conversation with an ice-breaker I'm sure she's used many times before. 'We're based in Geneva. You provide the ashes and we press them into something beautiful. Diamonds in white, green, blue, yellow, red and black. Or larger pieces that look more like a chunk of amber. You can have them set in silver or gold. Would you like to know more? Or may I show you some samples?'

'Why not?' Zoe says. Then to me, 'I'm fine. No need to babysit me. Thanks for the chat.'

I'm still digesting my encounter with Zoe when Dad bounces up. 'That death and cremation simulator, it's astonishing!' he declares. 'I know it's only virtual reality, but I swear I started sweating when I was on the conveyor belt that leads to the oven. Definitely the star of the show! Other than you, I mean!'

Dad's enthusiasm is a big relief. It was Jason Chung who tipped me off about the simulator. At first, I dismissed it as one of his tricks to get me into trouble. But when I investigated, I was intrigued.

'The original's in a Chinese theme park,' I tell Dad. 'Like a Disney ride with a difference. The cousin of an ex-colleague owns a franchise, so he's set it up here, hoping for publicity. I'm still a bit worried people will think it's in bad taste.'

'No, it's brilliant. Nearest you can come to dying and live to tell the tale! Just look at that queue.'

Thirty or forty people are waiting patiently in line.

'Morbid curiosity, if you ask me,' Dad continues. 'Nothing

wrong with that, and it's started a big debate about burial versus cremation. I think I'll stick with the worms and the daisies when my time comes.' My father speaks with the light-hearted confidence of someone in good health, and my thoughts return to Edo and Dele Dier.

'Anyway, your young man's entertaining some TV people over by the funeral foods display. They're after an interview with you.'

'He's not my young man!'

'That's not the way he tells it.' Dad looks pleased. 'He seems very nice. Invited me to go powerboat racing on the Solent.'

'Careful he doesn't talk you into waterskiing while you're at it.' I pull a wry face. 'I'd better catch up with the media people. See you later?'

'I've promised your mother supper in Marylebone, so we'll catch up with you tomorrow. Great job, Nina. I knew I was right to invest in you. We'll all be millionaires by Christmas!'

Dad's Del Boy imitation is pretty good and the way things are going, solvency no longer seems like an impossible dream. I go in search of the TV team but, before I find them, I notice Barclay standing with his back to The Wall of Death.

Until today, The Wall of Death was simply a large white canvas with a bunch of Post-it notes and pens alongside it. At the top of the canvas, Edo has stencilled the words: 'BEFORE I DIE I WANT TO ...' leaving the rest of the space clear for people to share their ambitions:

Go to Peru
See my grandchildren grow up
Have a tidy house
Learn to tap dance
Stroke a giraffe

Be happy
Delete my internet history
Sleep under the stars

Unaware I'm observing, Barclay slips his Post-it note in among the others. I take two discreet steps forward to see what he's written:

Wake up every morning with my girlfriend in my arms.

Chapter 43

The Final Celebration had been due to close at ten o'clock but by the time the last of the exhibitors had finished telling one another what a great time they'd had, it was well past eleven and Barclay was nowhere to be seen.

It's not until I'm locking the doors of the community centre – doing a rotten job of pretending to myself not to be disappointed – that he reappears, accompanied by Chopper.

'Gloria's rushed off to the hospice,' he explains. 'Dele's still holding on but she wants to be there for Edo. And we can't leave Chopper on his own all night, can we?'

Without further discussion, Barclay and I walk back to Chalcot Square, holding hands all the way.

'Chopper can sleep in the kitchen,' Barclay says when we arrive. 'Nice and warm in there. I'll go raid the linen cupboard. See what I've got to make him comfortable.' He returns with duvet and pillows, arranging them into a makeshift bed.

But Chopper shows no sign of being ready to turn in for the night. He thinks the bedclothes are props for a game of hide and seek. Every time we swaddle him in the duvet, he stays put for a count of five, then shrugs it off and paces the kitchen in search of a midnight feast. We ply him – and ourselves – with cheese and ham from the fridge, then try again.

'Do you think he needs a bedtime story?' Barclay asks. 'Once upon a time, there was a large, insomniac dog called Chopper.' Chopper thumps his tail on the floor in recognition of his name.

I'm thankful for the interlude, because I'd be a liar if I said I wasn't nervous.

This isn't going to be another blame-it-on-the-booze one-night stand.

This is different.

This is important.

This has been worth waiting for.

Thank God I'm wearing decent underwear.

'I think the best thing is if we leave Chopper to his own devices,' I say finally. 'He'll settle down eventually. There's nothing in here he can damage. And if we close the door, he can't get into the basement.'

'Or upstairs,' Barclay says softly. 'Do you want to go ahead of me? I just need to power down my laptop.'

Barclay uses the kitchen as an office and, judging from the pile of folders stacked on the draining board, he's had a busy day. 'Don't want Chopper sending emails in the middle of the night, do we?'

My about-to-be lover is talking nonsense.

I realise he's nervous too ...

Thirty minutes later, Barclay and I are sitting up in bed discussing the events of the evening with an easy familiarity. We've waited so long for this moment but now it's finally here there seems no need to rush.

'Really? Zoe's planning to have me turned into a diamond geezer?' Barclay snorts when I recount my unexpected encounter with his sister. 'Priceless!'

'Actually, it'll set her back about ten grand. Plus the cost of the setting.' I snuggle a few inches deeper into the crook of his arm.

'That death ride,' Barclay says. 'The virtual reality thing. It's weird. I'm still thinking about it.'

'So romantic,' I tease. 'Any chance we could talk about something else?'

'Seriously. It's made me realise how important it is to get my priorities right.'

'Are we about to have a deep and meaningful conversation?'

'Is there something else you'd rather be doing?'

I reply with a deep kiss. Barclay tastes of minty-flavoured goodness. I pull him closer. 'Not quite so fast.' He shifts position, then traces my neckline with his lips.

I'm wearing a T-shirt that says, *Never Done This Before*. Grabbed from the chest of drawers in the corner of the room.

'So now you're stealing my lines as well as my clothes!' Barclay accused when he saw me in it. By way of response, he chose one declaring, *This Way Up*.

Our conversation peters out, and although I'm enjoying the thrill of Barclay's inquisitive fingers working their slow way down my backbone, my body's still playing second fiddle to my brain. There's so much I don't yet know. Is he a cuddly sleeper, or will he retreat to his own side of the bed? Which *is* his side of the bed? Am I in his space? And, dear God, what's that terrible noise?

'You hear that?' Barclay shoots out of bed.

Chopper.

Howling as if he's being disemboweled.

'Be careful,' I yell. If there's an intruder downstairs, I don't want Barclay or Chopper getting hurt.

Before I can get properly dressed, Barclay's back in the bedroom. 'It's the basement. On fire. I think it's serious,' he gabbles. 'Too much smoke for me to get down the stairs and put it out. Fire brigade on the way. We need to get the hell out of the house. Right away, in case it spreads.'

I throw on the rest of my clothes and follow Barclay downstairs to the kitchen. Chopper is still howling in terror and the stench of burning is overpowering, but I know we're all safe, and it could have been so much worse.

I grab Chopper and put him on the lead while Barclay rescues his laptop and the tower of files next to it. Together, the three of us make our way downstairs, and into Chalcot Square.

'It's going to be fine.' Barclay seems to be talking to himself as much as to me. 'The important thing is that no-one's hurt. And the fire hasn't gone beyond the basement.'

The wail of sirens draws closer, and lights appear in several windows nearby.

'Should I alert the neighbours?' I ask Barclay.

'Let's leave it to the fire brigade. How about you take Chopper and wait in the shop? Or would you prefer to go home?'

'I'll go to Happy Endings,' I say. 'It's closer. Don't worry, we'll be fine.' Chopper is pawing the pavement and pulling on his lead. Looking intently at us both.

Two fire engines edge their way into the narrow thread of road that surrounds the square.

'Will you take these?' Barclay yells above the noise of the sirens, holding out his computer and his work files. He adds drily, 'I guess we know now what I'd rescue if the house caught fire. Other than you and Chopper, I mean.'

I take Barclay's belongings and kiss him on the lips. 'See you later,' I shout, before realising the sirens have been turned off and two firemen are walking towards us.

Chopper can't wait to get a safe distance between himself and the dangerous beast that's trying to break out of Eddie Banks's ruined redevelopment. By the time we get to the corner of the main street, I'm almost jogging to keep up with him and I'm slightly out of breath by the time we get to Happy Endings.

I'm reaching awkwardly into my pocket for the keys – juggling computer, folders and dog – when another fire engine, blue lights blazing and siren at full volume, announces its imminent arrival in Primrose Hill. The noise spooks Chopper, who lurches away from me and knocks me off balance.

Bugger!

Barclay's belongings fall to the pavement.

I open the shop door, which calms Chopper and brings him back to my side. I slip his lead and he retreats to the safety of my desk, curling up underneath it in a big round ball of fur. I turn on the lights, then go back outside to retrieve Barclay's stuff.

The computer's aluminium casing is dented, although if that's the only casualty of the evening, we've got off lightly. I stoop to collect the twenty or so folders that are scattered on the ground, smiling to myself as I notice each one is neatly labelled in Barclay's handwriting. Beneath his happy-go-lucky exterior, he's clearly very well organised.

What the—

In my right hand, I'm holding a folder.

A big, thick folder.

The label on it reads: 'HAPPY ENDINGS/NINA SHERWOOD'.

I put it on top of the pile, and go back inside the shop with everything I've just picked up.

Then I sit down at my desk and begin to read.

Chapter 44

I'm still reading forty-five minutes later. I've been through the entire file once and now I'm studying some of the documents again in what I feel is almost an act of self-harm, given the words and phrases that are already seared into my brain:

Naïve.

Foolish.

Nina Sherwood is exactly the person we need. Overoptimistic, inexperienced, and far too trusting.

Ignorant.

Perfect scapegoat.

Out of her depth.

Gullible. They should have added that to the list as well. Deep down, I've always known someone like Barclay Banks wouldn't be interested in someone like me. My instincts were almost correct as it turns out he *was* interested in me, but for all the wrong reasons.

Barclay and his bloody family have been plotting against me from day one.

All of them.

Making sure my business would fail.

Setting traps.

Engineering setbacks.

And – unspeakably – going after Dad.

Eddie Banks, it turns out, has been sitting in the sunshine of Monte Carlo pulling strings. He asked one of his construction industry cronies to make Dad redundant, expecting me to return what was left of his pension fund and close the business. And if it hadn't been for Dad's insistence, that's exactly what would have happened.

Eddie Banks even nudged Mrs Happy, reminding her that under the terms of the lease, I was responsible for half the cost of roof repairs. The man's got blood on his hands.

I'm about to take another look at the plan to 'invest' in Happy Endings when there's a rattle on the door. Alerted by the sound, Chopper unwinds himself from underneath the desk and lumbers up to greet Barclay. Before I can decide whether or not to let him in, he's standing in front of me.

'You ought to keep that door locked,' he says. 'Never know who might be on the prowl.'

I say nothing.

'So the basement's been made safe, but there's a huge amount of damage,' he continues. 'And I'm pretty sure it's not going to be covered by the insurance. You don't happen to know the scrap price for gold?'

I say nothing.

'I'm such an idiot,' he says.

And such a conman.

'It's entirely my fault,' he says.

I'm to blame, too. Naïve Nina. That's me.

'If only I'd listened to you, my love,' he says.

If only I'd listened to my head instead of my treacherous heart.

'You kept telling me the hoverboard's dangerous,' he says.

Not as dangerous as you.

'I left it downstairs on charge. Bloody thing exploded. Dreadful to think what might have happened if Chopper hadn't raised the alarm,' he says.

You got that damn right.

Barclay pauses in the face of my continued silence.

The two of us make full eye contact. I think he mistakes my expression for delayed shock and zones in to give me a hug.

'Don't touch me,' I spit.

'What's wrong?'

Wordlessly, I hand Barclay the file with my name on it and gesture at the paperwork spread across my desk.

'So ... You know.' His voice is flat, weary, and as he backs away from me, I realise he reeks of smoke.

'Nina. It's not what you think it is. I swear.' Barclay slumps into the chair opposite mine. 'You *have* to let me explain.'

This is Ryan Sherwood all over again. Here I am in the same shop. Just a different man with his different lies. So why does it hurt so much more?

I manage to compose myself. 'Your notes speak for themselves, wouldn't you say?'

'Yes but—'

'It's quite simple. Your father made sure I got this shop because he thought an undertaker's would never succeed in such a fancy neighbourhood. And just to make sure, he enlisted you and Zoe to give failure a helping hand. I've got to admit it. You've played a blinder, Barclay. Even setting me up with Alice's funeral so you could get the police onto me for scattering so-called human ashes in the park. Very clever.'

'You've got it all wrong!'

'Including the hoax call about Kelli being dead? You seem to have forgotten to write a report about that.'

'That was nothing to do with anyone in my family. I swear.'

'And I suppose I've misunderstood the end game, too. Genius! The council wouldn't grant planning permission for yet another café along this street, but your father reckoned there'd be an outcry if an undertaker arrived, and that after I'd been ruined, a coffee shop would seem like an excellent idea.'

'Yes,' Barclay admits. 'That was the plan. Originally. But you don't know the half of it. Please, Nina, you have to let me explain.'

Barclay speaks so vehemently, I can almost taste his sooty breath.

'Sure. You go right ahead. Knock yourself out.' The scorn in my voice makes Barclay flinch as if I've thrown an actual punch.

I can't bear to look at him, so I stand up and start to pace the room.

'So yes,' Barclay begins. 'My father did have ambitions for the shop. And he thought a funeral parlour would be all black drapes and granite. Dull and dreary. Easy to get rid of. And yes, he asked me to keep tabs on you. I'm guilty of that, and I'm so sorry. But from the moment we met, we hit it off. You know we did.'

You were only obeying orders, Barclay. I get it.

'As I got to know you better, I realised what a brilliant job you do. Yes, I did put the dog's funeral your way, because I wanted to give you a helping hand. I made the mistake of telling Zoe how fantastic you'd been and I'm afraid she tipped off the police and that environmental health officer. We had a hell of a row about it, and all I can do is apologise on her behalf.'

'And that makes everything okay?'

'Of course not.'

'And my dad? He's going to get another job? Just like that. So that's okay then?'

'That was outrageous. The tipping point. I realised my old man was losing the plot. Don't you remember, that night I cancelled dinner at the top of the Shard. Told you I'd been called away on urgent business?'

I do remember, yes.

'So I confronted my father. Told him we were going to leave you alone to turn Happy Endings into the success it deserves to be. But he's stubborn to the core. Wouldn't listen. Next thing I knew, you got that solicitor's letter, threatening you with a lawsuit for lowering the tone of the neighbourhood and wanting compensation. Remember?'

I nod my head.

'So I went back to France. Told him again that enough was enough. That I was through with doing his bidding. That I'd see the basement through to completion, and then I was done with the family business. He threatened to disinherit me, of course. The old man changes his will more often than he changes his shirts. But he wouldn't give in. Proper bee in his bonnet. Determined to sue you. In the end, I told him to go right ahead. Said I'd see him in court all right. And that I'd be representing *you*.'

I never did hear any more from the solicitors.

'Why should I trust you when you admit you've been trying to stitch me up?'

'I made the court case go away. I got Gloria out of trouble. I've helped you with the Funeral Expo.' Barclay is talking faster and faster, louder and louder, and his eyes are glittering with intensity. 'And because I love you.'

I want to believe him. I really do.

'Nina, could you possibly sit back down? All this pacing, it's making me dizzy. I need to tell you everything.'

Even if he's telling the truth – and I think he is – what kind of a future could we possibly have, after this?

I sit back down.

'The reason I printed everything out is because I'm going back to see my father. To finish this once and for all, I needed a lawyer's dossier. Look, my father emailed me boasting about his real intention. Once he's opened a coffee shop, he's going to slash prices to the bone, put the competition out of business and snap up their freeholds for a song. And having demonstrated to the council that retail businesses are no longer profitable, he'll turn them all into hugely profitable luxury houses.'

'But that would destroy the entire character of Primrose Hill! Turn it into just another minted London suburb.'

'Yes, and unless he abandons the whole crazy idea, I'm going to the media. If the thought of journalists investigating his business empire and its creative tax arrangements doesn't bring him to heel, nothing will. And then I'm done with the family business. High time I did something more valuable with my life.'

Barclay puts his elbows down on my desk and props up his head with his fists. 'So that's everything,' he says. 'Now you know the full story.' Without looking up, he adds, 'Talk to me, Nina. Please. Even if it's only to tell me to fuck off.'

Could I ever forgive him? Or would this always be in the way?

'Earlier tonight – last night, I mean – when Zoe and I were talking, she said something about you planning to go travelling?'

'Yeah. I was going to do something called flyboarding. You do it in the Caribbean. It's a cross between water-skiing and flying. You wear these jet-propelled boots for thrust and, if you do it right, you shoot fifteen metres up into the sky.' Barclay looks up, and for an instant, I see a flash of the man I thought I knew. 'It's a twelve-week instructors' course. They only take eight people a year. But I've already decided—'

'Sounds brilliant,' I interrupt. 'You should definitely go. Don't bother to send me a postcard.'

Funeral Number Five

In Memoriam
DELE DIER
1942–2019

††††

BBC BREAKING NEWS ALERT
Acclaimed conceptual artist Dele Dier has died at a London hospice, aged 77

Dier studied at the Courtauld Institute of Art, and was twice nominated for the Turner Prize. Fellow artist and lifelong friend Joshua Kent said: 'The art world has lost a towering figure. Always creative, often controversial, he was one of the most compelling artists of his generation, widely admired and striving to his final breath to explore the essence of art.'

For more details see the BBC News website.

LONDON EVENING STANDARD
Paid mourners take 'corpsies' at artist's bizarre farewell

Traffic along some of North London's busiest roads came to a standstill today when 100 mourners dressed as Grim Reapers marched in procession, escorting a horse-drawn

318

glass hearse to Highgate Cemetery where the funeral of renowned artist Dele Dier took place.

The Reapers, who were paid £50 each, were recruited on social media by friends of Dier. Spokesman Edo Clarkson explained: 'Earlier this year, Dele attended a joyless funeral with only a handful of mourners. He already knew he was terminally ill and immediately amended his own plans to ensure the ceremony replicated the person he was in life. Namely someone with a wicked sense of humour and no blood relatives remaining. He was amused by the idea of professional sobbers – and I know he would have been thrilled that someone, presumably dyslexic, turned up as a Grim Rapper.'

Far from sobbing, the black-clothed, scythe-wielding mourners stood at the graveside singing 70s hit '(Don't Fear) The Reaper', and swigging 'dark and deadly' Grim Reaper cocktails consisting of vodka, gin, tequila and wine. 'We consulted a top London mixologist who says the ingredients represent the Four Horsemen of the Apocalypse,' explained Dier's friend, fellow artist and triple Turner Prize winner Joshua Kent.

A further unusual element of the funeral was Dier's coffin, which was wrapped in gold paper, tied with a scarlet ribbon and inscribed with a date – 1st December 2019 – and website address: www.deaddeledier.info.

'All will soon become clear,' Edo Clarkson added. 'Before the coffin went into the ground, we took plenty of corpsies – selfies featuring the coffin – and I'm authorised to say that a website is currently under construction. Our intention is to remind people that life continues after death, and that Dele will go on in the afterlife. I'd like to thank the

awesome, innovative funeral start-up Happy Endings for
doing such a great job.'

A spokesperson for Highgate Cemetery declined to
comment.

Chapter 45

B arclay has gone. Vanished.

It's been almost a month since fire swept through the basement, destroying bricks, mortar, solid gold sheeting – and my life as I knew it.

On the day of Dele Dier's funeral, five days after I saw Barclay that final time, workmen arrived to board up the entire Banks house in Chalcot Square. The neighbours are still furious, complaining a derelict property will affect the value of their own homes. Which is more than a touch ironic. Something Barclay and I could laugh about together, if only he ...

I get stabbing pains in my stomach every time I think about Barclay.

'Nina!' Gloria's voice from downstairs. 'You can't hide in your room forever! Besides, you've got a visitor. Arriving in three minutes.'

Gloria is interrupting my new hobby. After work, I come here to the sanctuary of my bedroom to stare at the ceiling for hour upon hour, lost in feelings of treachery, loathing and confusion.

By way of variety, I also indulge in parallel fantasies.

There's one where Barclay never leaves his files in the

kitchen, we survive the fire, he stops his father's evil plan, and we all live happily ever after. Another where he convinces me he meant every word he said that hideous night about putting things right and cutting his ties with the family business. And – my current favourite – the one where Eddie Banks stands in front of me, apologising at length for his wickedness.

What's this about me having a visitor? I'm not expecting any callers tonight. Chopper, perhaps, but that's it. Gloria must have made a mistake.

I drag myself downstairs to find out what's happening.

Gloria's in the kitchen, putting crisps into a bowl. 'Eat!' She waves the bowl under my nose. 'Sweets, you're wasting away.'

Finally, I have found the weight-loss plan that works best for me. The Catastrophe Diet. Six pounds gone – sadly, from all the wrong places – in less than thirty days. The tang of salt and vinegar flavouring wafting up from the Pringles makes me nauseous.

'What's this about a visitor? Who are you expecting?'

Gloria plonks a glass of wine in my hand and looks shifty. Before she can enlighten me, the doorbell rings. 'Just keep your cool,' she says and dashes from the room before I can ask any more questions.

A moment later, two voices murmur in the hallway. One belongs to Gloria, the other is familiar, but I can't quite put my finger on—

No!

Zoe Banks is in our kitchen. To be fair, she looks as thrilled as I am. As for Gloria ... she didn't even warn me to brush my hair. I know I look terrible.

Zoe, however, looks worse. Wretched. Her lips are no plumper than my own. She's wearing nothing more fashionable than an old sweatshirt, jeans and trainers – trainers! – and her eyes are ringed by dark circles.

Gloria issues Zoe with a glass of wine. Then she tops up my glass and says, 'You two need to talk. That's why I invited Zoe over. I'll leave you to it.' Before either of us can say anything, far less object, Gloria flees.

Zoe and I eye one another warily, like boxers who have just stepped into the ring. Finally, I say, 'We might as well sit down.' I follow my own suggestion, and a second or so later, Zoe does the same, taking the chair on the opposite side of the kitchen table.

Zoe lands the first blow. 'Barclay says he's never coming back.'

Her words hit me in the pit of my stomach. 'You've spoken to him?' I manage. 'When?'

'The last time was three days ago. We Skyped. But now he's not even answering texts.'

'Where is he?' Ten days ago, in the middle of the night, I weakened and called Barclay's mobile, withholding my own number. I still don't know what I'd have said if he'd answered. All I got was a foreign dial tone and voicemail.

'Barclay's in Australia. Learning to do something called parkour.' Zoe clocks my blank expression and explains. 'As far as I can tell, it's the most dangerous sport on the planet. He's holed up in a warehouse near Melbourne, learning how to scale skyscrapers, run across rooftops, and the like. It's one step off skydiving, only without a parachute. I'm out of my mind with worry.'

'I'm sure he'll be fine,' I lie. 'Guys like Barclay always land right side up, wouldn't you say?' Zoe flinches from the scorn in my voice.

'He's so ashamed,' she mumbles. 'We both are.'

'That makes everything okay then.'

'Of course not.' This time, Zoe sounds irritated. More like her old self. 'Look, Nina. I genuinely didn't want an undertaker in Primrose Hill. The whole death thing gives me the creeps. You know that. So it was easy for me to go along with my father's instructions about not letting you join the Traders Association and the like.'

'By which you mean reporting me to the police and the council. That sort of thing. All in a day's work for you, is it Zoe?'

'How many times do I have to say I'm sorry?'

Zoe's twisting the stem of her wine glass so hard I'm sure it's going to break. I'm relieved when she plonks it down on the table and dives into her handbag to produce what looks like an email printout.

'I know you think my brother and I are scum, but we're trying to make things right. We'd have done it sooner, but the man we needed to get hold of was out of the country.'

Zoe passes what turns out to be five sheets of A4 across the table to me and for the next few minutes, while I scan the correspondence, the only sound in the kitchen comes from Chopper, slurping at his water bowl.

When I've finished reading I look at Zoe and ask, 'Does my dad know about this?'

'He'll be informed tomorrow. I hope the promotion and the pay rise go some way to redress the injustice.'

Eddie Banks's friend – the one who made my dad redundant – has been generous. Dad's about to become a Regional Project Manager with a forty per cent salary bump.

'I appreciate what you've done.' Zoe and Barclay are trying to buy me off.

'I've never seen Barclay so enraged as when he discovered our father was trying to get at you with the redundancy thing. He's been determined to put that right ever since.' Zoe absentmindedly pops a crisp into her mouth. 'Father's always been one to bend the rules. But he's gone too far. He seems to think he's Tony Soprano. As for his crazy plan to ruin the high street by driving all the shops out of business ... that's never going to happen, I assure you. In fact, we've forbidden him to set foot in Primrose Hill for the foreseeable future.'

Okay, so it's not Eddie Banks grovelling as he does in my fantasy, but Zoe is definitely apologising. To my surprise, she takes another handful of crisps.

'These are delicious!' she declares. 'It's been years since I had junk food. You want some?'

She pushes the bowl across the table, and I take one, if only to be companionable.

'You're trying to decide whether or not this is a genuine apology, aren't you?'

Zoe Banks has many faults, but I knew as soon as I set foot in her palatial home that she was a shrewd operator.

'Yes,' I say, simply. 'I need to work out what would have happened if it hadn't been for the fire. And if I hadn't seen the file. Would your father still have found a way to put me out of business? Or would you and your brother have stopped him?'

She doesn't exactly answer the question. Instead, she says, 'By way of sincerity, I'd like to invite you to join the Traders Association. Our next meeting's in January. I hope you'll be able to make it.'

Wow!

'And if you need any help marketing Happy Endings, just let me know. Although I have to say you seem to be

325

doing very well on your own. I saw all the media coverage about that artist guy's funeral. I'm starting to understand what it is you do, Nina ... funerals that manage to be uplifting. In their way. Although Barclay says you're not charging enough.'

Zoe eats another crisp, as if to stop herself from saying anything more. But then she mumbles, 'The other thing. Look, it's really personal, but I know that you and my brother ... well, I know the two of you ... he never took you to bed, did he?'

I can feel my face turning the colour of every fire engine that came rushing to Chalcot Square that night the basement burned.

'Believe one thing if nothing else,' Zoe gulps, 'I don't want to be having this conversation, either.'

After I have poured us generous third helpings of wine, I busy myself popping a steady supply of crisps between Chopper's eager jaws so I don't have to look at Zoe while she continues to address the kitchen table.

'It was when Barclay told me how serious he is about you. I implied you were just the latest in his long line of conquests and there'd soon be someone else. He went very quiet.' Zoe's confession has a ring of truth to it. 'Not cross, just quiet. Then it all came tumbling out. He said he was he was crazy about you. Believe me, Nina, I've spent hours listening to my brother describe your virtues.'

At this, I look up from my crisp-feeding duties and the two of us exchange not unfriendly glances.

'Barclay knew he had to do the right thing. The honourable thing. Lord knows, neither of us is perfect, but I think we might have inherited a sense of common decency from our mother. Barclay said he woke up every day diminished by the fact he was still working for our father.' Zoe pauses to claim a handful of the diminishing supply of crisps.

'He was about to tell you everything,' she continues. 'Make a clean breast of it. Hope you'd forgive him and start over, with you.'

If only I'd never read that ghastly file. If only events had unfolded the way Zoe says he intended, then – most likely – I'd have been able to forgive Barclay for the sins of his father.

'So what's with the never coming back? Didn't he plan to go for just eight weeks?'

'He wasn't going to go at all. Not until you told him to take a hike. And now he's discovered parkour. Look at this.' Zoe whips out her phone, taps on the screen and passes it to me.

A video.

A smiling man jumps confidently across a series of knee-high fence posts, spaced a couple of feet apart. So far, so good. Until the camera pans to reveal this feat of athleticism is taking place on top of a high office block. If he misjudges a single step, he'll become road-kill on the motorway below.

I shudder.

Now a teenager waves at the camera from his vantage point at the top of a crane looming high over a city. Berlin? The kid pops a yellow lollipop into his mouth, then works his way along the horizontal bar of the crane, hand over hand, until he reaches the outer edge. Next – and by now, I can barely look – he hoists himself onto the ledge of the bar itself, which seems no thicker than his own arm, in order to perform a handstand.

It makes a James Bond stunt look tame.

'I love my brother.' Zoe's voice is wobbling. 'I don't want him coming home in a box.'

Chapter 46

That night, after Zoe and I sank two bottles of wine and Chopper ate almost his entire body weight in crisps, I went back to my bedroom and stared at the ceiling for even longer than usual.

Eventually, I bowed to the inevitable.

According to my World Clock app, it was lunchtime in Australia. This time, I didn't withhold my number. I wasn't sure exactly what I was going to say – something between, 'Come home, most is forgiven,' and, 'You're scaring your sister to death!' – but when Barclay's phone went straight to voicemail I got so lost in the sound of his voice I forgot to speak at all.

It was thirteen – unbearable – days before I got a reply.

A text: *Dropped phone off Tasmania's tallest building. Only just got replacement. Sorry to have missed your call.*

I can't get past the fact that Barclay's polite acknowledgement of my attempted call is minus even a single kiss. Something that hasn't encouraged me to try again, so I suppose we're currently at stalemate.

In the meantime, I'm doing my best to get on with my life. This afternoon, I've had two 'Know Before You Go' clients – one of them a lovely man in his seventies who wants to make sure that if he dies first, his wife will receive a red rose from him every Friday without fail – and I've just posted a piece on the Happy Endings Facebook page about the recently departed Labour MP whose coffin was made from recycled copies of the *Guardian*.

Now, before I call it quits and go home to enjoy Edo's cooking, there's one final phone call I have to make. Kelli's widower, Keir Mahoney, is in Houston and I want him to know I'm thinking about him.

Keir picks up after a couple of rings. 'Nina, how are you? How's Primrose Hill?' He sounds pleased to hear from me.

'Cold,' I say. 'Ice all over the park every morning this week. Chopper's still trying to work out why his paws come under attack every time he steps on the grass.'

'Beautifully sunny here. Clear blue skies. Couldn't have wished for better weather for my lovely Kelli.'

'I just wanted to say I hope everything goes well.'

'They're wonderfully efficient. And the rocket looks amazing. Blast-off in four hours. Drink when I get back?'

'I'll look forward to that. Take care.'

I put on my coat and decide to walk home, even though the temperature has barely risen above zero all day. On the way, my thoughts are with Kelli.

After her funeral – since which one hundred and thirty thousand people have signed the organ donation register – Keir came to me with his rocket-to-space idea.

'Tell me if I'm crazy,' he'd said. 'But I'm thinking about sending Kelli's ashes into space. You know at the start of her career she had a role in *Star Trek*?'

Keir had already done his homework. He'd come across a firm that offers to deliver ashes to the surface of the moon. Another whose package includes an app that allows you to 'track your loved one's journey in orbit'. Finally, after I agreed Kelli would have been up for an adventure up among the stars in deep space, Keir chose the Texan company that's been providing memorial spaceflights for more than thirty years.

'I want to set her free to soar,' was how he'd put it.

As I turn the corner into our street, I hear Kelli's wonderful laugh. Clearly, as if she were walking alongside me. *'Twinkle, twinkle.'* She arches an ironic eyebrow. *'If it makes my darling husband happy. Well ... beam me up!'*

This isn't the first time I've heard – or seen – Kelli. We've had plenty of other conversations. In fact, we've been talking to one another almost since the day she died. And no, as I've explained to Gloria and Edo, it's not the same as that movie-in-my-head-thing of Ryan's imaginary funeral.

That was on a loop, the same scene over and over again.

Kelli and I ... well, we just hang out together. I know she's dead, but honestly, I hear an authentic version of my friend.

It's actually pretty common. I've had more than a dozen clients tell me they still see and hear people they've lost. Maybe we're all hallucinating. Or letting our imagination run riot.

My head tells me our exchanges are a way of processing my grief, but in my heart, I'm just so thankful Kelli hasn't vanished from my life.

'Have a great flight!' I silently say to her. 'Come back soon.'

'Bye for now. Love to Edo and Gloria.'

I'm not the only one who's been spending a lot of time in their bedroom.

Edo's been doing the same thing.

We all cope with anguish in our own way, and Edo's way has been to work incessantly on his tribute website to Dele Dier.

It goes live at midnight.

But first, Gloria and I are about to get a preview.

I've just finished clearing the table – Edo's supper turned out to be a selection of microwavable delights from Marks and Sparks, but none the worse for that – and Edo's fetching his laptop.

'Now look,' Gloria says. 'What Edo's been doing ... it's going to come as a bit of a shock. You need to get past that.'

'You've seen it?'

For a moment, I feel betrayed. But I'm aware, too, that Edo and Gloria have grown really close. They're even talking about setting up some sort of project that combines art, gardening and the local community. Gloria sees it as a not-for-profit, but Edo has other – more commercial – ideas.

Before I can ask Gloria anything else, Edo reappears, laptop in hand. He puts it on the table and says, 'Sooooo.'

Then silence.

'Edo, you have to tell her.' Gloria moves to Edo's side and puts her hand on his shoulder. 'Maybe if you just show her the Sky News piece?'

'The *what?*' Now I'm apprehensive, as well as confused. 'What's your website doing on the news?'

'It's not my website.' Edo's voice is little more than a whisper. 'It's Dele's.'

'A tribute to him, right?' I reach for the computer, but Edo shoves it beyond reach.

'Not exactly,' Edo manages. He looks at Gloria who gives him a nod of encouragement. Then continues, 'Remember my project? Design for Death.'

'Of course.'

'Well, Dele *is* the project.'

331

'I'm not understanding.'

'You know how some people leave their bodies to science?' Edo tries again. 'Well, Dele's left his body to art.'

For all the sense he's making, Edo might as well be speaking Serbo-Croat

'His grave at Highgate Cemetery ... it's more of an installation.'

'You're planning some sort of sculpted tombstone, you mean?'

Edo takes a very deep breath. 'No,' he says. 'That's not what I mean. I've created a multi-media show. I put Wi-Fi-enabled cameras inside Dele's coffin. The afternoon before he died, he swallowed five microchips with cameras. They'll be automatically activated once they're broken down in the stomach.'

'You *what?*' Before Edo can explain himself further, I think back to the aftermath of Dele's death.

The three of us, accompanied by Joshua Kent, had brought Dele's body from the hospice to Happy Endings, placing him to rest safely in my eBay fridge – which continues to behave itself perfectly.

Unlike Edo.

Now I'm remembering how, on the morning of the funeral, Edo had requested some 'alone time' with Dele's body. To say goodbye, or so I presumed.

Far from paying his last respects, Edo had been rigging the corpse of Dele Dier with cameras that would show—

'Do you have any idea what happens to a body when it goes into the ground?'

'Of course.' Edo actually manages to look self-right-eous. 'Right now, Dele's corpse is teeming with life. It's the cornerstone of a complex ecosystem that's going to flourish and grow as decomposition proceeds.'

'On camera?'

'I've set up a dedicated live stream on the new website. And there's going to be a YouTube channel. Should be really useful for artists and scientists alike. But that's only one strand of the installation.'

If there were a register for undertakers – and I've always thought there should be – this in itself would be enough to get me struck off.

'What else?'

'Immortality,' Edo announces with a half-smile. 'Dele Dier is going to live forever on social media. I've built a digital doppelgänger. Like an avatar, only more advanced. All that time I spent at the hospice, Dele and I were working together on my project. We recorded thousands of words and phrases. He's given me his entire photo collection, plus access to his Facebook and Twitter and Instagram accounts. By the time I've finished programming everything, Digital Dele Dier will have been trained to speak and interact with people. He'll be able to answer questions. Initiate conversations, even.'

Gloria touches Edo on the shoulder again. 'How about you show Nina your TV interview,' she prompts.

Edo fiddles with his laptop. The screen of which fills with a picture of Edo – dressed in a suit – and a voiceover saying something about a collaboration between a famous, recently deceased artist and his associate.

Edo begins to speak. 'The installation is called Liquidated Assets,' he tells the camera. 'It won't be to everyone's taste, and I expect some will find it downright offensive. But art has been controversial throughout history. And Dele's not the first to use parts of the human body for art itself. Do you know about the sculpture of a human head … made with the artist's own blood?'

I have to hand it to him. Edo is doing for art what Brian Cox does for science and Mary Berry does for cakes. He's expert, authentic and hugely likeable.

He might just get away with this.

Edo pauses the interview. 'It'll be going out after midnight,' he says. 'I hope you're not too angry with me. It's what Dele wanted. He signed papers with his lawyer to say so.'

I straighten up from the laptop and give Edo a hug. 'If you'd told me what you were going to do with the cameras, then yes, I'd have stopped you,' I admit. 'I'm not sure how Highgate Cemetery's going to respond, but I'll do my best to smooth things over. And Edo,' I add, 'you're right. Dele would have loved this. He'd be proud of you. And so am I.'

Chapter 47

Edo is famous. And to a certain extent, I am basking in reflected glory.

Liquidated Assets – Edo's Digital Dele Dier installation – has divided the media, not only in this country but across the world.

Including Australia.

A couple of days after the website went live, Barclay texted me a couple of links to the *Herald Sun*. In one story, a group of Melbourne funeral directors were praising me for my 'innovative approach' to undertaking, and in the other, Edo was referred to as 'the enfant terrible of British art'.

Great to hear from you, I cautiously replied. *Glad you're safe. How's it going?*

A day passed. Then another. Until Barclay responded with a photo of himself doing a standing somersault in the middle of a sunny meadow. *Life's still up in the air*, he said. *I miss you.*

'It's obvious,' Gloria said when we analysed his text. 'He wants you to tell him to come home.'

Something's stopping me doing that.

It has to be Barclay's decision.

But at least now we're communicating every few days via email and text. I've learned parkour isn't as dangerous as Zoe feared. *It's more like a martial art*, Barclay reassured me. *We try to get through obstacles in the quickest way possible, by jumping, climbing or running. Thinking of setting up a training school when I get back. Either that or buy a football club – been offered one that's struggling. What do you think?*

I think I have never missed someone so much in my life. I ache for him.

Yet instinctively, I know not to put any pressure on Barclay. More than that, I have no ambition to control him. I just want what's best for him. And if that turns out to be travelling the world while leaping from one extreme sport to another ... with a bit of luck Zoe will order him home some time soon.

At least Barclay's missing this freezing weather. I snuggle deeper into my coat and pull my scarf tighter as I turn the corner into the high street.

Most of the world seems to be celebrating Christmas, even though it's only four in the afternoon and there are still ten days to go. There's a big group spilled out onto the pavement outside the pub, and a couple of people wave at me as I steer a path around them.

I'm part of the neighbourhood, now.

An accepted part of the neighbourhood.

The year seems to have passed so quickly.

I'll soon be off to Southampton for a family Christmas – Mum reports Dad's projecting a laser Nativity display onto the front of the house this year – and, having had three funerals this month, I could certainly use a break.

That's right.

Three funerals.

One came by way of the hospice, the others from families

that read about me in the papers. I've also been on television three times, talking about what the media is starting to call the modern way of death.

If only Barclay was here to share in my success.

I point my camera at the Christmas lights in the high street and take a photo. Once I'm back inside the shop, I send it to him. *Take it you'll be spending Christmas on the beach?*

I spend the next few minutes looking again at the photos Barclay sent me yesterday – flyboarding in a turquoise ocean looks like a lot of fun – then force myself to focus on today's paperwork. I've got business rates to pay, and it feels great to pay them out of cashflow, rather than Dad's money.

The radio is playing Christmas music in the background when, a few minutes later, I look up from my desk, disturbed by some hullabaloo going on in the street. It seems to involve a huge white van, double-parked on the pavement, and reminds me of that first day in business, when Edo climbed on top of his van to hammer my shop sign into place.

This time, the van in question is being used to move furniture. I sit and watch while two armchairs, packing cases, and a hideous stone statue are loaded up.

Just as I realise the furniture is being decanted from the flat above The Primrose Poppadum, Ned Newman appears in the street. He notices I'm watching, and after a moment's hesitation, comes into the shop.

'Ned, how are you?'

'Stressed out. My first house move in twenty years.'

Ned Newman – Mr Happy – looks anything but stressed. What a transformation! At least two stone lighter, he's clearly been working out. He's sporting a winter suntan and has undergone a sartorial transformation, exchanging those buttoned-up tweedy suits he wore when his wife was alive for jeans and a hoodie. The combined effect makes him look ten years younger. I'm so pleased he's making a fresh start.

'Where are you off to?' I enquire.

'All of five streets away. To Princess Road. Once you live in Primrose Hill, it's hard to move away.'

I'm wishing Ned luck when we're interrupted by the driver of his removal van – Rob the Roofer – who opens the shop door and warns, 'The traffic warden's threatening to send in the tow truck unless we shift. Chop chop.'

'See you around,' Mr Happy says. 'And Nina, I'm glad your business is doing well. Thanks again for all you did for me when, well, you know, with Sybille.' Before he can say anything further, Rob beeps the horn from inside the van, and Mr Happy embarks on the next phase of his life.

Christmas Eve.

The days have flown past. The bookies got it right ... there's going to be snow for Christmas.

In fact, there's heavy snow already, transforming Primrose Hill into an enchanted winter wonderland. At this time in the morning – a few minutes before five a.m. and still dark – I have the whole park to myself, like a huge private garden. And although I thought the temperature couldn't fall any further, I heard on the news it's been colder here than in Moscow, with still no sign of a let-up.

I slip Chopper's lead from his collar. 'Off you go!' I coax. Chopper is a wimp. Or maybe in a previous life he lived somewhere sunny. He loathes these Arctic conditions. But he needs to be exercised and I'm hoping to tire him out before we set off on what's likely to be a slow and torturous journey down the M3 to Southampton, even with an early start that hopefully puts us ahead of the festive traffic.

I work through my mental list of Christmas stuff. Presents for Mum and Dad, gift-wrapped, sitting in the boot of my van. Chew sticks for Chopper, to give him something to do while I'm driving. Extra clothes, in case it gets even colder, although if I'm forced to put them on I really will look like the Michelin Man. Thermos of coffee. Sat nav fully charged. What about—

The snow makes it easy to see what's happening in the park. Which, I had assumed, was nothing more interesting than Chopper, gingerly relieving himself against the trunk of a tree.

But look.

There's Father Christmas.

At the top of the hill.

Complete with toboggan.

I turn around to look for the film crew, ready to act nonchalant when I see them.

No cameras.

But plenty of action.

Santa has launched himself into the snow and he's picking up plenty of speed. He's heading in my direction. And he's a moron. I'm no fan of winter sports, but even I know you're supposed to park your butt in the seat of a sledge. Not stand astride a sliver of plastic while racing down a steep, snow-covered slope.

At least there are no obstacles in the way.

Other than myself.

I'm standing frozen to the spot, and I'm going to get run over unless I move right—

I leap out of the toboggan's flight path just as Father

Christmas abandons his vehicle, performing a perfect back-flip as he does so.

He shakes ice crystals from his red robe, looks me up and down and says, 'You look like a snow princess.'

Then Barclay Banks unbuttons his costume to reveal a T-shirt that's got an image of a Santa hat and *Tell Me What You Really, Really, REALLY Want* written underneath.

Before I can say a word, Chopper forgets his hatred of the weather and lumbers joyfully towards Barclay, enveloping him in a shower of ice flakes when he rolls over on his back and wriggles around to make a canine snow angel. Barclay responds by stooping down to pack fresh powder between his hands. He lobs his snowball towards the children's playground and Chopper gallops off in pursuit.

'I knew you'd come sooner or later,' Barclay says. 'Three days I've been waiting in this freezing park.'

'Really?' Barclay had texted yesterday to say he was looking forward to Christmas, but hadn't elaborated. I'd replied with a chirpy – true-but-false – *Me too!*

'In the end I called Gloria and swore her to secrecy. She said you'd be here walking Chopper before you left for Christmas.'

'So did you take a wrong turning on your way back from the beach?'

'Are you disappointed?'

'No,' I admit. 'Not in the slightest.'

'You've got to listen to me.' Barclay is suddenly urgent. 'I admire you so much. The work you do. The way you make people feel better when they're going through hell. You're ethical. You're amazing. You're beautiful. And I'm such a coward. But I promise, there's a decent human being inside me – at least I think there is – and I'm desperate to live up

340

to your high standards. All of my life, I've been searching for something. Testing myself with every extreme sport ever invented. But now ... I want to be by your side, doing ordinary things. Watching Netflix. Looking at your childhood photographs. Rearranging the furniture. Standing in the park before dawn on Christmas Eve, freezing three-quarters to death.'

Barclay stares into my eyes with the most tender of looks. Without taking his eyes off me, he rummages in the pocket of his red robe, produces a hefty sprig of mistletoe, pulls me close and holds it above our heads.

'Here's what I've realised,' he says. 'I've never been more certain of anything in my life. Nina Sherwood, you are my greatest adventure. And I want – more than anything else on the planet – to be yours. What do you say?'

Chapter 48

Sixteen months later ...

I've always hated being the centre of attention. But today, there's no getting away from it.

'You definitely need more eye shadow,' Zoe Banks frowns. If you ask me – and neither Zoe nor Gloria is interested in my opinion – less is more.

'And perhaps an extra dab of colour to the lips and cheeks,' Gloria suggests. 'To make sure there's enough colour to compensate for the whiteness of the dress.'

Before I can protest that the test run surely featured a far more natural look, Zoe reaches for a fresh selection of brushes and bronzers, moisturisers and mascara, powder and pens.

'Keep still,' she scolds. 'You've got fabulous eyelashes, by the way. And the longer hair suits you much better, especially the caramel highlights.'

Finally Zoe seems satisfied. 'What do you think?' A question addressed to Gloria rather than me.

'Fabulous!'

Just as I think I'm going to weep with frustration – and ruin all her hard work – Zoe produces a mirror so I can finally see what she has done to my face.

I stare back at myself in wonder. 'I look like ... I look like an impossibly glamorous version of myself. Thank you so much.'

'My pleasure. Smile!'

The three of us pose for a Big Day selfie, which Zoe posts immediately on Instagram.

I'm starting to feel nervous. The car taking Dad and me to the ceremony is due to arrive at any moment. In fact, it's here!

'Take your time, sweetie,' Dad's excited voice crackles through the intercom. 'The traffic's not too bad at all.'

Twenty minutes later, when it seems the Euston Road has been turned from one of London's major roads into a car park, I'm glad we left nothing to chance and built in a margin of error for the journey. In an effort to distract one another, Dad and I sit chatting about business.

'Have you given any further thought to expansion?' Dad asks.

'I've thought about it. A lot.'

'And?'

'Not yet. Perhaps not even at all.' I slip my hand into Dad's. 'For now, I'd rather stick to what I'm best at. Taking care of people and organising funerals. The moment I open a second branch, let alone a third or fourth, I'll be forced to do more of the business stuff and less of the funeral stuff. Are you disappointed?'

'Not in the slightest.' Dad squeezes my hand. 'But you'll keep going with the media work?'

'Unless they fire me! It's only once a month so it doesn't eat up too much time. If you'd told me a year ago that I'd have a regular spot on national television to talk about modern funerals, I'd have thought you were crazy. But it's fun. It gets the message across that there are as many types of funeral as

343

there are people. And best of all, our Fair Funerals campaign means there's less chance of customers being ripped off.'

Our car is finally on the move again, and a few minutes later, we arrive at our destination. Gloria, Edo, Zoe and Mum have managed to arrive ahead of us. There they are, sharing a joke with my two guests of honour ... Anna Kovaks and her gorgeous baby son, Kazimir, who seems to have had his first 'grown-up' haircut since I last saw him, a few weeks ago.

'Barclay's inside,' Gloria says. 'Waiting for you.'

And with that, she flings wide a pair of oak doors that lead into a gorgeous wood-panelled room.

I take in my surroundings, and with Dad by my side, walk slowly toward Barclay.

'You've never looked more lovely,' he whispers by way of a greeting. Before he can say anything else, the ceremony begins.

An hour later, I am named Most Promising New Funeral Director.

I forget every word of the speech I was supposed to make.

All I can manage is, 'I'd like to thank the Good Funeral Awards for this huge honour. The support from my family and friends has been amazing. I'm the luckiest woman in the world.'

We Invite You to
Celebrate Our Wedding
9 May 2020
RSVP

'Good afternoon everybody and welcome to Kenwood House.'

I'm still the luckiest woman in the world. Sometimes I get scared just because everything's going so well. 'Trust the timing of your life.' That's what Barclay tells me.

This is such a cool place to get married. The Orangery is a lavishly ornate room with super views of Hampstead Heath through the floor-length windows. Intimate yet spacious. And Julie's flowers are, as always, amazing.

'Please rise to meet our happy couple.'

If you'd asked me to put money on it, I'd have guessed Edo would be the groom at the next wedding I attended. Wrong! But what an amazing time he's having.

From art student – and squatter – to Turner Prize winner – and homeowner – in less than two years. Liquidated Assets was described by the judges as 'the ultimate selfie'. And by the *Daily Mail* as 'a ghoulish example of everything that is wrong with art today and the vainglorious frauds who masquerade as artists'.

Which left Edo laughing all the way to the bank.

His YouTube channel continues to live stream from Dele's plot in Highgate Cemetery, generating a startling amount in advertising revenue every day, while Edo's own works already fetch stratospheric prices. He gives ten per cent of everything he earns to the hospice.

'Please face each other and take each other's hands. These are the loving hands of your best friend, holding yours on your wedding day, as you promise to love each other for so long as you both shall live.'

Edo and Gloria make such a great couple. She's a qualified lawyer now, still working at the community law centre. She intends to carry on working when the baby comes, in August. Hopefully, she and Edo will have finished their new home by then.

Zoe and Barclay kept their word. Told their father he was banned from Primrose Hill. Then Barclay sold the house in Chalcot Square – burned-out basement and all – to Edo, who promptly gutted the lower floors and turned them into free workspaces for recently graduated artists, while living upstairs with Gloria.

'Beloved partner, for so long, we were halves unjoined. Today, I merge my freedom with yours.'

One thing led to another. Barclay and I took out a mortgage on Gloria's house in Kentish Town and set up home together. Chopper is delighted to have two homes and four people acting as his willing slaves.

Having disentangled himself from the family business, Barclay bought that football club. They're in one of the lower leagues, not at all glamorous, saddled with tons of debt. He's now in the process of raising capital for a new stadium that will double as a Parkour Centre of Excellence for local kids.

Last Christmas, he tried to set up a ski jump competition on Primrose Hill, thrusting the people in charge of the Royal Parks into collective nervous breakdown. He's agreed to all sorts of health and safety precautions if they let him do it this year,

Mind you, Barclay's still getting over the shock of coming second in this year's Go-Kart Derby. Guess who won? I'll give you a clue ... it was me!

'Please place Robert's ring on the tip of his ring finger and repeat after me ... I, Edward Jeremy Newman ...'

As for Happy Endings, on average we've been arranging four funerals a week. More than enough to be profitable. I've taken on two members of staff, plus an intern who knows almost as much about social media as Edo.

Zoe and I are also working together, planning this year's Winter Fair. Barclay's made me swear I'll never tell her he owns a Father Christmas outfit.

'I, Robert Redmond Cole, take you Edward Jeremy Newman, joyfully, to be my partner and my husband.'

And here's Kelli in my head, saying just a bit too loudly, *'Rob the Roofer and Mr Happy! He definitely looks a lot happier than he used to. They make a great couple. But you must have wondered, Nina. About Mrs Happy. Did she fall, or was she—'*

'Shhush!' I say sternly. 'This is neither the time nor the place.'

Kelli was awarded a third – posthumous – Best Actress Oscar for her final film. Keir insisted I accompany him to LA for the ceremony. We both wept buckets, but in between the tears, we had such fun.

'I now pronounce you married. You may kiss your husband.'

As the wedding reception gets underway, Barclay quietly

347

steers me into a corner of the beautiful room. 'I've got something for you,' he says, 'I bought us one each.'

Barclay fastens the white strap of a cool-looking watch around my left wrist. I take a good look at the three rows of digital numbers on the display. They definitely don't tell me the time.

'What are they for?' I ask.

'The top row shows your life expectancy,' Barclay says. 'I worked it out to ninety-nine years four months and five days. And these numbers,' he taps the clock face, 'they show how much longer you've got left. The idea is to remind us that time is our most precious asset. So we can make good choices about the best way to use it.'

Barclay leans in closer. 'I think we should spend the next two minutes – at least – doing this.'

He leans in for a kiss.

Life is good.

Acknowledgements

Thanks first – and always – to my dear friend, mentor, and fellow novelist Beverly Swerling. Beverly, I miss you every day and I'm so sad that you are not here to celebrate publication with me.

Thanks also to Jo Barnett, Richard Barnett, Roberta Burke, Mel Croucher, Francesca Drake, Randy Haunfelder, Paula Jarvis, Lynne Orton, John Reiss, Judy Rich, and Tim Whiting.

I would also like to thank my editor Molly Walker-Sharp and her colleagues Hannah Todd, Sabah Kahn, Elke Desanghere, Rachel Faulkner-Willcocks, Helen Huthwaite, Katie Loughnane, Tilda McDonald, Beth Wickington and Lauren Tavella. I am thrilled to have received such an enthusiastic welcome into the Avon HarperCollins family.

Special thanks are also due to Tracy Fenton, tireless overlord of THE Book Club (TBC) on Facebook, and to Phoebe Morgan, who posted a message in the group ... had I been working rather than procrastinating that day, then *Five Wakes and a Wedding* might never have seen the light of day.

I am also grateful to the various funeral directors who were kind enough to give me their time, help, and advice on the road to publication; all factual errors are mine.

One final point. While Nina got a rough ride from some

of the retailers in my parallel universe Primrose Hill setting, those who work so hard to keep my neighbourhood's real life shops going – despite the crippling burden of business rates – are responsible in no small measure for maintaining and enhancing the unique village atmosphere of the charming London backwater I am proud to call home.

Nine Book Club Questions and a Suggestion

Life, death, love, heartbreak, a bottle of wine – or three – along with some nibbles and chocolate and a chat about this month's novel. If that sounds anything like your own Book Club, then here's a few questions to get you started.

1. How would you feel if a funeral home opened up on your local high street, or near your home – and have your views changed as a result of reading the book?

2. Did you have any sympathy with the council official who tried to insist Nina should take down her window display?

3. Towards the end of the book Zoe explains how a childhood bereavement has shaped the personalities of her brother and herself. Did you feel one way of coping was better than the other?

4. Is Barclay a worthy hero – or just a man-child with a too many toys and T-shirts?

5. Which of the five funerals affected you the most – and why?

6. One of the stallholders at Nina's Funeral Expo says, 'There's so much more you can do with ashes than just scatter them or keep them in an urn.' Did any of the ideas take your fancy?

7. Who's your favourite character?

8. Is there a relationship between death, art, and gardening?

9. Has the book prompted you to think about writing down your wishes for your own funeral – or do you feel that would be tempting fate?

Now let's open another bottle of wine and play Fantasy Casting! Who would you pick to play the main characters?